RAGE
AGAINST THE
NIGHT

BRIMSTONE PRESS

Other works by Shane Jiraiya Cummings

Anthologies edited:

Black Box

Australian Dark Fantasy & Horror Volume One

Shadow Box

Robots & Time

Magazines edited:

Midnight Echo Issue #2 (Guest Co-Editor)

Black: Australian Dark Culture Magazine

HorrorScope

Books authored:

The Mist Ninja

Apocrypha Sequence: Deviance

Apocrypha Sequence: Divnity

Apocrypha Sequence: Inferno

Apocrypha Sequence: Insanity

Requiem for the Burning God

The Smoke Dragon

Phoenix and the Darkness of Wolves

Shards: Damned and Burning

Shards

RAGE
AGAINST THE
NIGHT

EDITED BY
SHANE JIRAIYA
CUMMINGS

BRIMSTONE PRESS

National Library of Australia Cataloguing-in-Publication entry

Title: Rage against the night / edited by Shane Jiraiya Cummings.

ISBN: 9780980567755 (pbk.).

Subjects: Short stories, Australian.

       Horror tales, Australian.

Other Authors/Contributors:

       Cummings, Shane Jiraiya.

Dewey Number: A823.4

Print edition, published March 2012.

(E-book edition published December 2011).

PO Box 4, Woodvale WA 6026, Australia

www.brimstonepress.com.au

For Rocky: You're a champion, mate.

Through your efforts, you brought horror communities from around the world together. *Rage Against the Night* is a token of our gratitude to you.

Special Thanks

The editor would like to thank the wonderful contributors who donated their stories, time, and goodwill to this anthology. Thank you for your generosity. Thank you for supporting Rocky.

In particular, thanks to Hodder & Stoughton in London and Scribner in New York for their kind permission to reprint Stephen King's story, "Fair Extension", which was specifically requested by Rocky Wood for inclusion in this anthology.

Thanks, too, to Angela, for your endless patience and support under sometimes trying circumstances.

CONTENTS

INTRODUCTION:
RAGE FOR ROCKY

There is usually little hope in the horror genre. The courageous protagonist often finds him/herself overwhelmed by the forces of darkness, and too often, the struggle to defeat evil is futile. Horror is about fear, about rising dread and unknown terrors, and in the face of such nightmares, the acts of good people can seem insignificant.

Not so in *Rage Against the Night*.

In this anthology, you will find stories of brave men and women standing up to the darkness, staring it right in the eye, and giving it the finger. These are stories of triumph, but triumph doesn't necessarily come without cost. To conquer evil, sacrifices must be made. Battles may be lost to ultimately win the war. Heroes may fall to inspire the masses. Many stories in this anthology fall into this category of sacrifice for the greater good. A few even subvert the trope and offer a grim or somewhat tangential view of what constitutes triumph against evil. Overall, though, the forces of darkness meet their match in the pages of *Rage Against the Night*. Read on to see who (or what) gets their comeuppance.

There is another reason for the theme of triumph over darkness—a guy named Rocky Wood. All proceeds from the sale of *Rage Against the Night* will go to Rocky. He is the President of the Horror Writers Association, one of the world's leading scholars on the works of Stephen King, and a Bram Stoker Award-nominated author. For many years, he has toiled in the background, bridging the horror writing communities in Australia with our cousins across the Pacific. Like a true and selfless gentleman, he has devoted himself to strengthening the international horror community, while at the same time, chronicling the career of his favourite author, Stephen King. To better understand Rocky's devotion to the works of King, I would urge you to buy and read one of his books.

But Rocky is fighting his own battle with dark forces. Earlier this year, Rocky announced he had been diagnosed with Motor Neurone Disease (MND), also known as ALS or Lou Gehrig's Disease. For specifics, you can look up MND on Wikipedia, but suffice to say, it is a nasty disease that progressively shuts down the muscles in the body, and the prognosis is always fatal. Rocky is a great bloke, and when I heard he had chosen to sell his extensive collection of Stephen King books and memorabilia (one of the largest collections of its type in the world!) to pay for his medical expenses, I was outraged and devastated on his behalf. So I did something about it and contacted a few mates.

Rage Against the Night is the international horror community's effort to repay Rocky for his years of behind-the-scenes service. As a testament to the high esteem in which Rocky is held, you will find the megastars of dark fantasy and horror in this anthology. I was especially pleased Stephen King could contribute "Fair Extension", which Rocky specifically asked to have included (given his affinity for the protagonist). Having Steve involved in an anthology for Rocky has a nice circularity to it, given Rocky's books about Steve.

Your hard-earned dollars in buying this anthology will help Rocky purchase an eye gaze machine. This marvel of technology will allow Rocky to communicate as his disease progresses. An eye gaze machine will be a lifeline that will improve Rocky's quality of life as his health deteriorates. The machine costs $25,000, and I reckon we can make a big dent in this target.

Join me and the contributors in our rage against the unfairness of life. Help us give the finger to darkness. As Dylan Thomas wrote: *Do not go gentle into that good night ... Rage, rage against the dying of the light.* Join us, and rage against the night!

Shane Jiraiya Cummings
Perth, Australia, December 2011

FOREWORD

When Shane Jiraiya Cummings approached me with the idea for this anthology, my first reaction was, 'Why Me'—a not dissimilar reaction to when the specialist gave me the awful news that I had Motor Neurone Disease (ALS in North America). It seemed to me I was no more special than any other person who suffers from a terminal illness and therefore undeserving of a signal honour such as this.

But then I got to thinking—thinking about the many, many people who were offering to help me and to help my family as they heard about my illness. Of course, some of them were old friends and family members—the sort of close people in your life you help yourself in times of need. But there had been, and has continued to be, a flood of offers from my wider range of friends, associates, and people I had only met once or twice. And another flood of support from people I really hadn't known at all before I was diagnosed. What did all this mean?

I thought then and I now know it means all the good things about humanity that we often talk about, and hear of, and even contribute to, but oftentimes don't really understand how much it means to those who receive it. It's humbling, it's moving, and it's deeply helpful when one tries to come to terms with one's mortality, and in the case of MND/ALS, the difficult path one must follow. I made a decision to accept these offers of help to fund an Eye-Gaze Device, which enables profoundly disabled people to communicate. MND sufferers generally reach a point where they cannot move at all, except for their eyes, and this relatively new technology allows them to communicate through that eye movement. For a person whose whole life has been communication, the discovery of this device has, to be frank, kept me sane. I made the decision to sell my Stephen King collection so that I was myself contributing to gathering the required funds. And I have ensured the device will be passed on to another sufferer, whose family cannot afford the $25,000 or so that this technology costs.

I have come to embrace the love and help so many people have so freely offered me and have tried to return it in any way I can.

Anyone's life is marked by phases, and in some ways, defined by the varying communities we choose to be part of. In my life, I've had the great fortune to be a member of many communities—sometimes even as a leader—my family, my Rugby Union mates, my cricket teams, my political affiliations, my involvement in the study of whether this Earth has been visited in the past by aliens, certain employers where I made lifelong friends, and of course, writing.

Writing: the art of putting words on paper that someone else actually wants to read, and then enjoys! A strange pastime—in many ways, a very solitary one. But the last community I want to talk about is quite the opposite of solitary—it is welcoming, and that's the horror writing community. When I decided to resume my writing career a decade or so ago (I had earned good income as a freelance journalist outside my corporate career back in the late 1970s and into the 1980s), I chose to write about Stephen King and all his works.

Little did I know then that making that choice would lead me deep into the welcoming heart of the horror writing community, exemplified by the Horror Writers Association (HWA), presenters of the famous Bram Stoker Awards, and the Australian Horror Writers Association (AHWA). I joined HWA and began to build a small network of online friends and then was fortunate enough to receive a Bram Stoker nomination for *Stephen King: Uncollected, Unpublished*, that led me to attend the Bram Stoker Awards Banquet and World Horror Convention in Toronto in 2007. And just like that, I was introduced to dozens of people who became literally instant friends and our friendships continued to build online.

It's rather obviously a long way from Australia to North America, so we Aussies and Kiwis (I get to be both) don't get to do the convention circuit that so many in America and Canada do, where they might attend two or three, or even a half dozen of more 'cons' every year and catch up with their friends and colleagues. But I enjoyed my first overseas horror con so much I never looked back, going to WHC in 2008 (Salt Lake City, Utah), 2010 (Brighton, England), and 2011 (Austin, Texas) and the Bram Stoker Weekends in 2009 (Burbank) and 2011 (Long Island). I expanded my group of horror writer, editor, and publisher friends each time and even got a new publisher through attending one of these cons.

And of course, being me, I volunteered to help HWA, which snowballed to the point where I became President in 2010! I've enjoyed giving back to the genre—history's oldest; and I hope to continue to do so in the remaining time I have, as we expand the reach of HWA in support of dark fiction's writers, publishers, and readers.

When I look at the Table of Contents for this anthology, I realise I'd never been in contact with a single one of these fine authors a scant decade ago but now I can call almost all 'friend'. I am humbled that Stephen King donated "Fair Extension". If you don't know the story, perhaps you should read that first, as you will soon see why I empathise with its protagonist. Steve has been very kind not only to me but to untold thousands over the years through his generous support of the genre, the publishing industry, literacy, and the art of storytelling. He is one cool dude!

There are many ladies in our genre—and I mean 'lady' in the way one would say 'gentleman'—people who earn respect not just through their work but the way they carry themselves through life. I was fortunate to meet Quinn (Chelsea Quinn Yarbro) for the first time at a convention here in Melbourne, Australia. She is one of the most interesting people I have ever met, and she is generous with her time and advice. Lisa Morton has become one of my dearest friends—and now a co-author in our graphic novel project, *Witches!* A fine writer, a lover of books and movies, and the hardest working member of any voluntary Board I have ever served on. Sarah Langan, Nancy Holder, and Alex Sokoloff are all great writers who give more back to the literary world than they will ever take. I am deeply honoured all these ladies have contributed.

As to the gentleman, even reviewing the names is a little awe-inspiring. I have been reading Peter Straub since not long after I took up my King habit, but I did not get to meet him until early in 2011 at the World Horror Con in Austin, following which I got to host him as Special Guest of Honour at the Bram Stoker Weekend two months later. As with the ladies, the word gentleman attaches itself to Peter with little fuss but a lot of meaning. Here is one of the world's most brilliant wordslingers (a King term) who treats all around him with respect.

Others on the list I would describe more as 'mates' in the Australasian vernacular—guys I've grown to enjoy having a drink with, shooting the breeze, and considering the wider philosophical questions of life in the small hours of a convention: Gene O'Neill (who memorialises the underclass so well), the slightly dangerous Wes Ochse, Joe McKinney (I suspect he has more spine than any of us), F. Paul Wilson (the life of every party), John Little (a man with a very special writer's viewpoint), Jeff Strand (a guerrilla funny man), Bev Vincent (a fellow SKEMER from way back), Dan Keohane (a class act if ever there was), and Jonathan Maberry, the hardest working writer I know, a man who deserves all the success that is now coming his way like a freight train.

Nate Kenyon, Scott Nicholson, Gary Braunbeck, David Niall Wilson, David Conyers, Joe Nassise (a fierce proponent for our genre), David Conyers, Stephen Irwin, Gary Kemble and Ramsey Campbell are gentlemen I know more through our online interaction but each is a fine writer, committed to our genre and the sort of person one would want on one's side if there really was a zombie apocalypse (although we all need Maberry on our left, McKinney on our right, and Ochse on point if that ever comes to pass).

I thank all these authors for their generosity in donating their wondrous stories for your reading pleasure and to assist with my fundraising. I am sure you will enjoy every word.

Finally, let me thank Shane for conceiving this anthology, putting it together, and getting it into your hands. You are a legend, mate.

Motor Neurone Disease/ALS is an awful disease—one with no cure. And no treatment but one—the love of friends and family. As to that treatment, my glass is full to overflowing.

Rocky Wood
Melbourne, Australia, November 2011

THE GUNNER'S LOVE SONG
Joe McKinney

For Manly Wade Wellman

Sheriff John Morison was a big man, six-three and two hundred and sixty pounds in his boots, slack-brimmed Stetson cowboy hat, and chocolate brown suit. He had a strong, proud chin, a drooping, Teddy Roosevelt-style mustache, and sleepy, nut-colored eyes that had seen much and feared little. People around Sabine County said he'd come home from the Great War with his eyes like that—sleepy, yet with an intensity behind them that withered most men.

He was the only man from my youth with the stones to stand up to my Daddy when Daddy was on one of his benders, and growing up, I respected him, and even feared him, because of that power he seemed to have over other men.

And now, sitting in his office, a lazy metal fan turning on the windowsill with a steady *clack, clack, clack*, I had those eyes focused on me again.

Two days before I'd been in a hotel bar in New York City, sipping mint juleps with a lovely flaxen-haired gal from Iowa, the two of us enjoying my recent release from the Army, when I'd received a telegram from Morison telling me my cousin Mike had got himself into some serious trouble.

Now my cousin Mike has a problem. He stutters. People hear him talk and they think he's retarded, which he ain't. When the two of us were kids, folks took to calling him Machine Gun Mike. He hated it, and I hated hearing it.

Still, it was pretty accurate, far as nicknames go, because his stuttering makes him sound like he's spitting bullets.

But when Morison told me why I'd just raced halfway across the country, I nearly laughed in his face.

War will do that to you. The giants of our youth become merely men, and sometimes even the objects of our pity.

"A girl?" I said, staring Morison square in the eye. "You called me back here because Mike is having trouble with a girl? Is that why you got him locked up?"

"That's for his own protection."

"From who?"

He held up both hands and patted the air like that was supposed to calm me down. "Let me explain," he said.

"I bet it'll be a riot," I said.

And it was, too, because what he told me was a lunatic's tale.

Recently, there'd been seven murders along County Road 153, the dirt road that winds north past my cousin's house, into the pine forests of northern Louisiana, and from there to God knows where.

Mike and I had wandered that road many times in our youth, and I knew most of the folks who lived along it. They were all poor, just good old fashioned backwoods folks, their homes simple weather-beaten shacks that were even smaller and humbler than the little house Mike and I had shared with his Dad after my Daddy died. All seven victims had come from those simple folks, two men and five women.

The bodies had been chewed to pieces, like a pack of wild dogs had done it, and the whole county was up in a roar.

Armed men started patrolling the road at night—hard drinkers with rifles, most of them.

Two nights before my arrival, at the same time I was enjoying the company of my flaxen-haired Iowa nurse, those patrols had seen a large doglike thing skulking through Myrtle Ferguson's back yard.

They shot it, and they saw it fall, but when they checked to see what it was they'd shot, all they found was the naked body of a young, black-haired woman named Rosalinda Villalobos.

"Now there were witnesses," Morison assured me. "All those men swear up and down that what they shot was a dog. Or a wolf. Something like that."

"They were drunk," I said, unimpressed. "They made a mistake."

"Yeah, I know," he said. "I thought of that. First thing, that's what I thought. But you see, this Villalobos woman, she had a reputation."

"What kind of reputation?"

He sighed. "People 'round here claim she was a witch."

"A witch?"

He nodded.

"I see." I looked briefly at my fingernails, then back at Morison. In that moment I realized the number of sacred monuments from my youth had just been reduced by one. "Do you mind telling me what this has to do with Mike?"

"She's the one Mike was involved with," Morison said. "He was crazy in love with her, Tom. I mean crazy. You know the way some men get? Wild in the head."

That floored me. My first instinct was that this girl had talked Mike into doing something illegal. It hadn't even occurred to me to think of Mike falling in love. I guess even I hadn't figured he had that kind of emotional sophistication. Not the Gunner.

But then the implications of what I was thinking hit me, and I was ashamed.

I lowered my voice. "Has he tried to hurt himself?" I asked.

"No, not yet."

"So why did you put him in a cell?"

Morison looked down at his desk and pushed the blotter around, fidgeting with it. "Look, Tom, it's like this. Folks 'round here believed that woman was bad news. I don't believe she was a witch any more than you do, but those people were terrified of her. Still are. After they killed her, they chucked her body in the peach orchard up near the start of the pines.

I licked my teeth while I thought about that. The peach orchard hadn't been a working orchard since before the War with the Union. Sabine County's always had a lot of poor people, both black and white, and the peach orchard was where the blacks buried their people that didn't have family or friends to pay for a grave marker. For those people up in the pine country to toss a white woman—even a white woman with some Mexican blood in her—into an unmarked grave in the peach orchard, they must have really hated her.

Morison went on.

"Mike was real upset by that, Tom. Sometime during the night, he went up there and dug her up."

I wanted to scoff at him, to tell him that Mike would never do something that stupid or crazy, but when I looked into his sleepy, world-weary eyes, I knew every word of it was true.

"A couple of boys found her body the next morning."

"Where?" I asked.

"Mike's front yard."

My stomach turned over.

"Folks up in the pine country was plenty pissed. They took the body and pitched it back into the peach orchard, then they came back lookin' for Mike. When I got there, they was fixin' to lynch him."

My mind raced through the options, trying to figure out what, if anything, I could do for Mike. The old big brother instincts I'd always had for Mike were stronger than ever, like I'd never been gone at all, and I knew the only I could do to help him was to keep him close.

"You mind if I take him home?" I asked.

"I was kind of hopin' you would," Morison confided.

He led me back to the cells, which I remembered well from all those horrible Sunday mornings when I'd wake up to Sheriff Morison banging on the screen door of our house, yelling for me to get dressed and come with him to fetch my Daddy.

Little had changed. Many of the same faces looked out at me, their hands gripping the bars, their faces staring at me like morose, drunken butterflies in some grotesque bug collection.

Morison opened Mike's cell and Mike came out, head hung low, shoulders stooped. He looked like he wanted to disappear into the shadows.

He was sadder than I'd ever seen him before, which was maybe why he looked older than I remembered. But little else had changed. He still wore his pants hitched up too high and his skin still had that flabby, unhealthy paleness to it. He hadn't combed his hair.

I pulled him into the yellow circle of light that an overhead lamp made on the floor and straightened his hair.

"You okay?" I asked him.

He muttered something.

One of the other prisoners yelled at him. "Hey Gunner, what day is it?"

I hadn't heard anybody use his nickname out loud since Mike and I started to run around together, and the sound of it snapped something inside of me.

Mike looked up at the man with watery eyes that wanted so much to be liked. "S-S-S-Saturday," he stuttered, and that brought a loud, braying laugh from the cells.

I went over to the man's cell and punched him through the bars, laying him out on the floor.

The laughing stopped.

"You mind if I take him home now, Sheriff?" I asked.

"No," said Morison, staring at the man in the cell, who was on his back, breathing noisily through a red, blossoming flower of blood that had once been his nose. "Go ahead."

We drove back to Mike's house in the '27 Ford his Daddy had left him and stopped in the driveway, a cloud of white dust settling across the trash strewn yard ahead of us. Mike hadn't said a word since leaving the jail, and I didn't push him. I figured he'd come around sooner or later.

The house where I had grown up was an absolute wreck. Mike's Daddy had been a good man, a kind man, but not a strong one. In the last years of his life he'd let his home slide into shabbiness, and when Mike took over, the slide just sort of kept on sliding, but at an accelerated rate.

I looked up at the gray, two story wood frame house and sighed. A corner near the kitchen window had been threatening to cave in since I was a kid, but still hadn't fallen. It drooped over the yard like the brim of an old hat. The porch sagged in the middle and its support beams tilted at uncertain angles. The roof, no doubt full of holes, looked like a checkerboard of black and gray tar strips and the whole place was up to its waist in yellowing alkali grass.

I was wondering how bad it was inside when Mike finally spoke.

"I been m-m-meanin' to p-p-paint it," he said.

I put my hand on his shoulder and guided him towards the front door. "It's okay," I said. "We'll do it together."

The inside was as bad as I'd thought, so crowded with ruined furniture that I barked my shin with every step. Water had come through a hole in the ceiling and the wood floor near a far corner of the living room was dark and probably rotted through. I made my way to the kitchen and sat down while Mike made us coffee.

Outside the sky was coloring with the pink and gold and darkling purple of an East Texas sunset, the kind I'd missed so much during the war. A cool breeze stirred the curtains of an open window in the dining room and I smelled the scent of country pine mingled with the dust.

"Tell me about her, Mike?" I said.

Mike put our coffees on the table and sat down next to me. It occurred to me then that the truly remarkable thing about Mike was the honesty of his expressions, for another man might have tried to hide the naked pain of lost love I saw in his face.

"I l-l-loved her," he said with a stiff set to his mouth and chin that almost dared me to challenge him. "And she loved m-m-me."

That seemed to say everything that needed to be said in his mind, and I nodded.

"Okay," I said.

"Okay," he answered back, like we'd settled something.

I waited.

"I have a p-p-picture," he said. He got up suddenly and went into the living room. When he came back he put a picture frame in my hand.

I took it and studied the girl I saw there.

"This is Rosalinda?" I said.

He nodded.

She wasn't an attractive woman, to be sure, but her eyes were full of a vital spark that gave her face character, and kindness. They were as black as her hair, tucked in beneath a large, heavy brow line that shaded her face with one continuous, unbroken eyebrow.

He told me how they met. She'd wandered onto the property, looking for milkweed root, and came upon him while he was trying to fix the burned valves on his tractor's motor. The two of them talked all afternoon, and by the time Mike went to bed that night, he was hopelessly in love.

It was at that point I realized how unfairly I'd judged him when I doubted his ever falling in love, for he clearly loved Rosalinda Villalobos in that same absolutely honest and genuine way in which he expressed all his emotions. He was like a child in the uncomplicated purity of his heart.

Yet he moved from one emotional extreme to another with furious speed. As he told me how the mob had denied Rosalinda a decent burial—even as he knelt over her dead body and pleaded with them—he became so angry I thought for a moment he might start throwing things around the room.

"They t-t-told me she d-d-deserved to rot in the s-s-street like a d-d-dog," he said, his voice thick with sobs.

I looked him straight in the eye and asked him if he'd dug up her body.

"No," he said, and the word sounded like a judge's gavel pounding the bench.

"Then how?" I asked.

"That was her," he said. "She was trying t-t-to come b-b-back to me."

I let out a long sigh, seeing a long road to recovery ahead of him. I tried to reason with him, asking him all sorts of questions designed to get at the truth, but the honesty never left his face. He stood firmly by the belief that death was not the end for his beloved Rosalinda, and that not even the grave could keep her from coming back to him.

Though I never lost my patience, I finally got to that point where I couldn't listen any more.

I sent him to bed.

As for myself, I slept only in fits, tossing and turning on the couch all night.

The next morning Rosalinda's body was waiting for us on the front lawn.

I was angry, and for the first time in my life, I yelled at Mike, convinced now he'd lied to me. I accused him of sneaking out behind my back, of digging up that poor girl and dragging her corpse back here.

But his motives were a mystery to me, for he flatly denied any wrong doing, and though the words 'sick' and 'perverted' lingered on the tip of my tongue, I couldn't bring myself to say them.

"Let me see your hands," I said, taking them in my own and studying his fingernails for tell-tale signs of dirt.

I saw none.

"Come with me," I said, and led him upstairs to his room. I searched everywhere, looking for sweaty clothes or dirty boots or anything that would confirm my accusations.

"She c-c-came back to me," Mike said. "I t-t-told you she would."

"Shut up," I roared at him. It took us both by surprise, the anger in my voice. He backed into a corner and hung his head while I ran my hands through my hair, wondering what in the hell to do.

"Tell me the truth, Mike," I said. "Did you dig that girl up?"

He shook his head.

"Look me in the eye and say the words," I said.

He did. He looked me straight in the eye and pleaded innocent.

"She came b-b-back to m-m-me," he said. "She loves m-m-me."

"Okay," I said. "Come on."

"Where are w-w-we going?" he asked, following me down the stairs and out onto the lawn like a puppy.

"We're going to bury your girl good and proper."

Looking at Rosalinda's face, I felt a tinge of panic. This was not the same girl I had seen in Mike's picture frame the night before—or, rather, she was, only changed.

Those eyes, those eyes that had seemed to possess such kindness in the photograph, no longer seemed kind. They were bloodless and mean, wide open and fixed. To my surprise, they hadn't milked over with cataracts, the way they usually do in a dead body. I looked deep into them and shuddered.

The prominent brow ridge was gone too, and with it, the single eyebrow. In its place was a delicate, decidedly feminine brow, high and smooth, sensuous.

She was pale. I expected that, of course. But not the rosy, shapeless patches on her cheeks. Those seemed unnatural, definitely not right.

I knelt down next to her and looked at her hands. Her fingernails and the palms of her hands were caked with brown ditch mud, the kind found all through the peach orchard further up the road. Her simple white dress was stained with dirt, too.

"What are you d-d-doing?" Mike asked, as I ran my finger along the leading edge of Rosalinda's top teeth.

"Nothing," I said, and took my hand away. But it was at that moment that a new thought took shape in my mind.

Back in the war, my platoon was part of Patton's spearhead through France. At one point, we got so far ahead of the main force that we had to stop and spend two days in a little town on the banks of the Saone River.

As I washed the dust from my hands at a pump on the side of our house and watched an angry crowd of about twenty men coming up the gradual rise of the front lawn, I thought about those simple folk in that French village and all the funny superstitions they'd shared with me over dinner and endless bottles of wine. I didn't find those superstitions quite as funny now as I had then, though.

Mike, whose face was still glowing with the childish faith that his lover had come back to him, smiled stupidly from the porch down at the lynch mob.

I grabbed an axe handle and came up next to Mike as one of the men was mounting the steps to the porch. I hit the man in the gut with a hard backhanded slap that doubled him over. Then I kicked him in the face and sent him sprawling onto his back at the feet of the crowd.

Two more men charged us. A moment later, both were on the ground, one holding his shattered knee, and the other on his hands and knees, swaying drunkenly while he spit out teeth and blood onto the grass.

"Get off our land," I said, walking down the steps toward the crowd.

They backed up a few steps before somebody in the back yelled, "That retard done crossed the line."

There was a murmur of agreement as the others took courage from the defiant voice and stopped retreating. Several of them muttered threats.

"Bring us that witch's body," somebody yelled.

"She's not here," I said. That was a lie, of course. She was underneath a tarp in the woodshed, waiting to be buried.

"We know that retard dug her up," the crowd shouted.

"Look," I said, staring at each of them in turn, "I've just come back from the war and I'm having a rough time of it. If you don't get off this land I'm liable to shoot the lot of you and tell the sheriff I thought you was all a bunch of Germans. Now get yourselves gone."

I did my best to look insane, and I think more than a few of them bought it. I am Tom Gilley's son, after all. The apple don't fall far from the tree. They took a collective step back.

One of the crowd, I couldn't tell who, shouted that our house was likely to catch fire one night soon. I looked around for the one who'd dared to say it, but before I could respond, a single rifle shot split the morning air.

Everybody wheeled around, and there stood Morison, a smoking rifle on his hip, his sleepy eyes shining.

"There ain't gonna be no fire," he said. "You folks get back to your homes."

A murmur spread through the crowd, but the rifle shot seemed to have broken their resolve.

"Go on," Morison said.

Slowly, grumbling their frustration, they started to disperse.

When they were gone, Morison stepped on to the porch, looking with disapproval at my axe handle.

"Some men," he said, "they come back from a war and they still got the war in their heads. How about you, Tom? You still got the war in your head?"

I handed the axe handle to Mike and told him to put it back in the shed.

We both watched him go.

"I'm pretty well adjusted," I said, once Mike was gone.

Morison spit in the grass. "Well?"

"Well what?"

"Don't play dumb with me," he said, his finger in my face. "That's twice I've had to do this, so don't. You know what I want to know."

"He didn't do it," I said.

Morison looked deep into my eyes. "I have your word on that?"

"You do."

"Okay," he said, his voice softening to a husky grumble. A few minutes later he was gone, a cloud of white dust in his wake.

23

We buried Rosalinda in the backyard, beneath a majestic, moss-covered black elm. No more peach orchard for her.

Mike went out to the roadside to gather blackberry blossoms for her grave while I sat on the porch, whittling one end of the axe handle to a sharp point with my knife.

That night, I put Mike to bed and promised him when he woke the next morning, everything would be just fine. Then I went downstairs, opened the back door, the one that looked out on Rosalinda's grave, dropped down on the couch, and waited.

It was nearly two o'clock in the morning when I heard footsteps on the back porch.

Without bothering to get up I said, "Hello, Rosalinda."

"Hello," she said, and smiled wickedly. Two sharp white points poked out from under her upper lip.

"Come in. You're invited."

Her smile widened.

"Where is Mike Gilley?"

"He's upstairs," I said. "Sleeping."

"I want to see him."

"Yeah," I said, sitting up, "I bet you do." I reached under the couch and pulled out the axe handle. "But that ain't gonna happen, Rosalinda."

She glared at the pointed end of the stick and then at me. "Fool," she said. "Who do you think you are?"

"His guardian angel."

"I love him," she hissed. "And he loves me. I've come for him."

"I know you loved him," I said, standing up. "And for that I thank you. But you can't have him."

She ran at me, dagger-like fingernails slashing the air between us. I ducked the blows and plunged the point of the axe handle into her heart. She died, this time for good, with a scream still trying to escape her lips.

By sunrise I was done reburying Rosalinda, and as I brushed the dirt from my clothes, I wondered what I would tell Mike. How could I make him understand the murky complexity of superstition when my own mind was stretched to the breaking point trying to take it all in? I could tell him of creatures of the night, how a werewolf killed in her animal form is doomed to return as a vampire, but what would be the point? He was too fragile for that, and it might cause him to snap.

But then, as I mounted the stairs, it occurred to me that I didn't need to tell Mike anything. He had all the answers he needed. He'd loved honestly and deeply, and had been loved in his turn. That was a prize few men could ever claim. For hadn't Rosalinda, of all the possible places she could go, chose three times to return to Mike's door?

I imagined her struggles to claw her way out of the ground, and then the long, moonlit walk to Mike's door, before she ran out of the cover of night and the morning's light caused her to shut down, to slip into a catatonic state just a few steps short of her destination, and her lover's neck.

Mike didn't need to know any of that. He only needed the assurance that his love had meant more to Rosalinda than death itself. Let him take strength from that.

And let time cure him of his grief.

KEEPING WATCH

Nate Kenyon

—1—

My sister wrote to me the other day. Since the letter arrived and I risked the frigid stretch of road to fetch it from the mailbox at the end of the driveway, I've been sitting in pretty much the same spot. Front door locked tight. Shades closed. This chair in the corner of my dark little living room in my dark little house is the only place that seems safe to me anymore.

But I'm going to have to get up soon and do something about it, one way or the other. I can't live the rest of my life this way. Lately I've begun to wonder if it couldn't get out and come after me, even here. And that, my friends, is nightmare enough to drive anyone insane.

The letter is addressed to me, with the words *please forward* scrawled in my sister's spidery hand across the front.

> Dear David: I hope this finds you well. People are dropping like flies out here in Colorado—worst flu in twenty years, they say. Most of the deaths are old people who have gone the winter with little or no heat in their mountain cabins. Reminds me of the old days, waking up at 3 am with the fire out and my toes like blocks of ice, even with the three blankets and the dog on top of that. Do you remember?
>
> Where to begin? We haven't spoken in years, and I suppose it's my fault—I'm the one who left. I always hoped that you would leave too, but somewhere in my heart I knew you wouldn't. You still feel responsible, don't you? And so you stay in Maine. And I keep running.
>
> I have to know. Is it still there? God, I shiver when I think

26

about that black water. I still can't sleep at night. I think about it shriveling up under the sun, or somebody coming along with a bulldozer and turning it into a parking lot. But that would be too easy, wouldn't it? So I sleep with the lights on and I try not to dream.

And there's something else. I think it's awake again. I have them send the White Falls Gazette out here to me—I read and I hold my breath and I look for you, David, I look to see if you've gone missing. Well, I haven't seen your name and I thank God for that every single night, I do. But if you're still alive and still there then you know why I'm writing because you read it too.

She goes on a while longer, but the rest is not important. Because I do read the paper, and I do know about the little boy who disappeared last Friday in the woods.

I think Alley is right. It is awake again. I think about the lake out there, black as coal in the moonlight, and I remember.

Lord help me, I remember everything.

—2—

We found the lake for the first time during the early spring of 1995.

I was ten, and Alley was eight. The winter had been rough; those days we pumped our water by hand from the well behind the house, and I remember it kept freezing up every night about twenty minutes after the sun went down. Dad tried to keep it warm by running a light and packing it with hay, but that cold just wouldn't be refused when darkness fell.

The coldest days in Maine are the ones where the sky stays an icy blue, the ground is swept bare in places from the wind and the grass snaps like glass when you step on it. The cold came early that year, and by late December we'd been pounded by three major storms, and had about two feet of snow on the ground.

But around March we had a thaw and we could get outside. I think we'd just about driven Dad crazy by then, chasing each other around inside and playing with Alex, our nosy little Lab mutt. Dad was probably glad for a few hours of peace. We didn't have much; our mother had died of cancer two years after giving birth to Alley, and Dad worked in the mill for ten bucks an hour. He was gone a lot, and we mostly took care of ourselves, and made do with what we could find.

So on that early spring crisp and clear afternoon we filled a thermos with hot chocolate, threw on our coats and went out to find something to do.

Past the house and short stretch of pockmarked, bare dirt (Dad called it a lawn, but we referred to it as The Moon), the ground dropped off quickly to where a stream ran through the bottom of a shallow ravine. We'd been down there many times before, playing in the water. But we'd never gone much farther than the top of the other bank. Our folks had always told us it was dangerous in that part of the woods, and for some reason, we believed them. Certainly it stretched for several miles without another house or road, and so I suppose we were afraid of getting lost. Anyone who grew up in Maine knew that losing your way in the woods was bad news, with a capital "B."

As we stood in the shadows of the trees at the foot of the ravine watching the water run black and silent under its coat of ice, Alex ran right over it and up the other bank through the brush. I shouted after him but he didn't come, so I crossed as carefully as I could and fought my way back to the top, following his paw prints as Alley scrambled up behind.

The woods were deathly silent up there. No birds, or deer, or even wind to shake the trees. Alex might have scared the wildlife away, but the silence seemed unnatural to me. Winter in Maine is a desolate time, but there are all sorts of sounds in the woods if you know how to listen.

Those sounds were gone now.

Not too far away I saw a break in the trees. Nothing more than a deer trail, covered in a foot of snow, crisscrossed with the tiny light prints of rabbits and little birds. But I thought maybe Alex had gone down there.

"What do you think, Alley? Want to go for it?" I asked.

"I will if you will," she said.

I will if you will. Her typical response. "Would you jump off a bridge if I went first?"

She shrugged, and so I smiled and turned to follow the path, and Alley brought up the rear.

The brambles, so sharp and thick in summer, were brittle now and snapped as we brushed past them. I looked back at Alley once as she dragged her heels through the snow, staring down at the tips of her yellow boots. She wore one of my old jackets that made her look like a big marshmallow, and her cheeks were blotchy pink circles and icy lace from her breath clung to the brim of her hat.

A boy at the age of ten doesn't waste much time thinking about how he loves his sister, but I remember thinking it then, all right. Our daddy was gone most of the day and night, our mother was dead, and she was all I had.

I will if you will. It made me smile. She was willing to follow me to the ends of the earth, and at that moment, it almost seemed like we'd get there.

We'd been walking maybe ten or fifteen minutes when water began to seep up under a thin layer of ice that snapped and popped under the snow.

The sounds were like gunshots echoing in the cold air. I glanced up as we took a bend in the path and caught a glimpse of something flat and dark through the tree trunks. I stopped short, and I heard a short "humph!" and felt Allie's hand on my back.

Thing was, I hadn't stopped in surprise. It was shocking to see such open space in the middle of dense woods, sure. But it was the feeling I got that made me freeze in my tracks. The kind you get when a big hairy bug crawls out of the shower drain near your foot. A feeling of mindless disgust.

"David, what *is* it?" Alley said.

"It's a lake, dummy. Haven't you ever seen a lake before?"

"But what's it doing out here?"

I didn't answer. Her questions were silly, but I knew what she meant—a lake was the last thing I had expected to come upon, no more than a fifteen minute walk from the house. The chances were actually pretty good that this lake was a well-kept secret. I had certainly never heard of it before, and I doubted if my father had either. This was something that existed apart from and in spite of the human noise that surrounded it; Route 27 maybe twenty miles east, Brunswick with its Air Force base forty or fifty miles away.

Whatever was in that lake could have lived there untouched for years. The thought chilled me in a way the cold never could.

The trees around the lake were all bare, except for the stretch of pines that grew along the far edge. Their razor-sharp needles reached up and cut into the sky, while the others, bare-backed against the snow and ice, seemed to turn inward. Along one section of shore, a series of huge black stones reared out of the shallows like the back of some ancient beast.

I walked to the lake's edge. The bank was gently sloped, the water still and flat. Strangely, there was little ice here. I reached out a hand.

"Don't touch it!" Alley cried.

At the sound of her voice I jerked my hand back like it had been scalded. "Don't be stupid," I said. "It's only water. You don't see Alex getting all freaked out about it, do you?"

That was true enough; Alex was splashing in and out of the shallows, running along the bank and barking furiously at whatever invisible things dogs barked at. But I climbed back up the bank and didn't touch the water with so much as a boot tip.

We walked around a portion of the lake, sometimes losing sight of it in our efforts to climb over dead brush and fallen trees, always coming back to it again. It was much the same all the way around. We found nothing, not even a discarded beer can or gum wrapper. If anyone had been to this pond before us, they had left no trace behind.

By the time we had explored the whole area and come back around again, the sky above us had turned leaden, the kind of heavy gray that means a coming storm. That was when we both realized that Alex hadn't been around in a while. I hadn't heard him crashing around in the underbrush, either.

I got this feeling in the pit of my stomach, a sort of twisting in my guts, like I *knew* something was wrong. I would feel it again later, when Julie went under and I went in after her—but right then I had never felt such a thing before, and I panicked. I started yelling for the dog. I guess Alley must have felt the same way, because she started shouting along with me.

I yelled myself hoarse but Alex never came, and it seemed like the water was laughing at me. Dark and still and black as coal but somewhere, deep below the surface (and I knew it was deep, all right), something was saying *you want your dog? Come a little closer and I'll give him to you. But you might not like what you see. He doesn't look much like a dog anymore.*

I looked at Alley and she was crying. "We'd better get home," I said. "It's going to storm. Alex knows the way. He'll turn up at the house."

As we got back on the path I risked a turn and looked back at the lake through the trees. I could have sworn that right then I saw something move in the shallows. Something as big and black as that awful water, sliding back into the depths like a wave that had reared up and broken against the rocks.

I turned back and hurried home, my heart in my throat, and didn't mention what I had seen until years later, and by then, of course, it was too late.

—3—

Alex never did come back. Not that night, or the next day, or the next. The years did pass, too quickly. When I turned thirteen I started going to the high school in the next town, and Alley and I began to drift apart. I made my own friends, and she hers; a brother and sister can be close as children, but as they go through those early teenage years there are things they cannot discuss together, at least until the awkwardness of that age has passed.

But at fifteen, when I entered the ninth grade and Alley started her first year at the new school, we were together again for a while. We found some of our old affection for each other, and though it had changed into something we held at arm's length instead of in our guts, it was still good.

And then I met Julie.

Julie was one of my sister's friends. She lived on the other side of town. She visited our home for the first time on one of those beautiful spring days where the grass turned green and the day lost the final trace chill of winter.

The last of the snow had melted about three weeks before, and now the ground was muddy and thick, but the sun was out and things were waking up and moving around, preparing for summer.

Julie was a pale, pretty little thing, with dark shining hair and bright blue eyes. I saw why my sister liked her so much. She had a way of looking at you that could melt your heart, and when she laughed it was like the world had gotten a little brighter. I guess you could say I fell for her, and pretty hard, but she was two years younger and my sister's best friend, and I didn't have much experience with that sort of thing.

I guess I wanted to impress her, because walking home from the bus I started talking about the lake. I told her about how we discovered it as kids and my sister listened and didn't say a word.

"It sounds so cool," Julie said. "I can't believe you never went back."

I wasn't sure I liked where this was going. Things began coming back to me, the way the water looked under a gray sky, the feeling of the woods, and ... something else. Something I had tried to convince myself I hadn't seen; that movement in the shallows, a shape slipping back under the surface.

"It's out in the middle of nowhere, Alley," she said. "Hidden away. That's so neat. Clean enough to swim in?"

Alley wrinkled her nose in disgust. "Swim in *that?* No way."

"I don't know," I said. "Might not be so bad." Maybe I just wanted to disagree with my sister, or maybe it was the thought of Julie and me getting into swimsuits and splashing around together. Dad had probably been right about the dog. A bear had gotten it or some hunter had downed a few too many beers and mistook it for a deer. The point was the sun was shining and all the things that used to haunt my sleep seemed so silly and childish.

It took a few minutes of persuasion but my sister finally gave in. "I will if you will," she said, looking at me and smiling a little. I guess she hadn't changed much over the years. Still my baby sister, right?

Alley found Julie a suit and we filled another thermos, with sweet coffee this time. We found the path with no trouble, though it was marshy in places with long feathery ferns hiding the wet, sucking mud of the season. I pushed away small branches of alder and birch as I passed through, enjoying the smell of damp earth and old wood. The shadows painted dark lines on the tree trunks and underbrush. Fresh brambles at the edge of the trail caught and pulled at our clothes, and the trees were thick with leaves uncurling in the warmth.

The lake remained hidden until we were almost upon it, but the ground got wetter until we were stepping out of our shoes in the muck. I walked ahead of them both, and again the woods went silent around us. I remembered the feeling that had come over me years before and it got me thinking. The woods in spring are always full of life. Birds, mice, chipmunks and squirrels chasing each other up and down mossy tree trunks. But now, hell, even the bugs were gone.

It was almost enough to make me turn back. But one look at Julie, and I kept going. I didn't want to seem like a coward.

The path ended at a big mound of grayish clay that marked the end of a little tributary leading into the lake. I didn't remember it being there before. Spindly weeds grew out along the water's dark edges. And Jesus take me if it didn't look wrong. *Unnatural.*

Julie came up next to me. I said something like it didn't look too good to swim in after all, and she went right down to the lake's edge and crouched. "It's *warm*," she said, dipping her fingers in the murky water. "Like, eighty degrees, at least. It's like a big bathtub. And the bottom looks kind of sandy in places."

"Yuck, it smells," Alley said, and I got a strong feeling of déjà vu. Suddenly it was like I was ten years old again, and my sister was standing next to me in her puffy marshmallow jacket, her cheeks glowing pink with the cold.

"Could be leaches in there," I said. "Or snapping turtles. Big, mean bastards. They can take off a toe or two if you're not careful."

But Julie didn't seem to hear me. She was already pulling off her baggy shorts and top to reveal a black and white striped swimsuit underneath.

I sat down on a dry spot with the thermos of creamy coffee and poured a cup. Alley shrugged and sat down next to me, and we both watched Julie as she tiptoed around the water's edge to the point where the big black rocks reared up five feet out of the water. Smooth and slippery from the looks of them. She jumped up on one, hugging her arms to her chest, and peered into the water.

Then she took a deep breath and before we could say anything she threw herself off the rock.

I sat there with a cup of coffee in my hand and I couldn't move. I was suddenly sure that Julie wasn't going to surface at all, that the lake had reached out a weed-wrapped hand and pulled her down, kicking and screaming, into the depths. But a moment later she came up sputtering and laughing, shaking big drops of water from her hair, which hit the stone and sketched designs of darker black along its side.

"Come on in, you wimps," she called. "Water's fine."

"Knock it off, Julie," Alley said. "It's gross." Her voice was tight. Julie ignored her and scrambled back up the big rock. She smiled at me as she stood on the top of it and yanked up the straps of her suit. I could see the gooseflesh on her arms. Her hair stuck to her forehead and hung down the back of her neck in shiny black strings. The blackness of that hair against her pale skin was shocking. A thrill ran up and down my legs.

"How about you, Dave?" she said. "Or are you a wimp, too?" Then she took several short steps forward and flung herself out over the water, drawing her legs up before she hit with a splash.

I set the half-full cup down on the grass. Saw Julie, as she climbed up once again and perched on the top of the rock; she took one step and then one leg flew up and she fell backward with incredible speed, her head snapping down and hitting the rock with a sickening crack. I stood frozen as her limp body slid down quickly and slipped into the dark water.

My sister screamed, and then I was running, leaping over the stream and kicking my shoes off in the mud. I flung myself towards the water and hit with my right shoulder, scraping the shallow bottom, and the water was warm, God it was almost *hot*. I pushed off hard with my left hand and came up, half stumbling through the waist-deep water towards the place where Julie had disappeared, choking, my mouth full of brackish liquid. It was deeper there, and I felt blindly for her body with my right hand, my left grasping a crack in the slippery rock, but I couldn't feel anything and I let go, *she wasn't there*, I was kicking down under the surface, grasping handfuls of slimy mud along the bottom but finding nothing. I came up for air and Alley was still standing in the same spot, hands on her face, pale white and shaking.

I went back under and farther from shore, and I finally caught a glimpse of Julie through the murky water, arms out and head lolling to one side. She had slid several yards away from where she went under, down into the section of the lake that got deep very fast, and the strange currents of the water had kept her tangled in the long weeds along the bottom. She was caught between what looked like two huge rocks.

I came up for a gasp of air and went down again. That was when I felt something move.

I go over and over this part in my mind; the sudden rush of fear prickling my skin, opening my eyes in that cloudy, algae-infested filth, straining to see past the floating weeds like fingers in the darkness. And this is where I stop, and think that what I saw must have been a hallucination brought on by stress and adrenaline, because nothing, *nothing* in this world could have been that alien and horrible. But deep down I know that what I saw was real. And that, I suppose, is why I stayed here in Maine all these years, watching and waiting.

Beside Julie's body, a fissure in one of those rocks suddenly split to reveal a huge, rolling yellow eye.

I drew in a great mouthful of dirty water and pushed myself backward. The entire floor of the lake seemed to erupt under me as something monstrous and black and horrible came up out of the mud. That eye grew larger, unblinking, reptilian, foreign, surrounded by wrinkled flesh, moving closer through the dim water. I surfaced, choking and sputtering, and lunged back out of the shallows, throwing myself up on the bank, and a moment later the middle of the lake begin to boil and churn as that thing came up like a creature from the deep.

As its ragged, moss-covered hump broke the surface, we turned and ran. The branches whipped at my face and stung my skin, but I kept going, crying helplessly and numb from what I had seen at the last instant.

It had come up with Julie in its hooked jaws. Julie was bloody and screaming.

God forgive me. She was still alive.

There are things in nature that no one will ever understand, I guess. And things natural that have become corrupted, turned unnatural over time. I don't know what is in that lake, but I have my ideas. I'm willing to bet that whatever it is had existed there for centuries, unmolested and in a state of hibernation, until Alley and I and Alex the dog came upon it one day years ago. And then perhaps it was only waiting after that, sleeping lightly in the muck at the bottom of that cursed lake and waking up every spring, until we came along again and Julie lost her life.

We told our father, of course, and brought him out to the lake. The police chief came out the next day. They talked among themselves and decided Julie had hit her head on the rock and drowned, and Alley and I had cracked under the stress after watching it happen. A couple of divers went in the lake but they never found her body.

I didn't expect them to find it. I expected them to find something much worse.

It was funny. I remember one of the divers coming up out of the water and telling the police chief that it was useless and they had to stop. "Muddy and deep as hell out there in the middle," he said. "Can't see more'n a foot. The floor's unstable, too—started shifting on us a little."

That was when I started screaming at them and thinking of that huge yellow eye and the doctor had to give me a shot and put me to bed, and everyone agreed that it had been a bad idea to let me come out with them.

Alley ran away from home not long after that. She had her own reasons,

I guess, the main one being the sleepless nights we both had, thinking of that thing so close by. A year after she left, Dad died in an accident at the mill, and by that time I was seventeen and able to take care of myself, and I stayed on at the house, which might seem crazy to you but I had my reasons. The main one was guilt, guilt that I had brought Julie out there and then I had run like a coward when that thing came up with her in its jaws. I felt I had to stay and keep watch, in case it woke up again.

But there are other reasons.

And so I've taken the time to write all this down before I go out there, in case I don't come back. I'm leaving my sister's letter too, and the article about the boy who disappeared last Friday, so people won't think I'm crazy (though they probably will anyway). I'm taking my shotgun and I'm going out there because I have to do something about it now.

Alley, in case you ever read this, I want you to know that you were right; it's awake again, and this time maybe it's awake for good. You're probably wondering why I'm going alone, and not calling in the troops. It has nothing to do with wanting to be a hero. God knows I'd rather just run. But you can't always run, Alley, and I guess I've been running from this just like you, in my own way. Besides, something tells me that if I brought someone with me, we wouldn't find much more than an empty puddle. I think it knows I'm here and it's waiting for me, Alley. I can feel it. It wants me, and me alone.

If you read this after I'm gone, I want you to know that I felt like I had no other choice, and that I did my best. And I want you to know one other thing. I never blamed you for leaving. You're my flesh and blood. I love you, kid.

A couple more things, before I go. I said there were reasons other than guilt why I stayed around and kept watch. The first one is that I saw something in that yellow eye, as alien as it was; I saw a craftiness, something sly that said *I know exactly what I'm doing, boy.* Intelligence, that's what it comes down to, I guess. And intelligence in a creature like that is a horrible thing, indeed.

The second one I'm only guessing at, and I might be wrong. Lord knows I hope I am. But when I think about that lake the first time I saw it, and then the second time a couple of years later, something had changed. Something was there that hadn't been there before. It took me a while but I think I finally got it.

The pile of clay, you see. At the end of the trail where you come out, just above the water's edge.

That pile looked just like a snapper's nest would look, if the eggs were three feet around.

LIKE PART OF THE FAMILY
Jonathan Maberry

"My ex-husband is trying to kill me," she said.

She was one of those cookie-cutter East Coast blondes. Pale skin, pale hair, pale eyes. Lots of New Age jewelry. Not a lot of curves and too much perfume. Kind of pretty if you dig the modeling-scene heroin chic look. Or if you troll the anorexia twelve-steps or crack houses looking for easy ass that's so desperate for affection they'll boff you blind for a smile. Not my kind. I like a little more meat on the bone, and a bit more sanity in the eyes. This one came to me on a referral from another client.

"He actually try?"

"I can *tell*, Mr. Hunter."

Yeah, I thought and tried not to sigh. *What I figured.*

"You call the cops?"

She shrugged.

"What's that mean? You call them or not?"

"I called," she said. "They said that there wasn't anything they could do unless he did something first."

"Yeah," I said. "Can't arrest someone for thinking about something."

"He threatened me."

"Anyone hear him make the threat?"

"No."

"Then it's your word."

"That's what the police said." She crossed her legs. Her legs were on the thin side of being nice. Probably were nice before drugs or stress or a fractured self image wasted her down to Sally Stick-figure.

Skirt was short, shoes looked expensive. I have three ex-wives and I pay alimony bigger than India's national debt. I know how expensive women's shoes are. I was wearing black sneakers from Payless. Glad I had a desk between me and her.

"Your husband ever hurt you?" I asked. "Or try to?"

"*Ex,*" she corrected. "And ... yes. That's why I left him. He hit me a few times. Mostly when he was drunk and out of control."

I held up a hand. "Don't make excuses for him. He hit you. Being drunk doesn't change the rules. Might even make it worse, especially if he did it once while drunk and then let himself come home drunk again."

She digested that. She'd probably heard that rap before but it might have come from a female case worker or a shrink. From the way her eyes shifted to me and away and back again I guessed she'd never heard that from a man before. I guess for her men were the Big Bad. Too many of them are.

It was ten to five, but it was already dark outside. December snow swirled past the window. It wasn't accumulating, so the snow still looked pretty. Once it started piling up I hated the shit. My secretary, Mrs. Gilligan, fled at the first flake. Typical Philadelphian -they think the world will come to a screeching halt if there's half an inch on the ground. She's probably at Wegmans stocking up on milk, bread and toilet paper. The staples of the apocalypse. Me, I grew up in Minneapolis, and out in the Cities we think twenty inches is getting off light. Doesn't mean I don't hate the shit, though. A low annual snowfall is one of the reasons I moved to Philly after I got my PI license. Easier to hunt if you don't have to slog through snow.

"When he hit you," I said, "you report it?"

"No."

"Not to the cops?"

"No."

"Women's shelter?

"No."

"Anyone? A friend?"

She shook her head. "I was ... embarrassed, Mr. Hunter. A black eye and all. Didn't want to be seen."

Which means there's no record. Nothing to support her case about ex-hubby wanting to kill her.

I drummed my fingers on the desk blotter. I get these kinds of cases every once in a while, though I stayed well clear of domestic disputes and spousal abuse cases when I was with Minneapolis PD. I have a temper, and by the time they asked for my shield back I had six reprimands in my jacket for excessive force. At one of my IA hearings the captain said he was disappointed that I showed no remorse for the last 'incident'. I busted a child molester and somehow while the guy was, um, resisting arrest he managed to get mauled and mangled a bit. The pedophile tried to spin some crazy shit that I sicced a dog on him, but I don't *have* a dog. I said that he got mauled by a stray during a foot pursuit. Even at my own hearing I couldn't keep a smile off my face to save my job. Squeaked by on that one, but next time something like it happened—this time with a guy who whipped his wife half to death with an extension cord because she wasn't 'willing enough' in the bedroom—I was out on my ass. He ran into the same stray dog. Weird how that happens, huh? Long story short, I already didn't have the warm fuzzies for her husband. We all have our buttons, and when the strong prey on the weak all of mine get pushed.

"Did you go to the E.R.?"

"No," she said. "It was never that bad. More humiliating than anything."

I nodded. "What about after the divorce? He lay a hand on you since?"

She hesitated.

"Mrs. Skye?" I prompted.

"He tried. He chased me. Twice."

"*Chased* you? Tell me about it."

She licked her lips. She wore a very nice rose-pink lipstick that was the only splash of color. Even her clothes and shoes were white. Pale horse, pale rider.

"Well," she said, "that's where the story gets really ... strange."

"Strange how?"

"He—David, my ex-husband—*changed* after I filed for divorce. He's like a different person. Before, when I first met him, he was a very fastidious man. Always dressed nicely, always very clean and well-groomed."

"What's he do for a living?"

"He owns a nightclub. *The Crypt*, just off South Street."

"I know it, but that's a Goth club right? Is he Goth?"

"No. Not at all. He bought the club from the former owner, but he remodeled it after *The Batcave*."

"As in Batman?"

"As in the London club that was kind of the prototype of pretty much the whole Goth club scene. David's a businessman. There's a strong Goth crowd downtown, and they hang together, but the clubs in Philly aren't big enough to turn a big profit, and not near big enough to attract the better bands. So, he bought the two adjoining buildings and expanded out. He made a small-time club into a very successful main stage club, and he keeps the music current. A lot of post-punk stuff, but also the newer styles. Dark cabaret, deathrock, Gothabilly. That sort of thing. Low lights, black-tile bathrooms, bartenders who look like ghouls."

"Okay," I said.

"But this was all business to David. He didn't dress Goth. I mean, he wore black suits or black silk shirts to work, but he didn't dye his hair, didn't wear eye-liner. Funny thing is, even though he was clearly not buying into the lifestyle the patrons loved him. They called him the Prince. As in Prince of—?"

"Darkness, yeah, got it. Go on."

"David was more fussy getting ready to go out than I ever was. Spent forever in the bathroom shaving, fixing his hair. Always took him longer to pick out his clothes than me or any of my girlfriends."

"He gay?"

"No." And she shot me a 'wow, what a stereo-typically homophobic thing to say' sort of look.

I smiled. "I'm just trying to get a read on him. Fastidious guy having trouble with a relationship with his wife. Drinking problem, flashes of violence. Not a gay thing, but I've seen it before in guys who are sexually conflicted and at war with themselves and the world because of it."

She studied me for a moment. "You used to be a cop, Mr. Hunter?"

"Call me Sam," I said. "And, yeah, I was a cop. Minneapolis PD."

"A detective?"

"Yep."

"Okay." That seemed to mollify her. I gestured to her to continue. She took a breath. "Well ... toward the end of our relationship David stopped being so fastidious. He would go two or three days without shaving. I know that doesn't sound like the end of the world, but I never saw David without a fresh shave. Never. He carried an electric razor in his briefcase, had another at home and one in the office at the club. Clothes, too. Before, he'd sometimes change clothes twice or even three times a day if it was humid. He always wanted to look fresh. Showered at home morning and night, and had a shower installed in his office."

"I get the picture. Mr. Clean. But you say that changed while you were still together?"

"It started when he fell off the wagon."

"Ah."

"When I met him he said that he hadn't taken a drink for over two years. He was proud of it. He thought that his thirst—he always called it that—was evil, and being on the wagon made him feel like a real person. Then, after we started having problems, he started drinking again. Never in front of me, and he always washed his mouth out before he came home. I never smelled alcohol on him, but he was a different person from then on. And he started yelling at me all the time. He called me horrible names and made threats. He said that I didn't love him, that I was just trying to use him."

"I have to ask," I said, being as delicate as I could, "but was there someone else?"

"For me? God, no!"

"What set him off? From his perspective, I mean. Did he say that there was something that made him angry or paranoid?"

"Well ... I think it was his health."

"Tell me."

"He started losing weight. He was never fat, not even stocky. David was very muscular. He lifted a lot of weights, drank that protein powder twice a day. He had big arms, a huge chest. I asked him if he was taking steroids. He denied it, but I think he was trying to turn into one of those muscle freaks. Then, about a year and a half ago he started losing weight. When he taped his arms and found that his biceps were only twenty-two inches, he got really angry."

"David has twenty-two inch biceps?" Christ. Back in his Mr. Universe days, Arnold the Terminator had twenty-four inch arms, fully pumped. I think mine are somewhere shy of fifteen, and that's after three sets on the Bowflex.

"Not anymore," said Mrs. Skye. "He lost a lot of muscle mass. Really fast, too. I was scared, I told him to go to a doctor. I thought he might have cancer."

"Did he go to the doctor?"

"He said so ... but I don't think he did. He kept losing weight. After six months he didn't even have much definition. He was kind of ordinary sized."

"Was he drinking by this point?"

"I'm sure of it."

"That when he started putting his hands on you?"

"Yes. And he became paranoid. Kept trying to make it all my fault."

"How long did this go on?"

"Well ... after the first time he, um, *hurt* me, I gave him a second chance. After all, he was my husband. I figured he was just scared because of his health. But then it happened again. The second time he knocked me around pretty good. I couldn't go out of the house for a few days."

"Was that when you left?"

It took her so long to answer that I knew what her answer would be. I've done too many interviews of this kind. If self-esteem is low enough then victimization can become an addiction.

"I stayed for two more months."

"How many times did he hurt you during that time?" I asked.

"A few."

"A few is how many?"

Another long pause. "Six."

"Six," I said, trying to put no judgment in my tone. "What was the straw?"

She looked at her hands, at the clock, at the snow falling outside. If there'd been a magazine on my desk she would have picked it up and leafed through it. Anything to keep from meeting my eyes. "He choked me."

"I see."

"It was in the middle of the night. We were ... we were ..."

I almost sighed. "Let me guess. Make-up sex?"

She nodded, but she didn't blush. I'll give her that. "He'd been sweet to me for two weeks straight without getting mad or yelling, or anything. He acted like his old self. Charming." She finally met my eyes. "David has enormous charisma. He makes everyone like him, and he always seems so genuine."

"Uh huh," I said, wondering how that charm would work on a blackjack across his teeth.

"We sat up talking until late, then we went to bed. And in the middle of the night ... things just started happening. You know how it is."

I didn't, but I said nothing.

"I was, um ... on top. And we were pretty far into things, and then all of a sudden David reaches up and grabs me around the throat. I thought for one crazy moment that he was doing that auto-whatever it's called."

"Autoerotic asphyxiation," I supplied.

"Yeah, that. I thought he was doing that. He talked about it once before, but we'd never tried it. He's really strong and I'm pretty small. But ... I guess I thought he was trying to change things, you know? Create a new pattern for us. A fresh start."

Naivety can be a terrible thing. Jesus wept.

"But it wasn't sex play," I prompted.

"No. He started squeezing his hands. Suddenly I couldn't breathe. It was weird because we were so close to ... you know ... and David kept staring at me, his eyes wide like he was in some kind of trance. I tried to pull his hands apart, but it just made him squeeze tighter. That's when he started calling me names again, making wild accusations, accusing me of destroying his life."

"How did you get away?"

Her eyes cut away again. This was obviously very hard for her.

"I threw myself sideways and when I landed I kicked him in the, um ... you know."

I smiled.

"Good for you," I said, but she shook her head.

"I grabbed my clothes and ran out. Next day I drove past the house and saw that his car was gone. I had a locksmith come out and change the locks and change the security code on the alarm. I hired a messenger company to take a couple of suitcases of his clothes to the club. Next day I rented a storage unit and had a moving company take all of his stuff there. I used the same messenger service to send him the key."

"I'm impressed. That was quick thinking."

"I ... I'd already looked into that stuff before. Until that last stretch where he was nice I was planning to leave him. I'd already talked to my lawyer, and I filed for divorce by the end of that week."

"What did David do?"

"At first? Nothing except for some hysterical messages on my voicemail. He didn't try to break in, nothing like that. But after a while I started seeing his car behind mine when I was going to work."

"Where do you work?"

"I'm a nurse supervisor at Sunset Grove, the assisted living facility in Jenkintown. Right now I'm on the four to midnight shift. I've spotted David's car a lot, sometimes every night for weeks on end. I've seen him drive by when I'm going into the staff entrance, and his car is there sometimes when I get back home, cruising down the street or parked a block up."

"What makes you think he's planning to do more than just harass you?"

"He's said so."

"But—"

"He didn't say or do anything at first ... but over the last couple of weeks it's gotten worse. About three weeks ago I came out of work and stopped at a 7-11 for some gum, and when I came out he was leaning against my car. I told him to get away, but he pushed himself off the car and came up to me, smiling his charming smile. He told me that he knew who I was and what I was and that he was going to end me. His words. '*I'm going to end you*'. Then he left, still smiling."

"Did anyone see this?"

"At one in the morning? No."

Convenience stores have security cameras, I thought. If this thing got messy I could have her lawyer subpoena those tapes. I had her write down the address of the 7-11.

"That's how it went for a couple of weeks," she said. "But last night he really scared me."

"What happened?"

"He was in my bedroom."

"How?"

"That's it ... I don't know. The alarms didn't go off and none of the windows were broken. I heard a sound and I woke up and there he was, standing by the side of my bed. He's really thin now and as pale as those Goth kids at his club. He stood there, smiling. I started to scream and he put a finger to his lips and made a weird shushing sound. It was so strange that I actually did shut up. Don't ask me why. The whole thing was like a nightmare."

"Are you sure it wasn't?"

She hesitated, but she said, "I'm positive. He pointed at me and said that he knew everything about me. Then he started praying."

"Praying?"

"At least I think that's what he was doing. It was Latin, I think. He was saying a long string of things in Latin and then he left."

"How'd he get out?"

"The same way he got in, I guess ... but I don't know how. I was so scared that I almost peed myself and I just lay there in bed for a long time. I don't know how long. When I finally worked up the nerve, I ran downstairs and got a knife from the kitchen and went through the whole house."

"You didn't call the cops?"

"I was going to ... but the alarm never went off. I checked the system ... it was still set. I began wondering if I *was* dreaming."

"But you don't think so?"

"No."

"Why are you so sure?"

She fished in her purse and produced a pink cell phone. She flipped it open and pressed a few buttons to call up her text messages. She pointed to the number and then handed me the phone.

"That's David's cell number."

The text read: *Tonight.*

"Okay," I said. "Let me see what I can do."

"What *can* you do?" she asked.

"Well, the best first thing to do is go have a talk with him. See if I can convince him to back off."

"And if he won't?"

"I can be pretty convincing."

"But what if he won't? What if he's ... I don't know ... too crazy to listen to reason?"

I smiled. "Then we'll explore other options."

43

The Crypt is a big ugly building on the corner of South and Fourth in Philadelphia. Once upon a time it was a coffin factory—which I think would have been a cooler name. Less trendy and obvious. The light snow did nothing to make it look less ugly. When we pulled to the corner, Mrs. Skye pointed to a sleek silver Lexus parked on the side street.

"That's his."

I jotted down the license plate and used my digital camera to take photos of it and the exterior of the building. You never know.

"Okay," I said, "I want you to wait here. I'll go have a talk with David and see if we can sort this out."

"What if something happens? What if you don't come out?"

"Just sit tight. You have a cell phone and I'll give you the keys. If I'm not out of there in fifteen minutes, drive somewhere safe and call the name on the back of my card." I gave her my business card. She turned it over and saw a name and number. Before she could ask, I said, "Ray's a friend. One of my pack."

"Another private investigator?"

"A bodyguard. I use him for certain jobs, but I don't think we'll need to bring him in on this. From what you've told me I have a pretty good sense of what to expect in there."

As I got out my jacket flap opened and she spotted the handle of my Glock.

"You're not ... going to *hurt* him," she asked, wide eyed.

I shook my head. "I've been doing this for a lot of years, Mrs. Skye. I haven't had to pull my gun once. I don't expect I'll break that streak tonight."

The breeze was coming from the west and the snow was just about done. I squinted up past the streetlights. The cloud cover was thin and I could already see the white outline of the moon. Nope, no accumulation. Typical Philly winter.

I crossed the street and tried the front door. Place didn't do much business before late evening, but the doors were unlocked. The doors opened with an exhalation of cigarette smoke and alcohol fumes. There was probably an anti-smoking violation in that. Something else to use later if I needed to go the route of making life difficult for him.

It was too early for a doorman, and I walked a short hallway that was empty and painted black. Heavy black velvet curtains at the end. Cute. I pushed them aside and entered the club. Place was huge. David Skye must have taken out the second floor and knocked out everything but the retaining walls of the adjoining properties. The red and white maximum occupancy sign said that it shouldn't exceed four hundred, but the place looked capable of taking twice that number. Bandstand was empty, so someone had put quarters in to play the tuneless junk that was beating the shit out of the woofers and tweeters. Whoever the group was on the record they subscribed to the philosophy that if you can't play well you should play real god damn loud.

There were maybe twenty people in the place, scattered around at tables. A few at the bar. Everyone looked like extras from a direct-to-video vampire flick. The motif was black on black with occasional splashes of blood red. White skin that probably never saw the sun. Eyeliner and black lipstick, even on the guys. I was in jeans and a Vikings warm-up jacket. At least my sneakers and my leather porkpie hat were black. Handle of my gun was black, too, but they couldn't see that. Better for everyone if nobody did.

The bartender was giving me *the look*, so I strolled over to him. He knew I wasn't there for a beer and didn't waste either of our time by asking.

"David Skye," I said, having to bend forward and shout over the music.

"Badge me," he said.

I flipped open my PI license. "Private."

"Fuck off," he suggested.

"Not a chance."

"I can call the cops."

"Bet I can have L and I here before they show. Smoking in a public restaurant?"

Another smartass remark was on his lips, but he didn't have the energy for it. He was paid by the hour and this had to be a slow shift for tips. I took a twenty from my wallet and put it on the bar.

"This isn't your shit, kid," I said. "Call your boss."

He didn't like it, but he took the twenty and made the call.

"He says come up." The bartender pointed to another curtained doorway beside the bar. I gave him a sunny day smile and went inside.

There was a long hallway with bathrooms on both sides and a set of stairs at the end. I took the stairs two at a time. The stairs went straight up to his office and the door was open. I knocked anyway.

"It's open," he yelled. I went inside; and as I looked around I hoped like hell that the office décor was not modeled after the interior landscape of David Skye's mind. The walls were painted a dark red, the trim was gloss black. Instead of the band posters and framed '*look at who I'm shaking hands with*' eight-by-tens, the walls were hung with torture devices and S and M clothes.

45

Spiked harnesses, leather zippered masks, thumbscrews, photos from Abu Graib, diagrams of dissected bodies. A full-sized rack occupied one corner of the room and an iron maiden stood in the other, one door open to reveal rows of tarnished metal spikes. The only other furniture was a big desk made from some dark wood, a black file cabinet and the leather swivel chair in which David Skye sat. He wore a black poet's shirt, leather wristbands, and a smile that was already belligerent.

"The fuck are you and the fuck you want?"

The man was a charmer. I could just taste the charisma his wife had mentioned flowing like sweetness from his pores.

I flipped my ID case open. "We need to have a chat. It can be friendly or not. Your call."

"Go fuck yourself."

So much for *friendly.*

"That whore send you?" he demanded.

I smiled but didn't answer.

He had a handsome face, but his wife was right when she said that he'd lost weight. His skin looked thin and loose, and he had the complexion of a mushroom. More gray than white.

"Did my wife send you?" he said, pronouncing the words slowly as if I'd come here on the short bus.

"Why would your ex-wife send me?"

His eyes flickered for a second at '*ex*-wife'. I strolled across the room and stood in front of his desk. He didn't get up; neither of us offered a hand to the other.

"She makes up stories," he said.

"What kind of stories?"

"Bullshit. Lies. Says I slapped her around."

"Who'd she say that to?"

He didn't answer. He did, however, give me the ninja secret death stare, but I manned my way through it.

"What are you supposed to be," he said.

"Just what the license says."

"Private investigator. Private *dick.*"

"Yes, and that was funny back in the 1950s. Why do *you* think I'm here?"

"She's probably trying some kind of squeeze play. The club's doing okay, so she wants a bigger slice."

"Try again," I said, though he might have been right about that.

"Oh, I get it ... you're supposed to scare me into leaving her alone."

"Do I look scary?"

He smiled. He had very red lips and very white teeth. "No," he said, "you don't."

"Right ... so let's pretend that I'm here to have a reasonable discussion. Man to man."

Skye leaned back in his chair and stared at me with his dark eyes. It was a calculating look, and I'm sure he took in everything from my slightly threadbare Vikings jacket to my cheap black sneakers. Put everything I was wearing together and it would equal the cost of his shirt. I was okay with that. I don't dress to impress. Skye, on the other hand, smiled as if our mutual understanding of my material net worth clearly made him the alpha.

I smiled back.

"What does she want?" he asked.

"For you to leave her alone."

"What is she afraid of?"

"She thinks you're trying to kill her."

"What do *you* think?"

"What I think doesn't matter. I'm not a psychic, so I don't know whether you're trying to kill her or if you're playing some kind of mindgame on her. Whatever it is, I'm here to ask you to lay off."

"Why should I?"

"Because I asked real nice."

He smiled at that.

"Because it's illegal and I could build a harassment case against you and you could lose your club and sink a quarter mil into legal fees. Because I know inspectors who can slap you with fifteen kinds of violations that will hurt your business. I can have your car booted by *accident* three or four times a week, every week."

"And I could have you killed," he said, the smile unwavering.

"Maybe," I said. "You could try, and I might fuck up anyone you send and then come back here and fuck you up."

"Think you could?"

"You really want to find out?" When he didn't answer, I took a glass paperweight off his desk and turned it over in my hands. A spider was trapped inside, frozen into a moment of time for the amusement of the trinket crowd. I knew he was watching me play with the paperweight, wondering what I was going to do with it.

I put it back down on the desk.

"Really, though," I said, "how long do we need to circle and sniff each other? We don't run in the same pack and I don't give a rat's ass what you do, who you are, or how tough you think you are. We both know that you're either going to stop bothering your ex-wife and go on with your life; or you're going to make a run at her—either because you have some loose wiring or because I'm pushing your buttons by being here. If you back off, we're all friends. I'll advise my client not to file a restraining order and you two can let the divorce lawyers earn their paychecks by kicking each other in the nuts."

"Or ...?" he asked. Still smiling.

"Or, you don't back off and then this is about you and me."

"Nonsense. You're no part of this. This is about me and—"

I cut him off. "I'm *making* this about you and me. Maybe I have a wire loose, too, but once I tell a client that I'm going to keep her safe, I take it amiss if anything happens to her."

"'Amiss'," he repeated, enjoying the word.

"But that's a minute from now. We're still on the other side of it until you give me an answer. What's it going to be? You leave her alone? Or this gets complicated."

"What were you before you started doing this PI bullshit?"

"A cop."

He grunted. "You sound like a thug. An asshole leg-breaker from South Philly."

"Thin line sometimes."

He steepled his fingers. It was one of those moves that looked good when Doctor Doom did it in a comic book. Maybe in a boardroom. Looked silly right now, but he had enough intensity in his eyes to almost pull it off. He gave me ten seconds of *the stare.*

I stood my ground.

His cell phone rang and he flipped it open, listened.

"I'm in a meeting," he said and closed the phone.

His smile returned.

I heard the footsteps on the stairs even though they were quiet.

I sighed and turned. There were four of them. All as pale as Skye, but much bigger. "Really? You want to play that card?"

"It's one of the classics. Though, to be fair, it'll be more than a typical beating. I ... hm, am I wrong in presuming you *have* had your ass kicked?"

"That cherry was popped a long time ago."

The four men entered the room and fanned out behind me.

"So, our challenge, then," Skye said, "is to put a new spin on this. Something surprising and fresh so that you'll be entertained."

"Mind if I take my jacket off first?"

"Go right ahead."

I heard a hammer-cock behind me.

Skye said, "You can put your jacket on my desk here, and take off your shoulder holster and put that—and your piece—on top of it."

"Sure, whatever," I said. I shrugged out of the jacket. I bought it the year the Vikings took their eighteenth division title. I'll buy a new one if they ever win the Super Bowl. Or when pigs sprout wings and learn to fly, whichever comes first. I folded it and set it down, unclipped my shoulder rig, set that down. If I was going to ruin my clothes, then at least nothing I was currently wearing had sentimental value.

I leaned on the desk. "Let's agree on a couple of things first, okay?"

"Sure," he said with a grin.

"When I'm done handing these clowns their asses, then you and I dance a round or two."

"That would be fun," he said, "but I doubt I'll have the pleasure."

"Second, if I walk out of here on my own steam, then it's with the understanding that you will leave the lady alone."

"If you walk out of here? Sure. But, tell me something," he said, and he looked genuinely interested, "why do you care? What is she to you?"

"Maybe I'm the possessive type, too. Maybe now that she's asked for my help, it's like she's part of the family. So to speak."

"Part of the family? You fucking kidding me here?"

"Nope."

"You Italian? This some kind of dago thing?"

"I said it's *like* she's part of the family. My family," I said, "and I protect what's mine."

"That's it? It's just a macho thing with you?"

"No, it's more than that," I admitted. I gestured to the torture and pain motif in which his office was decorated. "But, seriously, I doubt you would understand."

"Mmm, probably not. I'm not into sentimentality and that bullshit. Not anymore."

"What happened? What changed you?"

His smiled faded to a remote coldness. "I learned that there was something better. Better than family, better than blood ties. Better than any of this ordinary shit."

"You found religion?" I said.

"It's a 'higher order' sort of thing that I really don't want to explain and I doubt *you'd* understand."

"I might surprise you."

"I don't think that's possible. But *we* might surprise you. In fact I can pretty fucking well guarantee it."

"Rock and roll," I said.

I straightened and turned toward the four goons. They took up positions like compass points. The office was big, but not big enough to give me room to maneuver. They were going to fall on me like a wall, and they knew it. The guy with the gun even snugged it back into his shoulder rig. They were *that* confident, and they were smiling like kids at a carnival.

"You shouldn't have bothered Mr. Skye," said the guy in front of me. He was the gun who'd holstered his gun. He stood on the East point of the compass. "You should have—"

I kicked him in the nuts. I really didn't need to hear the speech.

I'm not that big but I can kick like a Rockette. I *felt* bones break and he screamed like a nine year old girl. Dumbass should have kept his gun out.

I stepped backward off of him and put an elbow into West's face. It had all of my mass in motion behind it. That time I heard bones break and he went down so fast that I wondered if I'd snapped his neck.

That left South and North. South spent a half second too long looking shocked, so I jumped at him with a leaping knee—the only Muay Thai kick I know—and drove him all the way to the wall. By the time North closed in I'd grabbed South by the ears and slammed him skull-first into a replica of a torture rack. Blood splattered in a Jackson Pollack pattern.

I pivoted and rushed to intercept North who was barreling at me with a lot of furious speed; so I veered left and clothes-lined him with my stiff right forearm. He did a pretty impressive back flip and landed face down on the black-painted hardwood floor.

If this was an action movie everything would switch to slow motion as the four thugs toppled to the ground and I turned slowly looking badass to face the now startled and unprotected villain.

The real world is a lot less accommodating.

I caught movement behind me, figuring it for Skye going after my gun, so I whirled and made ready to launch into a diving tackle.

Only it wasn't Skye.

It was East and West getting to their feet. West's face was smeared with blood from his broken nose, but he was smiling. As I watched he took his nose between thumb and forefinger and *snapped* it into place, then spit a hocker of blood and snot onto the floor.

North was chuckling as he rose; and behind me I could hear South shifting to stand behind me again. I turned in a slow circle. They were all smiling. They shouldn't have been *able* to. They should have been sprawled on the floor and I should have been giving some kind of smart-ass speech as I closed in to lay a beating on Skye. That was the script I'd written in my head.

What the hell was this shit?

"Surprise!" said Skye dryly.

"What the hell are these fuckers *taking*?"

"You wouldn't believe me if I told you?"

"Try me."

"Blood," he said.

"What the—"

And I looked more closely at the smiles. Lots of white teeth. Lots of long, pointy white teeth.

"Oh, balls," I said.

"Yeah, kind of cool, huh?"

"Vampires?" I said.

"Yeah."

"Actual vampires."

Skye laughed. The four—well, let's call a spade a spade—*vampires* laughed with him.

Even I laughed.

"Geez. When shit goes wrong it goes all the way wrong, doesn't it," I said.

"On the up side," said Skye, "you did win the first round. Nice moves."

"Thanks."

The four of them circled me. My pulse jumped from 'uh-oh' to 'oh shit'. It was cold in his office, but I was starting to sweat pretty heavily.

"I guess I shouldn't be surprised," I said. "You're one, too? Am I right?"

"A recent convert," he admitted.

"So ... that whole weight loss, going all weird on the missus that was—?"

"A transition process. It's not like they show in the movies, you know. Takes weeks. The whole metabolism changes."

"No kidding."

One of the vampires faked a lunge to psyche me out and I jumped a foot in the air. I'm pretty sure I didn't yelp like a Chihuahua, but I wouldn't swear to that in court. They all laughed at that, too. I didn't.

"Which explains why you lost all that weight."

"Who needs steroids and free-weights," he agreed and spread his hands. "This package comes with honest to God super strength. I'm like Spider-man and Wolverine rolled into one. Super strong and I heal from damn near anything."

"Could you be more specific on that last point?"

"Cute."

"Worth a try." I looked at them, at their grinning, evil faces. My nuts were trying to crawl up inside of my chest cavity. I mean ... *fucking vampires?*

"Weird thing was," I said, "I was starting to build a case in my head about your wife. You losing weight and getting pale, blaming her for it all, and you saying you *know* what she is. Is she a vampire, too? Is she the one who bit you?"

Skye laughed. "Christ no. And she's not a succubus either. She's just a nagging, soul-draining, passive-aggressive, codependent bitch."

"Wow. You're really a chauvinistic prick, aren't you?"

"Better than being pussy whipped."

I dropped it. I had bigger fish to fry than trying to bring this macho jackass into the Twenty-first century. Namely the fact that I was in a roomful of vampires.

I know I keep harping on that, but really ... it's not the sort of shit that happens all the time to me. Or, like ... *ever.*

"Say, man," I said to Skye, "any chance we can roll back this tape to the point where we were still friends? I just walk out of here and we all call it a day?"

Skye made a face as if pretending to consider it. "Mmm ... no, I don't see that happening."

"You want to make a deal of some kind?"

"Nah," he said. "You got nothing I want. Except the O-positive."

"AB neg," I corrected.

"Never tried that."

"You wouldn't like it. Goes right to your hips."

The wattage on his smile was dimmer. Jaunty banter can buy only so many seconds and then it's back to business.

I tried to keep my face neutral, but my pulse was like a jazz drum solo.

"I'm going to throw something out here," I said. I could hear a tremor in my voice. Fuck.

"Oh, please." He gestured to the four killers and they started forward.

"Wait! Just hear me out. What have you got to lose?"

The thugs looked at Skye. West gave a 'why not?' kind of shrug.

Skye sighed. "Okay, what is it? Last words? A little begging?" he suggested.

"Mm, more like last threat."

"This I got to hear."

The five of them looked genuinely interested.

"Okay, so here you are, five vampires. That's some really scary shit, am I right? I mean creatures of the night and all that."

He nodded, nothing to disagree with.

"To most people that's enough to make them go apeshit crazy. I mean ... vampires. Not your everyday thing. It opens up all kinds of metaphysical questions. If vampires exist, what *else* does? If there are supernatural monsters, does that mean God and the Devil are real? You follow me?"

"Sure. We get that a lot."

"And I'm outnumbered here. Five to one. Tough odds without you fellows being the undead. So ... why am I not I scared?"

His eyes narrowed.

"I mean, yeah, my pulse is racing and I'm sweating. But do I look as scared as I should be? I don't do I? Now ... why is that?"

"So you put up a good front. It'll be a good anecdote later," he said. "For us."

"Maybe he's got a hammer and stake," suggested West.

That got a laugh.

"Nope."

My heart rate had to be close to two hundred. It was machinegun fire in my chest.

"Coupla garlic bulbs in your pocket?" asked East.

"Nah. I don't even like it on my pizza."

"You don't have any backup," said North. "And you don't got your gun."

My blood pressure could have scalded paint off a battleship. I wiped sweat off my brow with my thumb.

"Okay, jokes over," snapped Skye. "What's the punch line here? Why aren't you as scared as you should be?"

I smiled.

"I'll show you."

The first time it happened, way back when I was thirteen, it took almost half an hour. I screamed and cried and rolled around on the floor. First time's always the hardest. Each time since it was easier. My grandmother and her sister could do it in the time it took you to snap your fingers. My best time was during a foot chase back when I was with Minneapolis PD. I was running down the guy who'd beaten his wife with the extension cord. He saw me coming and ducked into his apartment. I kicked the door and he came out of the bedroom with a gun and opened up. I went through the change in the time it took me to leap through the doorway. Like the snap of my fingers. One minute me, next minute *different* me.

I tore the shit out of him. I lost my badge and pension and had to make up all sorts of excuses. On the plus side, I didn't die, which *would* have happened if I hadn't managed the change so fast. I'm only mortal when I look like one.

That night in Skye's office wasn't my best time. Maybe third or fourth best. Say, two, three seconds. It felt like an explosion. It hurts. Feels like my heart is bursting, like cherry bombs are detonating inside my muscles. It starts in the chest, then ripples out from there as muscle mass changes and is reassigned in new ways. Bones warp, crack and re-form. Nails tear through the flesh of my fingers and toes, my jaw shifts and the longer teeth spike through the gums. It's bloody and it's ugly and it hurts like a motherfucker.

But the end result is a stunner. A real kick-ass dramatic moment that wows the audience.

I think all four of the thugs screamed. They jerked back from me, looks of shock and horror on their faces. If I wasn't so deeply into the moment I would have smiled at the irony. Monsters being scared by a monster.

I crouched in the center of the room, hands flexing, claws streaked with blood, hot saliva dripping from my mouth onto my chest.

It would have been cool and dramatic to have said "Surprise!" to them the way Skye had said it to me, but my mouth was no longer constructed for human speech. All I could do was roar.

I did.

And then I launched at them.

Vampires are strong. Four or five times stronger than an ordinary human.

Werewolves?

Hell, we're a whole different class.

I slammed into West with both sets of front claws. He flew apart like he was made of paper and watery red glue. North and East tried to take me high and low, but they'd have done better to try and run. I brought my knee up into East's jaw as he went for the low tackle and his head burst like a casaba melon. I caught North by the throat and squeezed. Red geysered up from the stump of his neck as his head fell away. South backed away, putting himself between me and Skye, arms spread, making a more heroic stand than I'd have thought. I tore the heart from his chest. Turns out, vampires *need* their hearts.

Skye had my gun in his hands. He racked the slide and buried the barrel against me as I leaped over the desk. He got off four shots. They hurt.

Like wasp stings.

Maybe a little less.

I don't load my piece with silver bullets. I'm not an idiot.

He looked into my eyes and I would like to think that he saw the error of his ways. Don't fuck with the innocent. Don't fuck with my clients. My clients are *mine*, like members of my pack. Mess with them and the pack leader has to put you down. Has to.

So I did.

She saw me coming from across the street, her face concerned and confused. I was wearing a different pair of pants and different shoes. My own had been torn to rags during the change. Stuff I was wearing used to belong to the bartender. He didn't need them anymore. He'd been on the same team as Skye and the four goons.

I opened the door and climbed in behind the wheel.

"Are you all right, Sam?" she asked, studying my face. "Are you hurt? Is that blood?"

I dabbed at a dot on my cheek. Missed a spot. I pulled a tissue out of my jacket pocket and wiped my cheek.

"Just ketchup," I said.

"You stopped for *food?*" she demanded, eyes wide.

"It was on the house. I was hungry. No biggie."

She stared at me and then looked at the club across the street. The snow was getting heavier, the ground was white and it was starting to coat the street.

"What happened in there?"

I put the key into the ignition.

"I had a long talk with your ex. I told him that you were feeling threatened and uncomfortable with his actions, and I asked him to back off."

"What did he say?"

"He won't be bothering you anymore."

"Just like that? He agreed to leave me alone just like that?" She snapped her fingers.

"More or less. I told him that I had some friends on the force and in L & I. Guess I made it clear that I could make his life *more* uncomfortable than he was making yours. He didn't like it, but ..." I let the rest hang.

"And he *agreed?*"

"Take my word for it. He's out of your life."

She continued to study me for several long seconds. I waited her out and I saw the moment when she shifted from doubt and fear to belief and acceptance. She closed her eyes, sagged back against the seat, put her face in her hands and began to cry.

I gripped the wheel and looked out at the falling snow, hiding the smile that kept trying to creep onto my mouth. I was digging the P.I. business. Fewer rules than when I was a cop. It allowed me to be closer to the street, to go hunting deeper into the forest.

Even so—and despite what I'd said to Skye—I *was* pretty rattled that he'd been a vampire. I mean, being who and what I am I always suspected other things were out there in the dark, but until now I'd never met them. Now I knew. How many vampires were there? *Where* were they? Would they be coming for me?

I didn't have any of those answers. Not yet.

I also wondered what *else* was out there. I could feel the excitement racing through me. I wanted to find out. Good or bad.

I reached out a hand and patted Mrs. Skye's trembling shoulder. It felt good to know that one of the pack was safe now. It felt right. It made me feel powerful and satisfied on a lot of different levels. I knew that I was going to want to feel this way again. And again.

The snow swirled inside the thickening shadows.

Inside my head the wolf howled.

THE EDGE OF SEVENTEEN

Alexandra Sokoloff

The B Building was burning.

Anna could barely catch a breath through the smoke stinging her eyes and lungs. The wide dark halls were thick with it, curling, wafting.

A chemical fire? Those morons from Litwack's 3rd period lab, trying to shut down the building? There had been a dozen fire drills since the beginning of school ...

But why were the lights out? The only illumination was from the red EXIT signs above the side stairwell doors. The whole building was dark ... just the drifting smoke, tinged red from the neon.

Alarm bells were ringing, but far, far away.

And why was she alone?

Anna looked around her for what oddly felt like the first time, blinking through the smoky gloom. The cavernous halls were empty, no one in the open classrooms either.

There was the sound of sobbing, though, from somewhere, resonating faintly in the tomblike dark.

And softly, softly, screams. *Screams.*

She glanced down the center aisle of the classroom to the left of her, down the collapsing fiberglass curtain that served as a wall between classrooms—and froze.

Male legs in khaki pants and reindeer socks stuck out from under sweet Mr. Brooke's desk. The legs were stiff and still. Anna thought absurdly of the Wicked Witch of the East, how she'd run screaming from the living room when she was five and had first seen *The Wizard of Oz* on TV and those black-and-white-striped witch legs had curled up and rolled under the house ...

In her peripheral vision, a dark shadow ran suddenly past.

It was fast, so fast. Sinuous, snakelike.

Anna whipped around, staring down the corridor. Silence, stillness—but a heavy stillness, live. She held her breath, watching ... and the shadow fell again across the wall. A chill ran through Anna's entire body.

It had two heads.

Anna unfroze and ran for the main staircase. It felt unbearably slow, like running through sand. Like running—

In a dream.

The alarms started to shrill, piercing, pulsing beats.

Her breath was coming faster, her legs moving even more maddeningly slowly. Her pulse was pounding in her head, the sound distorted and visceral. She knew the shadow was behind her—she could hear a double breath ...

Madness ...

She reached the edge of the main staircase, grabbed the rail to pull herself forward onto the stairs—

At the foot of the staircase, on the landing, Tyler Marsh stood looking up at her, as real as she was, perfect profile and long dark silky hair falling into his eyes. The alarms pulsed around them, vibrating through her body.

"Run", he said, without opening his mouth.

And she woke up.

The clock alarm was bleating in shrill pulses, five a.m blinking redly from the digital screen. The morning was pitch black. Anna's heart was still pounding crazily in her chest, shaking the mattress. She reached clumsily for the clock to silence it, then lay back, dazed and groggy. The dream was gone.

The stench of smoke was in her nose.

Shower to wash away the lingering smell of smoke, then way too long with the hair dryer—reluctant to shut off the warmth. She mostly avoided her own eyes in the mirror, but sometimes, with her thick dark hair blowing around her, she was almost pretty.

She negotiated the tiny but labyrinthinely cluttered living room by the light of the TV screen. Her father was passed out and snoring in the huge vile LaZBoy, empty beer bottles scattered at his feet.

Anna grabbed a Diet Coke from the kitchen fridge, grabbed her backpack from the hall, and plunged out the front door into the chilly dark.

She made it to the corner just in time to catch her bus, and rode in pre-dawn, alone with the bus driver and two Latina housekeepers, over potholed streets, under the towering silhouettes of palms and old-growth trees, through sleeping San Gorgonio.

San G was a base town, or had been until the base was shut down in the closures of the nineties, plunging the city into economic depression. The war in Iraq had not revived the base. The dying town sprawled in a semi-desert ringed by mountains, pocketed in a valley which trapped heat and smog for the entirety of the summer, only somewhat relieved in fall by the winds Raymond Chandler famously described as "those hot dry Santa Anas that come through the mountain passes and curl your hair and make your nerves jump and your skin itch." And brought asthma and arson and wildfires, Anna knew all that. But the winds also signaled change and excitement, and sometimes, even, magic—like that fall in first grade when she for some reason had brought an umbrella to school on a cloudless Santa Ana day and discovered, walking home through the gusts, that she could fly, actually fly off the ground like Mary Poppins, with the umbrella open against the winds ... flying. And for one day, she was magical—

She sat up on the cracked bus seat with a gasp.

She'd dreamed about Tyler Marsh last night. Definitely. Definitely something about Tyler. Something she couldn't quite remember, but so intimate it made her stomach flutter.

But the dream hadn't been good. That much she remembered. Not good at all.

Her chest tightened with anticipation and unease as the bus shuddered to a stop in front of the high school.

SGHS was the town's original school, boasting several vintage buildings and a decrepitly grand auditorium surrounding a faded brick plaza, a core around which more modern buildings, if you could by any stretch of the imagination call the 1970s modern, had sprouted. There was the open-classroomed, two-story windowless monolith of the B Building, along with rows of "temporary" trailers that had constituted a significant portion of the school since the late sixties.

Anna made her way through the empty quad in the pre-dawn dark. The buildings were looming shadows around her, no lights on yet. Zero period, 6 a.m., existed so that seniors could get in their class hours for graduation while still being able to leave school early enough to work. Anna was cramming in all the credits she could in the desperate hope of graduating early. After fourth period she left the school to get downtown to her job at the Inland Center Gap—anything to avoid going home.

The long shining corridor of the A Building was dim and deserted, only one lit classroom at the far end of the hall. Anna's zero period, Problems of Democracy, was a graduation requirement, and unlike most other classes in the school, which were tracked according to student test scores, POD was taught on only one level, which meant classes were mixed in a way they simply were not for any other class. POD was technically a senior course, and Anna was a junior, but the class was easily the least challenging she'd ever taken, possibly in her life. The scattered students in the large, militantly undecorated room were the absolute dregs of the school: the dumbest of the football team, linebacks or whatever the biggest ones were called; a few slutty girls who seemed physically incapable of picking up their feet and consequently shuffled noisily when they walked; some sweet-faced Latino boys who no one seemed to have noticed didn't speak more than ten words of English. A good three-quarters of the class was sleeping, heads down on their crossed arms on their desks—including the teacher: pale, doughy Mr. Doyle. It all looked like the courtyard scene from *Sleeping Beauty* after the fairies had put the whole castle in suspended animation while Beauty awaited the awakening kiss of the Prince.

Despite herself, Anna stole a glance around the room for Tyler, the closest thing SGHS had to a prince—the only thing that kept Anna coming to POD at this ungodly hour. No sign of him.

The only other moving thing in the room was Carrie Thorne, the school's most unfortunate dwarf. "Little person" was the PC phrase, but Carrie was undeniably a dwarf: three foot ten, a hundred and fifty pounds, with a froglike face, lashless eyes. She wasn't retarded, exactly, but there was something not right about her mind, either. The jocks were merciless, pretending to be her friend and then mimicking her duck walk and turtle blink behind her back—barely behind her back. Carrie surely knew she was being mocked, but waddled after them anyway, trying to keep up with the young gods on her stumpy legs.

It was the height of teenage cruelty: Darren Elwes, captain of the football team, school sociopath, the ringleader, ostentatiously flirting with her, going on and on and on obscenely about taking her out to the drive-in, about what base they'd gotten to the night before, about jerking off to the memory afterward. Disgusting ... and unbearably, it seemed to excite Carrie. She'd stagger away in a flushed stupor as Darren mugged behind her in panting imitation of her froggy face ... the lettermen and any stray cheerleaders laughing uproariously.

Except for Tyler, who never laughed, but sat beside them, a million miles away, as if on another planet. Never entirely present, always at the edge of the group, dreamily aloof or (Anna wasn't stupid) drugged.

So different. So different—from Them. But he never left them, and at the lunch bell or the last bell he would get into Darren's car or Darren into his, and they drove off together to their childhood homes, three houses apart from each other.

Anna quickly took a seat between two sleeping students to avoid engaging in conversation with Carrie, whom she pitied, but not enough to endure her desperate, disjointed chatter.

The bell rang (such an assault at this hour) and Mr. Doyle blinked awake at his desk. The class slept on. Doyle licked his lips, growled, "Get out pencils for a quiz. No books."

Anna fumbled in her backpack—and then felt someone looking at her; the back of her neck was hot.

What an odd thing to think—that you could feel someone looking at you.

But the back of her neck was hot.

She turned to the row of tables behind her.

Tyler Marsh sat behind her, alone at one of the two-person desks as if he'd materialized from—

A dream ... the dream ...

He was looking straight at her, his long dark hair falling around his face. Their eyes locked in an electric moment.

It all came flooding back to her, the smoke-filled halls, the ominous dark shape darting in the classroom behind her, too quick to be human—*two heads.*

And Tyler, at the foot of the stairs, looking up.

She was there, then here—then both at once, realities layered on top of each other.

Tyler locked in to Anna's gaze from across the room. Chills ran up her back as he slowly nodded.

What? What?

"I was there," he said without speaking.

She caught her breath, looking into those eyes.

And then Doyle stepped in front of her, and slapped a paper down in front of her, beginning the test.

At the sound of the bell Anna raced out of class to catch up with Tyler, running into a chair and bruising her shin in her hurry to escape the room. But outside POD the halls stretched out endlessly, filled with nothing but the shuffling corpses of her other classmates. He'd disappeared.

Daylight had brought the Santa Anas gale force, gusting and crackling through the palms.

Anna walked through the quad, prime real estate for jocks, cheerleaders and other socies. Wannabees hovered hopefully on the periphery, always looking for an opening or whatever miracle it would take to join the inner circle. She saw Tyler as soon as she hit the bricks of the inner quad. He was in the usual gang seated around the central planter, Darren never far from his side.

It was a childhood connection, that much Anna understood: the two of them growing on the same block of Valencia, the broad main street of town, prime real estate for society parents, facing the golf course, a short drunk walk to or from the Country Club, kids growing up with golf and Junior League and SUVs and iPhones and iPods and an inbred sense of entitlement. Big fish in a small, small pond.

Tyler was in his place on the south side of the planter, as always at the edges of the group, smiling slightly, never quite participating in Darren's antics. Today, some sort of air guitar recounting of a concert, with lots of tongue involved.

Anna drifted more slowly, willing Tyler to look at her. He had spoken in her head, as clearly as if he had been on the phone. Could she speak in his?

Try it, why not? Nothing to lose, everything, everything to win.

She breathed in, and said it in her head.

Tyler.

She kept her eyes on him, every cell within her concentrating, focused on one thought.

Tyler.

She saw him blink, frown, look up and around him. She was barely moving, barely breathing.

Then Darren cavorted closer, shoved him. Tyler struck out and hit him so quickly even Darren looked surprised. Then Darren burst into manic laughter, echoed by everyone around them.

"You are one crazy motherfucker," Darren crowed, feinting back at Tyler.

Tyler did not once look at Anna. She dropped her eyes and walked quickly on, her face a mask.

So maybe it hadn't happened at all. Maybe none of it had.

Maybe *she* was crazy. As crazy as her father.

The morning dragged on: her hated Algebra II class, Mr. Maitland with his too-tight shorts and crawling eyes; then third period Chem: the dark, windowless second-floor lab soporific as always, Litwack spacing out behind his desk, mug of coffee well-laced with Vodka.

As the class practiced titration, Anna could see more than the assignment bubbling at a back table: Darren and a couple other football guys huddling too industriously over a beaker. Darren suddenly looked up, straight across the room at Anna. His lip curled and his eyes went colder than their usual glacial blue. The menace in his face made Anna look quickly down at her own notes and try to disappear into them.

It was not two minutes later that the beaker exploded. Blue smoke spread instantly through the room, noxious, suffocating. Startled back to semi-sobriety, Litwack barked orders at the hapless TAs and ordered the students out of the room "In an orderly fashion."

In the halls, chaos. Alarms shrieked as students poured from the science and math and computer labs, pushing and shoving. It was instantly clear that the school population far exceeded the evacuation capacity of the building. A wall-to-wall river of bodies undulated in excruciating slow-motion toward the main staircase in the front of the building. Anna turned instinctively toward the side emergency stairs. A clutch of students was squeezed against the doors, voices rising in a spiraling frenzy. From where she was, Anna could see that some idiot had twisted a bike chain around the doors of the back emergency exit.

This was planned. It's a setup.

The students twisted, fighting to turn where they stood. Teachers shouted over the chaos, adding to the madness.

The river of students surged forward. The sound of crashing glass, blue smoke, shrilling alarms surrounded Anna; she was carried through the corridor on a wave of déjà vu.

In the pushing, shoving horde, someone fell into step with her, and she looked up to see long silky dark hair, deep wary eyes, perfect skin in profile. Tyler. He put a hand to her elbow and held her, keeping her beside him in the jostling crowd. They moved in tandem, saying nothing. She was dizzy with the reality of him.

There was a logjam at the stairs, an ocean of students. Anna and Tyler inched forward.

"Good thing it's not for real," Tyler said with casual cynicism.

"It was a fire, last night," she said. For a moment she thought he would not speak. Then—

"It was something."

Their voices were soft in the din of wired chattering and occasional shrieks. She could hear him perfectly. She looked up, into his eyes, as if she had every right to do it. They were green, like the sea. "We had the same dream."

He shook his head slowly. "I don't dream."

"Everybody dreams," she said automatically. "We'd all be completely psychotic if we didn't." She'd read it somewhere, or maybe it was one of those classroom movies that have a strange way of sticking, random facts popping up when you least expect it.

"I don't dream," he repeated. "You were in my bed last night."

She was flooded with heat and confusion until she realized he'd said "head" not "bed". *You were in my head last night."*

The smoke was thicker—people all around them were coughing, crying.

"The smoke was in the beginning," she said, the dream flashing with crystal clarity in her mind. "There were people dead."

He looked down at her a long time, then nodded without speaking.

"There was someone. Someone dark and fast in the halls. Someone ... with two heads." She'd actually said it aloud. He didn't react. "Did you see?" She asked urgently. She couldn't believe she was talking to him like this. They had never spoken before.

He frowned slightly, "No." There was not a trace of skepticism in his voice.

The crowd moved them closer to the stairs. People around them were coughing and crying. If someone tripped, they would be trampled.

Anna glanced toward Mr. Brooke's classroom to the left of the stairs, remembered the legs sticking out from under the desk, and shivered.

"People are going to die," she said softly.

Algebra II. Maitland, with his bristly red beard and red mouth, tennis shorts with their insinuating bulge, rubbing past her in the aisle as he lectured, standing with his crotch at her eye level as he paused to "check her work".

They were studying probability, and Anna vaguely realized that there was something potentially magnificent about it, something philosophical and profound. But Maitland's leering and covert groping made it impossible for her to concentrate; her mind just shut down. She stared down at her textbook, trying to block him out as he cruised the aisles. She copied a definition onto her worksheet, a list of probability terms:

Sample Space: The set of all possible outcomes.

She sat up straighter, with a thrill of significance. Right there, for example. *Sample Space.* Wasn't that where she and Tyler were right now, in a set of all possible outcomes? She scooted up farther on her seat and flipped pages to find the definition of the next phrase.

Probability: The likelihood of the occurrence of an event.

Again, she felt a chill. And that's what they were struggling with, the likelihood of the occurrence of an event. *An event* ... Her mind skittered away and she hurried on to:

Conditional Probability: A probability that is compiled based on the assumption that some event has already occurred.

Some event that had already occurred. *The fire alarm in their dream ... and then in reality ...*

The next term on the list made her heart leap.

Impossible Event

That was it. That's what she needed to know. Her eyes raced over the chapter text looking for the explanation as if—as if—

As if lives depended on it.

She looked down at the page and the line suddenly jumped out at her.

"An impossible event has zero probability of occurring."

She stared down at the page bleakly. *Well, that's self-evident, isn't it?* But if an impossible event had zero probability of occurring, then probability had nothing to do with what was happening, because it was *all* impossible—

A shadow fell on the page. Maitland was standing above her, his eyes glittering down. Anna froze as his hand moved down to his crotch and he began to stroke himself.

She stared up, hating him—

And his head exploded. Blood and brain drenched Anna's dress and Doc Martens. She gasped, recoiled from the coppery stink and slime of blood.

Headless, brains stem exposed, Maitland turned in slow motion as if to confront his killer ...

... then crumpled to the floor.

Anna stood from her desk, awash in red. She was alone in the classroom, Maitland's body at her feet.

She looked around her. No, not alone. There were others, slumped at desks, holes in their heads and chests.

Smoke and blood were everywhere.

In the hall behind her, the shadow skittered. Fast, so fast ...

Anna ducked down beneath the desk, and crouched there, her ears filled with the thudding of her own heart and the faraway pulse of the alarms. She peered through the smoke toward the hall. Nothing moving. She took a breath and crawled along the edge of the fiberglass dividing curtain to the wall-less back of the Algebra classroom.

More smoke in the corridor and more fallen students. She felt movement, turned her head to see a figure down the hallway, almost obscured by the smoke. She caught a glimpse of legs in jeans and snakeskin boots, a rifle at thigh level and the shadow on the wall, its two heads bobbing.

A dull boom rocked the building, jolting Anna onto her hands and knees.

Around her there was screaming and screaming and screaming, and then the crackle of flames. The smoke surrounded her, hot and intimate and oppressive.

She crawled along the wall, eyes streaming.

There was another body in front of her, crumpled, not moving. Dark silky hair pooled on the carpet around his head. And blood, so much blood.

No, God, oh no, no ...

Her heart was in her mouth as she crawled to Tyler, oblivious of the shadow creature. He was still, so still, and pale. She lifted his head, cradling him in her arms. Blood was sticky on her hands, running through her fingers. The back of his head was soft, like melted Jello. Her pulse spiked sickly, feeling the ooze.

He opened his eyes, found her gaze. She saw recognition ... longing, relief ... He shuddered, and she held him harder.

"Help me," he whispered.

Her eyes swam with tears. His hand moved beside her leg, touched her fingers and picked up her hand. He raised her hand to his mouth; she felt his lips brush her palm—

Behind them, the two-headed shadow loomed on the wall—

"We have to stop it."

She spoke with utter calm. In her head was her own screaming from the dream.

They were sitting on the stairs at the side of the auditorium, privacy from the traffic of the quad, its cliques and gossip. They sat close, legs touching, as if they had known each other forever. *As if, as if ...*

"What is 'It'?" Tyler said. His voice was mocking but his eyes were not.

"You know," she said, and still hesitated. "Like Columbine." It felt odd to say it aloud. Had she ever said the word before?

It can't happen here it can't happen here it can't happen here

"What do you suggest we do?" He said reasonably. *And there's the rub, isn't it?*

"Tell someone." Her voice grated, as if she were irritated. As if irritated could begin to describe her feelings.

"Tell who? Our *parents?*" There were layers of complexity in the way he said the word.

"No," Anna said quickly, and he smiled without amusement.

"No," he agreed. A vision of her father, stumbling drunk and raving, flashed in Anna's mind. Tyler flinched, as if he saw. Their eyes met and she knew they had much more in common than she had ever guessed.

Then he looked away, and shrugged. "What's there to tell, anyway? 'We had a *dream* ...'"

"It was more than a dream. You know it. You know it. People don't dream the same thing."

He didn't answer—he didn't need to. She looked out at the wind rippling the nets of the tennis courts, and continued, feeling her way. "We're dreaming something real ... something that could be real."

After a moment he said, "So how are we supposed to stop the future?"

She shook her head, intent. "We don't know it's *the* future. I think ... it's *one* future." She visualized the probability equations from the dream. She'd looked them up in the morning and they were there in her textbook, exactly the same. "It's a possible outcome. One of a number of outcomes. It's Sample Space." She knew she was babbling, but his eyes flickered with sudden interest.

"Sample Space."

"A set of all possible outcomes," she said, though she knew he'd already gotten it. "Maybe ..." she paused to grasp at a thought that was just out of reach ... "Maybe we're being shown for a reason. So we can make a different outcome."

His grin twisted. "Maybe *you* can. I'm dead, remember?"

"*No.*" She said so fiercely she saw him jump.

"No," she said more softly.

He leaned forward and put his hand against her cheek, his forehead against hers, his hair falling against her face, and breathed her in.

She walked for English in a dreamy daze, the touch of his hands and head running under her skin. She rounded a corner and ran into someone tall and hard.

Darren's fingers dug into her shoulders, his ice eyes shone down at her. Her first thought was that he had seen her with Tyler.

"Watch it, cunt." So casually malevolent.

She looked at him steadily and saw the ice turn to rage. "Better watch those eyes, little girl," he breathed. "Someone might put them out."

Anna took a sudden step forward, startling herself and him. He didn't flinch, exactly, but his balance shifted, and he no longer seemed quite so tall. "I'm not afraid of you," she said softly.

Darren's face was blank and still. He seemed to have gone someplace else altogether. Then his eyes focused again, and narrowed to slivers. "You should be, little one."

The screaming was louder. And the curling smoke.

She was following feathers on the floor, past little piles of carnage: a head of a bird, twisted from its body. The glowing eyes of a cat, with its organs spilled out all around it. A charred lump of something that was once a dog.

Oh God. Oh God ... it was so much worse than she'd thought. It was years ... years of madness ... hidden from everyone. Who—What—could do that to an animal?

She felt herself becoming hysterical, though she had no real concept of the state, and she forced herself to breathe in, to focus.

Tyler. Must find Tyler.

She started to run past spreading pools of blood on the floor.

A shadow loomed up behind her. The two-headed thing stalked her in the halls. Anna bolted around a corner and drew up short with a gasp.

Carrie stood under a cottonwood tree that had somehow sprung up in the upstairs hall of the B Building. She stared up at Anna, oversized head bobbing on her neck, lashless eyes blinking. She wore black-and-white-striped stockings and black shoes that curled up at the toes.

"You're playing with fire," she intoned.

"Where is it?" Anna gasped, only she wasn't sure if she's said *Where?* or *Who?*

"You know," said Carrie. Her legs curled, rolling up underneath her, then she disappeared in a puff of smoke.

The winds blew trash across the blacktop as Anna ran through the scarred green picnic tables that lined the asphalt passage between the Vocational Arts building and the student parking lot. She'd overslept and missed her bus, subsequently missing POD, but it was not quite first period yet and she still had time to get there and catch Tyler before class let out. She pulled up short when she saw the cottonwood. There were more than one of the scraggly trees struggling defiantly up among the picnic tables, but the sight of this one hit her like lightning cracking through clear sky.

Carrie sat beneath it, at a picnic table. Her stumpy legs stuck out in front of her on the bench, her toes turned up. There was a bilious assortment of junk food spread out in front of her on the table—Cheetos, Snickers bars, Red Vines, Peppermint Patties.

Anna walked slowly to the table and sat down opposite her. Carrie looked across at her, and they were both still, as perfectly alive and awake as in the dream.

"You were there," Anna said softly.

"There where?" Carrie said. But her smile was knowing.

Anna took a breath. "What did you mean?"

Carrie stared at her without blinking.

"Last night. What did you mean?"

Carrie's eyes shifted craftily. She licked chocolate off her fingers, leaned across the table toward Anna. "Is it worse to be ugly inside or outside?"

"Inside," Anna said, and looked away.

Carrie snorted, a phlegmy laugh. "Liar. Everybody lies." She reached for another candy bar.

Anna leaned forward urgently. "Carrie, where is he?" Only she didn't know if she'd said "where" or "who".

"You know," Carrie said, exactly as in the dream, and bit into the chocolate.

Anna shook her head. "I don't—"

"Liar," Carrie said again. "Why does everyone lie?"

Anna swallowed. "Carrie, is it Darren?"

Carrie laughed, and kept laughing, rocking back and forth on the bench. Anna grabbed her backpack from the table and fled.

She got to POD just before the bell. Tyler was not in class.

Nor was he on the planter in the quad. Darren watched Anna walk by, like a snake watching a mouse. Her heart was racing, her backpack clutched close to her chest. She held her head high and straight, not looking at him.

Mr. Brooke was grading papers in his upstairs history classroom, decorated with maps from World War II battle campaigns, *National Geographic* history charts. Anna had had his American History last year as a sophomore and secretly adored him. Brooke was close to retirement, just a few wisps of hair left on his shiny head, but still as wiry and enthusiastic as a little boy. That enthusiasm and his off-the-wall humor had kept him a favorite through decades of students. True to form, he lit up when Anna walked in, springing from his chair and spreading his arms wide.

"Sullivan, Sullivan, such a good Russian name. Splendid to see you." He frowned, taking her in. "But you look disturbed. Nay, perturbed. Yes, a definite aura of perturbation. We can't have that." He waved grandly to the rows of empty desks. "Have a seat. Unburden yourself."

Anna opened her mouth, and to her chagrin felt tears just behind her eyes. Mr. Brooke saw, because his face lost its jolliness and reassembled itself into something so concerned and fatherly she very nearly broke down altogether. She swallowed through the ache in her throat. "I think I know something. That something bad is going to happen." She knew she had to say more, but nothing would come. The words hung in the silent classroom.

"Something bad?" Brooke said.

She nodded. The silence deepened.

"What is it?"

"I don't know." Appallingly, she started to cry, then.

Brooke looked alarmed. "Sullivan, are you in danger? Are you being hurt, or threatened—"

"No. No, no," she choked out, took a shuddering breath. "It's not about me—exactly. I don't know what it is, exactly."

"To someone else? Is it a police thing? A family thing?"

"No. No." She tried to get hold of herself. "It's a probability. Right now we're in Sample Space, but the outcome-"

Brooke looked confused. "Is that algebra? I never was much good at math."

"Not math." She kept shaking her head, sobbing. "I don't know. I can't figure it out. I don't know what I'm supposed to do. I don't know. I don't know."

Brooke came around to the front edge of his desk, in front of her—not too close, like Maitland, but just the right distance. She could feel his concern, like warmth rolling off him. He was wearing faded but neat khaki pants, and when he sat on the desk, the cuffs hiked up to reveal reindeer socks.

Anna froze, staring at the reindeer. *The legs under the desk. The blood ...*

There was smoke in her nose, and screaming in her ears.

Brooke was speaking, right into her eyes, and the tone of his voice brought her back.

"Sullivan, you know a whole lot. You are so much stronger than you think you are. There is a world of good inside of you. You can trust yourself to do the right thing. I have no doubt."

The bell rang. Anna jumped up to leave, blinded by tears. "I have to go," and he stood with her.

"You come talk to me any time you're ready. I'll always be here."

But you won't, she cried inside. And for a moment he had an odd look, but then it was gone.

"Trust yourself," he said.

Probability (P) is the likelihood of the occurrence of an event (A). If all outcomes are equally likely, then:

P(A) = Number of outcomes in event A
Number of outcomes in the Sample Space

Blood bloomed over Anna's algebra paper, drenching it with crimson.

She stood from her desk, awash in red and the cloying stench. She was alone in the Algebra classroom, Maitland's headless body at her feet.

She looked around her. No, not alone. There were others, slumped at desks, holes in their heads and chests.

Smoke and blood was everywhere.

Behind her, the shadow skittered. Fast, so fast ...

She ducked down beneath the desk, and crouched there, her ears filled with the thudding of her own heart and the faraway pulse of the alarms. She peered through the smoke toward the hall. Nothing moving. She took a breath and crawled along the edge of the fiberglass dividing curtain to the wall-less back of the Algebra classroom.

More smoke in the corridor and more fallen students. She felt movement, turned her head to see a figure almost obscured by the smoke. She caught a glimpse of legs in jeans and snakeskin boots, a rifle at thigh level ... and the shadow on the wall, its two heads bobbing.

A dull boom rocked the building, jolting Anna onto her hands and knees. Around her there was screaming and screaming and screaming, and then the crackle of flames.

The smoke surrounded her, hot and intimate and oppressive.

She crawled along the wall, eyes streaming. The screaming was louder, all around, and the curling smoke. Pools of blood spread on the carpet. She was following a trail of feathers on the floor—past the head of a bird, twisted from its body, the glowing eyes of a cat with its organs spilled out all around it ... a charred lump of something that was once a dog. Small fires were lit everywhere.

She strained to see through the thickening smoke and gasped.

Tyler sat against the wall, slumped and still. He was drenched in blood, head down, long hair falling around his face

No, God, oh no, no ...

Heart in her mouth, she crawled to him, now oblivious of the shadow creature. She reached Tyler, touched him frantically. Blood was everywhere, but she could find no wounds. She looked over his chest, down his legs ...

And froze- seeing his snakeskin boots.

Tyler stirred.

Behind him, the two-headed shadow slithered on the wall. It lifted its two heads as he lifted his.

Tyler opened his eyes and found Anna's gaze. She saw recognition, longing ... relief. He shuddered, and she held him harder.

"Help me," he whispered. His two-headed shadow was motionless on the wall.

Anna's eyes swam with tears. His hand moved beside her leg, touched her fingers. He picked up her hand and clasped his fingers around hers. She felt something cold and heavy and hard in her palm.

"*No—*" she said.

He looked into her face, his eyes as green as the sea. "Help me," he whispered. He closed his hand around her fingers and put his mouth around the barrel of the gun.

She closed her eyes, and he squeezed her hand.

She woke with her ears still ringing. She did not move for minutes, felt no desire to move ever again. Her chest felt as empty and hollow as a tomb.

After a time her hands moved at her sides and she wiped the blood onto the sheets.

The quad was buzzing with rumors like wildfire, like the Santa Anas rippling through the palms around the courtyard. Cheerleaders were sobbing, freshmen looking scared and disoriented.

One of the football guys was speaking with dazed incomprehension. "Marsh shot himself. His old man came into his room in the morning and found his brains all over the wall."

Anna walked by them without turning her head.

She sat in Algebra II with her test paper in front of her and no thoughts in her mind but the numbers in front of her. The numbers were a relief. If only she'd never have to think again.

> *Probability is the likelihood of the occurrence of an event.*
> *For any event A, O < P(A) < 1*
> *P (impossible event) = 0*

Maitland's hairy legs moved in front of her. Anna looked up from her test paper. His eyes glittered down at her, wet red mouth working.

Anna stared into his face. In her mind she saw his head explode in blood.

Maitland's eyes widened and he stumbled back in shock. Around them, the class turned to look, curious.

Maitland moved quickly away from her, mumbling, "Good work, looks fine."

Anna watched him without moving as he fumbled his way back behind his desk and dropped into his chair. He shuffled papers in front of him with shaking hands.

Anna dropped her gaze to her paper. She scratched out the equation she'd written and wrote instead:

Probability does not equal Possibility

She put down her pencil, stood, and walked out of the classroom, out of the building ... into the wind.

THE VIEW FROM THE TOP

Bev Vincent

The carnies who bark at Cliff as he approaches and recedes from their booths like an uneasy tide want only one thing: the precious roll of tokens in his pocket in exchange for a chance to tempt fate. Ordinarily an easy mark, Cliff is so focused on searching for what he needs that he's oblivious to their seductive banter. He tears around corners and threads his way through the crowd, flitting from booth to booth like a bumblebee in a field of daisies.

As he races past the ring toss booth, something catches his eye. Dragging his sneakers through the gravel, he skids to a halt. Nestled among stuffed bears and rabbits is a telescope, the type ancient mariners used when searching for land. Fluorescent light reflects from its golden barrel. The other toys piled around it pale by comparison.

It's exactly what he's been looking for.

Sprigs of oily hair emerge from beneath the battered derby of the skinny man working the booth. He looks like he hasn't shaved since Groundhog Day. The vertical yellow stripes on his rumpled brown suit shimmer in the booth's preternatural light. He turns toward Cliff. "C'mon, kid. Give it a try. This'll be easy peasy for a strapping young lad like yourself."

Cliff digs out a token and pushes it across the countertop. His first throw lands amidst the forest of pegs. His second ricochets and rolls to the ground.

"So close," the barker grunts. "Once more and you'll have it." His voice is a deep growl punctuated by phlegmy coughs.

The muscles in Cliff's stomach tighten. His hand quivers. Sweat drips from his underarms. It takes twelve tosses before he finally loops a ring over a peg near the back. "We have a winner!" the barker announces, using Cliff's accomplishment to draw in more players, more tokens. He reaches for a stuffed giraffe. "Congrats, kid."

"No. That." Cliff stabs his finger at the answer to his prayers.

The man's hand falters. He spits on the ground and strokes his face before plucking the telescope from its resting place.

As if seeking a blessing, Cliff holds out his hands. The barker slaps the barrel into his palms but maintains his grip on the other end. Cliff is forced to meet the barker's gaze. One of the man's eyes wanders, but the other is steely cold. "Use it well, kid," he says.

Cliff blushes. It's like the barker knows why he wants it. This time when he tugs, though, the man relinquishes. Without stopping to examine his winnings, Cliff dashes toward the rotating Ferris wheel, which beckons to him like the hand of destiny. On the way, he rips a purple ticket from a folded strip tucked in his front pocket.

He joins the queue and grits his teeth when the cutoff comes not two or three people up, but right in front of him. He rocks from foot to foot while he waits for the wheel to make four ... five ... six ... seven ... eight revolutions. His right knee vibrates like an overwound watch spring. At last the wheel slows and the operator, his barrel chest covered by a filthy white shirt and suspenders, starts to simultaneously unload and load the carriages for the next ride.

The three kids behind Cliff are together, so he gets a carriage to himself. The operator says, "Have a good ride, kiddo. Enjoy the view from the top." He winks as he double-checks the safety bar and swings the carriage for luck.

Cliff inches upward as the wheel fills with boisterous kids and young couples. He inspects his telescope for the first time. Extended to full length, the tin barrel curves perceptibly in the middle. The plastic lenses are cloudy with age. He peers through the eyepiece, trying to make sense of blurry images. His shoulders sag. What a waste of time—and tokens. He's tempted to pitch the piece of crap into the bushes, but that will likely get him ejected from the ride, if not from the carnival altogether. He'll have to make do.

The Ferris wheel stops and starts every few seconds. Throngs of people mill about below, interweaving like gears. Lights flicker and pulse. Hurdy-gurdy music carries waves of shrieking laughter to his ears and beyond. He's barely aware of any of this, though. He has his telescope. It may be shoddy and cheap, but it's better than nothing.

When his carriage clears the cluster of trees at the edge of Murchie's field, Balsam Ridge springs into view. Cars crawl along the residential streets, many heading toward the carnival parking lot.

His best opportunity to use the telescope will be during loading. He puts the viewfinder to his eye and sweeps the barrel back and forth, orienting himself with the flag on his school's roof. The magnified image is far clearer than he expected. He can almost read street signs. Next, he picks out his home, where a light burns outside the back porch. His parents said they'd catch the fair another night. They seemed anxious for him to go. Mushy stuff, he figures.

Steeling his shoulder muscles to keep his hands steady, he darts from one landmark to another. He has just located Jane's window when the wheel lurches and starts moving again.

He and Jane aren't going out, exactly, but three days ago, in social studies class, she patted the chair next to her when he passed. He accepted her shy invitation, pretending not to notice everyone staring at them. Despite Eddie and Greg's incessant teasing, Cliff sat beside her the next day and every day since.

The timing of the carnival's arrival was perfect. On Tuesday evening, fliers were stapled to telephone poles and taped up in store windows. Rides and booths sprang up overnight at the edge of town as if someone had planted magic Tilt-a-Whirl and Scrambler seeds and watered them with fairy dust. Now it looks as if the carnival has always been here ... as if the rust at the base of the Free Fall ride is formed out of the very earth on which it sits ... as if the ropes holding up the Bingo tent poles have been attached to the same pegs in this spot since the beginning of time.

The past two evenings, Cliff rehearsed in front of the mirror. "Do you want to go to the carnival with me? Would you like to go to the circus Friday night? Hey, I have an idea. Let's go explore the Hall of Mirrors tomorrow night."

When the crucial moment arrived, though, his tongue turned into a lifeless lump of muscle so thick it filled his mouth. His heart pounded, his face grew warm, and the blood rushing through his ears deafened him. Jane's face, alive with wide-eyed anticipation, collapsed to a puzzled frown. She lingered when the bell rang and the others scattered to class, risking a tardy slip from Mr. Comeau, but after a few moments she, too, had to go and Cliff was left standing alone in the hall. Mr. McPhee didn't look up from his lecture notes when Cliff snuck into the classroom, took his seat, and buried his head in his hands.

Instead of embarking on the adventure of a lifetime, Cliff settled for tagging along with his goofy friends, determined to have a good time. This was the carnival after all. People shrieked as they subjected themselves to thrilling torture. There was music everywhere. Who knew that cumulus clouds of spun sugar had such an enticingly pink aroma or that popcorn butter actually smelled yellow? He was convinced he could even smell the ice cream. And the lights! Multicolored bulbs flashed and popped, deliriously disorienting.

Magic filled the air, dancing like static electricity from the tips of his hair. A shiver ran down his spine as he absorbed the overwhelming sensations.

Cliff and his friends fired cork guns at metal ducks, smashed into each other in bumper cars, yelled at the tops of their lungs when the swinging pirate ship reached its apex and froze momentarily in space, and screamed as they surrendered to gravity on the Free Fall machine.

Despite the excitement, he couldn't stop thinking about Jane. When Eddie and Greg dragged Bryan toward the Tilt-a-Whirl, Cliff said he'd catch up with them later. His friends would have said the Ferris wheel was for little kids. Properly equipped, though, Cliff saw it as an opportunity.

Now that he has his telescope, he suffers a momentary pang of conscience, reinforced by the ring toss barker's leering wink. It's not like what he's doing is wrong, exactly. He's just going to look at Jane's house. That's all.

When the wheel stops to admit more passengers, Cliff's carriage rocks. Is that her upstairs window with the light on? He tries to compensate for the motion as the window swings across his lens like a pendulum. The babble below fades into the background. Time stops when Jane materializes in his eyepiece. Cliff recognizes the clothes she had on at school today—when he'd been unable to get his mouth to work. She's leaning on her windowsill, staring toward the carnival, or so it seems. She sways back and forth as if she's listening to music. She looks close enough that he could reach out and touch her. Instead of spying on her, he should be sitting beside her. Her head should be resting on his shoulder. When they reached the top, they might even have kissed. He curses his shyness and wonders if she'll ever speak to him again.

The Ferris wheel starts moving, carrying him haltingly back down to ground level. Soon Jane is gone, stolen away by gravity. He clutches the telescope as he begins to rise again, smoothly and without interruption this time. The higher he rises, the more his heart pounds.

Once he's clear of the trees, his telescope finds Jane's window almost immediately, but she's no longer there. All the air empties from his lungs and his shoulders slump.

An unexpected jolt deflects his aim so that he's looking through the window of a neighboring house. He recognizes Mr. Goldman, the soft-spoken school librarian. Mr. Goldman doesn't have any clothes on and the woman he's with doesn't look anything like Mrs. Goldman, unless she's lost a lot of weight and gotten a boob job since the last time Cliff saw her. He blinks and wipes his eye to make sure he's not imagining what he's seeing.

Another jolt, another deflection. Mr. Comeau, the English teacher, is pounding on the back door of Mr. McPhee's house. Mr. McPhee appears a moment later and the two men engage in an animated discussion. Cliff's carriage drops behind the trees just as Mr. Comeau punches Mr. McPhee in the face.

Cliff's mind races. What should he do? Mr. McPhee might be hurt. The Ferris wheel seems to be crawling along. He wills it to return him to the top so he can find out what's happening. He hears his name and looks over to see Greg and Eddie laughing and pointing. Bryan is lying on a bench near the Bingo tent, vomit puddled on the ground beside him. Cliff ignores them as he braces for the next pass across the top.

Pull it out one more notch.

Startled, Cliff twists his head to locate the source of the voice, which seems to come from someone sitting behind him. But that's impossible—there's nothing behind him but a spider web of metal. He would have sworn he felt hot breath accompanying the words into his ear.

Cliff looks down at the flimsy telescope in his lap. It appears to be fully extended but he grasps it in both hands and tugs.

Pop!

The telescope elongates to reveal a previously undetected segment. The extra length provides much greater magnification. Nearing the top, he scrambles to find his target. Through the lens he sees the two teachers wrestling on the ground outside Mr. McPhee's back door. He can even make out the gashes on their faces and spittle flying from their mouths.

The carriage lurches, bumping Cliff's view to a different house. Though the living room curtains are pulled, Cliff can see through a gap. He recognizes Eddie and Greg's fathers, but he doesn't know the third man, the one tying a rubber hose around Eddie's father's bicep. When a needle plunges into Mr. Duffy's forearm, Cliff looks away.

As he approaches nadir, he rises from his seat and yells at his friends, wondering if he can climb down without getting tangled and crushed by the wheel's lumbering, relentless force. The operator shouts at him to sit.

A familiar figure is standing next to the barrel-chested man: the skinny carnie in the derby and the striped suit who runs the ring toss game. The man stares at him with dark intensity. His lips move, but the carnival's cacophony drowns him out. *Turn it around*, a voice whispers in his left ear. Cliff finds the barker's eyes. The man nods, as if to confirm the instructions.

Cliff sits, clutching the aluminum telescope hard enough to dent its flimsy body. He doesn't want to see more. He wants off. Still, when he approaches the peak, he reverses the tube and stares through the wide end.

Time screeches to a halt. The hurdy-gurdy music recedes, as if playing underwater. The flashing carnival lights all come on at once and stay on.

Somewhere far, far away, water drips from a tap into an empty bucket, the only sound Cliff hears.

Through the reversed telescope, he can peer into just about every window in town. He spies Mr. Jamieson, the town banker, hiding a set of accounting books beneath the floorboards in his home office. Peter Fearon is beating up his girlfriend. Donny Moore is sitting cross-legged on his bedroom floor, dumping the contents from wallets and purses piled around him. Miss Hamilton, the single mother who lives up the street, is shaking her screaming baby so hard that its head whips back and forth. Terry Cook is watching a snuff film and taking notes. Mrs. Hickey is adding something from a small, brown bottle to her husband's coffee cup. Everywhere he looks, people he thought he knew are doing terrible things.

At last, he returns to Jane's window, now seemingly a thousand miles away. Even so, her tiny bedroom—decorated with pink lace and movie posters—fills the viewfinder. She's lying in bed, her long hair splayed across her pillow. A man is sitting beside her, stroking her cheek. If she wasn't naked, it might seem a tender scene. Tears stream down her face as she pleads with the man and tries to push him away.

Cliff's jaw clenches so hard his face aches. An artery on his forehead pulses. Blind hatred seethes through his body, filling his veins with lava and vitriol.

The man collapses on top of Jane, burying his face in her hair. She turns away and stares out the window. She seems to be looking straight into Cliff's eyes. *If only you had asked me out*, she appears to be thinking. Trapped atop the cursed Ferris wheel, Cliff's heart tears. His hands tremble as the trees once again interrupt his view. The telescope tumbles to the floor of the carriage.

Murmuring voices fill his head, screaming at him to do something. *Get them all*, one says clearly in his ear. *Make them all pay.*

The Ferris wheel slows down, too soon for many, but not fast enough for Cliff. He leaps out before it stops, his feet in motion before they touch the ground. This time, he's on a different kind of quest. He knows exactly where to find what he needs—his father's gun case.

He rushes past his friends without a word. The last of his tokens and a long strip of purple tickets stream from his pockets as he runs as fast as winged Mercury. Burning embers of hatred displace his thoughts.

At first it sounds like firecrackers going off in the distance. Soon, though, sirens pierce the night, overwhelming the calliope and the other carnival sounds. People fall silent as wail after wail join together in a single, discordant aria.

The ring toss barker slaps the Ferris wheel operator on the back, spits on the ground and returns to his booth, the telescope clutched in his left hand.

Steve stands fuming in front of the carnival game booths. Carla, his bitch girlfriend, canceled their date at the last minute. Something came up, she told him.

"I'll bet," he mutters. "And I'll bet that something's name is Phil." He's long suspected Carla of cheating on him. If he ever catches them together, he'll make them pay.

His gaze falls on the prizes at the ring toss booth. A telescope is nestled between a pair of stuffed animals. He tilts his head to one side and regards the Ferris wheel towering over the fairground. An idea begins to gel in his beer-addled brain.

He reaches into his pocket for a handful of tokens and slams them down on the counter. "Set me up," he tells the geek in the stupid-looking hat and striped suit who runs the booth. "I'm gonna win me a prize."

AFTERWARD, THERE WILL BE A HALLWAY

Gary A. Braunbeck

> "About suffering they were never wrong,
> The Old Masters: how well they understood
> Its human position; how it takes place
> While someone else is eating or opening a window or
> just walking dully along."
>
> —W.H. Auden
> "Musée des Beaux Arts"

(... fingers barely brushing the surface of her skin but still her eyes fall through their sockets and into the back of her skull with soft, dry sounds ... touching her cheeks, wanting to hold her face as a lover should, whispering that everything will be all right, it will, you'll see, she only has to come back, please, please come back, don't leave again, dearGodplease, but her head collapses inward, flesh crumbling apart, flaking away, fragmenting, becoming slivers, becoming specks, becoming dust, her face sinking, splitting in half, disintegrating ... staring helpless as the rest of her crumples and decays, revealing nothing within, the parched shards of what were once her lips holding their form only one more second, long enough to say that it's time ...)

"... to get up, sleepy-head! *C'mon*—it's Wednesday and it's gonna start in a couple hours."

"You've only reminded me ten times since last night," I mumbled, head still buried underneath the sheet, a preview of that day when the sheet would not be pulled back and I'd be lying in a cold drawer in a cold room in the cold basement of some hospital like the rest of them. Someday. Just not today. As with most mornings, I was ambivalent about how I felt on the subject of that particular eventuality.

I had not been dreaming—I rarely dream these days; no, I'd been lying there envisioning what *might* happen if I were to chance touching—

—don't. Just ... don't. You know better than to do this to yourself, Neal, my man.

I sat up, rubbed my eyes, and focused on the little girl standing in the doorway to my bedroom. Seven—no, wait, just turned *eight* years old. She still wore the Scooby-Doo pajamas underneath the white hospital robe, and those SpongeBob SquarePants slippers that looked cute from a distance but were in fact unbelievably creepy when you saw them up close. Her complexion was a sickly shade of yellow-white, with dark brownish-purple arcs under her eyes. Her left hand rose up to scratch at the padded, custom-made bandanna covering her bald head. The chemotherapy must have been hellish. Every time I looked at her, I wondered if I could have held on as long as she did.

She stared at me for a moment, then asked: "Can we open it now?"

"You've only been here two days, you know my rule."

Hands on hips, one foot impatiently tapping, lower lip sticking out in defiance. "But it's a *dumb* rule! A *whole* week? How come I gotta wait a whole week?"

"Because I ..." I rubbed my face, feeling the first twinges of pain behind my left eye; a sure sign that a migraine was going to visit me today if I wasn't careful. "Would you please come over here, Melissa?"

"Not until you start calling me 'Missy'. I asked you, like, what? A *hundred times*."

"Oh, don't be so dramatic—this is only the second or third time and you know it."

"Still ... you better not think it's dumb. Mom called me Missy because it sounded like 'messy' and she was always saying how my room was such a disaster area. 'Messy Missy.' I liked it. So you call me that, okay?"

I actually managed a small grin. "Your wish is my command, oh Messy Missy." I pointed to the foot of the bed. "Now, would you come over here and sit down, please?"

She hesitated for only a moment before doing as I'd asked. I imagine her mother had warned her about strangers, about never, ever talking to them, let alone sitting on their beds.

I turned on the nightstand light, blinking against the sudden bright burst. "Missy, have you ever gotten mad at one of your friends and said something that you felt bad about later?"

"Well, *duh*. Who hasn't?"

"My one-week rule is sort of my way of ... of making sure something like that doesn't happen with you and your stuff, *duh*."

She cocked her head to the side and squinted at me. "You know that doesn't make any sense, right? God, you're weird."

I sighed. "Okay, look at it this way. It's like—and I am *not* weird."

"Yes, you are."

"Am not."

"Are too."

"I am not."

"*Shut! Up!* You are too! I've seen weird people before, and you're a freakazoid, mister. You don't have any friends except for that lady who's asleep in the other room and she's never awake so for all I know, she hates your guts, nobody ever calls, you don't go anywhere except to drive around all day stealing boxes, you almost never smile and when you do, you look like you're trying to poop but can't—you're *weird*."

Yep. Lost that one.

Something in my face must have alarmed her, because after a few moments she leaned forward and said, "I'm sorry. Really. I didn't mean it in a *bad* way, y'know? You're weird, but it's a *good* weird, I think."

"You don't have to apologize, Missy. You're right, I *am* weird and I *don't* have any friends."

"Not even that sleeping lady?"

I knew she'd get around to exploring the guest room sooner or later; I'd been hoping for later. "I don't know. I don't know how she feels about me."

"Who is she, anyway?"

"Her name's Rebecca. She was my wife."

"How long's she been dead?"

"Three years this Friday."

"She doesn't look very good. Her breathing's all wheezy and her skin—"

"—could we get back to the subject, please?" I was more than aware of how Rebecca looked and sounded, unless things had worsened since I'd checked on her last night. Though I knew I should (and maybe even a part of me wanted to), I couldn't go back in there, not this morning. Seeing her last night—her hair still falling out in clumps, cheeks more hollow than the day before, lips cracked and parched, the black blotches on her skin that seemed to expand as I stood there watching—was bad enough. A second visit this soon was more than I could take.

Missy looked out toward the hallway, deep in an eight-year-old's thoughts, and then turned back to me and said, "I could be your friend."

"That's sweet, but you're not going to be around that long."

"Because of the one-week rule thing?"

"Yes. I know this seems unfair, but I'm only doing it for your own good." Dear God, did I actually just *say* that? "It's like when you do something or say something that seems like what you want to do or say *right then*, at that second, understand? So you say or do it, and then later on wish you hadn't because it was mean or inconsiderate or just plain dumb. You wish you could take it back, but you can't. Does *that* make sense?"

A shrug. "I guess."

"Well it's the same thing with your stuff, only it's a lot more important. Once we open that box, you *have* to choose something, and it's got to be the *right* something. If you pick the wrong thing, you'll be ..." I let fly with a soft groan of frustration; this was more difficult than I'd thought it would be. Throwing off the covers (I'd slept in my shirt and pants), I stumbled to my feet and crossed to the other side of the bedroom, pulling back the curtain covering the window there. "Come here. I want you to see something."

Her eyes narrowed. "It isn't something gross, is it? One time, this boy in my class, Eric, he said he had something real cool to show me, and it turned out he had this fat old slimy nasty water-bug that he'd squished open with his fingers. It looked like a big glob of snot with legs and pincers. I couldn't eat my pudding at lunch that day, and I *like* pudding. A lot."

"No squished bugs or anything like that, I promise."

She came over to the window and looked down at the street. I live on the twelfth floor of one of Cedar Hill's nicer apartment buildings, and the windows in my bedroom and living room all offer a good view of the downtown area.

I pointed. "See that old brick building down the street? With those stone steps?"

"Gargoyle Castle!" she shouted, giggling.

"Wha-huh?"

"Gargoyle Castle, you freakazoid. It's got those stone gargoyles up near the top, see? So I always called it Gargoyle—"

"—I follow the line of reasoning, thanks so much—and stop calling me 'freakazoid,' it's rude and gets old in a hurry."

She smiled. "Says you."

The truth was, I'd forgotten about the gargoyles that squat over the stone archway of what used to be the Building and Loan, so for a moment, I was seeing it through her eyes, and it was, as she might put it, *way cool.* But the feeling passed. It always did.

"Okay," I said. "Look down at the steps of Gargoyle Castle and tell me what you see."

She leaned closer to the window, concentrating for all she was worth, and then said: "That guy sitting there with that tin cup? Is he what you wanted me to see?"

"Yes. His name was Leonard but he liked being called 'Lenny'. Lenny fought in Vietnam, did two tours of duty. That cup—which is steel, by the way, *not* tin—belonged to him. It was part of his C-rations kit. You know what C-rations are?"

"Yeah. I saw this movie one time, with my mom, on TV, about these soldiers in World War Two. Lee Marvin was in it—Mom always watched Lee Marvin movies. She thought he was a hottie. I always thought he looked like someone who was mean but wished he wasn't. Anyway, they had those C-ration kits in the movie that they ate from." She seemed so very proud that she was able to answer my question, so I made sure to look suitably impressed.

I nodded toward Lenny. "He carried that cup inside a pocket of his vest. You can't see it from here, but there's a pretty big dent in the side. That's because it deflected a bullet that would have blown his hip to pieces and probably crippled him. He never went anywhere without that cup afterward. He called it his bad luck shield."

"His *what?*"

"His good luck charm."

"*Ahhhh ...*" She looked down at Lenny once again. "So when you guys opened Lenny's box, he chose his cup, his good luck charm, right?"

"Not exactly. The cup was the first thing Lenny saw, and he was ... he was *really* happy to see it again, so he just grabbed it without thinking."

She gave a soft but genuine gasp. "It *wasn't* the thing he was supposed to pick?"

"No, and because he grabbed the wrong thing without thinking, he's stuck here. He hangs out on those steps ... always. And he always will. Maybe not those same steps, but he'll always be waiting around ... somewhere."

"Because he can't take it back?"

I nodded. "Because he can't take it back."

"That's so sad. Does he have anyone to talk to?"

"I talk to him almost every day. Sometimes other people like him come by."

"Really?"

"You'd be surprised how many people like you and Lenny wander the streets around here, Missy."

"And you see all of them?"

"Oh, no, not even close. When Lenny's got a visitor whose ... I mean, I can only see and talk with those whose belongings ... wait a second—look." Sure enough, Lenny, ever the social butterfly, was chatting away.

"Hey," said Missy. "Who's that pretty lady he's talking to? Oh, wow ... isn't her hair *beautiful?* She looks like she's going to the Oscars or something fancy like that." She looked at me. "Don't you think she's pretty?"

"I have no idea. I can't see her."

"But she's *right there!*"

"I don't doubt it, Missy, honestly, I don't. But the thing is, whoever she is, I wasn't the one who took care of her personal effects."

"Her what?"

"Her things. I wasn't the one who picked up the box of her stuff."

"'Kay ... so how come I can see her?"

"Because the dead can all see each other."

"Huh." She stared for a moment longer, and then her face brightened. "So it's kinda like a secret club? That's *so cool*. Hey, can we go around today and see how many I can spot but you can't? It'll be like a game you play in a long car trip, 'Bury the Cow' or 'I Spy.'"

"We can do whatever you want, Missy. Speaking of—" I dropped the curtains back into place. "—are you *sure* you want to go to your own funeral?"

"Yep. I wanna see Mom again ... and I wanna see if mean old Eric feels bad now about what he did to me with the water bug. That was *so disgusting*." She gave an overly-theatrical shudder. When that got no reaction from me, she repeated it, only this time throwing one arm up, the back of her hand pressed against her forehead. "Oh, *suh*," she said in a not-bad imitation of a Southern Belle, "I do believe I ham about to fa-haint."

"'Ham' is right," I said, trying to stop my (according to her) constipated smile. "That's some fierce overacting, *mah de-ah*."

She flung herself against my dresser, one hand still plastered to her forehead, the other now pushing forward to fend off the eee-vell Yankee. "You *must* leave me my *honor*, suh! You *must* show some *decency!*"

I applauded, and she took a broad, grandiose bow.

"I was gonna be an actress on the soaps."

"You're certainly pretty enough. I'll bet you would have been great."

"Me too." No sadness, no regret, just a simple statement of fact. Most of the people I deal with usually crack at a moment of epiphany like

(*Me too*)

this, their bitterness, anger, fear, and grief reducing them for a time to a crumpled handful of spoiled human material whose potential they now knew would never be realized. I'd been listening to it for nearly three years now, this cumulative symphony of human misery, hurt, loneliness, terror, rage, despair, all of it in search of an outlet, something to give it purpose, an endless sonata of sorrow and hopelessness composed by those whose existence has ground to a halt in a series of sputtering little agonies, leaving them with nowhere to go, nothing to hold onto, and no one to speak with except some stranger whose job it is to gather the detritus left behind by the odd ones, the damaged and devastated ones, the ruined ones, the old, the alone, and the forgotten.

Yeah, I'm a real party monster, a walking chuckle-fest. Just ask my wife. Maybe she'll answer *you* ... if there's anything left of her.

Melissa was the youngest I'd dealt with, and she still had all the pent-up, eager, impatient energy of a child. It was probably that very impatience that caused her to show up so soon after her death; when I retrieved the discarded box of her personal effects from beside the hospice dumpster, her body still lay inside her room waiting to be picked up by the funeral home. I put the box in the trunk of my car, drove home, and found her sitting in the middle of my living room when I walked through the door.

"Hey," she said softly to me now (as she did then). Something in her voice warned me she was about to ask a question I didn't want to answer.

"We need to start getting ready—well, *I* need to, anyway." I started toward the bathroom and was mere inches from a clean getaway when Missy asked:

"How did Rebecca die?"

And there it was.

But I was ready. Snapping my fingers as if I'd just remembered something, I made a sharp right turn into the hallway and called back, "I almost forgot—I have a surprise for you."

"A *surprise?*"

She was in the living room before I was, her sudden presence startling the hell out of me.

"Ah, damn—*Missy!* I asked you to please not do that anymore." Three years, and it still unnerves me, the way they can pop in and out of a room whenever they want.

"I'm sorry," she said. "I just got all excited when you said—"

"It's all right. Now ...

"Close your eyes."

Find me the kid who can resist those three words. Missy did as I asked, bouncing up and down on the balls of her feet. If I listened hard enough, I bet I could have heard her etherial molecules going, *Oh, goody, goody, goody* ...

I pulled the wrapped package from its hiding place behind the television and held it out to her. This was as much an experiment as it was an evasive tactic. "Okay ... open them!"

She did, her eyes growing almost absurdly wide as she jumped up and down, practically squealing, "Oh, *goody! A present!*"

And took it from my hands.

So I was right: if it's an action they performed without thinking when alive, they could continue to do so after death.

I'd expected her to make quick, ferocious work of the wrapping paper as would any child thrilled over a present, but instead she looked it over, studying it. "This is *real* nice paper. You did a great job wrapping it. The ribbon's beautiful." She studied it a little more, a jeweler determining the carat-value of a diamond, then held it up by her ear and gave it a little shake. "Hmmm ... I wonder what it is."

By now *I* was ready to tear the paper off the damned thing, but then just as quickly realized she'd not only reaffirmed one of my theories, but also just shown me what an extraordinary little girl she was. Had been. She knew, at age eight she *knew* that a surprise equaled a mystery, and any good mystery was to be savored as much as solved. I froze at the sight of her smile; I had never seen such a radiant smile before ... or if I had, was too full of myself to

(*You don't have any friends except for that lady who's asleep in the other room and she's never awake so for all I know, she hates your guts* ...)

notice it. It was the kind of smile that told you she'd just been let in on this Big Secret, something so wonderful and great and full of happy promises that nothing would ever seem bad or sorrowful to her again; and standing there in my living room, nailed to the spot by the sight of her smile, her joy, her ability to savor the wonder and anticipation, my defenses taken by surprise, dumbstruck by the sudden rush of emotions, I fell a little bit in love with her.

Don't misunderstand, there was nothing even remotely sexual about it, nothing physical or lustful or perverted; I fell in love with her the same way some people fall in love with a piece of music, or a certain time of day or season of the year—twilight in autumn—or even an idea. It was the kind of startling, forceful, promise-of-salvation love a person experiences maybe two or three times in their life, should they be graced with a long one. My breath caught in my throat and my arms would not move. I refused to blink. Everything I'd once believed to be good and pure and redeeming of life stood less than two feet away from me, in the form an eight-year-old girl who would never know her first kiss, her first dance, or the first time she held a boy's hand; for her there would be no late-night study sessions cramming for the big exam, no prom, no graduation parties; no first job, first paycheck, first promotion; none of that for Messy Missy. For her there was only this moment, this breath, in this place, with this wonderful mystery wrapped in shabby-looking paper I'd grabbed from a discount bin at the last minute before getting in the checkout line.

"Are you okay?" she said, taking a step toward me.

I blinked, wiped at my eyes, exhaled, and took a step back. "Uh, um ... yes, yes. I'm fine. I guess my mind just wandered off for a moment." I flashed my best Constipated Smile. "Well, go ahead—open it."

"Okay." Even then she didn't rip the paper to shreds; she carefully unwrapped it—a corner here, a corner there—until the paper was loose enough for her to reach in and pull out the gift, which she did with her eyes closed.

"Oh, this is gonna be *good*, isn't it?"

"For the love of God—*open your eyes and find out!*"

"Geez, don't bust a vein." She opened her eyes, saw what it was, and then squealed loudly, jumping up and down while simultaneously twirling. "*The SpongeBob SquarePants Movie!*"

"You said you never got to see it, right?"

"No, but I'm gonna watch it while you take your shower!" She stopped her twirling and held the DVD against her chest as if she expected some stinking pirate to come sailing out of nowhere and be a-relievin' her of her treasure a-fore makin' 'er walk the plank, yar. "Oh, no—wait! Wait! Hang *on!* You know what would be great? Oh, this'll be *way cool!* Listen—we could make popcorn tonight and watch it then. Mom and me, we had this special recipe for buttered popcorn, I could make it for us. You'll love my popcorn, you will, you will, I *swear* you will!"

I pointed at the television. "But I thought you wanted to watch it now."

"Well, *duh*, I do, but SpongeBob, he's more fun to watch with someone else, not just all by yourself. We could—oh, hey! Hang *on!* We could maybe see if Rebecca feels like watching it with us—we could even invite Lenny and his new girlfriend." She gasped, eyes growing even wider. "We could *have a party!* Oh, *rock* out! Let's do that, okay? Let's have a party tonight. A SpongeBob/Missy's Funeral party!"

"You want to have a party to watch SpongeBob and celebrate your funeral?"

She turned into a human Bobblehead figure. On way too much sugar. "It'll be *so awesome!*"

"And you called *me* 'weird.'"

"Oh, this is, like, one of the awesomest presents *ever!* You rock! *Thank you so much!*"

And before I could move, she ran forward and gave me a great big hug and the next thing I knew I was

(*... crying out but there was no sound no matter how much she tried, and she wondered what had happened to her voice and why wasn't anybody here she had to go to the bathroom and ohGod, it hurt, it hurt, ithurtithurtithurt so much, and she tried to roll over and press the button so the nurses would come but she couldn't move her legs and there was sudden liquid fire spreading down the backs of her thighs and she started crying because she'd just soiled her bed again and ohGod it burned so much when her bowels let go and she closed her eyes and tried to think of something funny, something cool, like winter snow and goofy snowmen, but then there were arms, strong arms, helping her up, but she vomited all over herself and the nurse and Mommy, where are you, I hurt, Mommy, I hurt, and now it was me that hurt, I felt all of it, the sickness and pain, the vomiting and pissing and shitting, then she'd get so cold and couldn't stop shaking and it felt like her teeth were going to smash to smithereens every time they chattered together, but then came the shot and she felt warm, so warm again, with fresh sheets and a new gown and her SpongeBob slippers keeping her feet snug, and she began to fade away for a little while, then awoke to see Mommy sitting beside her bed, holding her hand, telling her that she was being such a strong, brave little girl, that she'd feel better soon and did she want another shot, they could give her another shot now if she wanted, and Missy said yes, please, and could I have some pudding, too, I like pudding a lot, I promise not to spill any ...*)

on my hands and knees on the floor, my body still wracked with the physical agony of her last few hours, but it would fade, I knew it would, this is why I always made it a point to never touch any of them, or to let them touch me; there were always remnants, some strong, some weaker, but none of them coming close to what had just chewed through me.

"Omigod!" shouted Missy, dropping to her hands and knees beside me. "Omigod, I'm ... I'm *so sorry!* I am. Please don't be mad. Is there anything I can do? Do you need me to get you—?" She reached out.

"*Don't* ... don't touch me, please? It'll happen again." I turned my head toward her and tried to smile but it hurt too much. "It's not that I didn't enjoy the hug, okay? It was really sweet. But ... you ... you can't ... *I* can't ..." I couldn't finish, and so lay stomach-down on the floor.

Missy leaned down and whispered, "Is it okay if I stay with you?"

"... sure, hon, whatever you want ..."

"Then I'll be right here."

"... okay ..."

"Hey, Neal?" It was the first time she'd called me by name.

"... what is it ...?"

"I'm sorry that Rebecca killed herself."

The other reason I try to avoid touching or being touched by them: they always pick up on some remnant within me.

"... so'm I ..." *Christ*, why wasn't the pain fading yet?

"Do you know why she did it?"

I shook my head, which—considering the threat of the migraine on top of the rest of it—was perhaps not the best course of action. "... don't know, Missy ... I really don't ..." I said, lying.

"Shh, there-there. You rest, okay? I'll be right here when you wake up."

"... don't know why she did it ... there's ... so much I don't know ..."

The pain became a wave of cold nausea, and I passed out beneath its force.

Here is what I *do* know:

They come to me as they were at the moment of their deaths, that is the only thing on which there has never been any variation; they retain their five senses (if they had all of them while still alive); until Missy, the usual period between death and turning up in my life was between ten days and one month (it was exactly twenty-three days after her suicide that Rebecca showed up in the guest room, where I'd found her body), but there are at least a dozen who have *yet* to show up, even after three years; most of them don't like to talk too much the first few days, Missy and Lenny being the exceptions there; and—again, excluding Missy and Rebecca—all of them died alone and forgotten, some in the hospital, some in the nursing home, some in the hospice, no one coming forward to claim either their bodies or the boxes containing their personal effects.

Here is what I have learned:

Death is not instantaneous. The cells go down one by one, and it takes a while before everything's finished. If a person wanted to, they could snatch a bunch of cells *hours* after somebody's checked out and grow them in cultures. Death is a fundamental function; its mechanisms operate with the same attention to detail, the same conditions for the advantage of organisms, and the same genetic information for guidance through the stages that most people equate with the physical act of living. So I asked myself, if it's such an intricate, integrated physiological process—at least in the primary, local stages—then how do you explain the permanent vanishing of consciousness? What happens to it? Does it just screech to a halt, become lost in humus, what? Nature doesn't work like that. It tends to find perpetual uses for its more elaborate systems, and that gave me an idea: maybe human consciousness is somehow severed at the filaments of its attachments and then absorbed back into the membrane of its origin. I think that's all they are by the time they come to me—the severed consciousness of a single cell that hasn't died but is instead vanishing totally into its own progeny.

"I don't have the slightest goddamn idea what you're talking about," Lenny had said to me on his third night in my company. We were sitting at my kitchen table, putting a pretty good dent in a bottle of Glenlivet I'd bought earlier that day, knowing it was Lenny's poison of choice.

"Not all of your cells have died yet," I said, only slightly slurring my words, "and the ones that're still alive *remember* you. And as long as just *one* cell remembers, you're tied to the corporeal—to the physical body—in some form. But when those final cells finally give it up—" I snapped my fingers as if I had actually made my point.

"I'm guessing you weren't a big church-goer," said Lenny, tamping a smoke out the pack lying on the table and lighting up.

I leaned back in my chair, grinning. "Okay, smartass, let me ask you something, then. How is it you're still able to smoke a cigarette?"

Lenny looked at the smoke he held between his fingers as if it were something he'd never seen before.

"You don't remember doing that, do you?"

He shook his head.

"That's the answer—or at least part of it. There's a thousand things we do every day without thinking—walking, eating, breathing, lighting a cigarette, picking up a pen, taking a piss. All done by rote. We explain it away by saying that we do it 'unconsciously,' but the truth is it's our *cells* that remember this stuff for us, that tell the rest of our body how to lift a phone receiver or add a little more sugar to the iced tea because it's not sweet enough. Don't you get it, Lenny? You're here with me because those cells in you that are still alive haven't figured out yet that you're gone."

"Horseshit. I bought the farm almost a month ago. You're not really going to sit there and try to tell me that buried under the ground in Cedar Hill Cemetery there's some part of my body that's still *alive* on a cellular level, are you? I'm here, that's that, and it don't mean nothin'."

I was on my fourth drink—well past my limit of two—and feeling no pain. "You remember Medgar Evers?"

"The Civil Rights leader from Mississippi? Betcher ass, I do! Helluva guy. Took 'em thirty years, but they finally put that bastard Beckwith away for his assassination."

"Remember when they exhumed Evers' body before Beckwith's third trial in '94? How there was almost no decomposition after *thirty years* in the ground?"

"Yeah ...?"

"I saw this cable special one night where one of the medical examiners who studied Evers' body was being interviewed, and he talked about how, on a routine examination of some tissue, he detected the smallest amount of cell activity. An embalmed body, thirty years in the ground, and there was *still* cell activity in the tissue. So don't say 'Horeshit' to me, buddy."

He crushed out his smoke, poured himself another shot, and lit up a fresh cigarette. "It ain't exactly like these can hurt me *now*, is it?"

"Is that your way of saying that maybe, *maybe* I'm right?"

"It's my way of saying that maybe, *maybe* you're not full of shit right up to the eyeballs, but that's as far as I go. You know, you remind me of this chopper pilot I once caught a ride with from Two Corps in Pleiku. Son-of-a-bitch musta *loved* the sound of his own voice too because, *man*, he could go on and on about anything and most of what he talked about, he didn't know *jack*, but did that stop him? *Hell*, no ..."

It was because of Lenny that I discovered they don't sleep. I found out later that night when I heard him cry out from the small room that I laughingly call my office. I was still in the process of cataloguing the contents of his personal effects and had left the lid off the box. He wandered in there, saw his C-rations cup, and without thinking, picked it up.

They can touch and hold those inanimate things that had meaning for them while they were alive, even if these objects weren't among their final personal effects—a favorite book or magazine, a record or CD, a toy or knickknack, even, believe it or not, kitchen utensils and equipment. I once had a wonderful older lady—Grace (never was someone named more appropriately)—who all but danced a jig when she saw that I had an old-fashioned stand-mounted mixer, and insisted on baking cookies and a cake. Once she saw the mixer, everything in the kitchen took on meaning for her, and she puttered around in there for days. It was actually comforting, listening to her occupy herself; the clinking of dishes, the rattle of spoons, the sounds of the mixer working overtime ... it reminded me of when I was a child, sitting in the living room at Christmastime listening to my mother work her magic over the holidays. Grace even hummed while she baked, an old lullaby that my mother used to sing to me when I was young:

You can take the Toy-Town Trolley and meet the jolly Times Express,
No one there is melancholy, it's an isle of happiness.
Don't you keep your dreamboat waiting, hope you have a pleasant stay
On Hush-a-bye Island on Rock-a-bye Bay ...

Yes, it's corny as hell, but I don't care (hey, *Sinatra* recorded it, so don't get *too* high and mighty); it was nice, during Grace's stay, to feel something of my mother close again.

Lastly, here is what I hope: I hope ...

... ah, mmm, *well* ...

... on second thought, let's skip that last one. I would have been pissing in the wind and praying for rain, anyway.

A photograph of Melissa, taken at her seventh birthday party, had been enlarged and set on an easel near the head of the closed casket. Even from the back of the crowded room, you could see her sweet, grinning face and know how much had been lost.

There must have been at least seventy-five people there, possibly more. I was dressed in my best suit and trying to look like *I* was wearing *it* instead of the other way around as I walked up to the polished-wood podium holding the guest book and signed Lenny's name.

"That's not very nice," Missy whispered to me. "You really ought to sign your own name."

Looking up to make sure no one was watching me, I whispered as softly as I could, "We *talked* about this, Missy."

A sigh. "I *know* ... 'I can't talk to you once we're inside, Missy. People might think I'm *ca-ra-zeeee*.' This sucks." She looked toward the closed casket. "How come the lid's shut like that? And—oh, *God*, I can't believe she used that picture! I look like a pug!" She stared for a moment, touching her hospital robe, and then her trembling hand moved slowly toward her bandanna. "Do I look that *awful?*" The tears were evident in her voice before they appeared in her eyes. "I didn't think I looked *that* ugly, not so ugly that Mommy wouldn't ... wouldn't want people to *see* me!"

I reached out to take hold of her hand but pulled back almost at once; I couldn't chance another episode this soon.

It had taken the better part of twenty minutes for the pain to subside as I lay on the floor of my living room, and true to her word, Missy never moved away from me the entire time. When I was at last able to speak in almost complete sentences, I asked her to go into the bathroom, get into the medicine cabinet above the sink, and bring me one of the boxes containing the pre-measured shot of Imitrex I took when a migraine hit—and make no mistake, once Missy's pain had faded away, the full-blown migraine was there in all its shimmering, aura-soaked, drilling, nausea-inducing glory. I listened as Missy ran into the bathroom, threw open the cabinet door, and knocked over most of the contents within as she grabbed the Imitrex. I could hear her tearing open the box as she came back to the living room.

"You sure you can hold this thing?" she asked. "You seem real shaky—here, I'll do it."

"P-please don't—"

"Shut. *Up*. Dummy. I'm not gonna touch you. How do you—this doesn't look like any needle I've seen. How'm I supposed to ...?"

I explained, not once having to repeat myself, and she administered the shot like a pro. It took about thirty seconds before it began its voodoo, and then I realized there was something I'd forgotten to tell her.

"I am *so* ahead of you," she said, setting the emptied waste-paper basket by my side as I struggled into a sitting position.

"You might ... might want to look away for this next part," I said.

She shrugged. "Don't bother me to see somebody else puke."

I would have said something witty and Noel Coward-like in response, but by then my head was buried deep in the plastic basket and things were taking their natural course. If I don't take the shot in time, if the migraine's in full-tilt boogie mode by the time the medicine enters my system, I vomit. Unconditionally. Like this time; I wouldn't have been surprised if I had seen my *shoes* land in there.

Afterward, shoving the basket away, I fell back on the floor and lay there shuddering.

"You're all sweaty," said Missy, picking up the basket and marching back into the bathroom. I heard her empty its contents into the toilet and then flush it away; after that, she rinsed it out in the bath tub, then did something else at the sink. A few seconds later she was kneeling beside me again and placing a warm, damp washcloth against my forehead. I began to protest but she cut me off.

"I'm not touching you," she said, applying the slightest pressure. "There's a wet rag between us."

True enough. She kept her hand there, maintaining pressure, until the warmth began to sink into my flesh. She'd gotten the temperature exactly right, and I liked the feeling of her hand against my forehead.

"You're taking good care of me," I said, managing to produce a second complete sentence in less than three minutes. Things were looking up.

"Well, a lot of people took real good care of me, and I always paid real good attention, so I learned how to do it, too. Hey, maybe I could've been a nurse, huh?"

"Florence Nightingale's got nothing on you."

"I'll bet you think I don't get that, don't you? Well, I *do*, I know all about Florence Nightingale from school, so there!"

I laughed and it hurt. She laughed, as well.

"Better yet?" she asked.

"Yes, yes it is."

"If you wanna tell me where your suit is, I can go and lay it out for you. I used to lay out Mommy's work clothes for her at night so they'd be all ready when she got up in the morning."

I opened my eyes, relieved to see that the shimmering aura surrounding her and everything else was nearly gone. "There's a tan garment bag hanging on the left side of the closet in my bedroom."

"Your shoes in there, too?"

"Yes."

"You picked out a tie yet? If you haven't, can I pick it out for you?"

"That would be very nice of you."

She stared at me a few moments longer. "Y'know, if I didn't think it'd give you another bad fit, I'd kiss your cheek. You look like you could use a kiss on the cheek."

"I appreciate the thought, though."

"Yeah, well ..." Then she did something marvelous; she removed her hand from the wash cloth, bent down, and pressed her lips against it, kissing my forehead through the still-damp cotton. "That worked okay, I guess."

"I liked it."

She shook her index finger at me. "Mommy warned me that's what all dirty old men say before they start perving on you, so you just watch it, buddy."

"I'm not *that* old."

"No, but you *do* need a shower. *Phew!* Dude, you stink. Go deal with it."

Then she was off to lay out my suit and shoes, choose my tie (a silk number in a soft, muted shade of red), my socks (black), and wait for me to pull myself together and shower.

Now, standing in the main viewing room at Criss Brothers Funeral Home, she was crying and feeling embarrassed and humiliated because she thought she looked so ugly at the end (which meant she thought she looked ugly now), and I'd just chickened out on taking hold of her hand and maybe, *maybe* helping her to feel a little bit better.

I knelt down, acting as if I were re-tying one of my shoes. "Stop it, Missy." My teeth were clenched together and I was trying not to move my lips, so it emerged sounding like *stotitnissy.*

"I didn't wanna be *ugly.* Oh, lookit Mommy! She's *so sad* ..." And the crying—which before had been only sniffles and a few cracked words accompanying stray tears—now threatened to erupt into body-wracking sobs. She was so scared and ashamed and confused, and me, I just knelt there, scolding her, useless, awkward, self-conscious, ineffectual, and inept, having just denied her the one gesture that might have told her was still beautiful, that no one was ashamed of her, she wasn't repulsive and never had been—

("... I'm sorry that Rebecca killed herself ...")

—*no*, I thought. *It will not be this way, not within reach of my arm.*

Maybe if I'd been able to summon this kind of backbone sooner, Rebecca wouldn't have ... *wouldn't have.*

I reached out and took hold of Missy's hand, prepared for the onslaught of sensations and memories I was sure were going to kick my ass into next week. That is when I discovered what happens if I mentally prepare myself for the consequences of touching them before doing so:

I felt only the hand of a frightened little girl. Missy looked at me, tears streaming down her cheeks, and tried to say something, but all that emerged was a pained splutter of nonsensical sounds as she gave my hand a squeeze, let go, and threw her arms around my neck. "I'm n-n-not u-ugly, am I, Neal?"

"No, honey, *of course* you're not. Shhhh, there-there, c'mon, Missy."

An old woman seated in a chair near the back row heard me, and turned around to stare. Seeing that I was talking to myself, her eyes narrowed in disgust.

"I'm sorry," I said to her. "I just ... I knew Missy and it's just a terrible thing." The emotion in my voice wasn't as much of an affectation as I thought it would be.

The old woman's eyes softened and the slightest ghost of a smile crossed her face. She gave me a slight nod—*Maybe the poor fellow's really broken-up*—and turned away, leaving this stranger to his grief.

Missy pulled in a thick, snot-filled breath, and then laughed. "Boy, *that* was a close one. Don't say anything, freakazoid, or somebody'll call the nuthouse to come get you." She gave me a quick kiss on the cheek and broke the embrace, wiping her eyes and nose on the sleeve of her gown. "I'm gonna go over and see Mommy, okay?"

I gave a quick nod as I rose to my feet again. Missy didn't cross the room, she simply did her imitation of an electron, bounding from point to point without traversing the space between. Her mother sat in a chair off to the side of the casket and photo display. Missy was now by her side, looking uncertain what to do.

As soon as Missy appeared, the area she occupied, as if by silent understanding, became at once forbidden to anyone around her. Maybe people were just giving Missy's mother a little space—God knew the woman looked exhausted from trying to put on a strong face as she listened to mourners tell her how sorry they were about her loss—but my guess was that Missy was unconsciously emitting some sort of energy that made others nearby sense a sudden *otherness* in the room, and it might be best to just keep their distance for a few minutes.

I moved along the wall, trying to be as invisible as a living person could be, never taking my gaze off Missy and her mother. I caught a millisecond glimpse of the old woman who'd been staring at me: she was leaning over and whispering something to a well-dressed man who had just enough detached concern about him to be easily labeled an employee of the funeral home. I knew without actually looking that both the old woman and the man were talking about me.

—*Do you know him, ma'am?*

—*Never saw him before today. I'm not sure, but I think he maybe ought to be watched. I think he's really broken up, poor fellow—he was talking to himself. Not trying to start any trouble, you understand.*

—*I do, ma'am, and I'll keep an eye on him.*

Great. The last thing I needed was to have any attention drawn to me.

Missy was reaching out to take hold of her mother's hand. The funeral home employee was moving away from the old woman and making a beeline in my direction (I couldn't get mad at the guy, he was just doing his job). I didn't have many choices, and what few I did have were depleting fast.

Moving away from the wall, I made my way through the clusters of people toward the casket. A prayer bench had been placed close to its side, and I knelt down, making the Sign of the Cross as I did so and then folding my hands, lowering my head. Even if the funeral home employee did think I was trouble, he wouldn't dare interrupt me while I was praying—not that I *was* praying, but I knew damn well how this looked, and right now the appearance of prayer was good enough to buy me at least two minutes of safety.

I did not close my eyes; instead, I began turning my head in small, slow degrees to so that I could see Missy and her mother, at least peripherally.

At first all I managed to do was get the great-grandmother of all neck cramps, but as soon as I saw what was happening, the muscle strain seemed trivial.

Missy was squeezing her mother's hand. The woman's head snapped up, her eyes widening as she gasped. Several people turned in her direction but no one approached.

"Neal?" said Missy, not bothering to whisper because she knew I was the only one who could hear. "Please come over here. Please come right now."

I crossed myself, rose, and with a left-right-left sidestepped the funeral home employee who'd been lurking in wait nearby.

I approached Missy's mother, who looked directly at me, smiled, and said, "*Lenny!* Oh, I'm so glad you could make it."

Missy gave me a quick glance, indicating that I needed to take hold of her mother's *other* hand, which I did at once. Her skin was simultaneously sweaty yet cracked and calloused.

"Lenny," said her mother, gesturing with her head for me to lean down; instead, I got down on one knee. She moved her lips close—but not *too* close—to my ear. "I know how most people would take this, but I think you'll understand ... I ... I *feel* her near me, right this second. It's so *wonderful.* She's fine. She feels fine. She isn't suffering anymore."

I smiled and looked into her eyes; where before they had been red-rimmed and glossed with that heart-numbed luster from having shed too many tears, now their shine was one of utter bliss, of an inner-peace that transcended anything I had ever experienced, and if I'd fallen in love with Missy's joy and innocence before, I felt an equal rush of emotion toward her mother. I had no idea what Missy was doing—or even how she was doing it—but it was obvious that this grief-stricken woman would end the day not with the same broken heart and spirit that had been her only interior companions since the death of her daughter, but with a sense of tranquility, even serenity, that would get her through this.

Even now I cannot tell you what Missy's mother (Cynthia) and I talked about; I had become, for lack of a more subtle simile, Missy's ventriloquist's dummy; she was filtering her feelings and memories and thoughts through her mother into me, compelling me to put those feelings and memories into my own words (more or less) so that, for the dozens of people who slowly and cautiously gathered to listen, it sounded as if Cynthia and I were old friends, sharing private moments and recollections about Missy. If there had been any doubt in anyone's mind that I *wasn't* a friend of the family, those doubts were erased over the next twenty minutes.

When at last Cynthia noticed that we'd gathered an audience, she smiled, wiped her eyes, stood, and said: "Everyone, I'm sorry—this is Leonard Kessler. He was Melissa's—*Missy's*—kindergarten teacher."

Everyone—including the old woman who'd been watching me, and the funeral home employee—said hello and shook my hand and told me how wonderful it was that I'd come. I discovered, much to my surprise, that Missy had given me a cache of specific memories to share with each person, *detailed* memories exclusive to the individual with whom I spoke.

Finally someone—possibly the minister—announced that the service would be starting in five minutes, and everyone should take their seats. I gave Cynthia a hug, she kissed my cheek, and I wandered (read: half-staggered) toward the back row where Missy stood waiting.

Looking at her now, I realized that I knew her better than I'd known my own wife—hell, I knew her better than I knew myself; she might have filtered her feelings and memories through her mother in order not to chance another physical incident like the one earlier that morning, but it in no way lessened the way the information and sensations both effected and affected me.

"Don't you say a word," she said to me. "I've decided I don't want to stay for the service. I—oh, wait, hang on." She made her way over to a well-dressed woman who'd just entered holding the hand of a slightly plump boy who was roughly Missy's age. The little boy was practically sobbing. Missy walked up beside him, took hold of his free hand, and whispered something in his ear, then kissed his cheek.

The kid looked as if he'd just shaken Spider-Man's hand. His face *beamed*, and the tears just—*viola!*—stopped. He looked to his right, where Missy stood, and smiled. Missy smiled back, then returned to me.

"That's Eric, the guy who did the gross bug-thing," she said. "I told him I wasn't mad so he didn't have to feel, y'know, all guilty and stuff. Then I told him he looked real handsome and gave him a kiss." She looked up at me. "Some kids say he's fat, but you know what I think? I think he's gonna be a real strong football player someday with lots of fans and millions of dollars, and nobody'll make fun of him anymore." She studied him for a moment. "I'll bet he grows up to look like a cross between Johnny Depp and George Clooney. He'll be yummy."

I almost laughed, but she shot me a look that said, *Don't you dare, not in here, freakazoid*, then said, "I learned that word from Mommy—she thought Lee Marvin was 'yummy,' so don't look at me like that. I'm gonna touch you now, so get ready," and grabbed my hand, dragging me toward the door.

"I figured it out," she said as we made our way out into the parking lot. "If one of us sort of … *prepares* … y'know, if we make ourselves ready for touching the other person, then we don't gotta worry about sending you into fits like before."

"'Fits'?" I said.

"Well, that's what it was, wasn't it? All that shaking around and kicking your legs and gagging on the floor and puking in a wastebasket." A shrug. "Looked like a fit to me."

"Missy, why don't you want to stay for your funeral?"

"I told Mommy everything she needs to know to feel better. The rest of its just going to be a bunch of boring prayers and people crying and it'll be *soooo* depressing." She stopped by the car, looked me straight in the eyes, and said: "And I changed my mind about one other thing. I want you to call me 'Melissa' from now on, okay?"

"Absolutely. I think it's prettier than 'Missy,' anyway. May I ask why you?"

Her eyes glistened ever so slightly, but she did not cry. "I never knew that it was my grandma's middle name. Mommy wanted to name me after Grandma—I never met her, she died before I was born—but I ... I gave her crap about it being such an old-lady sounding name. That's what I said: 'It sounds like an old lady's name.' I shouldn't have done that."

"But your mom, she knows now, right?"

Melissa nodded her head, firmly, once. "You. Bet. And she's gonna feel better now. I mean, she'll miss me—" She then posed like a classic movie star, one arm cocked so that the hand was behind her head, the other hand on her hip, legs crossed at the ankles, Carole Lombard hamming it up for the press before putting her handprints in cement in front of Grauman's Chinese Theatre. "—c'mon, look at me, who *wouldn't* miss all this? But Mommy will be okay." She put down her arms and looked at me. "So what about you?"

"What about me?"

"What's gonna make you okay?"

"This isn't about me, Miss—uh, *Melissa.*"

"It is if I say so—you said this day was my day, that we could do whatever I wanted, *your* rules, not mine, smarty-pants—and *I* want to know what I can do to make you feel okay."

I got into the car and clipped the Bluetooth cell phone receiver to my ear; it makes it look less weird when I'm talking to no one ... well, no one that anyone else can see. Yes, it's a waste of money, but it keeps me from landing in the bin.

Melissa was already sitting on the passenger side, arms folded across her chest, glaring at me, impatient.

"I *asked* you a question, Mr. Gloomy Gus."

"If I'm going to call you by your name, then you have to call me by mine. It's only fair."

"Like your stupid one-week rule thing is fair? *That* kind of fair?"

I stared at her. She stared at me.

"I'd like to see you have fun," I replied.

"*Huh?*"

"There's a nice little playground not too far from here, Dell Memorial Park, you know it?"

"No. Does it have a teeter-totter?"

"Yes, and a Jungle Gym, and a slide, and a bunch of other stuff."

She waved the rest of it away. "Not interested in those other things. Give me a teeter-totter any day. Seriously, dude—uh, I mean, *Neal.*"

I started the car. "Then to Dell Memorial Park it is. You going to meet me there?"

"Nah," she said, settling back into the seat. "Think I'll just catch a ride this time."

"Seatbelt," I said.

She stared at me. "Dude—I mean, *Neal.* Think about who you're talking to. Seriously."

"Oh, yeah ... right. Sorry. Never mind."

"Well, *duh.*"

There has always been something about playgrounds that strike me as simultaneously joyful yet also sad and eerie, despite however many children are running around, shrieking and squealing and laughing their heads off, having a high old time as loving parents sit on the benches off to the side, watching Jimmy or Suzy or Billy or Amy or (insert child's name here) burn off some of that seemingly everlasting energy that could power a small Third-World nation were one to harness it properly. Despite the joy and enthusiasm and laughter, I always see playgrounds from a palimpsest sort of view; while everyone else looks at the children and the life and the brisk activity, I imagine I can see beneath the surface to where the other playground waits, the deserted one, the one that exists late at night when everyone has gone home; a silent, shadow-shrouded place of swings with no occupants moving almost imperceptibly back and forth with the evening breeze, empty teeter-totters that somehow still manage to squeak at the hinges, and metal slides that quietly rattle as something small but hard falls from a nearby tree and rolls down to the ground.

Told you before, I am a walking circus of mirth.

But *this*, what I was watching now, this would have given even the most steely-nerved person a case of the willies.

Melissa was running all over the playground, hitting the teeter-totter, the Jungle Gym, the slide, the swings, all of it (despite her protestations that she didn't care about the rest of the playground's offerings), laughing her head off, having the grandest of all grand times, playing with at least five other children ... none of whom I could see. I wondered how the scene looked to those people who drive by; the teeter-totter going up and down with no one on it, unoccupied swings moving back and forth, some of them snapping up fairly high ... they must have thought they were imagining things.

Watching Melissa play with the unseen children, hearing the chime of her laughter, seeing the happiness on her face and how she looked like such a normal, healthy, vibrant, *living* child, I don't think I've ever felt so lonely.

After a few more minutes, Melissa ran over to me, still giggling over something one of her playmates had just told her, stopped, caught her breath, and said: "This isn't working, is it?"

"What do you mean?"

"You still look like a Gloomy Gus. The *Gloomiest* Gus."

"I'm fine."

"I'm gonna hold your hand again, so get ready."

I prepared myself, and she did as she'd threatened.

"You're so *sad*," she said.

"I'm just tired, Melissa. That's all."

"Huh-uh, buddy. Don't lie to me." A tear began forming in one of her eyes.

"Oh, hey, *Melissa*," I said, taking hold of her other hand. "Don't you get upset, hon, okay? I just ... get like this sometimes."

"You *are* like this a lot of the time. I can tell."

"It passes. You go back and play with your new friends, all right?"

She shook her head, her eyes unblinking. "No. I wanna go for another ride, see if I can spot people you can't."

"Whatever you want."

"What I *want* is not to be dead. What I *want* is for you to, I dunno, *smile* and mean it. It won't break your face, y'know."

"Well, then, why don't we go home—uh, go to the apartment and watch SpongeBob, then? I was promised miraculous buttered popcorn, as I recall."

"Oh, you'll get the popcorn, and you'll *love* it. Okay. Let me say good-bye and then we'll go back."

"You could stay here and play with them a little longer, you know. I mean, it's not like you *have* to ride back with me."

"You asked me not to do that popping in and out thing. It makes you nervous."

"Only if I'm not expecting it. This would be different."

Her eyes narrowed. "You trying to get rid of me?"

"Not at all. But you're having so much fun and ... and I'm not so much fun."

"Says you. Gloomy Gus."

"I think I preferred 'freakazoid.'"

She parted her hands in front of her. "I am fickle. *And* I am dead. So we do things my way. I'm gonna go say good-bye to the other kids, and then I want you to take me someplace before we go back to watch SpongeBob."

"Did anyone ever tell you that you were kind of bossy?"

"Yes, but I never listened. Like now." And with that, she ran off to have one more ride on the teeter-totter with her unseen friends, while I sat there trying to think of *where* she could possibly want me to take her.

"You're *not* serious?"

"Yep," she said. "I wanna see where you keep the other peoples' boxes."

We were driving around the downtown square where I suspected Melissa would be able to spot others like herself, but if she did, she said nothing.

"Why would you want to see ... I mean, there's nothing to—"

"I just think it would be interesting, that's all."

I made sure to watch the tone of my voice. "Look, Melissa, I don't go there unless I *have* to."

"Is that another one of your dumb rules?"

"No. It's just the truth." I stopped for a red light near the Sparta and found myself remembering when Rebecca and I first began dating, how we'd always start our Friday nights out at the Sparta for the world's best cheeseburgers. This was back when I was arrogant—or lazy—enough to believe that I knew her.

"Hey," said Melissa, pointing toward the traffic light. "Is there, like, a certain *shade* of green you're waiting for?"

"A—huh? Oh, right ... thanks." I pulled away, automatically heading toward the East Main Street Bridge that led into Coffin County.

"How come you don't go there unless you have to?"

My grip tightened on the steering wheel. "It's not exactly Disney World in there. It's a big, cold, depressing room filled with metal shelves and boxes full of dead peoples' personal effects—their *stuff*."

Melissa glared at me for a moment. "I remember what 'personal effects' are from when you told me before, so don't explain it every time you say it. I'm not stupid."

"I didn't mean to make it sound that way, I'm sorry."

She turned away from me for a few moments, waved at someone I could not see, smiled, then said: "Can you see that lady over there by that wall?"

Without really being aware of it, I'd driven over the bridge and into Coffin County. We were once again stopped at a red light, right at the corner where the Great Fire of 1968 began when a local casket company went up and took every business in a 3-block radius with it. The area never recovered.

There was an old but elegant-looking black woman standing in front of a brick wall. If I remembered correctly, this part of Coffin County—what used to be called 'Old Towne East'—used to boast a lot of nightclubs, small museums, and specialty shops. I wondered which type of business that wall had belonged to, and what memories the old woman associated with it.

"Yes, I see her."

She stood there with her arms spread apart, as if waiting for someone to embrace her. Her dress was a thing of tattered, faded elegance, and the gloves she wore looked ... cheerless. That's the only word I could think of.

"What's she doing?" asked Melissa.

"I have no idea, hon. There are a lot of ... lost people who live in this area."

As if to illustrate my point, a young but horribly disheveled man walked up to the old woman and began asking her, in a very loud voice, to cut something off of his face for him. After a few moments, the old woman smiled, patted his cheek as if he were nothing more than an upset little boy, and gave him a dollar bill from her purse. She then turned back to the wall, her arms spread open for the embrace, while the young man looked at her, looked at the dollar bill, and shuffled quietly away.

"You see him, too?" asked Melissa.

"Yes."

She leaned toward me. "I don't know why, but I got a feeling he might be the next person to come stay with you for a while."

"He's just one of the ... lost people here, Melissa, that's all. Poor guy's probably crazy or something, can't afford his medications."

The light changed and I drove on.

"Do you always do that?"

I looked at her. "Do what?"

She looked at the young man who was now stumbling around the corner, then shook her head. "Nothing. You're just a lot nicer than you want me to think you are."

"No, I'm not. But thank you, anyway."

"Hey, I'm bossy, remember? If I say you're nice, then you're nice."

"But—"

"Shut. *Up.*"

We fell into a comfortable silence for the next few minutes, Melissa studying the streets and buildings (and ruins of buildings) with an intensity that you are genetically incapable of after the age of 9, and me simply repeating a route I could drive in my sleep.

Cedar Hill Memorial Hospital, both of the city's nursing homes, and the County Hospice Center form an almost perfect circle from my apartment; what makes the circle complete is stopping by the "Old Towne East Storage" before heading back home. While this fact has always been present in my mind, I don't know that it ever really hit me as hard as it did as Melissa and I drove toward the OTES facility; for three years I had been driving and living in one ongoing circle; a moth around a light bulb, deciding whether or not to give into the temptation; a plane in a holding pattern, waiting for clearance to land; a humorless straight-man stuck in a revolving door in some silent 2-reeler from the 1920s, waiting for the punch line to the gag.

I pulled up to the locked gates and dug my key-card from my wallet. I was just getting ready to swipe it when Melissa said: "You'd really do it, wouldn't you?"

"Do what?"

She nodded at the gates. "Take me in there and show me the boxes."

"You said you wanted to see them."

"And *you* said that the place depressed you."

"No, I said that the room was big, cold, and depressing."

"Same thing."

"Technically, no, because—"

"Shut. *Up.* You'd really take me in there and show it to me, even if it makes you sad?"

I said nothing. There seemed to be no point.

"I'm gonna hold your hand for a minute," said Melissa.

She did, and for a few seconds I was *aware* of her being somewhere within one of my memories of the storage room. This wasn't anything like this morning or with her mother at the funeral home; this time, I felt ... comforted. Less alone.

She let go of my hand and gave a mock shiver. "Yeech, you're right. That is one *depressing* place, dude. Seriously."

"Told you."

"Can I ask you a question?"

"You mean besides that one?"

She giggled. "Don't be a smarty-pants. It makes me want to smack you."

"And your question ...?"

Her face became very serious, very adult-looking. "Why do you do this? How did you get this job? What do you do for money? I mean, jeez, it's not like somebody pays you for this, do they?"

"That's four questions."

She huffed. "What? You gotta be somewhere in, like, ten minutes or something? Okay, it's four questions, big deal. Will you tell me, please?"

By now I'd backed out and was heading to the apartment. I decided to take a few small detours. If I was going to tell her about this, it was going to be in the car, not the apartment. I had never spoken about this while in the apartment, and I never would. Something about Rebecca's presence made talking about it seem distasteful, as if I would be dishonoring my wife's memory. Or the memory of the wife I thought I'd known.

Melissa cleared her throat—dramatically, of course. "*Well ...?*"

"Promise not to interrupt me with a bunch of questions?"

She mimed zipping her mouth closed.

"I'm serious, Melissa. I've never told anyone about this, and I don't want you making jokes."

She raised her hand, unzipped her mouth, and said: "I'd never make fun of you. Not about something like this. I promise."

I flashed my most dazzling Constipated Smile. "Okay. If something isn't clear, *then* you can interrupt me. Deal?" I held out my hand.

"Deal," she replied, and we shook on it.

"Okay, I'm going to answer your questions in reverse order, if that's all right."

"Just so long as you answer them."

"I *don't* get paid for doing this. I live on my savings, the early-retirement benefits package from my job, and Rebecca's insurance money."

Melissa held up her hand. "Okay, I don't, like, mean to bring up something sad, but if Rebecca killed herself, the insurance company wouldn't pay."

I grinned and wagged a finger at her. "Oh, no, no, no—that's a myth that a lot of insurance companies do everything they can to keep alive. The truth is, there are several companies who *will* pay on a life insurance policy when the person commits suicide. They wait a year, and they pay only the face-value of the policy, but they *do* pay. Suicide is considered a result of undiagnosed mental illness. You'd be surprised at how many companies quietly do this."

"How do you know all that?"

"Do you know what I did for twenty-two years before Rebecca died and I took early retirement?"

Melissa shook her head.

"I sold life-insurance."

"Oh. My. *God!* That is *so* funny! That is, like, the goofiest thing I've heard all week! Is it okay that I think that's goofy?"

I nodded. "I've come to see a certain irony in it." I gave her a look.

"I know what 'irony' means," she said. "My teachers told Mommy I was 'gifted.'"

"I don't doubt that."

"Yeah, well ... what'cha gonna do? Hey—how old are you, anyway?"

"I'll turn forty-seven next month."

"Oh, *man.* Your *birthday's* coming up? Dude, I could *so* make you the *best* birthday cake."

"I stopped celebrating my birthday a long time ago—oh, no you don't, Melissa. No arguments."

She sighed, pouting. "Okay, you were saying ...?"

"Rebecca didn't have her policy through my company. *My* ex-company is one that won't pay out on a suicide."

"Well that sucks."

From the mouths of babes.

"Does that answer your questions about my financial state?"

"So you got enough money to live on for the rest of your life?"

"If I'm careful. The apartment is paid for. Rebecca and I made some good investments. I'm not rich, Melissa, but I'm okay."

"Cool beans." She turned toward me a little more and folded her arms across her chest. "So ... how did you get this job, and why you?"

"I don't think of it as a 'job,' Melissa. It's more like ..."

"Like what?"

My throat tightened a little. I coughed. "Could we go back to that one later?"

"Okay."

I pulled into the underground parking garage and had to dig out the card-key, then drove over to my assigned parking space near the elevators. I turned off the ignition, removed the keys, and sat looking at them in my hand.

"What is it?" asked Melissa. "C'mon, Neal, you were going real good there."

"Can I ask *you* something?"

"Sure."

"Why wasn't your dad at your funeral? You've never even mentioned him."

"My daddy's dead. He died before I was born. He had a big party with some of his friends right after he and Mommy found out she was pregnant. He was drunk and got in a wreck. He hit a tree. There wasn't anybody else in the car with him, though, so that was lucky." She looked down at her hands. "I only know him from, like, pictures and video tapes and what Mommy said about him. It's not the same, y'know? It sounded like he might've been really cool, kinda like you."

"You think I'm cool?"

A shrug. "Don't let it go to your head, though. You'd have been a pretty cool dad, I think."

For a moment we just looked at one another. Then she scooted closer to me and put my arm around her shoulder. "Is this okay?"

"This is good. I like this."

"Me, too."

No jolts, no visions, no sudden rush of sensations; just me with my arm around her shoulders, and she with her head resting against my chest. It was nice.

"Three weeks after Rebecca's funeral," I said to her, " I came back to the apartment and found her sleeping in the guest room, just like you saw her. That's where I'd ... found her body. She'd taken a bunch of prescription tranquilizers, crushed them up and mixed them in with a bowl of oatmeal so she wouldn't vomit. She'd been gathering the pills for months and I had no idea.

"At first I didn't know what to think—I mean, I'd watched the coffin with her body lowered into the ground, yet here she was, back in the guest room. The rotting part—if that's what it is, rotting—that didn't start for almost three months. But that night, when she first re-appeared, I couldn't stop looking at her. She was breathing, I could see her chest rise and fall, I could *hear* the air going in and out of her lungs, it was like she was just taking a nap. I just figured that I'd been holding it all in, you know? The grief. I'd been holding it in and I'd simply ... snapped. Gone a little crazy. So I pulled out a bottle of booze and got good and tanked, then went back into the room. She was still there. I decided that I was going to wake her up. So I stomped over to the bed and reached out and gave her arm a good shake. And that's when ... you remember what happened with us this morning, right?"

109

"Uh-huh."

"Something like that happened with Rebecca. It wasn't as strong as what happened this morning, but it was bad enough. I had a single flash of what had been in her mind during her last moments, and it ... it was awful, Melissa. She was so *lonely*, and I never knew. She felt like I was a stranger to her, had been for years." Even now, hearing myself say it aloud, I still couldn't quite grasp it.

"I mean, people like to think that when someone they love dies, that that person is thinking about them, about those they're leaving behind, right at the end." I shook my head. "Rebecca wasn't thinking about me at all. I wasn't even a *distant* thought. I had pretty much ceased to exist for her."

Melissa reached over and squeezed my hand. "I'm so sorry."

But I couldn't stop, not now. "But then something fell out of her hand." I lifted up the car keys. "A key wrapped in a piece of paper. It was a note, in her handwriting. It had an address on it, and a number, and the words, 'Look in your other wallet.'

"That's where I found the card-key to the storage facility. The other key was for the padlock on the unit door, Number 23."

"That's where you keep the boxes."

I nodded. "But that night, when I went to the place, there was only one box. It was filled with things of Rebecca's I never knew she had. Children's books, stuffed toy animals, a shadowbox of antique sewing thimbles, a watercolor pad filled with these gorgeous paintings she'd done—hell, I never knew she liked to paint. Fifteen years we'd been married, and I had no idea. There were notebooks of poetry she'd written, programs from theatrical productions she'd done in high school and college, it was just ... these precious keepsakes from someone I never knew.

"But the worst of it were the letters. She'd been having ... I can't call it an 'affair' because the two of them never ... uh ... they didn't ..."

"Have sex. It's okay to say something like that to me."

I couldn't look at her, I was too embarrassed. "They'd been high-school sweethearts and had met again about ten years or so after she and I were married. They talked on the phone a lot, met for lunch, but made sure they were never alone together. He was married, as well, with a bunch of kids, but the *letters* ... my God, Melissa, he loved her so much, and she loved him. She told him things she never told me. She had both his letters and hers—he'd sent hers back when he finally broke it off. It had just gotten too ... I don't know ... too painful for both of them. I sat in that damned room all night reading them, and by the time I finished the last one, I knew that I'd been the runner-up for her all along. I was the consolation prize for not getting the man she was meant to have been with.

"I wanted her back right then. I still do. I could have been a better man, the kind of man who deserved to be her husband. If I hadn't been so busy making sure we had all of our ducks in a row, everything paid for, always keeping track of the money, the investments, all that pointless bullshit ... then maybe I would have noticed how lonely she was. I loved her just as much as he did, but I was never good at showing it, expressing it with words like I should have. 'You're a very cautious man, Neal.' That's what she used to say to me. 'Cautious.'" I pulled in a deep breath, squeezed Melissa's shoulder, and pushed out the rest of it.

"After that night, I kept checking on her, and I kept finding new pieces of paper, with names on them and the addresses of the hospital, or nursing homes, or the hospice. It didn't take me very long to figure out what I was supposed to do. The first few were kind of tough. I had to dig through the dumpsters in order to find the boxes. But after I began figuring things out, the boxes ... they weren't so hard to find. They would be on top of all the garbage, or sometimes even setting beside the Dumpsters. I even know the schedules now. The hospital disposes of unclaimed personal effects every Tuesday night; the nursing home on 21st Street gets rid of them on Thursday; the retirement center puts their unclaimed boxes out on Friday; and the hospice—"

"Sunday night," said Melissa.

"Sunday night."

"So you've been doing this for three years, huh?"

"Yes."

"Must get lonely."

I thought of her on the playground, laughing with friends I couldn't see. "It does sometimes. Even when I've got visitors like you and Lenny and all the rest. I even tried to stop doing it once, but that's when Rebecca started to ... *deteriorate*. There, I said it. I keep hoping that if I get to peoples' effects right away that it will stop the process, that she'll start getting better. But then I remember ... she's dead. There's no 'getting better' from that."

"So why do you think you're the one doing this?"

I looked at her this time. "I don't know for sure, but I hope ... I hope that if I do enough, then she'll forgive me for not being there for her, for being such a bad person, for being so distant and unthinking and ... and ..."

"Cautious?"

I nodded. "Cautious."

"Maybe it's kind of like what the priests make you do after confession, Say an 'Our Father' or 'Hail Mary' or an Act of Contrition."

"Penance."

"Sounds like that to me. Mommy always used to say, 'If it walks like a duck, and quacks like a duck, it must be—'"

We were both startled by the sound of someone banging on the driver's-side window. I actually shrieked, which made Melissa giggle afterward.

"You ever going to get out of that damn car?" shouted Lenny. "I got something to show you." I opened the door but Lenny was blocking my escape.

"Got me a new toy today!" He held up what could only have been a digital camera, and a fairly expensive one, at that. "Some smartass yuppie-type left this at the library. I always wanted one of these, so I figured, what the fuck—oops, pardon the language, little lady."

Melissa grinned. "That's okay. I've heard worse."

We climbed out of the car. Lenny removed his hat and offered his hand. "My name's—"

"Your name is Lenny Kessler. Hi. I'm Melissa." She grabbed his hand and gave it a solid shake.

"Well, now, it's real pleasure to meet you, Melissa. I guess old Neal here's mentioned me, am I right? Tell me I'm right."

"You're right. Where's your lady-friend from this morning?"

"My lady—? Oh, you mean Theresa? The woman in the dress?"

"Uh-huh. I saw you two talking. I watched from the window. She's *pretty*."

"Pretty full of herself, but yeah, she's a looker. I'm afraid she and I didn't exactly hit it off." He looked at me. "Pity. I'd've given a year's pay for her to've unleashed the hounds and give me a look at those bazooba-wobblies under that designer dress."

Melissa giggled. "You're funny."

"Glad someone here thinks so." Lenny winked at her, then faced me. "So you were about to ask me why I was at the library in the first place?"

I sighed. "Lenny, it's already been a long day and it isn't even six yet."

"I see you're still your usual bucket of chuckles. That's all right, I'll tell you on the way up to your place. By the way, I hope you've still some of the good hooch left. I'm a bit parched."

The three of us headed toward the elevators. I pushed the UP button and waited.

"I was looking through this book at the library," said Lenny, "all about brain science and what the writers called the 'biology of belief,' right? They said that all our brains contain what they called a 'God area,' a place where the spiritual and the biological come together during moments of euphoria. And that got me to thinking about you and that 'your cells remember you' horseshit, so I—"

I held up a hand, silencing him. "You still have your wallet on you, Lenny?"

"Always." He pulled it from his back pants pocket. "Not much money in there, though."

"Gimme." I took it from his hand, opened it, and thumbed through its contents until I found what I was looking for. I pulled out the card, read it, saw Lenny's signature, and laughed.

"What?" said Lenny. "You find a naked picture of me or something? Sorry if you feel inadequate at the sight of it, but—"

"You were an organ and tissue donor, Lenny."

He pulled the card and wallet from my hands. "Yeah, so wha—? Oh, wait a minute ..."

"I don't know what they took and what they didn't, but according to that card, you agreed to donate your corneas. The rest of you could have been a godawful mess, Lenny, but corneas are among the first things they take from a donor."

He stared at the card, then looked a me. "So you were right? I mean, the cells in my corneas—?"

"Are still active somewhere in the sockets of some lucky person."

"Well, hell, don't that beat all?"

The elevator arrived and its doors opened. It was empty.

"I want to ask a favor of you two," I said, stepping in and holding the door open. "Would you two mind just popping on up to the apartment and letting my ride up by myself? It's nothing personal, but I just ... need a minute or two by myself."

"You're not gonna sneak out or something like that, are you?" asked Melissa.

"Where would I go?"

She nodded. "Good point." She grabbed Lenny's hand. "Okay, Mr. Gloomy Gus—we'll see you upstairs."

The doors closed. I pushed the button to my floor, waited a few seconds until I felt the elevator start moving, and then my legs gave out and I dropped ass-first onto the floor, burying my face in my hands and crying. *Goddammit!*

Three years. Three years it had taken me to get the walls built, to train myself *not* to feel anything, and in the course of two days Melissa had bulldozed right through them, and everything I'd been trying to avoid thinking about, confronting, admitting to myself, all of it followed right behind her, blasting into me like the heat from a furnace.

There should be a way to scrape the guilt and regret and sadness from the places in you where it builds up like plaque on your connective tissue, making it almost impossible for you to get out of bed and face the day because it hurts too much to even *move*; there should be a tool that you can carry for those times when a little undetected piece of that plaque breaks loose and begins moving toward your core, a tool that can enter the flesh without spilling blood or scarring tissue and simply scour it away, cut it out, and leave you in a safe oblivion where nothing touches you, nothing moves you, nothing matters.

"*Fuck ...*" I said aloud to no one and nothing. I pulled up my head, saw that I was almost to my floor, and got to my feet, wiping my eyes as best I could and hoping like hell that the damned elevator didn't stop at another floor for someone else to get on. I did not want anyone to see me this way.

The doors opened to my floor. No one was waiting there. I made a beeline for my door, key in hand, and slipped quickly inside.

In the kitchen, Melissa was gathering together the ingredients for her popcorn while Lenny poured himself a generous drink. I walked by them as fast as I could, claiming a need to use the bathroom, and that's when I heard Melissa sing:

"*A gentle breeze from Hush-a-bye Mountain
Softly blows o'er lullaby bay.
It fills the sails of boats that are waiting—
Waiting to sail your worries away ...*"

And I couldn't move.

"Hey, Neal," called Lenny. "You want a belt of this stuff?"

"That doesn't go with my popcorn," said Melissa. "Only soda pop. Or strawberry smoothies."

I pulled in a thick, snot-filled breath, went to my office, grabbed the box of Melissa's personal effects, and stomped back into the living room, dropping the box on the sofa. "It's time for you to pick something," I said, a little more loudly than I would have preferred.

Melissa stuck her head out from the kitchen. "It's time for me to *what?*"

"You heard me," I said, pulling the lid off the box. "Time to go, Melissa. Get in here and choose something right now."

She looked at the box, then at me. She was trying not to show it, but I could see that inside of her, something had crumpled.

"But that's not fair! You said that I had to wait—"

"My 'dumb' rules, remember? I can change them if I goddamned well want to. Now get your ass in here and pick something!"

"But ... b-but—"

"But *nothing!* I don't need this, I don't *want* this. Everything was fine until *you* showed up, with your questions and your 'dude' and 'freakazoid' and touchy-feely and 'You'd have been a pretty cool dad,' and all the rest of it. I—*look at me!* I'm not your dad, Melissa, he's *dead*, just like you, just like Lenny, just like Rebecca, just like I'll be someday—and the sooner the fucking better!" Even I was startled at how loudly I was screaming at her.

Lenny stood behind her, a hand on her shoulder. "Hey, Neal, buddy—what is this shit?"

"This shit is none of your business, Lenny." I threw down the lid and started toward Melissa, who backed up against Lenny, her eyes widening with fear.

I stopped again. Jesus Christ, what was I doing? She was actually *scared* of me. And she'd been having such a good time at the playground, too.

But of course I knew what I was doing. I was just being cautious. Remove the source of what makes me feel anything, and I would cease to feel once again, and all could continue as before.

I covered my mouth with my hand. "Oh, God ..."

"Have you been *crying?*" said Melissa.

"I think you need a belt of the good stuff," said Lenny.

I looked back at the box, at the lid on the floor, and realized what a horrible, terrible, vicious thing I had just done. Once the lid has been removed in their presence, they *have* to choose. I don't know why it's that way, it just *is*.

"Oh, God, Melissa," I said, pulling my hand away from my mouth. "I'm so sorry. I was ... I was upset because ...because ..."

"It's okay," she said, her tone neutral, her expression unreadable. She set down the bowl she was going to use for the popcorn, squeezed Lenny's hand, and walked right up to the box, examining its scant contents.

"All right," she said, the slightest quaver in her voice. "I made my decision."

"Can you forgive me?"

"We'll have to see about that." She turned away, picked up the lid, and placed it back on the box. "There's nothing in there I want. Sorry, freakazoid. Looks like you're stuck with me."

"What are you doing?"

"Making my choice." She walked over to me, gave me that I'm-gonna-touch-you-now look, and held my hand. "I choose to stay here with you. And I *know* you're not my dad, but I never knew him." She pulled on my arm, forcing me to bend down slightly. "But I know you. And I really wanna stay." And then she kissed my cheek. "You need somebody to take care of you, 'cause it sure looks like you can't do it yourself. I mean, *dude*, have you *looked* at that bathroom of yours? I mean, *really* looked at it? I've seen science experiments that were less gross."

We stood in silence for a few moments, and then all three of us turned in the direction of the guest room.

"Was that you, Lenny?" I asked.

"Yeah, been working on my ventriloquist act, learning to throw the sound of my coughing—*what the hell do you think, Cell-Boy?*"

I looked at Melissa. "She's never coughed before."

"You sure?"

"Yes."

"Well, then—maybe we ought to go check on her ...?"

The three of us moved toward the guest room. I opened the door and saw that the light of early evening, golden yet somehow gray at the same time, was filtering through the blind on the window, casting soft, glowing lines across Rebecca's body.

Melissa moved away from me and opened the blinds a little more—not all the way, just enough that Rebecca looked for a moment like a figure in a painting, the black patches on her skin looking more like deliberate shadows added toward the end by the artist's brush or charcoal pencil.

"There's less of them," I whispered.

"Yeah," said Melissa, walking over to the bed and sitting by Rebecca's side. "She still doesn't look too good, but she looks *better*, don't you think?"

I started to say something, but then Rebecca coughed again, a soft, dry sound, and moved her head ever so slightly to the right, as if getting more comfortable. I heard the bones in her neck softly crack as she did this, and then she released a small sound, a low, gentle, but satisfied sigh, *There, that's better.*

Melissa took hold of Rebecca's hand. "Huh, that's weird."

"What?" It was all I could do to say *that* much.

Melissa looked at me. "She's thinking about cheeseburgers."

"Oh, man," said Lenny from behind me. "Neal, you *have* to let me take a picture of her, of all three of you." Not waiting for a response, he powered up the camera and nodded for me to go over to the bed.

I moved as if drunk or drugged, and sat on the other side of my wife.

"Take her hand," said Melissa.

I hesitated.

"I'll make sure nothing happens," she said. "I promise."

I took Rebecca's hand in both of mine; it felt almost no different from the other times I'd dared to touch her hand; clammy, moist, lifeless ... but I could sense, far beneath the facade of her tissue, the façade that was ultimately all flesh, the tiniest wave of warmth struggling to swim to the surface.

"It's gonna be a long time, still," said Melissa. "But at least she'll have company. So will you." She leaned forward. "*Please* don't ever yell at me like that again. You scared me."

"I know."

"You hurt my feelings."

"Never again, hon. Never again."

Lenny aimed the camera, got us in focus. "You know, there are some cultures that believe if you take a person's picture, you steal part of their soul."

"Then take a lot of pictures," said Melissa. "You can keep all of our souls together in there." She smiled at me. "That way, we can be a family. Kinda. Does that make sense?"

"Works for me," I said, my voice suddenly hoarse.

"I'm gonna make chocolate cake for your birthday," said Melissa. "Chocolate's good for birthdays."

I thought of the rest of my life, knowing that there was now more of it behind me than ahead, and of the days I would spend in these rooms, watching over Rebecca with Melissa nearby to take care of me, and wondered if maybe I'd find that it had some meaning, after all. Maybe Rebecca would come all the way back to me, and maybe she wouldn't; but if there was even a chance I could win her heart as I should have, that I could love and treasure her the way I always should have, then I would not push it away. I would continue to collect the boxes of personal effects and help those who came to my door to find their way to ... wherever they went once their choice had been made. I would grow old with my wife and this little girl for company, and the day would come when I would find myself in a hospital, nursing home, or hospice bed, and I knew they would be there, as well, watching over me, whispering memories into my ear, singing lost lullabies as I release the final, relieved breaths, feeling the weight of purpose and meaning forever lifted from my eyes; and afterward ...

Afterward, there will be a hallway, its polished floor shining under the glow of overhead fluorescent lights, and into this hallway there will be wheeled a gurney with a sheet-covered body, and the wheels will squeak softly as it is rolled toward the far end where only one elevator waits, and this elevator goes in only one direction. As the gurney is wheeled away, another person, dressed in hospital or hospice whites, will shuffle from the room carrying a box with my name written on its side, and they will carry this box to the front desk, knowing that come Tuesday, or Thursday, or Sunday, it will be discarded with the other unclaimed possessions, left to time, the elements, or other mysteries best not dwelt upon for too long. It is, after all, only a box of *stuff*, of left-behind things, items with no meaning to anyone except the person who can no longer touch them, hold them, or tell the stories of how this book meant something, this ring was precious, this cross-stitched picture is beautiful *because* ...

But for now, right now, this moment, I hold my wife's hand, and Melissa holds her other hand, and in this way we are one, and it needs to be captured, to be noted, in order to make it true not only in the moment, but in memory, as well. I look at Melissa and smile and hope that all I want her to know can be seen in that smile, and hope—God, how I hope, how strange a feeling it is to hope—that we'll know in a few seconds, after Lenny takes the picture. I look at him and think, Take it. Take it as we are now. We are looking at you. As we are now. Take it. Take it. Take it.

FOLLOWING MARLA

John R. Little

"I just wanted you to know," Marla said. "It's not too late for you to change your mind."

We were in the back room of the church, just having finished the rehearsal. Most of the wedding party was hanging out in the foyer, waiting for us, but Marla had whispered something to the priest and then pulled me down the hallway to the back room.

"I just don't understand," I said. "You ... it doesn't make sense."

"I know."

She had those big brown puppy-dog eyes staring at me as she pursed her lips. She took a deep breath and said again, "I faked my own death."

"You're not kidding?"

Of course she wasn't. I could see that as clear as the candles surrounding us. She lowered her head a bit, and pushed her hair back. Tomorrow, she'd have some new hair style for the wedding, but I liked it just hanging long and straight, like she always wore it.

"It was two years ago. I was married to a monster in Boston. He just hit me one too many times, I guess. We'd been married almost three years, and every one of those thousand days was worse than the one before. He abused me in every possible way. Yelling, belittling me, hitting me so often I felt like a punching bag ..."

Marla started to shake and I pulled her to me. "You don't have to—"

"And he'd rape me after hitting me. Fuck me just to hear me scream. Sometimes, though, my mind just went blank."

She pulled back and looked up into my eyes. I didn't know what to say, so I said nothing.

"You wouldn't recognize me, Andy. I was a lifeless zombie, not caring if I lived or died."

She stopped talking, continuing to look at my eyes. I tried to imagine this vivacious, beautiful, strong woman in a marriage like she described. I couldn't see it.

Marla tried to smile, but it was forced. Even so, her smile always hit me like a hammer, and I kissed her forehead, still amazed that she would agree to marry me. She was definitely out of my league.

There was a knock on the door. We both turned to look as Michele poked her head through. "We're getting hungry, guys ..."

"We'll be a while," I said.

"We're ready now," said Marla. She whispered to me, "The rest can wait. I just had to tell you the hard part."

Now her smile was genuine.

The wedding was perfect.

I thought I'd seen Marla in her best form many times before, but when she walked down the aisle with her sister, I knew that I was marrying the most beautiful woman in the world.

We'd known each other for a couple of years, but our first date was exactly one year ago, on her 32nd birthday. It seemed only appropriate to marry on the same day a year later; I wanted the day to be devoted to her. For that matter, I wanted my whole friggin' life to be devoted to her.

It sounds terribly hokey, but I was head over heels in love, and I knew my sole purpose in the future would be to make Marla happy. That's God's honest truth. Marla was on my mind every waking minute, and my feelings were even stronger knowing now what she'd been through in Boston.

I wanted her forever. It all seemed guaranteed, until we were alone in our suite and somebody knocked on the door.

We hadn't even had time to change out of our wedding clothes. The reception was underway, dinner was over, and the speeches were all done. We were just getting changed into casual clothes to go for one last dance before ... well, before my fantasies would end and I would make love to her for the first time as my wife.

"Probably Janice," said Marla. "Not sure what she'd want, though."

Marla's sister was the only person who knew our hotel room number. I nodded.

She flipped the lock on the door and pulled it open. I heard her gasp and turned to see her try to push the door closed. "Ricky? No, it can't be—"

And then she was blown back, blood splashing out on her peach wedding gown. The gunshot wasn't loud, but it was very powerful. Blood covered everything, and Marla flew off her feet, landing a few feet behind.

She never moved.

I think I went a little crazy for a while. It was impossible to believe my whole life would be stretching forward without Marla.

I couldn't cry at her funeral. It was like I was looking at a jigsaw puzzle all broken apart with the pieces mixed up. The picture wouldn't come to me. It was simply not possible that the casket being lowered into the ground carried my Marla.

For a week after, I ignored the phone calls, the knocks on the door, even the cards that came in the mail from well-meaning friends.

All I knew was that I needed her back. And, yes, maybe I was *more* than a little crazy, because the only idea I came up with was to follow her. I had to follow Marla beyond death.

Before I did, I needed to talk to her sister, Janice. She opened the door at my knock and gave me a hug. She was a big woman, so different from my petite Marla that it was hard to believe they were sisters.

"I'm so sorry, Andy."

"I know."

"Would you like a drink?"

Marla always drank Chardonnay. "Do you have any white wine?"

She smiled and poured the drinks. "To her."

I touched glasses with her and took a sip.

"How'd she fake her death before?"

Janice looked at me and seemed to be thinking back. "It was so hard on her. She knew if she just left Ricky, he'd hunt her down. He was nutso crazy, but the cops could never do anything. One night we cooked up this plan. It took eighteen months to work."

"Why so long?"

"Insurance. She took out an insurance policy on herself with me as the beneficiary. Ricky was so stupid, he believed he was the one who would get the money, and that scared Marla even more. We didn't want it to ring any alarm bells at the insurance company, so we waited a long time before ..."

She stopped and took a sip of her wine.

"It's okay. She wanted to tell me. We just ran out of time."

"I know. Anyhow, the two of us hired a friend who owned a fishing boat. The story was that we all went out on the ocean for a day, and Marla fell overboard. We couldn't save her and her body was never found. Of course, Marla wasn't really there that day. She was on a train to Topeka. Eventually the insurance company paid me $250,000. I gave part to Billy, who owned the boat, and sent the rest to Marla. She used it to buy a new identity. A couple years later, I followed her here."

The house was silent except for a quiet song coming from a radio in another room. I think it was a song by the Bare Naked Ladies.

A tear rolled down Janice's cheek. "Ricky must have followed me. Somehow he must have known she wasn't really dead."

We finished the drinks, toasting my Marla one more time before I left.

I thought of having another drink or two, just to give me the courage I'd need, but no. I needed to be clear-headed if I was to follow Marla beyond death.

My kitchen

(our kitchen)

had many different knives. Marla brought a complete carving set when she moved in. They were some kind of novelty knives with long emerald-colored handles. There was a copper design snaking through them. Marla thought they were funny looking. I didn't much like them but the knives were long and sharp. The handles were firm and the blades serrated.

I took the longest one and placed it on our coffee table, staring at it from my easy chair.

"My name's Marla. Who are you?"

"Andy."

She nodded and shook my hand. That first day, she gave me that gorgeous smile. She was short, couldn't have topped five feet, but that smile shone through the whole room, making her the tallest person in the room.

"Do I know you?"

"Not yet."

I'd come to the party with my room-mate, just wanting to kill a couple hours.

Marla moved closer to me, staring at me.

"Is something wrong?" I asked.

"No, no of course not."

We kept our eyes locked. It was a once-in-a-lifetime kind of thing. Finding somebody you didn't even know you were looking for.

Ten minutes later, I held her hand. I didn't let go until I left her at three the next morning. I knew I'd found the woman I needed to be with.

The knife was in my hand. Thinking back to when we first met confirmed my decision. I couldn't let her go.

I used the blade to find a soft spot between some ribs and held the handle with both hands.

(What if I can't find her?)

I shook my worries away. I damned well *had* to find her.

My hands were shaking. I blinked and looked up at the ceiling, biting my teeth together.

And I slammed the knife into my chest as hard as I could.

Pain roared through me and pushed me down into the chair. I couldn't breathe. Somehow I'd let go of the knife but my hands tried to find it again, to pull the fucker out to stop the pain and to ... to rest ... and to rest ... and ... *Marla!* ...

I wanted to blink but I didn't seem to have the muscles to do that. I no longer felt the knife and I looked down to my chest.

There was no knife, no blood. I was wearing the tuxedo I'd worn to our wedding.

Around me was a light purple fog swirling on the ground.

Purple!

My nickname for Marla when we'd first met was Purple. She'd worn a purple dress to her birthday party and I mentioned an old poem I'd heard about a woman who promised to wear purple when she grew old.

"Marla?"

My voice didn't make any sound, but I could tell what I was saying. I called for her again.

"She's not here."

The voice came from everywhere. Or nowhere. I turned to see an old man in a wheelchair. I think he was black, but I wasn't sure. There wasn't much light.

"Who're you? Where's Marla?"

"Marla's dead. So are you. I'm the gatekeeper."

"Gatekeeper to what?"

He didn't answer, but wheeled around me. "You don't belong here."

"I had to follow her."

He didn't seem satisfied. "You shouldn't *be* here yet."

"Then let me find Marla and go back."

"Oh, if it were only that easy."

"You know who she is?"

123

"Everyone knows everyone here."

Here? I still didn't know where I was. Heaven? Hell? Purgatory? Were those even useful concepts for people who are really dead?

"I came to take her back."

The man just stared at me. Somehow I knew what he was thinking even though he didn't say it: *You're not the first to try.*

The purple mist floated around my ankles, my mind turning the swirling fog into cloud-like shapes. I watched for a few minutes, waiting to see what would happen next.

Purple.

My Marla. Sometimes I seemed to catch a glimpse of her face in the mist, but it was gone before I could truly see her.

"We don't just send people back for do-overs."

I looked back to the black man, who now was younger with long brown hair. His face seemed Oriental but he didn't have an accent.

He still sat in the same wheelchair.

"How do I get her back?"

He smiled and spun around. "You can push me."

What I *wanted* to do was to spin the damned chair around and grab the guy by the throat. I *wanted* him to tell how the fuck I could get Marla back. I *wanted* him to just let me love her.

I pushed his wheelchair forward, not knowing where we were going. The chair didn't need much pressure to move, and I was pretty sure that my pushing was an illusion.

"Why her?" he asked.

I almost answered "I love her" almost as a reflex, but I stopped myself. He knew I loved her. But why? What made this girl so special?

In my mind I ran through some random thoughts about her. She was pretty, she was smart, she was funny, sex with her was inventive, funny, and magic, she liked the same books and movies I did, she appreciated me, she worked hard, she played hard, she wanted to have two children like I did, she had simple tastes (preferring fried pork chops to filet mignon), she told me every morning that she loved me and every night, she rarely wore cosmetics, she loved to hear me compliment her, she had a gentle voice and a loud laugh, she would lay her head on my lap letting me stroke her hair while we watched movies on TV, she had that alarmingly beautiful smile, she taught me to play Sudoku, I taught her to play chess, she always held my hand while we were walking together ...

And a million other things about her ran through my mind.

I stopped and turned the guy around in the wheelchair.

"All my life I've built up an image in my mind of what my perfect life-companion would be. No woman ever came close. One would have the looks but no sense of humor. Another might be funny but a flake. I never found any one girl that ever came close to what I really wanted. I'd pretty much resigned myself to being alone, because there was never a woman that could meet my ideal.

"Then, a year ago, I found Marla. She didn't match *any* of my ideals. She's short. She's not blonde. So many things aren't what I thought I wanted, but I knew right away she was *it*.

"And it seemed I was equally her *it*.

"We were just meant to be together, and I am not going to fucking well give up on that now."

I'm not sure when the guy's hair had changed to white. He looked Scandinavian, I think. Long cheeks, blue eyes.

"Being without her isn't worth living," I added.

He nodded.

"You must prove that you truly will do *anything* for her."

I almost gasped. The first hint of a chance. "Anything," I repeated. "I'll do anything."

"We'll see. You must succeed at three challenges. One is physical, one emotional, and one spiritual. On my watch, there have been more than 10,000 people who've come to me as you have. Only 382 succeeded at the physical challenge."

"How many of them—?"

"13 succeeded at the emotional challenge."

I couldn't ask.

"And of the 13 ... well, maybe you'll be the first to pass all three challenges. I keep thinking there has to be a first time. What will you do to have her return?"

"I'll do whatever I have to."

"We'll see."

"Who *are* you?"

There was no answer. He turned his wheelchair around and started to roll away. "Your first challenge is to walk to the light."

I started to follow behind him.

"Not this way. Go to the light."

I didn't know what he meant until I looked around and in the distance I could see a bright flash. It might have been a spotlight or a flashlight or something. Or a star. There was nothing else to see except the purple haze, so I couldn't tell how far away it was. 100 feet? 500? A mile?

When I looked back to the wheelchair, it was gone. I was alone in the mist.

I started walking toward the light, wondering if something in the mist would try to stop me. My watch had frozen at 4:42 p.m. when I'd committed suicide, so I tried counting my steps. What else was there to do?

When I hit 2,000 steps I stopped. Had to be a mile, and I couldn't really tell if the light was any closer.

"Keep going if you want her."

I spun around, but there was nobody there. I wondered if I was being timed and if I didn't get to the light in time, would I forfeit Marla?

I started again, faster.

After another 3,000 paces my leg muscles were starting to hurt, but I didn't stop. I was almost sure the light was a bit brighter.

(Maybe.)

If anything, I walked faster, breathing heavily and really starting to notice the cramping in my leg.

I started to get discouraged after another 10,000 steps. Five miles? More?

And then somewhere after that, I lost track of how long I'd marched. The landscape was all the same rolling purple mist and the damned light never really seemed to get any closer.

"It's moving away from me," I said. When I realized that, I stopped.

Could I see the light move? No. But it had to be moving away, likely as fast as I was walking. How else could I not have reached it yet?

A wheelchair rolled around from behind me. A bald woman sat in it now. She had a lilting voice. "You don't seem to want her very badly. You've got a very long way to go."

"How long?"

"*Long.*"

"It's moving away from me, isn't it?"

She shrugged. "What does it matter? It takes as long as it takes, and if you keep going, you'll get there."

"But, I've got to know how long it'll take."

"No, you just have to know you want to do it."

She rolled back into the mist and disappeared.

I walked.

"How long has it been," I asked.

"Two days."

Could it be? I'd walked for two days?

I stared at the guy. He was Chinese. "You shitting me?"

"Two days."

My legs were cruel tortures all the time. They hated me. I didn't need to eat, sleep, drink water, or anything else I should have wanted. I was dead. But, my legs cried out in pain with every step.

I walked again.

Marla and I worked together at City Hall. I worked on computer problems and she was down the hall and around the corner. I saw her sometimes at our shared printer or in the cafeteria. I never had the courage to talk to her.

Besides, I thought I'd heard she was dating somebody.

But ... from a distance, I saw her. Saw her when she changed her hairstyle to wear pigtails, saw how she loved to pop a peanut M&M into her mouth as an afternoon snack.

For two years, I slowly fell in love with her, barely ever saying a word.

At her 32nd birthday, she originally seemed surprised to see me. I'd found a way to tag along with Dan, and when I saw her there ... I could see she was glad to see me. Some barrier just melted away that day; we became inseparable.

"How long?"

"Almost a year. Now you're making progress."

A year? I'd been walking for a fucking *year*, and the light wasn't any closer?

"Shit, this isn't working," I said. "There's got to be another way."

"Don't you want her badly enough?"

I hesitated for the first time. A year? But then in my mind, I saw her again, as clear as ever, that wonderful smile breaking me into little pieces.

I walked.

"How much farther?" I asked.

And I finally got my answer. "Another ninety-nine years."

And I walked again.

When I asked how long I'd been searching for Marla, it seemed impossible to believe the numbers. Two years, Ten years ...

Fifty-seven years.

And she was still fresh in my mind. I still needed to walk, to save her.

I loved her too much to let her die.

One hundred years.

The light grew brighter. It was a lighthouse after all. I reached the base where a naked woman in the wheelchair met me. She was missing an arm.

"You made it."

"Where is she?"

"Soon enough."

For the first time in a century I fell to the ground. My legs were jelly and it was hard to not just die. Except I'd already done that.

The ground was slightly inclined at the lighthouse and large rocks were scattered around. The weird purple haze didn't climb the small hill and so it looked like we were in the eye of a hurricane, only this was the eye of the fog.

"Do you want to stop yet?"

Stop? How could I stop? I'd just spent a *hundred fucking years* following the woman I love. I wanted to hit the woman, but I had no strength.

"No. I won't stop until I save her."

She nodded. "You may rest."

I don't have any idea how long I slept, or even if sleep was the right word. In any case my legs relaxed, my eyes closed, and I thought of Marla again.

At some point, the guy in the wheelchair used his walking stick to poke me in the ribs. "Get up, you lazy bastid."

He was dressed in a tuxedo like me, with his hair slicked back. He frowned, as if he was just wasting his time with me.

Fucker.

I stood, my legs still wobbly.

"Ready t' give up?" His face had deep lines etched into them, as if he'd spent his whole life frowning.

"I've come this far to bring Marla home. Nothing can stop me now."

"Ya think?"

"I know."

"Second challenge. Somebody's comin' out that lighthouse. You kill them."

"Kill them? Like with a gun?"

"Strangle. Don't piss around. Just do it. No matter what."

I looked at my hands. Could I actually kill somebody in cold blood? Maybe if it was Marla's ex-husband, Ricky. Anybody else? A stranger?

Of course I could. After walking about a million miles, this would be easy.

"When—?"

The wheelchair and its occupant were gone.

I waited.

It was a week after her birthday party that Marla and I decided we were going to marry. Just seven days. We'd spent those seven days together, almost every minute. We found we agreed on everything we talked about. We both loved frog's legs and escargot, but we also both liked a Big Mac with fries and a coke.

I liked that she wanted to dance even if there was no music. We just made our own. We hummed Billy Joel's song, "Just the Way You Are," to each other as we waltzed.

We knew we'd be together forever.

I don't know how long I stood there. I thought of lying down, but what if some guy came storming out of the lighthouse and attacked me when I wasn't ready?

So I watched and waited. I have no idea how much time passed. It could have been a day or another hundred years. I just knew I had to stay focused on the lighthouse.

Then the door opened.

I had developed a new understanding of patience and a sense of purpose like nobody else ever had. Time will do that.

A few minutes passed, and I wondered if another infinity would go by, but no, this time, only a few minutes passed and through the door toward me came Marla.

She hesitated and looked behind her as she moved out to me. I'm not sure she knew I was there. She seemed to startle when she noticed me. "Oh, my God ... Andy!"

We stared at each other and then she smiled. I hadn't forgotten that smile, and it melted my heart the same way it had more than a century earlier.

"Marla ..."

She rushed into my arms and we kissed, a long deep kiss, and this time I didn't care how much time it took. I ran my hands through her hair and smelled her and pulled her to me and stared into those amazing brown eyes.

"I can't believe you found me," she said. "I've been locked here so long."

"I know. I've been following you."

"But what do we do now?"

And then I remembered what the guy in the wheelchair said. *Somebody's comin' out that lighthouse. You kill them.*

"Andy?"

She kissed me again and I kissed her back. I licked her lips and sucked her tongue.

I couldn't ...

As I kissed her, my hands trickled down her hair and held onto her neck. I rubbed her throat as tears filled my eyes.

"Andy? What—?"

I pressed my hands harder and squeezed her neck. Her beautiful neck.

Marla realized what I was doing. She couldn't talk, but I could see the pleading in her eyes. *Stop.*

I didn't stop. I squeezed harder, even though every ounce of my being shouted at me to stop. I could barely see Marla through the tears, and I couldn't help but think I was betraying her. I just prayed that I was right, that this wasn't the real Marla, that I needed to kill this fake in order to save *my* Marla.

Her eyes continued to stare at me, begging me to stop. I wanted to stop so very much. She tried to fight me off, but nothing could loosen my grip after all I'd been through.

Eventually, her beautiful eyes glazed over and her arms fell to her side. She felt like a bag of raw meat. I lay her on the ground, but I kept squeezing her neck. I wasn't going to take any chances.

"She's dead."

I think she was Japanese, but I'm not sure. I was still covered in tears. "Tell me it wasn't really her."

The wheelchair moved around so the girl could face me. "I won't tell you any such thing."

"What?"

"Go into the lighthouse." She rolled into the door that Marla had come out of.

I looked down. Marla's body was gone.

Her lips had felt so soft on mine. I had to believe I'd done the right thing, and I followed the girl into the lighthouse.

There was an auditorium inside. I'd long ago given up any pretence at trying to understand how things worked here, so I just accepted that more than a thousand wheelchairs were all lined up with a thousand faces staring down at me. Maybe ten thousand. Or a million.

Behind me, on a table lay my Marla. There were no marks on her neck. She wore her peach wedding dress.

"Do not go to her. She is sleeping."

I turned back to the crowd. None of them had spoken; all of them had spoken.

"I need to take her back. She doesn't belong here."

Their voice was in my mind. "You've completed the first two challenges. Now the third waits for you."

"Just tell me what the fuck it is and let us go!"

A short pause. One of the wheelchairs came forward. In the chair was my mother. She'd died of Alzheimer's disease a decade before my suicide.

"Andy, this isn't easy."

"My God ... Mom?" I went to her and hugged her. The last time I saw her was in the hospital and she had no idea who I was.

"You have a decision to make, son."

"Mom, what is this place?"

"It just is. We may be able to chat later. Now you need to make your choice."

I stood back from her. Her dark eyes were as clear as they were when I was a teenager. She nodded as if listening to me tell her my grades.

"You can't both go back. Only you or only her. You need to decide which it'll be."

I turned to face Marla, moved a couple of steps toward her. She looked at peace. After all this time, we couldn't be together?

"That's not right," I said.

A murmur of laughter came from the people behind Mom.

"You should go back, son. Look at her. She's already dead and doesn't know you've come for her. She'll wake in her own wheelchair and she'll fit right in. You should just go back. Go live your own life."

"I need to help her."

I looked around. If one of us had to stay with the dead ...

"It won't work that way, son," Mom said. She reached out a hand and touched my arm. "You interfered. If you stay, you won't be with us. You'll be in an endless mist alone forever."

"What?"

"Exiled. For all eternity. No chair for you."

Marla's hand was cold, but I loved holding it anyhow. She was what I had wanted my whole life. Would she forgive me in time if I left her dead? My Marla ...

I stared into her face forever, touched her cold cheeks and put my hand on her breast for the last time.

When I turned back to my mother and told her my decision, my voice cracked.

We were just getting changed into casual clothes to go down for one last dance before ... well, before my fantasies would end and I would make love to her for the first time as my wife.

"Probably Janice," said Marla. "Not sure what she'd want, though."

Marla's sister was the only person who knew our hotel room number. I nodded, but inside me I felt panic. Something was very wrong.

"Marla, no!" I grabbed one of our emerald-colored knives and ran toward her.

Marla had flipped the lock on the door and pulled it open. I heard her gasp and turned to see her try to push the door closed. "Ricky? No, it can't be—"

I jumped and pushed her aside as the gun exploded and my guts fell out all around me. I gasped as I slammed the knife into Ricky's chest, and then I had no energy. I fell to the floor.

"ANDY! NO!"

Marla was lifting my head from the floor and screaming. I tried to touch her face one last time, but I couldn't lift my arm. I couldn't even say good-bye. A strange purple haze seemed to roll through the room, taking me away from my Marla.

I smiled, not knowing why.

MAGIC NUMBERS
Gene O'Neill

Today, the number is seven.

Despite common belief, late night sounds are not really muffled in heavy fog, quite the opposite: A siren shrieks sharply in the distance, a dog howls mournfully, nearby music is crystal clear, and a car roars by on Jefferson Street, its tires making sticking sounds on the wet pavement. Forgetting about the fog creatures, you stop, cock your head, and enjoy the night sounds, watching trails of mist swirl about your legs, which reminds you of a neighbor's gray kitten that archs its back, puffs up, and rubs against your ankles.

You almost expect to hear ...

Instead of the anticipated purr, you hear a gasp of surprise as three figures materialize out of the fog like black phantoms, their faces momentarily startled by your sudden appearance. Then quickly their expressions turn blank; and for a moment they stare at you in dead silence.

Your heart thumps rapidly and you begin to hyperventilate.

But thinking quickly, you extend all five fingers in the left pocket of your coat; and in the right pocket, you extend two fingers, the tips pressed down into the stolen silk panties at the bottom. The number seven restores your courage, your breathing and heartbeat quickly returning to normal.

"Whatcha doin' here, man?" the short, stocky one on the left asks in a deep voice thick with menace. He's wearing a Raider's windbreaker, the collar pulled up against the misty chill, his hostile black eyes peering at you directly.

For a moment your legs weaken, lose tone, but you repeat the number in your head: Seven, seven, seven.

"Yeah, white boy, whatcha doin' here 'cross Jeff'son?" the big guy in the middle says slowly, his speech softer, less measured, but the sentence full of implied threat. There is a sharp meanness to his features. And he is indeed huge, his shoulders wide, his white football jersey bearing the black number 66; but there is easily enough chest for another 6, which makes you shudder.

The guy on the right is wiry, his partially-hooded gaze making him appear sleepy, except his speech is hyper and jumpy.

"M-m-may-b-b—" He stamps his foot, which breaks the stutter, "Maybe this white boy t-t-that Lil Bo Peep dude, LeRoy."

Oh, no, you think, closing your eyes for a second, hoping one of the fog creatures will swoop down and swallow them up. Seven, seven, seven.

You blink, but they are still there.

"Yeah, whatta bout that, boy?" the big guy, LeRoy, asks. "You awful funny-lookin'. Now, you ain't that dude from the newspaper, one been sneakin' and prowlin' 'round over here, scarin' all of the women-folks, is you?"

"This little sucker him, alright," the one on the left butts in, before you can think of any answer.

"How you know, Sidney?" LeRoy asks, challenging the husky guy's statement.

"'Cuz, my ladyfriend, Clorinda, she done tole me what the muthafucka look like, man." He glances at you disparagingly, then nods his head. "Dude ripped off some of her stuff when he peepin' in her backyard last week, but her dog, Spike, he starts barkin', and she see him 'fore he do his Carl Lewis outta there, you know what I'm sayin'?"

Cautiously, you push the panties deeper into your right jacket pocket with the extended two fingers, hoping they won't think to search you.

"T-t-t-t—"

LeRoy turns to his left and snaps sharply, "Spit it out, Replay." Then he reaches out and puts his arm gently around the thin guy's shoulder. "C'mon, man."

"This is the dude, L-L-LeRoy," he says, almost flawlessly with his friend's arm around his shoulder.

But LeRoy lets the arm slide away.

"F-Fits the paper's d-d-d—"

"Description," the one on the left fills in impatiently. "Yeah, Replay's right, LeRoy. Just like Clorinda say. Real short ... kinda lop-sided, you know, with a little-dude body, big-dude head. This here Lil Bo Peep!"

Despite the seven fingers extended in your pockets, your bowels feel loose.

"O-kay," LeRoy says, stretching the word into sentence-length with the finality of a court judgment. He withdraws his hand from his pants pocket and flicks his wrist, the light glinting off the opened straight razor. "Let's carve us up a Lil Bo Peep turkey." He grins evilly, taking a step toward you. Then he stops, turning left, "What kinda meat you like, Replay?"

"I-I likes w-w-w-white—"

Even though you are protected by the aura of the day's number, you feel a strong surge of panic that enervates your legs; and as LeRoy waits for Replay to finish the joke, you suck in a breath and dart away as fast as you can ... leaving the trio of blacks standing in the fog.

You cross Jefferson Street heading west, and even though you can not see the goals, you know you are on one of the basketball courts of Olympic Park, the boundary separating black and white housing, because your feet slap against sticky blacktop, the sound rebounding in the mist, giving your location away.

The three must be able to hear it, too.

And you realize they will follow.

You weave erratically as you run across the grass beyond the courts, whispering and scattering sevens in your wake, hoping to attract at least one fog creature to cover your escape.

At last, ahead in the mist, the glowing orange streetlights of Franklin Avenue appear like blurry Japanese lanterns. You are finally back in the white business district, but too far from home. You must find somewhere close to hide and catch your breath.

Crossing the street, you spot the red neon of the Leaning Tower of Pizza blinking in the mist. You slow as you reach the sidewalk, debating the wisdom of seeking sanctuary in the restaurant. Looking through the window under the neon sign, you see no one in any of the booths, only a pair of tired young men leaning on the order counter, their dirty, striped-red aprons and wrinkled, chef hats looking anything but gay this time of night.

You shake your head and trot by, ignoring the closed Starbrite Videos next door, gazing ahead to the bright green, orange, and red sign glaring like a beacon in the mist: 7-Eleven.

You cry out with relief, almost stumbling into the convenience store.

But you come to a sudden stop in the doorway and glance back toward your unseen pursuers, realizing that you will be trapped in any store if the blacks catch you inside. So you take seven more steps up the street and pause at the mouth of the dark alley running between the 7-Eleven and a boarded-up storefront.

Suddenly, her voice speaks in your head.

Robert, this way, Robert.

It's the Lady of the Numbers!

And she seems to be directing you up the alley.

You move cautiously, the light here off the street very dim, only one shaded bulb over a side entrance to the 7-Eleven about halfway up the alley, doing little more than casting shadows, scary shadows.

Here, Robert, back here.

The voice leads you to the end of the alley, behind a dumpster. You peer warily around the container piled high with refuse.

Nothing.

Only a brick wall, its graffiti obscured by heavy shadows, the smell of urine strong in your nostrils. Yuck.

Then, you hear footsteps coming to a halt at the mouth of the alley. Quickly you squeeze back behind the dumpster, ignoring the smelly mess, trying to conceal yourself.

After a moment you peer back around the dumpster, out toward the street, and even though you can not see them in the fog, you know who has cornered you in the alley.

The Black Phantoms.

"L-L-Le—" a voice stutters in the mist, confirming your suspicion.

"Shhhh."

You are trapped.

No, the voice interrupts in your head. *No, you are not caught.*

It is her, the voice so soft and gentle, comforting.

Look, here, turn around.

You turn and the shadows along the brick wall seem to stir, to take on depth.

Still, you can not really see anything, but you sense movement, and some of the shadows are almost shimmering, like heat waves off asphalt.

Here, Robert. It is a cloak, a very special cloak. Turn, slip it on, pull the cowl over your head.

You turn and feel something slipped over your shoulders. And you shiver, but remember to reach back and pull the hood up over your head.

Good. Be still. No one can see you now, Robert. You are cloaked in shadows.

The footsteps approach warily.

The three must be carefully searching along both sides of the alley.

After a lifetime, you hear breathing just beyond the front side of the dumpster, and you recognize Sidney's voice. "LeRoy, that lil sucker jus' ain't back here, man. Dude disappeared, you know what I'm sayin'?"

"Yeah, well, he gotta be here, some place." You hear things being thrown angrily about. Then, after another eternity or so, LeRoy finally admits with a sigh, "You right, Sidney. C'mon, Replay, let's get on back 'cross the playground, 'fore the Man come 'long 'n' bust our raggedy ass."

"I-I-I hears ya, m-m-m—"

"Jus' move, Replay."

You wait, squatting in place behind the dumpster with aching legs, until the footsteps fade away into the misty night. Then you stand and stretch; and the wonderful cloak is lifted off your shoulders, taken back into the wall.

Today, the number is two.

It is early, and you are lying on your bed, listening to a tape by, The Cure, Robert Smith singing the second song, "Siamese Twins," the part about the girl's face in the window. You listen with your eyes closed, the crotch of your pants tight.

Suddenly you are disturbed by a knocking on your door.

"Bobby?"

Your mother breaks the mood, knocking again, before she jams her head in the door.

"You sure you don't want to go to the Beaumonts?" she asks, her voice hopeful you will change your mind. "Donna says Mary Ann would love to see you again."

You almost laugh. Mary Ann is a cow, a fat cow. She would love to see anyone again, even someone ugly like you.

But you answer back, your anger under control, " No thank you, Mother." Then you add the old clincher, "I have a big assignment in English to finish tonight, you know."

She nods, disappointment heavy on her face. "All right ..." But she hesitates a moment, then adds in a tentative voice, "I just thought it might be ... oh, natural for a seventeen-year-old boy to be interested in seeing a teenage girl."

You almost laugh at the irony. You are very interested in seeing women— small, attractive, young women. "Have a good time, Mother."

She nods. "Oh, don't forget your medicine."

"I won't, Mother."

She waves goodbye and reluctantly shuts the door. Actually it's ironic she is so concerned about your welfare, now. For years, when you were little and she had all the boyfriends, she denied your existence. She would bring them home, the men, eventually taking them to her room; and you would watch from the shadows of the hall through the open door, repelled but fascinated by the laughing, giggling, sight and sound of their sweaty coupling. So many of them, so much love for strangers, so little for you. Then the steady stream of men slowed down as your mother grew fatter, aged; and she began to turn to you for attention.

And eventually you responded, letting her closer, except you never let her know about your real life: The creatures in the fog, the Lady's voice in your head, the importance of the numbers, your night walks, and so on. No, you knew better. Those were all your little secrets, and you were sharing them with no one.

You have no intention of taking the terrible medicine from the talking doctor either. If you do, you won't be able to hear the Lady's voice; and of course, you must know each day's number.

For an hour or so, you listen to The Cure tape; then you fluff-up two extra pillows that have been hidden under your bed, and you stuff them beneath your bedcovers. Finally, you slip out the bedroom window into another misty night.

Carefully, you move down the alley near the 7-Eleven until you reach the dumpster that still hasn't been emptied. You edge in back in the narrow space, feeling the brick wall.

Lady, you think, concentrating.

The shadows deepen, like yesterday. Then:

Hello, Robert. You have come back.

Yes, I need the cloak, again.

For a long while nothing happens, and you are afraid that you may have overstepped a boundary. You shudder. Maybe the Lady is angry.

But eventually she speaks again in your head. *All right, but you must be very careful and return it before daylight chases the shadows away.*

I understand.

You feel there is more, some kind of admonition or warning if you do not come back before daylight; but you are too excited to ask, for again you sense something in the shadows, something blacker than night.

Turn around.

You feel the touch of the cloak draped over your shoulders.

Of course it is better than the darkest, starless night, better than the thickest fog. For with the cloak of shadows you are completely invisible. You can roam anywhere at night and see everything with complete impunity.

You drift across the playground, pause and watch a couple embracing on one of the park benches, the man clutching at the woman's breast; and for a moment your mind drifts back, you are watching your mother, again.

Abruptly, the young man stands, and leads the woman away, back around behind the restrooms. For a moment or two you debate whether you want to follow. But no. Tonight, you have something much better, more exciting planned than watching these two.

Yes, indeed!

You walk down Jefferson Street boldly, right in the middle of the black section, passing a group of boys, another couple, and a drunk and his dog staggering out from Yo Mama's, the bar on the corner near Addison. You almost giggle to yourself, as the mutt follows you a step or two, sniffing the air near your leg; then it offers a tentative growl.

"C'mon, Mr. Nixon," the drunk says, his words slurred. "Wha's the matta wif ya?" He stops and stares down at the dumb animal, which is still looking in your direction and whining. "Ya actin' lak ya seen a ghost, boy. C'mon, now. We late foh suppah."

You climb over the white picket fence and go around back of the one-story frame residence on the corner of Jefferson and Lamont.

Only once before, on a very foggy night, have you worked up the nerve to prowl this yard, because it is so well lit by the streetlights and the backyard so visible from passersby on either street. You walk cautiously up to the back of the house and listen carefully at the frosted window of what you know to be the bathroom.

Water splattering.

Someone is in the shower.

You pull the garbage can quietly in place and climb up on it. The top window, which is frosted too, is cracked about two inches. But stretching up on your tiptoes on the can you are able to peer down inside.

Oh, what luck!

It is her.

The girl.

Kris!

Your thoughts drift back in time ...

The number that day had been five, when you first saw her in your fifth period Trig class at school. She had moved here from overseas in January—the fifth month of school—her father in the Air Force. From that first glimpse

139

you were smitten. Kris was a black pixie, no taller than you. And her unusual eyes, almond shaped and glittering like emeralds.

But you have never been able to even speak to her, because Henry Johnson, the school's star basketball player, is always with her outside of class. Although once you thought she looked your way and smiled at you.

He is six foot two.

They look ridiculous together.

As you peer down into the tiny bathroom, Kris is just stepping out of the shower, and her nakedness takes your breath away. Your heart thumps in your chest, your mouth drier than a cotton swab.

She is exquisite, only the barest hint of curves contouring her boyish shape, tiny breasts but the aurioles dark, almost purple against her coffee-colored skin, the nipples pronounced in the cool air as she rubs them dry. Your gaze moves slowly down to the dark, triangle, almost velvetlike in texture. You watch for another few minutes as she slips on a nightgown and bathrobe. Then she turns, smiles almost knowingly, and peers directly at the slightly opened window with her sparkling eyes.

You duck down out of sight, holding your breath, until you realize it is too dark out here for her to have seen you. When you ease back up and peek back through the slot, she is gone. You blink twice, hoping the number two will draw her back to the bathroom for some forgotten thing ...

But she doesn't return, today's number not strong enough.

After another minute of watching, you finally give up and climb down, moving the garbage can back to its original location.

Then you retrace your steps back to the alley by the 7-Eleven, back to the wall, returning the cloak of shadows.

Today the number is one.

It is very late, the moon shining brightly, illuminating everything; but you are drawn back to the house on Jefferson and Lamont, the cloak of shadows with its cowl shielding your presence even in this almost daylight brilliance. You vault the picket fence easily and circle the house quietly. It is dark, everyone apparently in bed. You stop at her bedroom and suck in a breath, trying to calm your racing heart.

The window is open, the blind up halfway.

You blink, thinking you must be dreaming. It's like ... an invitation.

Then, holding your breath, you peer in, and freeze, for in the moonlight you can see Kris clearly. She is lying on her side on her bed, staring directly at you. You blink.

No. Her eyes are squeezed shut. It was only your imagination.

You reach up and test the window. It slides up easily and quietly. With a slight effort you pull yourself up and over the sill, dropping to the floor in her room. Crouched, you watch for any movement. But she remains asleep, a kind of coy smile on her face. She must be dreaming. You rise. Then, on tiptoes, you move noiselessly to her side.

Her chest rises and falls so gently, her face so serene.

Suddenly, she stirs, moaning, lifting up her arms.

She has heard you!

An icicle of dread stabs into your chest; you hold your breath, and will your heart to stop beating. One, one, one.

No, she has not heard you.

On her side now, Kris smiles—something in her dream?

You kneel, only a foot or so away from the sleeping pixie; and you gaze into her face, the features so elegantly crafted.

Your chest is about to burst.

On impulse you try to lean down and kiss her lips.

But you have forgotton the cloak, its cowl preventing any contact.

Frowning with frustration, you stand up, glance about, and listen to the house creaking in the night, the moonlight still streaming through the window and spotlighting Kris's loveliness.

You debate with yourself for a moment, questioning the wisdom of shedding the cloak. Should I?

You wait, hoping the Lady of the Numbers will advise you. But there is nothing but the creaking sounds of the house.

Finally, you decide, shedding the cloak, letting it slide to the floor at your feet. Then you just stand there a moment, watching her breathe rhythmically. So lovely, so beautiful. Quietly, you slip from the rest of your clothes, letting them slide to your feet into the pile of blackness on the floor.

It is time we are one, Kris.

You take one step forward and trip over the cloak and pile of clothes, falling and reaching out toward the nightstand to catch yourself. But you only slam to the floor, knocking over the nightstand with a loud shattering of glass.

You leap back to your feet, glancing nervously at the closed bedroom door.

Somewhere nearby in the house, a masculine voice shouts, "Kris, baby, what is it? Are you all right."

She is awake now, sitting up, with the bedsheets pulled up around her, looking surprisingly calm, a strange mix of exasperation and anger on her face.

Confused, but operating with animal instinct, you scurry to the window and jump through, running as your feet hit the ground. Vision tunnels, panic clutching at your thudding heart, but you keep moving. Run, run, run ... one, one, one, repeats like words from a song in your head.

The cool air suddenly reminds you that you are completely naked, vulnerable out here in the bright moonlight. Oh, no. You have forgotton the cloak, left it behind in Kris's room. The wonderful cloak of shadows. But you can not go back now; so you continue running across the playground, two black men watching awestruck as you fly by—a lopsided, nude sprinter.

Then, miraculously, you find yourself on Franklin Avenue, some of the lights off now, a few businesses closed; and, luck still holding, you pass no one very close, until you reach the 7-Eleven.

As you thunder by the store entrance you almost knock over a guy coming out with a bag, who shouts at you angrily, "Hey, what the fuck's the matter with you, kid?"

You dart up the alley.

Sirens whine nearby, the shrill sound rasping at your nerve ends, for you know the police are coming for you; and they will cage you like a mad dog.

You must get away, you think, gasping for breath in the dark alley, which is thankfully shielded from the moonlight.

You scamper to the deadend, and squeeze in behind the dumpster.

Lady, oh, Lady—?

But there is no answer, only a dirty, smelly wall in the shadows. *Oh, please, please, help me.*

Still, no movement in the shadows, no answer.

You squint, hold back the tears. Maybe there is no Lady, no numbers, no Land of Shadows.

Could that be?

The sirens whine shrilly, but they are off in the distance now, and seem to be moving away from you and the alley.

Could the talking doctor be right? you ask yourself.

Maybe you are nothing more than a weird little man, sitting naked in an alley, all alone. No numbers, no lady, nothing.

A footstep crunches nearby.

You bite your lip, steel yourself, and peek around the dumpster; then you gasp aloud.

There, just beyond the light, hovering in the air, are two orbs, glittering like green fire in the dim alley.

A fog creature!

"No," you whisper hoarsely, trying to convince yourself, "it's a clear night. No fog, no fog creature."

Your logical denial quickly disappears from consciousness, like a dream the next morning, and you begin to panic as the green ovals slowly move closer, closer ... stopping only a few feet away from the dumpster.

You begin to hyperventilate.

A giggle.

And a face appears in the alley dimness, like an apparition, but a familiar face.

It is Kris!

She is smiling and giggling at you.

Still confused, you blurt out a question, "What—?"

The question breaks off, as more of her body becomes visible.

And it eventually dawns on you, the whole thing clear.

She is slipping the cloak from her shoulders—the special cloak of shadows. She had been wearing it, the cowl shielding her face, only her beautiful green eyes visible as she followed you here and down the alley.

Puzzled, you whisper, "I don't understand, Kris?"

She slips from the rest of the cloak, and only then do you realize that she, too, is completely nude. She steps forward, her arms beckoning, her eyes burning expectantly, and she replies, "Today, the number is one."

You take her hand and slip back behind the dumpster, facing the brick wall. The shadows deepen, part slightly, and now you see the Lady of the Numbers—tiny, elegant, and so pale, as if carved from alabaster. *Robert ... and Kris. You are ready to come to me? No, not yet. You must shed your otherness.* And her pale hand reaches out from the shadowed wall, something glittering in the dimness.

A straight razor. *Drain the otherness, Robert.* You understand, taking the shiny instrument in your free hand. A momentary frightened expression on her face, Kris tries to jerk away; but you tighten the grip on her hand, smile calmly, and tug her closer ...

As you grow colder the otherness runs from your hands joining the crimson pool at Kris's feet.

Then the Lady speaks again, but her voice is only a gentle whisper. *Come, my children.* Weakly clutching Kris's hand, you stumble forward into the icy Land of Shadows, into the Lady's arms.

You, Kris, and the Lady are now one.

TAIL THE BARNEY
Stephen M. Irwin

I'm not partial to travel. I'm a home body. But when Florey told me the bloke had died, I did the ring around. We three decided, out of neighbourliness and out of friendship for a chap less fortunate than us, that we'd duck out and fetch Florey's blessed thing back. But if truth be told, we didn't do it for Florey. We did it for peace and quiet. Florey was quite the whinger. But he was *our* whinger, *our* neighbour. That's why we nipped out that night: to flog back Florey's trinket from the dead man.

I suppose it was my dart. But let me tell you about Florey and you'll understand why Reed, the girl, and I went a-thieving. Florey moved into our block some thirty-odd years ago. It was a council relocation; he had no one to look after him. At first I was pleased to have someone new to yarn with. Florey had been around the ridges, and I don't mind a listen. But cripes, talk! This and that; war and women; won so much, lost so much. I guess we got used to it, we neighbours. Fat Reed on my left. The young girl Lisa over the road (she's new). Dimity next door: my age. We got used to Florey's deepest scratch, the one about the chap who stole his thing. His brooch, his good luck charm, the loss of which sent his whole life down the box. Yes, we'd say, that's terrible; what a scoundrel, we'd say; let it go, we'd say. Dimity suggested telling Florey to plug it, but Dimity was more of a home body than me and she was always maggoty about something. And another chap you *would* have had a go at, but Florey had been in the war and he'd lost his legs in the flood, so I guess we just took pity. But what would we do for a bit of shush! Well, I guess this is about just what we'd do. What we *did* do.

What a night.

I'd had the daughter and her kids around that day. Little bastards. A chap reaches an age and I think that permits some frankness. I love my daughter, but her children are diseased little monkeys. Running around, throwing rocks, jumping the fence into Dimity's place and throwing more rocks (thank Christ Dimity's a deep sleeper or there'd have been hell to pay). They'd been swimming at Southbank, she said. Lauren talked and talked; lovely girl, but emotional. But you only get one family, so I listened politely, nodding in the right spots, tuning out of the babble and enjoying the view across the river. Finally Lauren took off, taking her Godless little marmosets with her, but then Reed's family came to visit him and I had to hear all their nonsense. Why can't people speak softly anymore? You'd think with mobile telephones and all this guff people would have evolved out of yelling, but no. Anyway, come evening all I wanted was an early kip. That's when Florey started up.

The chap who stole his brooch had died. I don't know how Florey knew this, but he come across so certain that I didn't doubt him. He'd died just this night, said Florey. He still had the brooch, said Florey. *My* brooch, said Florey. My good luck brooch. And the thief's family would get it now, and there was no hope then—no hope at all!—of getting it back. Woe was Florey. I patted Florey on his bony shoulders and there-there'd him and sent him home with the firm intention of doing nothing.

It was a beautiful night, and I would have been content to have sat out smelling the cinnamon of jacaranda bark and the tang of camphor laurel and watching flying foxes sweep like flakes of ash across the sky and watching the slow stars climb before retiring ... but an idea caught me. I couldn't rest. I couldn't sleep. It niggled. It itched so I felt like ants were crawling inside me. I had a plan. I went next door to see Reed. "Reed!" I called. He rubbed his eyes (him tired, too, from his family's yammerings) and listened to my plan to go and fetch Florey's tail-the-barney brooch from the dead man. Reed hummed and nodded and rubbed his feet. "I'm not too svelte," suggested Reed, blushing. He was very worried about his weight. "And you're, well, you're not so young ..." "Fine," I said. "We'll get Lisa." "Lesia," corrected Reed. "Fine," I repeated, and we went across to get Lisa.

Lisa was maybe thirty and had moved in a few years ago. I may be old, and I may not quite have the air to fill the balloon, but I am not blind, and the thought of watching Lisa wriggling through a window was the better part of my plan, and I congratulated myself on it. "It'll shut Florey up?" asked Lisa. Smiles never landed on Lisa's face. I said I thought it would. "Let's do it, then," she said. "I'll just do my face." "No time!" I cried. "The dead bloke's family are probably there already, pawing through his things! Let's go!" None of us thought to invite Dimity. Dimity would talk us out of it. And this was far too nice a night to be talked out of anything. So Reed, Lisa/Lesia and I went out to steal some peace.

In the early spring, the city's air is at once loose and tight, cool and warm, clear and full. In the pocket of the hill climbing Annerley Road one can feel toasty and pleasantly assaulted by fragrances of potato vine, cut grass and the distant tweak of diesel. But crest the hill and glimpse the sparkling night time spires of the city, suddenly you feel cold air rattling your bones, and the wind stealing all scent to the wide, dark river, to be wicked jealously away.

And that was as far as we three got—the top of Annerley Road, looking one way North to the city and one way South to the river and all of us feeling the chill wind tugging like children—when we realised we didn't know where we were going.

We three sat in the park there to discuss notes on Florey, his gewgaw, and the tormentor who stole it. Reed, puffing heavily, said he'd heard the chap who stole it lived in Taringa. I (not puffing at all) recalled hearing the dastard's name was Richard someone-or-other, and Florey was upset because the tail-the-barney was lucky. "What do you remember, Lisa?" I asked. "Lesia," she snarled, looking around nervously and already wanting to go home. I said we couldn't go home. Or, we could, but we'd be condemned to years of whining and we should see this through. She nodded nervously, hoping no one would see her with her face not made up, and explained that Florey told *her* the treasure was a pendant made in the *taille d'épargne* style, and was given to him by a grateful gypsy when he had entered Bergen Belsen with the British at the end of the war. That rang a bell with Reed and me. "And also," she snipped, "the scoundrel's surname was Richard. His first name was something dull and boring." "Bill!" cried Reed, remembering, and I grew offended because my name is Bill. Still, we had something to start with: William Richard, Taringa, thief of a gypsy's magical tail-the-barney pendant.

Taringa, as the crow flew (and as flying foxes now did, black leather brackets arcing silently west, winking out the cool stars as they passed) was not far. But for old bones like mine, it was a fair trot. "Let's catch a cab!" I suggested, and tottered out of the deep shadows of the pergola toward the whirring headlights and flitting shadows of Annerley Road. "Who's got some Oscar?"

Reed and Lisa looked at me blankly.

"Oscar Asche?" I asked.

Still the round, empty stares.

"Cash!" I shouted.

"Oh," they said, looking sideways at each other. "We're a bit younger than you, Bill." It transpired that Reed didn't bring any cash—he thought we were out for a stroll which was a good idea because he was feeling heavy and unsightly. Lisa didn't have any because she didn't even have time to do her lips fergodsake let alone hunt around for her purse. And I am old, and old people in Dutton Park don't carry money—everyone knew that. "Looks like we walk." Reed looked at his fat feet. Lisa looked up at the fingernail moon. "What?" I asked. Reed mumbled something about Saturday night and young ladies on their way to night clubs laughing at him, and Lisa/Lesia sneered something else about anyone going anywhere pointing at her and thinking she looked like a trollop. I sat beside them. "You," I said to Reed, putting one arm around him, "worry too much. You've been fat. I remember when you first arrived, you looked big. But I think you've got so used to thinking you're fat, you don't realise how sporty you look. And you," I said, wanting to put my arm around Lisa but instead just patting her thin knee once. "This is a beautiful night, and it is only more beautiful with you in it, not at home sulking."

My inspiring talk did nothing whatsoever, and they both suggested they might go home. "Well, you're not!" I snapped. "Let's walk!" "Which way?" ground Lisa. "There's a new bridge across to the University," suggested fatso. "No way, I don't do bridges," venomed Lisa. "Well it's that bridge, or it's the Grey Street Bridge, or that other new bridge, or it's a ferry where you can have half the population laughing at you, you fat-thin miseries." So, we started back the way we came, between the thin black shadows behind streetlights and the thick black shadows under a clear night sky toward the new bridge.

Years pass fast. You think you know a place, you think you know what kind of people live here, and what kind are drawn there, but if you stay still too long, the truth washes past like a tide, carrying new things past your drowsy eyes. When you break free of your reef and drift with the current, you see that nothing has stayed still except you—everything is different. Hills have been subtly reshaped. Roads widened. Trees cut down or planted. People cut down or planted or transplanted. Only the stars are fixed, and they are cold and far, far away. But some things, mercifully, change slowly. Once upon a time, one wouldn't go about on foot around Dutton Park at night for fear of violent drunks. I discovered one still should not go about on foot around Dutton Park at night for fear of violent drunks. "Yo yo yo!" said the young man who looked, in silhouette at least, like a penguin—all baggy britches, billed cap and swaggling arms. "Wassup wassdown wattavwehe-ya?"

I turned to Lisa and Reed, hoping for a translation. They each shrugged and took a subtle step behind me. We had been walking downhill through the park, talking about favourite foods (mine: shepherd's pie; Lisa/Lesia's: caffeine tablets; Reed's: anything starting with a letter of the alphabet) and didn't see the huddle of penguins on its park bench ice floe until we heard the voice. Then, the vapour wash of hot malcontent ran over us. The emperor strutted a bit closer. Only a circle of streetlight separated him from me.

"What did you say?" I asked.

"You a bit croaky old man," said the emperor, pronouncing the last word 'main'. "You need a drink." "Tell him to drink this!" shouted one of the shadow penguins, and I heard a fly unzip and laughter. I glanced back at Reed and Lisa. They were magically ten feet back already. I scowled.

"I don't like your attitude, son," I said. They laughed louder. I heard metal. Once, years ago, I'd been pretty fearless. As a tar boy I'd fought one of Brophy's lads in Charleville, and lost with great dignity. Then I grew older and scared. Why not tonight? I couldn't explain it. It was too nice a night to be scared. And I knew I would be all right. I had something to do: I had Florey's treasure to rescue, and nothing was going to stop me. All five penguins detached themselves from their nest and waddled up behind their leader.

"Righto," I said. "Rafferty rules with louts." I shaped up and stepped into the light. A siren sounded somewhere, growing louder. The boys looked at me from under their shadow bills. Their faces were all white as sand, their eyes dark as soil. The siren grew louder. They ran.

Pleased, I looked back to Reed and Lisa. They were amazed. "Still cut quite the figure," I said, throwing a punch at the air and wincing at the grinding joints. Reed cocked his head and looked at me, then looked at his own arms. Lisa looked at me and almost—not a word of a lie—almost smiled, I swear. The bridge was ahead, arcing batwings with steel veins soaring across the river into the night.

We were midway across the bridge when Lisa collapsed into a tight, shrieking ball. I tried to move her, but her arms and legs spat out like snakes, one hard knuckled thing striking me in the shin. I swore aloud (which I *never* do) and limped back along the bridge, leaving Reed to the hissing viper's nest. I was cranky. At this rate we'd never get to Bill Richard's house—certainly not before his peregrine-eyed beneficiaries began their greedy snatchings.

"What's the matter with her?" I asked Reed. "She says she ... what did you say?" He listened to her sizzle a moment. "She says she jumped off a bridge and that's why she hates them."

I rolled my eyes, put my hands on the cold rails, and looked out across the river.

It was a beaut. In my time I'd see the Yarra, the Torrens, the Margaret, the Gordon, and the Mary. This wasn't a pretty blue brook, or a wild rapid antelope. This river was wide and stately and slow to anger. She glimmered in the moonlight, a grand diva hiding her bulk behind shimmering silver and twinkling ice blue. Her mangrove flanks smelled like tears. I could just make out the cemetery, and the new galvanized steel rails of the roadside that separated the graveyard's ivory tombstone teeth from the black, plunging banks. There. That must have been where Florey lost his legs. Where he lost his trinket, and his luck.

As the river mumbled quietly below me, I let my mind drift back with it. Ten, twenty, thirty years. Back to 'seventy-four. And the floods. I remember the council men, wandering about, digging new holes while the rain thundered down. Laughing and occasionally vomiting, stomachs disgorging as their trucks disgorged. The river had swollen with the rain, rain, rain, and she'd grown very fat and hungry. She'd broken the banks in some spots, eaten the banks in others, one of them here at the cemetery. She'd risen up to the level of the tombstones and started chewing into the cemetery soil. You've seen film of icebergs shedding their sides and crashing into the sea? This was like that, only brown not blue. Slabs of soil, undermined by the racing brown-grey water, suddenly fell away into the current, exposing new, raw banks. From these began to poke caskets. The fierce rain would trouble the rotting flanks of coffins until they fell away, exposing perished linen and grey bones of corpses. Some caskets fell whole into the torrent and bobbed away, to be found days later caught by mangrove fingers or bouncing expectantly against flooded doorways in Eagle Street. But most simply filled with water and ejected shrivelled cadavers into hurried and unwelcome baptisms. The council was alerted to this problem. It wasn't a health problem; not compared to the bloated cows and bloated dogs among the flotsam. But it was a problem of perception. Bony hands and spidery legs and surprised skulls peeking out from the riverbank were unattractive to nose and eye. So they got in teams to exhume swiftly, and relocate the bodies before the river could. They were only half in time for Kenneth Dougal Florey. His coffin happened to be aligned in such a way that his feet hung out over the new drop created by the voracious waters. He lay there, pants ripped away, embarrassed as hell, half hoping to be saved and half hoping to be spared the shame by being pulled into the current. As was Florey's lot in life, he got half of what he wanted. His white phalanges, then metatarsals, then talus bones, then left fibula and right tibia then both femurs were sucked away before the two council workers got to him. It was William Richard who knelt on the bank, reached down, and yanked what was left of Florey up and out of his second, fetid womb. "He pongs!" shouted Richard, tossing the half-skeleton to his co-worker Dennis Chee, who giggled and caught Florey in an army surplus body bag. Florey was, naturally, doubly embarrassed by his aroma.

"Wait a second," shouted Richard over the rain, and Chee stopped zipping. Richard sloshed over and reached down. "No no no!" Florey told me he shouted, but the rain was too loud. Richard plucked the necklace and the beautifully wrought pendant from Florey's neck, snapping the silver chain. "You a dobber, Chee?" Chee, said Florey, shook his head "No, Mr Richard." Richard winked, and—for Florey—everything went black.

Others in their stygian cocoons in the back of the lorry told the fluttering and incensed Florey that the bloke's first name was Bill (that's what the chink called him when he wasn't in strife, said one—then a furious argument over racial invectives drowned Florey's pleading for help to regain his *taille d'épargne* pendant. The next day, Florey was moved into the row opposite mine, high on the hill. He'd been an insufferable whinger ever since.

"Here, Bill!" Reed's voice pulled me back into the cold night. He'd somehow gotten Lisa/Lesia to her white feet, and had one arm thrown around her thin shoulders. A silly wave of envy wriggled through me. "Here!" I hurried over, my own feet tack-tacking on the hard bridge surface. Lisa was shaking, sounding like a dozen frozen, chattering jaws. Reed and I exchanged a nod, and I put my arm around her, too, my bones creaking as we took her weight. "It's all right, Lesia," I said. "We'll have you off here in a jiff." "Story Bridge," she whispered. "Story Bridge. Story Bridge ..." I remembered, now, what Dimity had told me when Lesia had first moved in. She'd jumped from the Story Bridge, but the tide had been out and she'd landed head first in salty mud. She'd suffocated to death. It was rude, but one day he'd glanced at her stone: 'Beautiful daughter. Loving sister. Lost too soon.' "Here we go," I said, and we were over. But I kept a hold of her long after we were back on land, until she stopped shaking.

We walked through the university grounds, three unlikely haystacks of white shuffling between pools of light, footsteps echoing like dice rolls off the hard stone walls. I stared up at the buildings, feeling the wind tickle inside me.

Till now, I thought I'd seen a bit and done a bit. But all these big square buildings, filled with books and those computers and God-knows-what else, made me feel like I hadn't done a tap. I felt small. "We need a phone book," said Reed. "Oh! I should call my sister!" suggested Lisa. Reed explained we had no money, and Lisa nodded glumly. We tick-ticked through the sandstone canyons. We only saw one lad, one hand on one hip, gently swaying while he relieved himself against something that was either a rubbish bin or a sculpture. "Fella!" I called. "We need a telephone directory." He turned, saw us, grinned and held his head, and went back to contemplating his stream. "Fuck me," he giggled. We found a bank of glass booths near shuttered doors. The directory was chained to it, a ragged and beaten dog of a thing, and looked up 'Richard, W'. There was only one in Taringa, in Pike Avenue. We'd get directions as we got closer. We kept walking, and I was pleased to be out of that dismal mausoleum place.

We passed houses glowing prettily and warm as Tilley lamps. The Methodist church was dark. The Catholic church was lit, and singing came from within. I slowed. Human voices carried on the soft breeze, rising like fresh tide and falling like clean rain. How long had it been since I heard music? How long since I heard voices in joy, voices other than Dimity's or Florey's or Reed's, or my daughter's dripping weariness or my grandchildren's bored snatchings? How long since I'd heard voices talking without bitterness or confusion, with hope and brightness? "Bill?" said Reed, tapping his wrist. I nodded and we pressed on. The she-oaks in the school yard whispered as we passed. "Look!" said Lisa, delighted. On the bitumen parade ground, two dogs chased each other, tumbling. The smaller one grabbed one of the bigger one's ribs and ran off with it. The bigger one scooted after, bones and nails clicking. Lisa laughed and jumped the fence to chase the dogs, throwing the errant rib. Reed and I leaned on the fence, watching her. "Makes you wonder, doesn't it," said Reed. "About what?" I asked. Reed's dark sockets were thoughtful. "What happens to us. After we die." I watched him. "This comes next," I said. He looked at me. "Oh," he nodded. "Yes. Forgot." I called to Lisa: "Come on, sunshine." She was grinning, breathing hard. Her smile was as lovely as I'd imagined it would be, and that made me a bit glum. "Come on."

The smells! One becomes so used to the back palate of fresh cut grass, the front palate of fresh flowers, the mid-palate of distant salt or distant exhaust fumes. One forgets the smells of *life*. We passed houses, and we three sniffed, grinning at each other: wood smoke, said Reed. Mosquito coils, said Lisa/ Lesia. Rissoles! I moaned, licking airy lips. Oh, rissoles and fresh beans and butter! And here: steak and chips! (Porterhouse, specified Reed, and Lisa and I believed him). Lamb and Brussels sprouts. Coffee. Muscat.

We floated on aromas, nudging each other. Reed shook his head. I saw him run white fingers down a belly he remembered, growing sad. "Don't worry," I said. "This is window shopping. It's free!" He nodded gloomily, and I looked at Lisa. She shook her head. I changed the subject. "So, why do you think Florey misses this bauble so much?"

We compared notes, each digging into our lightly whistling heads for memories of mostly-ignored, one-way conversations with Florey. The pendant was beautiful, rose gold with black enamel tracery. When he and the other Brits had stumbled stiff-legged through the gates of Bergen Belsen, some of the walking skeletons had stared, some simply died with the shock of the horror ending, some had wrapped leather and bone arms around the soldiers. One had simply walked up to Florey and pressed the curio into his hand. Florey hadn't known if the naked thing was a man or a woman. "Once, once!" the creature had said, and winked, its smile revealing two teeth. "Romani. Yes? Good, good." And held up one twig finger—once! This we agreed. The second thing we agreed was recalling that Florey had wondered how long the thing had been in the gypsy's arse. The third was that, when he'd been demobilised, he went to a jewellers in Suffolk and talked a deal on a gold chain. That day—that very day he put it on!—had been the luckiest day of his life. In one day he 1) met the most beautiful woman he'd ever seen (who, ahem, became his wife); 2) was feeling so lively at meeting Imogen that he put one pound neat on a horse named—can you believe it?—Lucky Day, on the nose, at fifty-to-one and it *won!*; and 3) he took that money, wandered into a card game in The Old Bell and got a straight and won the keys to a very posh Ford Anglia de Luxe and a handful of petrol coupons! Happiest day, happiest day ...

"And then what happened?" asked Lisa/Lesia. We didn't know. He ended up here. He ended up broke. He died alone, buried by the Serviceman's League.

"Here," said Reed, pointing.

An old man was walking up the footpath toward us. Reed elbowed me. Lisa elbowed me. I stepped forward. "Good evening," I said. The man stopped and looked up. "Evening." He smiled. "Lovely night," he said. He wore a cloth cap and carried a white cane. I agreed it was, and asked him if he knew where Pike Avenue might be? Down the way I was heading, left at the corner, one right one left and there we were. Then he straightened. "You've not come for me, then?" Then I heard the tremor in his voice. "What makes you say that?" I asked. "You three click when you walk, and your voice sounds like wind blowing through old bottles on a forgotten beach. But aside from that, you seem very pleasant." I told him we were not coming for him, but thanks for the directions. He waved his cane with a cheerio, and kept walking.

This was Brisbane as I remembered it. Weatherboard houses with flaking flanks or proud gloss beige and white, hunched on spindle legs with batten skirts and dark tin bonnets, kind-eyed windows winking at a mild night where high-hissing gums and spider-fingered jacarandas scratched at the Southern Cross, polishing her bright. A wide fig spread her skirts over the whole road, knitting the breeze with her dark leaves. The houses were tucked behind hedges of roses, hedges of geraniums, low wire fences, low white timber fences. We started looking for the house the phone directory told us held the remains of William Richard. We didn't have to look hard.

The house was grey and in darkness. The yard was overgrown, wind-dried grass a foot high crunched like steel wool underfoot. The ancient paint on the cottage's fibro shanks flaked like eczema, and the downpipe was rusted through, hanging like a rotten tooth from the diseased gum of the equally rusted gutter. The place stank of bad luck.

"Well, we beat the family," said Reed. "Or they beat us," suggested Lisa. "Here," I said, and pointed to the overgrown path that bled toward the lattice veranda doors. The grass was unbent. We were first. "Nice work, Sherlock," said Lisa, and winked emptily at me. I smiled and pressed the doorbell. No sound came from inside ... but we all felt the loose air of regret shift around us. I didn't like this too much. "We could tell Florey it was gone," suggested Reed. His voice shook. Lisa nodded and skipped back toward the street, decided already. "No," I said. "We ought to try."

Bones do not have good grip. The green brass doorknob slipped under my fingers. "Bung idea, this," I said. "Round the back." Stepping high through grass dry as ash, we crept along the narrow yard under the yawning shadow of the unhappy house. At the back, a low set of sagging stairs rose to a bent landing and a tattered screen door. Lisa/Lesia nodded at me: you go first. One, two, three steps, and I was rapping softly on the aluminium frame dusted white with age. "Richard?" I whispered. "Bill?" Lesia and Reed stared back at me, white skulls tiny moons on shrugging shoulder bones. "Fine." I pulled the door open and crept inside.

Some homes are graves of the living. They are dust and sorrow. Lost time hangs like a caul, strung by cobwebs. Skittering things hide under dishes unwashed (who will see them?), clothes unfolded (who will mind?), floors unswept (who will visit?). A calendar from 1989 was crucified by one rusty nail to the hallway wall. I crept up, and four clacking feet followed mine. Ahead was the lounge room, a tiny box, a lifeless place split by icy moonlight slivered by dust-caked Venetian blinds. The air smelled of stolen tobacco, mice, and loneliness. "There," whispered Reed. Curled like an unanswered question mark on the floorboards was a man evaporated. "Bill?" I asked.

He blinked, staring with white, already sinking eyes. "Yes?"

"Bill Richard?" asked Reed. "Jesus, Reed, seriously," snapped Lesia. But the dead man answered anyway, "Yes. I can't move." "That's 'coz you're dead," said Lesia. Bill strained, and turned his head a notch, and saw us. A whiff of rot, of surrendered lungs, a sigh of surprise. "Oh." We told him who we were, how we knew Florey, and how we'd come to fetch Florey's tail-the-barney pendant. As we did, Richard's dead hand crept like a crab up from the floor, across the broken reef of his chest, to his throat, where it curled around something there on a chain. There it nested, guarding. "It's my good luck charm." "It's not yours." "It's mine!" "You stole it." "No!" "Give it over!" "Never!!" We all pried at Richard's closed crab hand.

We all four saw the yellow headlights flash across the front door glass; we all four heard the car door outside slam. A moment later, the front gate creaked. A moment after that, knocking at the front door. Through the dirty rippled glass, the silhouette of the visitor. Reed, Lesia, and I were perched above Richard, exchanging looks. "Ssh!" "SSSH!" "You be quiet!" "Quiet!" We listened. We waited. The visitor knocked again. "Dad?" she said. I looked down at Richard. "Oh," he whispered. "Oh, no."

At the front door, keys jangled.

"Hide!"

With an ivory clatter, we scurried. Lesia ducked behind the dusty genoa lounge. Reed cried, "I'm too fat! I'm too fat!" and ran down the hall to the toilet. I stood quietly, and crept back, back, back into the dark corner of the room. The front door groaned open, and the woman slipped inside.

"Dad?" She clicked the light switch, on-off, on-off. "Dad ..." she whispered, disappointed, unsurprised. She stepped deeper into the musty, hollow coffin room. And saw the curled rag figure on the dusty floor. Her breath sucked in sharply, and her steps were fast. She knelt over the body, hands fluttering like birds ... then perching still. "Oh, Dad ..."

She was maybe thirty, maybe a bit more. She wore a skirt and jacket and shoes as slender as calligraphy on her feet. Her hair had been worried by the wind. Her face was in shadow. She sighed, and it sounded like relief. And then ... "Hello," she said, quietly.

No, no! I thought.

She touched his covetous clam hand, and uncurled it easily. Again, her breath sucked in, and—had I lungs—mine would have, too. For even from across the room I could see the tail-the-barney, and it was beautiful. It was gold, dark gold with a hint of sunset and warm as fire. Its surface stretched with sensuous curls of black enamel, fine as hair mussed in love, but in the shapes of delicate vines that wrapped around a cunning gate that would, if gently pushed, open to a summer garden so breathtakingly lovely one would never, ever leave. "Daaad ...," she whispered, and reached for the clasp.

Then I pictured what would come next. She'd put it on. Tomorrow would be a wonder—a day of love and luck and laughter. But the next day after would be duller, and poorer. The next: anxious and desperate. The next: worried and angry and clutching. The next, the next, the next ... until she was curled in rags, empty as a kettle and alone as a dry well in a desert.

"You can't have it," I said, and stepped from the shadows.

She looked up at me. Her eyes widened. Then they rolled back in her head and she fell to the floorboards with a bang and puff of cinnamon dust. "Nice one, Bill!" said Lesia, rising from behind the couch. "Kill her?" "What was that bang?" shouted Reed, scuttling up the hall. I hurried to the girl. I touched her wrist. I touched her white, soft throat. Reed and Lesia hovered above me. I felt ... and found the lovely thudding beneath her skin. "She's all right." "Well, get it, then!" The girl's warm hand was tight around the pendant, just as zealous as her father's. "She won't let it go!" said Richard. "Shut up, you!" I hissed. "She's your daughter? Want her to end up like this? You ungrateful man, neglectful, ungrateful ..." I stopped a moment, and thought of my beautiful Lauren and her dirty marmosets. "This is not yours," I whispered. Then, the girl's eyes fluttered open, and found a focus. I am guessing what she saw was a bit much: three creamy skulls staring down at her, sockets wide and dark and full of wonder. Because her eyes rolled back again, and she hit the floor with a second solid thud. "Nice catch, Bill," said Lesia. But the woman had released her grip. I snatched up the pendant.

"We'll see you, William Richard," I said.

"You're thieves," he hissed.

I shepherded Reed and Lesia toward the front door. "Wait," I said. "Reed, here." "What?" I took him by the arm, and led him into Richard's bedroom.

Against the wall was a duchess, its walnut veneer lifting like tiny tectonic plates, its mirror back smeared with dark melanomas. "Here," I said, and led Reed to it. "Look." I positioned him before the glass, and made him see himself. For a moment, he was still as a crane, staring. Then, one hand lifted to a double chin that was gone, then slid to a belly that had vanished, then idled to buttocks that had sublimed into history. "I'm not fat," he whispered. "I know," I said, and Lesia and I smiled. "It killed me. Heart attack." I shrugged, "Well, you had to die sometime." Lesia and I watched the smile dawn on Thin Reed's wide, white face. "Come on, mate." I tugged his arm, and we flew before the girl could wake again.

We rattled down the streets of Taringa, clicked up the footpaths of St Lucia, covered Lesia's eyes with careful fingers and crossed the bridge, and slipped like white wind through the trees to the cemetery. "Florey?" we cried. "Florey!" Florey mumbled awake. "What? What?" "Close your eyes and open your hand," said Lesia. He scowled and didn't, so she punched him and stalked home. I watched her go. "Night, Lisa." "Lesia," she snapped, but when she turned back she was smiling, so that was good. "Well?" demanded Florey. "Reed?" I asked, and Reed put the pendant into Florey's hand. "Oh!" cried Florey. "Oh! OH!!" He clasped his hand tight, he opened it wide, he held the pendant high, he hugged it close. "Isn't it beautiful! Oh, it's beautiful! Did I tell you how I found it? It was 1945, and I was with the Eleventh—" "Tomorrow, Florey," I said. "Yes, yes, tomorrow," he fluted, spinning in the moonlight. I stepped away, and looked at Reed. He smiled at me. "Thank you, Bill," he said. "Maybe next week? Another trot?" I suggested. He nodded. "I'll tell Lesia." "Good night, Reed." "Good night, Bill."

Dimity was waiting. "Well, husband?" she demanded. "Well indeed," I replied, and kissed her and we held hands and watched the stars do their slow wheel, and sank into the cool earth to sleep.

THE NIGHTMARE DIMENSION

David Conyers

I

When I was woken by a thud sounding suspiciously like a dead body falling into my guestroom, I gave up any idea I'd sleep again that night.

I rolled towards the bed side table and checked my alarm clock. It was 1:00am. The darkest hour had just begun, when creatures of night liked to come a knocking.

I slid out of bed figuring I might as well get this unscheduled business meeting started. Yet in no hurry to seem eager, I stepped into the kitchen and poured myself a large glass of water. Then I sauntered across my apartment lounge area to the guestroom. I could have lingered longer and dressed for the occasion, but I was too tired to worry about my appearance, and my guests wouldn't likely care that I wore only pyjama pants.

I broke out in a sweat as I lingered at the door.. Sydney summer had been particularly hot this year, but nothing like the heat radiating from the guestroom door. The flames that cast flickering shadows through the cracks were more telling, as was the unmistakable stench of sulphur.

Taking a long deep breath that might be the coolest, cleanest air I might enjoy for the next couple of hours, and grateful that I had stopped to get myself a glass of water after all, I stepped inside.

"Gordon McColley," the demon I knew as Marcus Sempter greeted me in his perfectly clipped English accent. He stood straight-backed before his entourage of hell-spawned lackeys and picked at what I suspected was a morsel of human flesh he'd dug from beneath a fingernail. "I don't like to be kept waiting."

Behind him, a portal into the inferno of Hell had opened—the source of the flickering flames that illuminated Sempter and his followers in a halo of angry red light.

I pressed the cool glass of water against my forehead as I relaxed into the room's only chair, a leather lounge I'd installed last month. I'd grown tired of standing during these late night meetings, which could last for hours. My demonic guests stood not because I was stingy, but because they generally wrecked any provided furniture within the first few minutes of their arrival.

Sempter looked human enough, with his expensive three-piece charcoal suit, purple silk tie, slick dark hair, perfectly proportioned face and the physique of a twenty-year-old fashion model. But behind this façade lurked a high ranking demon who had willingly tortured thousands of souls since before the fall of the Roman Empire.

Two of Sempter's attending lackeys I knew as the voluptuously figured Torture Sisters, their nickname acquired due to their abilities in extracting information. The first demoness was composed entirely of ice, the second of hot embers, and that was the basis of their technique.

The fourth demon I didn't recognise. Perhaps he had been recently promoted from Hell's torture factories? This imposing creature resembled an ogre whose skin had been sewn together after a complicated dissection. In his club of a hand rested a meat cleaver the size of a combine harvester blade, while across his broad shoulders hung a helmet attached to a breastplate contraption forged from rusted iron.

"I see you brought some friends." I took a sip of water as sweat ran off me in streams.

Sempter didn't reply. He had just noticed he and his entourage were trapped inside the magical circle I had recently burnt into the floorboards, the only portal through which supernatural creatures could enter or leave my harbour view apartment. Displaying his disgust on his down-turned brow, Sempter then looked to me. "You should have dressed for the occasion."

"You don't like my pyjamas? With this heat, you're lucky I'm even wearing that."

A delicate, precisely directed finger pointed at my body. "It's the symbols tattooed on your chest, arms, and back that offend me, McColley."

I took another sip of water because it really was hot in here, despite Ice Sister's presence. "You should know better than that, Sempter. Without these magical symbols, your lot would have done away with me a long time ago."

Sempter gave me his famous grin agreeing that he'd always rather be eating my flesh than conversing. "It would be a short lived gain, as your soul is not yet promised to me for eternity."

"And it never will be."

His grin grew mischievous. "I see you've extended the same protection to your apartment." His thin finger pointed to symbols burnt into the floor, identical to those tattooed on my flesh.

"Your kind likes to surprise me in the middle of the night. And you make a mess. Better, don't you think, I keep you and your mess confined to one room?"

The demon's face and body contorted suddenly as if a million fish hooks had just yanked at every centimetre of his flesh when he said, "You need to assist me with a minor matter."

I smiled, finally understanding. His agony was because demons never liked to ask anyone for help, particularly not from mortals like myself. "What does the world's greatest demonic criminal mastermind want from me?"

He clicked his fingers. Immediately, his three companions stepped aside so I could see the naked, broken and bloody body of a young woman lying at their feet. A few hours earlier, she would have been in her mid-twenties, rather attractive, and probably a very happy soul.

I felt sickened seeing this human death, but I didn't show it. If I displayed any fear, it might excite Sempter, and he might decide that when he next had the opportunity, a short-lived torture was worth the mild distraction it would offer him from his own intense pain—pain that each demon suffered every second of their existence.

"Who is she?" I took another mouthful of water. At this rate, I'd have to go and get another glass.

"She interfered with my London operations."

"What, one individual?"

"She's more than that."

"She's one of the Awake?"

"Just. She knew enough that I was required to come to you."

"Played you, did she?"

Sempter, already clearly agitated, now literally fumed. Skin began to peel across his face and hands and then erupted with sulphur-laden smoke. The same acrid stench billowed from the seams and cuffs of his formally very nice suit, and it, too, was beginning to smoulder. "I can't find her soul," he admitted.

"Ah," I said, finally putting the pieces together of this rather sordid puzzle. As well as never asking for help, demons never liked to admit when they had been duped. "I take it she didn't enter into a soul contract with you, then?"

"Not every soul I claim has to be promised to me."

That was too true, hence all my protective tattoos and my magical fortress of an apartment.

"You need to find this soul, McColley."

I laughed. "Sempter, you control the largest crime syndicate in the world. No one shifts heroin and cocaine laced with Hell's Elixir in the quantities you do. Can't one of your many cronies find it instead?"

I pointed to his posse. Ice Sister had thinned, melted with the rising temperature. Fire Sister, in comparison, seemed more alive, as if petrol had been thrown on her, exciting the flames that ran like tiny dancers up and down the embers of her skin. The armoured demon at the back had said and done nothing since their arrival, yet he seemed the scariest of them all.

"My people aren't investigators for hire!" hissed Sempter.

"What about Synder? This is more his kind of work."

Synder was Sempter's most senior drug distributor for the Australian arm of his operations, and a mage like me. Sydner's magic was more overt than mine—and more powerful. He would have no trouble finding the poor woman's soul.

I could have been as powerful as Synder if I wanted to, but the price wasn't worth it. Synder had obtained his skills by selling his soul to so many demons he probably didn't even know that he'd once been a man with a conscience. I, on the other hand, had made no contracts with any magical entity and never planned to. I'd learnt magic on my own through many hours of hard study. It was the only way to survive in this slipstreamed world as one of the mortal Awake, both in this life and the next one. I wanted certainty that when the afterlife finally found me, it wouldn't take me somewhere horrific like Hell.

"Synder's indisposed at the moment."

"Really?" I raised an eyebrow. I'd have to look into that one.

"Are you going to do this job for me?"

"Perhaps."

"What do you want, McColley? You obviously don't plan to do this one for free? You never do."

Feeling hot, I raised the glass to my dry mouth only to find it empty. I'd finished it without noticing. "Oh you know; the usual."

"What? Not fucking Tanjar Karim's Seal again?"

Every muscle in Sempter tensed again just before his suit burst into flames. Then his skin melted, ran as bubbling, putrid liquid over bloody flesh interlaced with thousands of broken shards of ancient glass.

"Of course, Tanjar Karim," I said doing my best to ignore Sempter's temper induced spectacle. "You know me better than that."

Tanjar Karim was one of those great men of history. If he hadn't been a philosopher mage from Fourteenth Century India and one of the Awake, and if Hell's minions hadn't done their utmost to eradicate every historical reference to him known to exist, Karim would have been worshipped today by the Asleep in churches and temples the world over as another Jesus, Mohammad, or Buddha. In his time, Karim had convinced tens of thousands of his followers not to sell their souls to unscrupulous creatures of Hell. So successful was Karim that he almost caused Hell's hierarchy to collapse into anarchy and rebellion.

In desperation, Hell's Overlord (Sempter's boss) tried to make a deal with Karim. The Indian mage agreed to negotiate, for he was cunning, offering up his soul to the eternal torments of the Overlord's torture factories on the proviso that anyone who made a deal with any creature of Hell in his name, who acted selfishly for the good of another person or persons, then their own soul could not be claimed by Hell and would remain forever their own. Hell's Overlord, forgetting that there were plenty of good natured people on this Earth, thought he was the one who would come out on top in this deal. But the number of souls Karim has saved since his death more than six hundred years ago must now number in the hundreds of thousands.

One day, someone, somewhere is going to rescue Karim's soul. The Mortal Awake everywhere owe him big time, me included.

"McColley, forget Karim's Seal. I could offer you magic like you could never imagine. I could make you more powerful than Synder."

That was the second mention of my nemesis. I felt that something might have happened to Synder that I hadn't yet heard about, and this worried me.

I said, "You think I'd risk my soul for something so minor?"

Snarling, the demon didn't answer while his naked flesh crackled like slices of burning bacon. He would attempt any form of trickery to obtain a soul like mine, a mage who essentially worked as a private investigator for magical entities and Awake humans the world over. But I was never going to give him that chance. No bargain is ever worth the price of eternal torture and damnation.

"Very well," Sempter said, seeing that he was never going to win this argument, "how do you wish to use Karim's Seal?"

"To save a soul. What else?"

He snorted flames. "A soul for a soul. Whose soul?"

"No one I know to save at the moment, so I'll have to take a raincheck."

He grimaced through eyes without eyelids and grumbled through a clenched mouth without lips. "You have a deal then, McColley. Just find her soul—and quickly."

"Before you go Sempter, I need something of her to find her with." I pointed to the dead body they had brought with them.

Without instruction, the armoured demon took his cleaver to the corpse's hand, severing it with enough force to embed the rusted tip into my wooden floorboards, adding another soiling mark. With a hard yank, he pulled the blade free and then used the weapon to flick the bloody hand at me.

I didn't bother to catch the severed remains. If the dismembered hand contained anything harmful, it would not have been able to pass through the protective circle. So I let it hit the wall behind me, slide wetly down the wall leaving a smear of fresh blood before it hit the floor, then splattering crimson droplets across the room from the impact.

"Actually, just some of her hair would have been enough."

Again without instruction, the ogre swung his cleaver a second time. I looked up from the fallen hand just fast enough to see him flick a clump of bloody hair at my face, which I caught with ease.

"And what's her name?"

"Yvonne Adams, of London," snorted Sempter.

And then they were gone, shimmering into the portal that vanished like a heat mirage dancing in a desert.

Quickly the temperature dropped and the smell of sulphur lessened, and I was left with a name, a clump of hair, a severed hand, and a job to do.

II

With Sempter and his posse gone, I did a little cleaning, which included disposing of the hand with magic, and then took a shower. Afterwards, I dressed in my favourite two-piece suit and open-necked shirt and packed my laptop, travel case, and enough changes of clothes for a week. Then I magicked ten thousand Pounds Sterling into my bank account and credit cards.

It was nearly dawn when took a taxi to Sydney International Airport. At the departures terminal, I collected my one-way business class ticket to London via Hong Kong, also magicked into existence.

Only when I was in the air did I relax and take stock of my situation.

If I had a choice, I wouldn't normally work for demons, being the disgusting, immoral, depraved creatures that they are. But if I'm not useful to them, then they'll find a reason to do away with me. It's that simple. It's why I took the case.

Human mages, also known as the Mortal Awake, offend supernatural creatures like Sempter. We are like children in their adult world where they make all the rules and control all sources of magic. I am not magical in myself; I have to find magical energy to use it. A demon, or a vampire, werewolf, or a faerie for that matter, they are magic personified. When we mages use magic, we're essentially stealing a little of their essence and then destroying that essence to create our own wonders. Naturally, the supernatural don't like this.

On a more primordial level, demons regularly kill on a whim, often for distraction from the constant pains and discomforts they all suffer. The glass sown into Sempter's flesh is a minute component of his torment, for he continually suffers a multitude of tortures I will never understand.

Higher ranking demons like Sempter, however, have learnt self-control. Although such demons could torture me for a period of time on Earth, such pleasure is only ever finite. Similarly, they would have to inflict controlled techniques so as not to kill me too quickly. But if they can secure my soul in Hell where it is impossible for anyone to die, or even fall unconscious or asleep, even when dissected into a thousand pieces, there I could be tortured non-stop for eternity using whatever corrupted techniques they could imagine. Sempter and his kind wait in hope to inflict that kind of pain on fresh souls because fresh souls scream and beg more than any other.

So while I ensure Hell's hierarchy require my skills, I also never ask for anything for myself in return and follow the philosophy of Tanjar Karim. It's not like I need money or any other material reward. As a mage, I use magic to create the wealth I require when I need it. I pay only in the sense that I have to work for the creatures that are the source of my magic.

So twenty-four hours later, after a good sleep on the aeroplane, I was settled into an upmarket hotel in the heart of London and ready for the next step in my investigation.

I could have teleported myself to England and avoided the discomforts of a long flight, but there are costs if I do that. Despite the fact that such magic requires too many unwholesome deals with supernatural entities, more importantly perhaps, overt magic draws too much attention. If I cast subtle incantations, generally no one will notice, but if I dematerialise in Australia and suddenly turn up in England, then that does get attention, from Asleep authorities and magically entities alike.

I did use a strand of Yvonne's hair to cast a spell to find the location of her soul, but that turned up nothing, which was worrying in itself. Either she had hidden it extremely well, it had been destroyed, or more likely, it was no longer on this Earth.

After a quick search on Facebook, I discovered that Yvonne Adams was a student at the University of London's main campus completing her final year of veterinary science. It wasn't difficult to find the news reports that she was still missing, and that the London police still had no leads.

Since Yvonne apartment wasn't listed in the telephone directories, I found it by using magic, by throwing a London street directory into the air to see what page it opened to when it landed. Then I dropped a pin entwined with another strand of her hair onto that page and noted where it struck.

"I'm sorry to ask this of you," I said to the landlord when I arrived at Yvonne's last place of residency. I showed her my magicked private investigators licence and the hefty woman read its detail. "Yvonne's parents are worried to death about her. You'd be worried, too, wouldn't you, if your child was missing?"

The middle-aged lady couldn't help but nod in sympathetic agreement.

"Now that the police have given up, Michael and Helen's only hope is that I might find Yvonne." (This is technically true, even if Yvonne's parents have never met me.)

"I don't know," responded the tired woman. The landlord had eaten too much fatty food in her day to have any shape left to her or give her any cause to feel energetic about anything, even a murdered tenant. "The police were very clear that no one was to go inside." With effort, she pointed to the crime scene tags taped across the door.

I handed her another of my magicked creations. "Ah, but I have a permission slip, if you will."

As she read the faked letter from Scotland Yard, her brows met betraying that she was confused by the legal jargon, which was my intention. She was not confident enough to say she didn't understand or that she needed to make a call to verify it, so I was waved inside. "Just don't touch anything."

"Of course," I said when put my hand to my heart, gave a slight bow. "Thank you."

Inside, I shut the door behind me and found myself alone with the last spiritual presence of Yvonne Adams on this Earth. The room felt very sad, but oddly, there was no anger, no rage, not even a desire for vengeance.

Apart from the obvious signs of violence in the lounge area, complete with dried blood sprayed across the walls—a detail the police had not yet realised to the public—the apartment was otherwise conspicuously tidy.

I checked to find fresh food in the refrigerator and enough utensils to prepare home cooked meals. There was no meat in the freezer and only vegan cookbooks.

Yvonne's shelves were lined with textbooks on animal anatomy, physiology, and diseases, popular non-fiction titles on the state of the environment, the ethics of genetic engineering, books on animal rights, and travel guides to Costa Rica, Ecuador, and Madagascar.

There were many photographs of her with what I assumed were her parents and others with another man near her age who might have been her lover. When I spotted the family resemblance, I guessed he was her brother. Yvonne looked both happy and sad in their most prominent picture, while the brother looked haggard and withdrawn, with eyes like sunken grey pits.

I decided that a vegan who's interested in ethics and the plight of the world, and is obviously loved, is not the kind of person to get mixed up with illicit drugs, especially not Hell's Elixir. I guessed it was the brother who was shooting up and was a dealer, and it was he who had first been lured in the machinations of Sempter's criminal syndicate.

Had Yvonne tried to rescue her brother from an ever-downward spiralling fate, not realising exactly who, or what, she was going up against?

I felt sorry for Yvonne in that moment. She didn't deserve to be murdered by Sempter and his thugs. She didn't deserve to have her wonderful, meaningful life taken from her so suddenly and so violently.

Yet I still had a feeling that I was missing something important. How was it that her soul could not be found? The answer had to lie here somewhere.

It's damn near impossible to hide a soul on Earth. The only plausible answer to that question now is that it was hidden in another dimension where Hell can't reach it, but which one?

Not seeing anything obvious to guide me, I withdrew a bag of marbles from my laptop bag and scattered them on the floor. They were a gift I had acquired as payment from a rather self-centred faerie I had once done a job for, but that is another story.

A first the marbles rolled in random directions, into the bathroom and bedroom and everywhere else without leaving the apartment. After a few moments of busy exploring, they began to congregate, and within another minute, they had gathered at a blank corner of the wall. I was confused, at first, until they started climbing. Then I saw the heating duct and the missing screws on the vent.

I dropped the bag and the marbles fell to the floor with it, before rolling back into their home.

I pulled away the vent grill, and I saw what I was looking for: a book on the occult circa 1930s entitled *Defensive Magicks for the Cabalistic Sorcerer.* The yellowed pages turned easily enough, and I soon found a book mark. That page opened to a symbol partially resembling a cross but was actually more like a whirlpool or a tunnel.

I read on. Several words leap out at me immediately: homunculi, soul boxes, and unicorn blood tattoos.

I felt sick when I realised what Yvonne had done.

Two hours later, I was on an aeroplane bound for Nigeria.

III

Ask anyone who has been to Lagos, Awake or Asleep, and they'll tell you it is the worst city on Earth. It's crowded, hot, and muggy, and these are the city's most endearing features. The pollution crawls on your skin. Violent crime is a national pastime. A foreigner driving in the twenty-four-hour rush hour is offered the same odds of survival as playing Russian roulette. I came to Africa's most populous country only because there is nowhere else on Earth that would get me answers, and into other dimensions, faster.

Unfortunately, I arrived later than I intended, knowing that night is when the city is most dangerous.

At the airport, I used magic to find the most reputable taxi and then covered the rusted contraption with more protective wards than there are spines on a cactus demon.

"Where to man?" asked the driver through a mouth of yellowed teeth.

"Club Abiku, Ikoyi Island, you know it?"

His grin grew large. "Of course."

I didn't ask and he didn't tell me how he knew the nightclub. Some truths aren't worth knowing.

After a mad rush through the half-lit streets, we arrived at the club around midnight. African Reggae mixed with drum and bass reverberated through its entrance. The two muscles at the door packed semi-automatics and sparking fingertips. They knew me and so let me inside immediately.

The red-hued interior presented a mixture of patrons including crime lords, mercenaries prostitutes, entrepreneurs, backpackers, artists, and Internet spammers. I pushed through the crowd, not wishing for anyone to find reason to stop me because someone here was likely to recall that I owed a favour or two.

Every night here the patrons looked human enough, but about a quarter were supernatural entities, and they worried me the most. The group of agitated mercenaries guzzling beer were lycanthropic leopard men, identified only by their smell and claw-like fingernails. The frenzied kissing and cuddling from a group of smartly dressed Yoruba corporate types were actually vampires feeding on unsuspecting backpackers, young Europeans who looked to be writhing with ecstasy but were actually in a lot of pain.

At the back of the club, I give a quick nod to the barman, Henri, and gestured to a staff-only door. He nodded that it is okay for me to slip out the back, and I did so.

The studio room I entered was familiar—and much quieter. African masks representing most indigenous cultures of the continent, and some from other cultures never seen on this world, were on prominent display, hung besides studded, buckled, and chain decorated leather overcoats. In contrast, the furniture was modern, with smoothed edges and minimalist designs.

The tall, slender-legged woman wearing a shapely, expensive cocktail dress, seated on one of five leather recliner lounges that formed a pentagram in the centre of the studio was focused not on my entrance but on a central brazier expelling thick clouds of black smoke. Her eyes focused on an image shifting in the fumes, but she expelled the scene when she noticed my entrance, before I had time to identify what she was scrying.

"Pre-empting my arrival, Jezebel?"

I sat close to my fellow mage and watched the black cloud settle into a comfortable stream of gently twisting smoke that gathered on the ceiling.

She smiled briefly. "No need, Gordon, I knew you would show two days ago."

"So you know why I'm here, then?"

She shrugged. "I know you've been hired by Sempter."

"Word gets around fast."

"Or maybe you just don't hide what you are up to well enough."

She had me there, so I nodded in agreement. Sometimes, I feel Jezebel Bagayogo is too well informed, but finding information is her talent. That's why she built Club Abiku from the ground up, to draw the supernatural to her to trade with them, battering her visions of the future and glimpses into other dimensions closed off to the rest of us Awake.

"I need your help, Jezebel."

"Of course you do. You never come to my place just to be sociable."

"Well, you do choose to live in Lagos."

She shrugged again. "This favour you want?"

I didn't mind asking Jezebel for help because we are the same. She'd asked favours of me in the past and she'll do so again, and the reverse is just as true. In the balance of all things, we owe each other nothing. So I passed her the photograph of Yvonne and her brother that I lifted from the London apartment. "I need you to find these two, Yvonne and Ike Adams. They're siblings."

"You can't find them yourself?"

"Normally, I would have by now, but they are no longer on Earth."

She took the photograph, focused on it for the better part of a minute, and then said solemnly, "They're both dead."

I nodded because I was expecting this news. "I knew she was. I suspected he was, too, when I couldn't find him."

Jezebel stood, walked to a shelf at the back of her studio were she kept a large black wooden box, opened it, and scooped out a handful of black dust. (I've never been game to ask, but I suspect these are the funeral remains of the cremated dead.) Returning to the flaming brazier, while holding the photograph to her chest, she threw the dust into the flickering light. The dark clouds of black smoke again bellowed forth. Instead of looking for an image in the smoke, her irises rolled upwards out of sight to peer into her frontal lobe while the white of her eyeballs stared at nothing for several minutes. When she did finally return her focus to the studio, she was exhausted and fell into the lounge next to me.

I poured us each a glass of water. She gulped hers down quickly.

"Him," she pointed to the brother while she collected breath. "Ike Adams, he died today."

"Today?"

Her eyes roll back momentarily. "A couple of hours ago, actually. His soul is now in Hell."

I felt insulted. Ike had been alive when Sempter had hired me. Knowing this, I couldn't help feeling that his recent death was a direct outcome of my negotiations with Sempter.

"The boy sold his soul a long time ago, Gordon."

"Then he was a mule shifting Sempter's Elixir."

"And so you have your answer. There is nothing you could have done to save him."

I raised a questioning eyebrow. "What makes you certain I'm here to do that?"

She raised a higher eyebrow. "I may not look it Gordon, but I'm much older than you, more than a hundred years if you want to know. I've learnt a lot of life's lessons in that time that you are still to face. I have experience as a result, and that experience means that sometimes I'll know you better than you know yourself."

Deciding not to indulge this conversation by taking where she wanted it to go, I instead pointed to Yvonne in the photograph, which now lay on the lounge between us. "I came here to learn about her, not me."

"Yvonne is reachable, but you are not going to like where she is."

"Where, Jezebel?"

"The Underworld."

I swallowed hard and felt as if my confidence was fleeing screaming from me, leaving instead an empty space in my gut that could never be filled again. "The Nightmare Dimension, that's worse than Hell. Why would she want to hide her soul there?"

Jezebel grinned and said nothing, as if she was testing me. She did that a lot, and I felt then that she probably was over one hundred years old, even though she barely looked twenty-five.

"Do you know exactly where in the Underworld she hid her soul?" I asked.

"To within a localised area, I do. Everything is so confused in the Underworld, so uncertain, to be more precise."

"But you can get me close enough so that I can find her?"

"That is my power, my friend: to see into the other dimensions, and to other times and places. That is why you came to me."

I leant forward, a little afraid. If Hell can be likened to enduring a major dental procedure performed without aesthetic, then the Underworld is like being trapped in the waiting room beforehand, knowing what is coming.

"You ever visited the Underworld, Gordon?"

I was about to lie and say yes when I shook my head instead. "I haven't been to Hell, either." When she remained silent, I reluctantly added, "Okay, I've seen a lot in this world, but that's it. I've been nowhere else, despite the professional reputation I've been trying to cultivate of late."

She smiled like she had just caught me in a lie. "You are so very young, aren't you, Gordon? What, early thirties?"

I decided not to answer. I already appreciated what she was trying to tell me, what I feared already. Most mages don't make it through their first twenty years (I'd only been practicing magic since I was eighteen). Many mages, before they die, make it worse by first inadvertently offering up their souls to a torment they'll suffer through eternity.

Sometimes, I feel a part of Jezebel wants me to succeed and become successful like her, but another part is just watching with detached curiosity, ready to be bemused by my inevitable fall.

I, of course, wanted to prove her wrong. I want to prove all the Awake wrong.

"The biggest danger in the Underworld, Gordon, is your self. The Nightmare Dimension is the realm where the dead go when they want to forget or are made to forget. No one there knows themselves anymore, or where they are, or why they are so confused. Every moment is like waking from a terrifying dream, but that feeling never ends, ever."

"I'm not going there as one of the dead."

"But everyone there is truly lost, even visitors. You go there even as one of the living, anything you reveal about yourself will immediately be lost to who ever you share that information with. In the Underworld, you face the real danger of losing everything that defines you."

I wiped the sweat from my forehead, an action that did not go unnoticed, which she responded to with another bemused smile.

"The majority of the living who venture into the Underworld never came back. As a visitor, Hell is far safer, more painful perhaps, but much safer."

"I still need to find Yvonne's soul."

She looked sad, disappointed. "Are you doing this for yourself or for Sempter?"

"I need to see her for myself because Sempter will know if I don't—and because I might have let it slip that I can get into dimensions he can't," I added sheepishly.

"Well, you are a fool, then."

"But there is more to it ..." I hesitated, afraid that Jezebel might think me brash and naïve if I lay down too many of my true motives, and then pick them to pieces as she always did.

"Gordon, you've always wanted to play in the big league. You must feel that to return successful from this great expedition into the heart of the Underworld, that these demons will then respect you."

"No!" I shouted, unable to sit still. "That's not the reason at all."

Jezebel laughed at me. "You want to be able to respect yourself, then?"

I refused to answer, too proud and too agitated to do so.

"If you want me to show you the path into the Underworld, I at least need to know the truth to what drives you, otherwise I can't protect you."

I sighed. She had me there. "Yvonne had a book, *Defensive Magicks for the Cabalistic Sorcerer*. She was studying homunculi, soul boxes, and unicorn blood tattoos."

"Ah."

"You see the connection, too? I think she hid her soul where Sempter couldn't find it and that place was the Underworld, in a homunculi or a soul box, which one I'm not yet sure. Yet she bound herself to her hidden soul so she could claim it later, after her mission to rescue her brother was completed. That way Sempter couldn't claim her soul if he caught her. She tattooed linking magical symbols on her body using unicorn blood as ink, symbols I believe will match those painted on the homunculi-slash-soul box."

"Your argument makes sense. Demons cannot see the blood of unicorns. They wouldn't know what she had done."

"I didn't get to properly see Yvonne's body when Sempter brought it too me, but I'm sure those tattoos would have shown me exactly where to find her. That's why I had to come to you."

Jezebel formed a cage with her thin fingers. "That still doesn't explain why you want to find her. In the Underworld, now that she is dead on Earth, she won't remember anything about what she did or why she is there."

"She's an innocent, Jezebel. She tried to free her brother from Sempter's influence and corruption. Ike probably got himself into his own mess, perhaps he deserves to be in Hell, but not her."

"She's not in Hell, she's—"

"You know what I mean."

Jezebel stared at me. When she said nothing, I guessed she was waiting for me to say more. She wanted me to work all this out for myself.

"Sempter only wants me to find her soul. There was nothing discussed about me not helping Yvonne."

The Nigerian shook her head. "I've only lived as long as I have, Gordon, because I never played games as dangerous as the games you like to play."

I stood, tired of this conversation.

"I know how you talk to Sempter," she said urgently. "You're arrogant around him. Don't think he hasn't noticed. He may be ignoring your attitude for the time being, but he is playing you, biding his time. He'll get his revenge. He wants to see you fall. He'll make sure you do."

"Are you going to help me? Lead me to Yvonne?"

She stood, took a leather coat from the wall, and opened it so that I could slip my arms inside. I did so only reluctantly. Then she buckled the various studded belts, chains and hooks tightly until I resembled a walking bondage display case.

"You will need to be disguised."

"In this?"

She passed me the accompanying wooden African mask. Its beady circular eye slits and mouth were permanently etched with o-shaped expressions of surprise. "You need to hide everything that identifies you."

My trembling hands touched the wooden contraption, felt its coldness.

"You look nervous, afraid even, and I don't blame you. You don't have to do this, Gordon."

I took the mask. "Actually, I do."

IV

Five levels below Club Abiku, far deeper than the stinking, ineffective sewers of Lagos, and well below the low tide line of the Atlantic Ocean, I found myself in a secret chamber complete with muddy floors and dirty walls, and a pit at my feet dug from the stenchful earth. Because the pit was obscured in shadowed, I had no idea how deep it was, and Jezebel wanted me to jump into it.

Anything that identified me—driver's licence, passport, money, credit cards, keys and so forth were locked in an imp-safe back in Jezebel's studio. My only possessions were my clothes, the leather bondage overcoat, and the African mask now strapped to my face like I was about to attend some hideous masquerade party. In my right hand, I held a crystal vial sloshing with pure water. In my left, I held the photograph of Yvonne. The half containing Ike had been ripped off, and it, too, was upstairs with the rest of my possessions.

Jezebel, next to me, whispered in my ear. "Remember Gordon, when you want or need to return, smash that vial against your face."

"Won't it cut me?"

"Wearing that mask, you'll be protected."

"And the photograph, it will take me to Yvonne?"

"Yes, but don't show it to anyone down there, otherwise you could forget who she is, and why you are there. If you forget the all important 'why', you won't make it back home."

I looked into the pit that I could only imagine as being endless. "Will this really take me to the Underworld?"

"How else do you propose to reach the Nightmare Dimension? Fly? Take a bus?"

I gulped. I wasn't sure I could do this now, not when the reality of what I was about to do was staring back at me, like a gigantic all-seeing eye rising out of abyss. "I guess it is called the Underworld after all."

She didn't give me an answer. She pushed me instead, and I fell screaming ...

... and then I was standing in mud up to my knees, uninjured.

The world in which I found myself was dark and cold. I could see a sky, where lightning and rolling black clouds surged beneath the cavernous roof resembling a whole world inverted, seen thousands of metres above me.

At ground level, I was inside a roofless building. Its walls were no farther in any direction than a few metres, and they wiggled. Hundreds of eyes opened and as many tongues lolled. Thousands of naked corpses, as bricks, were pilled one on top of the other to form the walls. The stacked flesh reached about four metres in height whichever direction I stared. The unliving human wall was the internal structure of a labyrinth.

One of the corpses screamed when she saw me. I screamed back.

Another looked surprise, as if waking suddenly, and asked me where he was.

Soon hundreds had woken from a half-sleeping, half-awake state of inaction, to scream, wail, beg, and struggle. But they were all fixed in their places, glued by magic into their own supporting slot of this vast architectural horror.

"Who are you?" one middle-aged man asked. His scalp was raw where he had pulled out all his hair.

"Me, I'm—?" I almost told him my name. I almost gave up that core part of myself to this place, the first step towards the self-destruction that Jezebel had warned me against.

"What is this place?" asked a teenage boy, wide-eyed terror naked on his pasty face.

This time I held my tongue.

"Where is ... um, what was I asking?" said another.

"I don't know my name," said a third.

"How did I get here?"

"What is this place?"

An arm grabbed my elbow. I looked when I didn't want to, to see a child, about ten, tears in her bloodshot eyes, hanging onto me in desperation. "I'm lost," she pleaded. "Can you take me home?"

"Where is home?" I asked, not wanting to, or willing to connect with this fragile girl, but doing so anyway.

"Do I have a home? I'm so cold and afraid."

For a moment, she lost the idea that she was cold and afraid. But then she felt the chill again, and saw where she was, and became terrified all over again, the experience as fresh as it had been the first time.

When she really looked at me and my hideous mask, she screamed with the rest of them.

I could do nothing here, so I marched on, clutching the now crumpled photograph of Yvonne in my hands. I trundled through the muddy passages of the Underworld, letting my instinctive senses guide me. The multitudes of hands, arms, legs, even heads, they kept reaching out to touch, grab, punch, bite and kick me, and all the while I just had to pretend I couldn't see or feel any of them.

My stomach churned and my head pounded. I couldn't be here for much longer and not go insane, not lose myself amongst so much suffering and pain. If I failed here, I would become like them, to experience this horror *ad infinitum*, forever and ever.

After that realisation, I ran and ran until I coughed up torrents of acidic phlegm, until I collapsed and curled into a tightly wound ball.

They wouldn't stop screaming at me, the living wall. They kept asking for my help, accused me of all kinds of horrors, or pulled at my limbs and clothes.

173

When I felt ready again, I ran some more.

After an hour, or perhaps just a few minutes—it was hard to be certain about anything here, including time—I gave up on trying to solve the maze to instead climb up the human wall.

I did so with my eyes shut, pulling on arms and legs and breasts and other bodily appendages, all the while tightly gripping in one hand the torn crumpled photograph and vial of water, should I need either in a hurry.

The dead tried to pull me into them but I kept climbing, using my elbows more often than my hands to lock into the cold, pulseless flesh. I was bitten many times, licked, tickled, poked and groped, until I finally reached the top, and stood on many complaining bodies. I pretended I couldn't hear them and stared out across the macabre spectacle that was the Underworld.

It was worse up here, where so much more could be taken in all at once.

In one direction, the labyrinth vanished into a gulfing darkness. The other disappeared into a vast black expanse of ocean, lapping gently with dark, lifeless waters. Behind the ocean, black craggy mountains resembling bird claws eventually gave way to the vertical cliffs that stretched upwards until it became the cavern. Rain fell into the ocean from a vast tunnel in the roof, until I realised it was not water but the recent dead, dropping from up high in their millions, forever falling into perpetual, time-eradicated, and everlasting undeath.

The only place I could head towards that was distinctive was a temple, forged of stone rubbed smooth by eons of erosion. A light shone from within, a dull, soft blue illumination split into lines by the temple's pillared walls.

For many hours, I marched upon the complaining and screaming bodies of the labyrinth, jumping between one wall and the next when the distances were safe to speed my progress.

Eventually I reached the temple and walked on the first hard surface since my arrival. I took the stone steps two at a time until I entered the inner sanctum of the soul box.

Inside, a young naked woman sat alone, cross-legged in the center, immersed by the blue light. She trembled from both the cold and from her fear. Her eyes were black and haggard. Her skin was as white as ivory and riddled with sores. She had bitten her fingernails and toenails down to the point were each would have been bleeding, had there been any blood left inside her.

Unlike the other unliving corpses I had witnessed, she still had her tattoos, inked in luminous unicorn blood, and I finally understood the source of the eerie blue glow. What I had never understood was how she had first come to be in possession of such a rare commodity, and I probably never would.

"Can you help me?" she asked. "I don't know where I am. I don't know who I am."

She would have been beautiful once, when she was alive.

"Who are you? Have we met before?"

I wanted to tell Yvonne Adams that I would help her, but I didn't.

"I don't want to be alone anymore."

Instead I smashed the vial against my mask ...

... and I was thrashing about in a pool of putrid dank water that smelled like piss. It was in my mouth and eyes, and I screamed pathetically, tearing the mask from my face.

When my shoes connected with solid ground, I stood, spat and coughed, and gagged until I realised that the pit Jezebel had pushed me into was filled with dirty water, barely waist high, and that she was no more than a metre above me.

She reached down her hand, which I readily accepted, and she pulled me up.

"Who are you?" she asked forcefully.

"You know who I am."

"Then tell me."

"Gordon McColley, of course."

She smiled then, and asked many more questions.

I answered them all easily enough until she was convinced I had lost nothing of myself to the Underworld. While I talked, I stripped off the water-soaked coat, only to realise that its surface was now blank. Gone were the decorations, buckles, chains, studs and art motifs that characterised the garment. The mask too was similarly blank. The Underworld had stolen their identities.

"You came back," she sounded surprised.

"I always intended to."

Jezebel looked away, crossed her arms over her waist, a defensive gesture I had never seen her perform before.

"What's bothering you?" I asked. I had been wondering whether I should use overt magic to clean, dry, and de-stench my clothes and skin but decided against it. Cleanliness could always wait. She had something important to tell me.

"No one comes back from the Underworld, no one that I've ever sent anyway."

"But I wasn't really there, not physically at any rate."

"No, but the mind is powerful enough to get you into the worst of any troubles there. You lose your mind in the Nightmare Dimension, then your body dies in this one, and the end result is the same."

We headed upstairs where it was not so dark, dank, and cold. She offered me a shower, which I readily accepted. Afterwards, as I towelled off, she returned my clothes, clean and as good as new.

"I never told you, Gordon," she said later when we sat again in her studio drinking Nigerian beer together. "I've never been to the Underworld, either."

I felt a cold shudder run the entire length of my body. That revelation was a surprise to me. "Yet you sent me there, convinced that I was never coming back?"

"It's not like that."

"No, then how is it?"

She sipped at her beer. "Part of me wanted you to succeed, but if you didn't come back, you would be one problem gone from my life forever."

I stared, disbelieving in what I was hearing.

"I'm a scryer Gordon. Many times I have seen what you were becoming, what you still might become. I don't like what I see. Not many of us mages around the world like it, either."

I took another mouthful of beer, licked my lips before I said, "And?"

"Dealing with demons the way you do, eventually you will be corrupted and you will become just like them."

I felt insulted. "We all have to survive, Jezebel. That's all I'm doing."

"I know in your heart you intend to do good, but you do remind me of someone I once knew a long time ago."

"Who?" I prompted. I was tired of Jezebel slowly feeding me the barest morsels of information purely it seemed, for dramatic effect. "Are we talking about a younger you?"

"No, I'm talking about Synder."

I sneered. "Synder? I'm nothing like him."

"And neither was he, long ago. Sydner, too, started out doing favours for Sempter, just like you are doing now, thinking he could work the arrangement to suit his own objectives. Your enemy is dead by the way, murdered last month in the desert a few hundred kilometres outside of Kalgoorlie."

"Dead? You're joking?"

She shook her head adamantly. "He's in Sempter's torture factories now, and I think Sempter's very pleased about it. That's what the supernatural want from all of us eventually, to control us absolutely in their own realms where they can make all the rules."

I lent back, pressed the beer glass against my forehead. "No wonder you've been so cold and aloof since my arrival."

"But you did come back from the Underworld, Gordon. And something has changed, or could change, depending on what you do next. I've seen it."

"I still need to report to Sempter. You can't pull out of an agreement made with Hell before a conclusion is reached and expect no repercussions."

"Perhaps."

I stood, took my laptop bag and luggage. I'd had enough of her lecturing. "Thank you for your help, Jezebel. Let's hope I can return the favour soon." Furious, I turned to leave.

"Gordon!" she yelled at my back.

I turned, my dark eyes attempting to outstare hers.

"I wanted to tell you. For the first time since we met five years ago, I now think you might actually have what it takes to make it as a mage. You have changed, and for the better."

Grudgingly, I said, "Thank you, Jezebel. That does mean something to me. But it all depends on what I do next, right?"

She finished her beer. "Yes, exactly."

V

Marcus Sempter insisted I meet him at a rather expensive restaurant in the retail heart of St Petersburg. Despite the near zero temperatures, the Neva River being frozen over, the clumps of snow everywhere on the streets, he had also insisted on an outside table overlooking Baroque and Neoclassical buildings dating from the Eighteenth and Nineteenth Century. The setting would have been picturesque to behold had Sempter not brought his own corrupting taint to the scene.

I approached him reluctantly and tightened my overcoat against the chill. He sat outside alone because the weather was too cold for mortals. I noticed he wore a new skin and a new suit, for today he was Japanese. I could tell it was him because of his haughty mannerisms and brazen confidence.

He had ordered a fifty year old French wine and two beef steaks, both rare, but none of these details made me uncomfortable. It was the building across the road from the restaurant, destroyed by a terrorist bomb detonated not fifteen minutes earlier that left me anxious, apprehensive, and not a little terrified.

I saw the corpses on the street first. Then I spied the injured men and women staggering in a daze. Many bled profusely, while some supported broken bones and multiple burns. The injured, at least, were being attended to by the city's ambulance services otherwise I would have felt compelled to lend a hand. The police cordoning off the scene waved me away.

So I sat next to Sempter instead, trembling. He was the only patron still dining, as everyone else had poured outside to gawk at the death scene presented like some surreal movie or late night news feed. Other patrons, I suspected, had discretely disappeared home before they were questioned by the FSB, Russia's Federal Security Service, who would soon be all over the scene.

I did my best not to be sick, or allow my legs to shake, or faint from the shear shock of it all.

"This is your doing," I stated, afraid that my voice would fail me when I spoke.

The nervous waiter immediately placed a cloth napkin over my waist and then poured me a glass of wine, which I could not touch. When I smelt it, I finally vomited on the cobbled stone terrace.

Sempter kept eating.

After I finished expelling my breakfast, the waiter quickly cleaned my mess without utterance.

Sempter meanwhile savoured his wine. "Who can explain the mindset of Chechen rebels these days, to do such a terrible thing?"

I wiped my face with the napkin, unable to get the acidic taste from my mouth. I asked for a glass of water.

Across the road, I saw that the FSB had arrived and were taking control of the situation. I knew they wouldn't bother us. Sempter's connections would see to that.

"Not hungry?" the demon asked while he devoured his bloody steak while ignoring the vegetable side dish that had come with it.

My water arrived, so I sipped it at. "I found Yvonne—"

Sempter raised a finger, silencing me. Without seeing it actual appear, an ancient bladed weapon materialised on the table. Its purpose I immediately recognised.

"Before we discuss the outcomes of your assignment, McColley, you will need to yield to this truth blade."

I rolled my eyes as I placed my right hand on the table, palm down and fingers spread. Sempter then plunged the blade into my flesh, pinning me to the wooden surface.

I felt no pain, and no blood or injury was presence. Such is the nature of a truth blade: excruciating pain and crippling injuries would follow only if I told a lie.

Sempter returned to his meal and his wine. He had successfully ignored the carnage across the street, but I knew he was secretly enjoying every second of it as much as he was enjoying my displeasure at having to witness it.

"Did you find Yvonne Adams' soul?"

"Yes," I said quickly. Monosyllabic answers were always best as they were less likely to be open to interpretation and pain.

"Then where is she, McColley?"

"In the Underworld."

"Oh."

I could see he was disappointed. Yvonne had chosen well to hide her soul in the Nightmare Dimension, for it was the one realm that demons never liked to enter. Like the rest of us, there they could easily forget who they were and become just one more soul trapped in an eternal, forgetful afterlife.

"I'm impressed. I didn't think you had what it takes to enter and leave that realm successfully. You saw her yourself?"

"Yes."

He paused to consume another mouthful of the steak he seemed to be particularly enjoying. "How did she manage to hide her soul from me?"

Now I had a problem. I couldn't answer this question simply, so every word had to be chosen carefully. "I believe she tattooed magical symbols on herself that temporarily hid her soul in the Underworld. I believe this was to protect her soul while she infiltrated your organisation in order to rescue her brother."

I looked at my hand. There was no blood and no pain. I believed what I was telling him, which was good. That was the problem with truth blades: if I was lying to myself, it would know.

"How did I not notice these tattoos?" Sempter asked.

"The ink she used was unicorn blood."

"How the fuck did she get hold of that?"

"I have no idea."

"You'd like to though, wouldn't you? A mage with a supply of unicorn blood, even a miniscule amount, would be very powerful."

I said nothing. He hadn't asked me a question.

Sempter waited a few moments then yanked the blade from my hand, leaving me uninjured. I rubbed my hand anyway, imagined hurt there as I held it close to my chest.

Across the road, ambulance crews were attending the injured and covering the dead with bloodied sheets. The FSB were conducting interviews, some with sobbing onlookers who were probably family members or friends of the dead and maimed.

"Well, at least she's in the Underworld." He looked up from his food, caught my stare. "Scare you did it, McColley, what you saw in the Nightmare Dimension?"

Last time we met, I had been cocky with Sempter. This time, I couldn't be anything that resembled confidence. This assignment was no longer just a complex game to amuse my sense of ego. Jezebel Bagayogo had understood me completely: I was on the path to becoming another of Sempter's monstrous henchman. This meeting clinched the truth for me.

While Sempter kept eating, I finally found the courage to say, "We agreed as payment you would release one soul from Hell."

Sempter wouldn't look at me when he said, "Fair enough. Which soul did you have in mind?"

"Tanjar Karim."

He laughed so loud I thought we would draw attention from the onlookers at the bombing site, thinking that he was laughing at them. Thankfully, we were ignored. I don't believe I could have handled the embarrassment on top of every other emotion I was bombarded with right just then.

"That was your plan all along, McColley? You sure you're not getting something out of it? Think of the prestige you'll gather about yourself if it is learnt that you freed Karim."

I said nothing. I just stared feeling in the depth of my churning stomach that this was the moment of choice Jezebel had warned me of, where I could take the right path—or the wrong path—that would define me forever.

"Yes, I'm certain."

Sempter put down his bloody knife and fork, wiped his mouth delicately with his napkin. "First of all, I don't lay claim to Karim's soul. That privilege belongs to the Overlord."

"But you could make it happen, if you wanted to."

"I could extend my influence, but it would have to be worthwhile, for me."

Without me seeing, the truth blade was at my throat, or more precisely, inside it. Sempter's other hand gripped the back of my neck and held me immobile with his unhuman strength. My whole body went rigid with fear.

"I'll tell you what, McColley. You do two things for me. The first is that you promise me your soul for eternity when you die. The second is that you then tell a lie. Any lie, I don't care, whatever you want. If you can do both those things before I count to five, I promise I'll do my best to convince the Overlord to let Karim's soul go free. One ..."

He stared at me, waited for my answer. I stared at him, said nothing.

"Two ... Three ..."

I had a strong urge to pee. Only the greatest effort on my behalf stopped me from doing so.

"Four ... Five." He withdrew the blade and returned to his eating. "I knew you were too gutless to do it."

I felt defeated, defiled. I couldn't bear to be in this place of death and cruelty a moment longer, but I had to, just a few minutes more. I had to at least try and make good of this situation.

"Then Ike Adams' soul. I want you to release him."

He waved his hand in a gesture like a stage magician about to make a rabbit appear out of a box. "It's done."

"You killed him, though," I said accusingly, "after we last met, knowing that I'd have to choose him."

Sempter smile was thin and measured. "Adams was nothing to me, a mere cog in my operations, so I feel no loss here."

Without warning, I suddenly needed to throw up again, or tried to because my stomach was already empty. All the while the waiter hovered over me with a mop and a bucket. I wouldn't look at him, or Sempter, or the carnage. The scene was too surreal to feel any grip on the reality of what was unfolding around me.

"Where's Ike's soul now?" I managed to say when I managed to sit up again, and when the waiter had disappeared.

Sempter shrugged. "Who knows?"

"In Heaven?"

He laughed again, but not as loudly as before. "I don't know of anyone who knows if Heaven is real or not, not even the Overlord himself. I think you humans just made it up so you wouldn't all go mad without hope."

"So where then? Where is Ike now?"

"Not in Hell, McColley. That's all you asked for. That's all I'm giving."

VI

I found my own path back to the Underworld easily enough. Once you've been to another dimension, you leave a trace there, no matter how small, and so it's easier to return. This time, I used my own magic, projected my ghostly form via a magical conduit, created through a candle flame that I timed to burn out in exactly five minutes. That was all the time I was willing to risk for a second visit.

I returned directly to Yvonne Adams' soul box temple. She remained there alone as I had left her, curled up and terrified, shivering and pale. She had been crying, and her eyes were red.

"Who are you?" she asked me.

"I can't tell you that," I said from behind my full-faced masquerade mask and my outfit of black clothing. I stared down at the piece of paper I had brought with me, that said in very friendly and bright lettering at the top: KEEP READING THIS TO HER, BUT DON'T TELL HER ANYTHING ABOUT YOURSELF.

"I can tell you that your name is Yvonne Adams, and you are from London, England, Earth."

"What was that?"

"What was what?"

"You told me my name. Why?"

"Did I?" I saw a note before me, read the next line under the friendly letters that said: KEEP READING THIS TO HER, BUT DON'T TELL HER ANYTHING ABOUT YOURSELF.

"Don't tell me anything that I tell you," I repeated. "You need this information, if you are to have any chance of escaping."

"Escaping? Where am I?"

"What was that?"

I was confused. I was staring at a naked woman who was shivering alone in the Underworld, with a note in my hand that said: KEEP READING THIS TO HER, BUT DON'T TELL HER ANYTHING ABOUT YOURSELF.

"It says here that I'm to tell you that you died, and that your soul is trapped in the Underworld."

"Where?"

"Where is what?"

Whoever this naked woman was before me, she seemed pleased to have heard what I just told her. I knew I had told her something, but I couldn't remember what. Her back had straightened a little. Her eyes and face had gained a little colour.

I saw a note in my hands, and it said: KEEP READING THIS TO HER, BUT DON'T TELL HER ANYTHING ABOUT YOURSELF.

"You are protected by magical tattoos inked with unicorn blood," I read. "While it is no guarantee, it might be enough to protect you while you escape the Underworld." I looked up at her. "What place is this?"

She was about to say something, then changed her mind. "You were going to read me something."

"I was?" I looked at the note in my hand, which said in very friendly letters: KEEP READING THIS TO HER, BUT DON'T TELL HER ANYTHING ABOUT YOURSELF.

"It says here that your brother, Ike Adams, is dead, but his soul is no longer in Hell. It is free again."

I looked up, saw a rather attractive, naked shivering woman seated before me in a very cold temple, and I had no idea where we were, or why. I held a note in my hand. I read it and it said in very friend letters: KEEP READING THIS TO HER, BUT DON'T TELL HER ANYTHING ABOUT YOURSELF.

"Why am I reading this to you? Why can't I tell you anything about myself?"

"Don't!" she yelled, holding out a hand as if to stop me from coming any closer. "Tell me what I need to do? Tell me what you wrote down."

There were lots of blank spaces on the top half of the page where I felt there should have been writing, so I read what was on the lower half. "You need to escape, and to do that you need every edge I can offer ..."

... I think this is the gist of my conversation with Yvonne Adams, but I will never really know. The truth is I can't remember any of our conversation.

I only know that I found myself in my guest room, confused, dressed all in black wearing a ridiculous mask and not sure where I had been and what I was doing. There was a candle before me and it had just burnt out. Then I noticed the scrawled written notes in my own handwriting, thousands of them stuck to every surface of my Sydney flat.

They told me that I once worked for a particularly nasty high-ranking demon named Marcus Sempter, who was my enemy now and he would be after my soul. I had been hoping to save a young woman who hadn't deserved to die, and that she certainly hadn't deserved to be trapped forever in the Underworld, a nightmarish dimension where the souls incarcerated there had forgotten everything there was to know about themselves ...

In fact, I wrote everything that you have been reading here. You know as much as I do about this last week of my life.

All I hope for now is that I'm the person Jezebel Bagayogo wanted me to be, that I've taken the right path, not the wrong one.

And that the soul of Yvonne Adams might make it home one day.

ROADSIDE MEMORIALS

Joseph Nassise

A DRUNK DRIVER KILLED MY FRIENDS!
So read the sign now standing at the corner of Thunderbird and Main. It stood in almost the exact spot where Martin had pulled the bodies of two teenagers from the smashed wreckage of their yellow Nissan Xterra just two days before, shouting its message out to any and all who passed by. Around it was a haphazard collection of candles, flowers and photographs, laid out in commemoration of the lives that had ended so abruptly there.

"Freakin' morbid, that," his partner Giles said, but Martin barely noticed. He couldn't take his eyes off the memorial, stunned by the size of it. It had to be six feet square and the accident wasn't even 48 hours old yet. Where the hell had all this stuff come from? It was disturbing, uncanny even, how swiftly such memorials could appear. Back home in Philadelphia, he'd never heard of the practice, had never laid eyes on even one such marker, but here in the southwest they were practically guaranteed to show up whenever there was a fatal accident. They sprang up overnight like ravenous weeds. He wasn't certain where the tradition had come from or what those who created them hoped to achieve, he just knew that being around them made him uncomfortable. It didn't matter where the accident had taken place—back roads, city streets or the long stretches of road bisecting the desert—time and time again he would see them there, like soldiers standing solitary vigil in the darkness.

"... don't see what good it does."

"What?" he asked, as the marker swept behind them in the distance and he belatedly realized his partner was still speaking.

Giles waved a hand toward the rear of the ambulance. "Those stupid memorials. Those folks are dead, right? What good do those things do them?" He snorted in disgust. "Besides, I'd rather have folks visiting me in

184

the cemetery than in the middle of nowhere. Who wants to be reminded they'd died in the middle of a freakin' car wreck?"

Martin nodded, turning away from the window as the memorial slipped away behind them in the distance, but he wasn't really listening. It had been a long night; three car accidents, a knife fight, and two heart attacks, the most activity they'd had in one night in weeks. *And we aren't even halfway through our shift.* All he wanted to do was get back to the hospital and crash out for awhile before the next call came in.

At 36, Martin Jones was already tired of his so-called life. He spent his days sleeping, his nights cleaning up the messes left behind by other people's mistakes. Gone was the idealism that had gotten him into the EMT business in the first place, washed away by too many stupid accidents, too many senseless beatings, and more than his fair share of horrible car wrecks. It didn't help that his days were other people's nights.

Tonight was worse than usual, however. He'd felt an odd sense of unease all evening and the weirdness surrounding that roadside shrine didn't help. It was almost as if he could sense something, something looming just beyond the horizon; at any moment he knew it was going to come charging in to swallow everything whole.

It wasn't a comfortable feeling.

As Giles droned on, Martin leaned back in his seat and wearily closed his eyes. Tonight's shift couldn't end fast enough as far as he was concerned.

The call came in around two a.m. A tractor trailer rig had jackknifed out on I-17, taking out three vehicles before colliding with a bridge embankment. Traffic was stopped in both directions for miles. Ambulances from three different hospitals had been called in, including their own.

Martin was behind the wheel for this trip. Switching back and forth halfway through their shift kept them both from going crazy with the redundancy of the job and tonight he was glad for the change. He couldn't seem to get his mind off all the roadside memorials they passed, especially that large one he'd seen back at the beginning of their shift, and staring out the passenger window as they drove around all night wasn't helping. He'd never really paid much attention to the things before now, but tonight they haunted him. It was simply amazing how many of the damn things were out there. One hell of a lot of people where dying on these streets, that was for sure. At least driving would keep his attention focused on the road and not on those weird little shrines and the deaths they represented.

When they arrived at the crash site, they were updated on the casualty list. Eight dead, three wounded, and a truck driver with nothing but a scratch. Martin had long since stopped being surprised at the vagrancies of life. It was just the way things were. Still, he couldn't help but feel sorry for the lives that had ended so abruptly there. All those unrealized dreams.

Giles chatted up the female driver next to them while they all waited for the firefighters to cut the bodies loose from the wrecks and call them in. Judging from the condition of some of the vehicles, it was going to be awhile.

Three cups of coffee and two hours later, they were finished. Having been the last to arrive, they were the last to be loaded and most of the crews at the scene had already left by the time they got the body stowed away in the back, ready for transport to the morgue.

As they pulled onto the main drag a repetitive thumping could be heard from the right rear side of the ambulance. When Giles got out to investigate, he found a six inch piece of steel sticking out of the rear passenger tire. Cursing a blue streak, Giles prepared to change it while Martin went to tell the remaining officers they were going to be a few more minutes.

It shouldn't have been a big deal; after all, the guy in the back didn't have any place to be anytime soon. But something about the evening, something about the call, had Martin spooked. He found himself nervously drumming his fingers on the dashboard and gritting his teeth the way he did when he knew he'd screwed up. It was totally unlike him and that's what made him nervous. Something was wrong.

He could feel it, taste in the air.

That sense of impending doom.

He felt like he had a hundred pairs of eyes on him and several times he found himself searching the darkness around them, looking for persons unknown.

More than once he snarled at Giles to hurry up, only to receive blistering waves of swearing in return. Finally he couldn't take it any more. He jumped out of the truck, pushed his partner aside and finished tightening the bolts on the tire himself. He didn't know what was wrong; all he knew was that he wanted to be out of there as quickly as possible.

Unwilling to even take the extra time to properly stow the spare, Martin simply threw it in back next to the body. Climbing back into the driver's seat, he gunned the engine and pulled onto the road.

He made the mistake of looking back, however, as they left the scene.

Behind them, in the gray light of the early morning, he saw a figure dash out of the woods near the crash site, drop something on the spot where the tractor trailer had been, and then disappear back they way they had come.

Without understanding what he had just seen, Martin knew that the strange figure had been the cause of his unease.

And suddenly he desperately wanted to understand.

He slammed on the brakes.

Giles bounced off the dashboard as the ambulance skidded to a stop, not yet having had a chance to buckle in. "What the fuck?" he swore, but his question was left unanswered as Martin threw open the door and ran back toward the scene.

"Martin? What are you doing, Martin?" Giles called after him.

But Martin only had eyes for what was ahead. Even before he could see it clearly, he knew what it was.

A small white cross.

This one was of the Celtic variety, with the center point wrapped in a large circle. It was still swaying slightly from the force that had been used to plant it in the ground.

The sight of it sent the hairs on the back of his neck crawling.

The body hadn't even left the scene and someone was already erecting a marker on the spot?

What the hell was that all about?

He walked over and squatted beside it. It appeared to be fashioned of a couple of thin, wooden slats, like the kind that made up packing crates. The circle appeared to have been cut from similar material. The whole thing was painted white and from the looks of it, it had probably been done with a cheap can of spray-paint.

In other words, it was perfectly normal looking.

So why did it creep him out so much?

He didn't know.

He reached out a hand to touch it, but stopped short of doing so.

Very slowly, he stood up and backed away from the cross, in the same manner one would move away from a suddenly snarling dog.

When he was several feet away, he turned and jogged back to the truck, feeling like he'd just narrowly escaped a danger he didn't understand.

Behind him, the eyes of the living and the dead watched him leave.

Martin couldn't get the events of the previous night out of his thoughts, so he called in sick, determined to get to the bottom of what he'd seen. He'd made arrangements to borrow his brother's black Trans-Am and the car was waiting for him in the driveway a little after nine. Like the car, he, too, was dressed in black, hoping the dark clothing would help him blend in better and avoid being seen.

He spent an hour hanging around in the local Safeway parking lot, listening to the battery-operated police scanner he bought earlier that afternoon, and then he got lucky. A two-car accident on Highway 60. An elderly lady had lost control and smashed into another vehicle driven by a young woman. The girl was in critical condition and was being removed from the wreckage, the older woman was already dead.

That was all Martin needed to hear. The Trans-Am's tires smoked as he peeled out of the parking lot and raced for the scene.

Traffic was stopped a quarter mile from the wreck, a police officer rerouting traffic to the nearest off-ramp. Martin pulled over to the side of the road, parked the car in the breakdown lane and approached the officer on foot. He flashed his identification, saying he'd been called in to fill the right-hand seat on an ambulance that had gone out with only the driver, and managed to scam his way through.

As he neared the crash scene, he slowed and looked around. Several emergency vehicles were parked nearby, but no one seemed to be looking at him. When he was sure he wouldn't be seen, he jogged up the embankment and pushed his way into the scrub brush lining the noise barrier at the top. Once out of site, he continued moving until he was immediately above the scene itself.

From here, he could keep watch on everything going on.

And he could get a better look at the mysterious cross bearers.

If they showed up.

Scratch that. When they showed up.

They'd be here.

Martin settled in for a long wait.

From his position on the hill, he watched the ambulance load up the injured girl and the older woman's body and then drive off just shy of an hour later. The tow trucks and the police were there for another half hour and then they, too, left. Seeing their blue flashers fade into the distance, Martin moved into a crouch, ready to make his way down the hill to confront anyone that arrived.

It was good that he did. Only a few moments passed before a figure scuttled out of the ditch slightly further down the road, near the spot where the elderly woman had died.

Martin burst out of the shrubs and charged down the hill, intent on catching whoever it was and discovering just what was going on.

He closed the distance swiftly and the other didn't hear him coming. As he drew closer he could see that the figure was clothed in dirty robes and in its hand it held a white cross, like the one he'd seen at the accident site last night. As it raised the cross over its head, preparing to sink it into the earth, Martin snatched it out of its hands.

"What the hell are you doing?" he cried.

The other whirled around and Martin had his first good look.

What he saw sent his heart stuttering in his chest.

The thing had no face.

Only the slightest sense of features existed, as if it were an unfinished canvas given life before its time. Its eyes were shadowed indentations beside the nub of a nose and where its mouth should have been was only a flat expense of grey flesh.

"Holy shit!" Martin yelped, stepping back. He couldn't believe what he was seeing.

The creature rose to its full height, an odd tittering sound emanating from it. Martin had the disturbing notion that the thing was laughing at him and maybe it was. But where was the laughter coming from if the thing had no mouth?

Beyond a doubt, Martin knew he'd made a mistake.

Some things were best left alone.

This, this thing, was certainly one of them.

He had no idea what he had stumbled into, but he knew it was time he got the hell out of there. He turned to run and found a second, similar creature standing a few feet behind him, blocking his escape back up the hill.

Martin hadn't even heard it approach.

From the darkness around it, several more of the creatures suddenly appeared.

Martin stumbled away from them, out into the road, his hands held out defensively before him, praying they wouldn't follow.

A weird, haunting cry rose on the wind and the leader took a step toward him, causing Martin to back up ever farther.

That was when the delivery van roared around the corner, silhouetting Martin in its headlights where he stood by the side of the road. The driver slammed on the brakes, but it was too late. His rearview mirror clipped Martin on the shoulder and tossed him aside like a rag doll.

Martin never took his eyes off the creatures watching him. Their odd, featureless faces were the last things he saw as he slammed against the ground and the darkness closed in around him.

He woke up in a hospital bed, a swatch of bandages wrapped around his skull. His doctor told him it was only a minor concussion, but he'd have to stay a few days while they made certain there was no internal damage. Martin had no recollection of the events leading up to the accident and the doctor said it was unlikely he would ever recover more than bits and pieces of those few hours, but if that was the worst of it, Martin felt he couldn't complain.

Late in the afternoon of the third day they discharged him with a prescription for some codeine and orders to get more rest before trying anything strenuous. His boss gave him the week off without argument and he spent it lying around the house, recuperating.

The ride into the office went without incident and it wasn't long before he was down in the locker room, joking around with the other EMTs. Giles insisted on driving for the night, something Martin didn't blame him for, and the two of them settled back into their easy routine.

Their first call came in fairly quickly; an elderly man over at the Northside Rest Home had breathed his last. Martin and Giles were dispatched to pick him up and bring him in.

Northside was on the other side of town, but since they weren't in any hurry Giles took the scenic route. He wound his way through the city streets, taking as many of the back roads as he could to avoid the traffic that had fled the construction on the expressway.

Martin glanced out the window as they drove by the scene of an accident they had worked the month before and froze.

A white memorial cross now stood on the spot, draped with ribbons and flowers.

The sight of it terrified him.

The light turned green and Giles drove off, but Martin couldn't rid himself of the haunting image of that cross and the unexplained fear it stirred within him. As they passed others, his fear, unease, and disgust only seemed to grow. By the time they reached the nursing home, Martin was all but useless, cowering in the corner by the door, refusing to look anywhere but at the floorboards beneath his feet. He would not get out of the truck and so Giles was forced to handle the call on his own.

On the ride back to the hospital, Martin chose to sit in the back with the corpse, preferring the company of the dead to having to lay eyes on another of those crosses.

When they returned to base, Martin excused himself, apologized to Giles and his supervisor, and went home sick for the rest of the evening.

Martin spent the next day turning the events of the previous evening over and over again in his mind. He'd seen such roadside shrines more times than he could count. They'd never bothered him before.

What had changed?

He didn't know.

What he did know was that the crosses unnerved him. They frightened him. He sensed instinctively that they were dangerous, but wasn't able to put just why into words. All he knew was that they shouldn't, couldn't, remain.

Despite his fear, he felt driven to get rid of them.

Called to even.

Doing so proved much harder than he expected, however, when he tried to do just that later that night. The crosses were sunk deep into the ground, so deep that it was impossible to pull them loose no matter how hard he tried. He was forced to resort to cutting them off at the base, but even this wasn't easy. The wood seemed to have been treated with some kid of special chemical. An ordinary wood saw wouldn't even dent them and the hacksaw he resorted to using went through blades like they were butter. The need to do it all at night, when there was less a chance of getting caught, did not make things any simpler. Yet he persevered. Martin was on the road almost constantly once the sun went down, roaming the city streets, tearing down as many of the makeshift shrines as he could find, scattering far and wide the objects visitors had left behind.

He had no idea if destroying the memorials was actually doing any good, but the physical action made him feel like he was doing something, anything, and so he kept it up as long as he could each night, only stumbling home after the sun had risen in the east and the danger of being seen became too great.

The nights began to blur together as Martin pushed himself to the limit.

He was at the Mobil station at the corner of Thunderbird and Main early one morning, only feet away from the makeshift memorial that had started it all, when he finally cracked beneath the strain. He had finished filling his tank and was turning to replace the gas hose into the pump when he caught sight of a young girl adding a wreath made of photographs and flowers to the memorial on the corner.

Exhausted, dismayed, appalled at the seemingly endless array of these roadside shrines, Martin couldn't take seeing another person build them up any higher. He dropped the hose, ignored the splash of gasoline across his sandaled feet, and rushed the young woman, screaming at her to stop what she was doing. Snatching up a wooden sign that made up part of the memorial, he brought it cracking down across the woman's skull when she turned to see what the commotion was about.

By the time the police were able to tear him away from the victim ten minutes later, it was hard to tell just what she had once looked like. Blood ran thick in the gutter, coating her long blonde hair and the face of the nearest of the flower wreaths like some kind of organic spray paint.

Martin had begun screaming in tandem with the trapped souls standing in the midst of the memorial behind him when he'd begun striking the woman and did not stop until the responding officers shocked him into unconsciousness with their tasers.

"All rise. The Honorable Judge Prentiss Wilson presiding," cried the bailiff, as the judge returned to the room.

Martin dutifully rose to his feet beside his attorney, but he was barely aware of the proceedings. His trial had been swift; the jury's decision even swifter. Five weeks after the incident and here he was waiting to be sentenced. The public had wanted swift justice for the brutal and unprovoked attack and the district attorney had given it to them on a silver platter. Truth be told, Martin didn't care what happened to him any longer. He just wanted it to be over with so that he could go back to his bunk and curl up again, safe from those faceless thieves that had haunted his every waking minute since the accident. He'd been running ever since that night and he hadn't stopped until they'd locked him up inside.

The judge had been speaking for more than ten minutes when Martin's public defender nudged him in the side, telling him to pay attention. The judge was going to deliver the sentence.

"Mr. Jones, based on the testimony at your trial, it would appear that your behavior has been uncontrolled for quite a while. You've been physically violent, eccentrically erratic at best. Your attorney may have requested leniency due to the fact that this is your first such offense, but if I were to release you back into the public in your present condition, I'm afraid I would be remiss in my duty to the people. Never mind to that young lady still languishing in critical condition. Based on the findings of this court, I sentence you to five years confinement.

"For the time being, I'm remanding you into the custody of Mount Holy Oak Hospital for a thirty day psychological evaluation, the results of which will determine where you will spend your sentence.

"Questions?"

Neither side had any so with a crack of his gavel the judge rendered his sentence. Martin barely noticed. He'd drifted past the point of caring these last few weeks, knowing as he did what lay beyond these cement and steel walls. All of those crosses gleaming in the darkness ... it had become too much for him to think about. At least, inside the walls of the courthouse and its adjacent jail facility, he did not have to seem them standing there, mocking him with his impotence.

No, as far as he was concerned, they could keep him locked up forever.

They put him in irons with the other prisoners for the walk out to the transport vehicle. Hands chained to the waist, feet chained together, prisoner after prisoner chained to each other. He shuffled along with the rest. At the door to the bus they checked his ID once again, matching his photo to his face, and then they were loaded up, the guards pushing them gently into seats in every other row, the shorter length of chain that had tied them to one another now used to secure them to a large ring in the floor of the bus in front of each seat.

The windows were covered with a thick, steel mesh and a guard rode on either side in the front seat, their shotguns out and ready. The driver, too, was armed; Martin could see the butt of his pistol from where he sat a few rows away. Martin was relieved; he'd been dreading the move from the jail to the hospital facility. Fifteen, maybe twenty minutes and he'd be safely inside the hospital walls with enough dopamine coursing through his veins to get him to forget he'd ever seen such things.

As the bus pulled away from the curb and merged with the traffic around it, Martin, his head down, keeping his gaze focused on the floorboards in between his feet, determined not to see another of those damned crosses if he could help it. So earnest was his concentration that he wasn't aware there was a problem until the guard a few seats ahead of him began cursing and shouting out the window.

"Hey asshole! Get the fuck away from us, this is a government vehicle."

Martin looked up. The sun had set. They were out in the middle of the desert, halfway to their destination, nothing to be seen in the harsh glow of the streetlamps ahead of them but four lanes of blacktop and an occasional cactus that dotted the dirty landscape around them. Martin followed the guard's gaze to the left and turned just in time to see a black El Camino come swerving back across three lanes of traffic to hang directly off the driver's side of the bus. The car's passenger side window was open. Martin watched as a long, dark muzzle appeared from within its depths. Before he could shout a warning, the gunman fired.

Three quick shots, one immediately after another.

The bus driver's skull exploded, showering the windshield with a smattering of blood, brains, and gore.

The El Camino swerved in one direction.

The transport bus went in the other.

One moment they were traveling sedately down the road, the next the driver was dead, the guards were bouncing around the front seats, a shotgun went off, accidentally or otherwise, and by then the bus had left the blacktop. It jolted over an irrigation ditch, careened off a large outcropping of rock, and soared off the edge of a deep canyon before smashing roof down into the desert floor some hundred feet below.

When Martin opened his eyes the first time, he had a moment to glimpse the crumpled wreckage of the bus around him and then a wave of pain washed over him, pain so intense that it stripped him of his ability to breathe, to see, and he was quickly drowned in its wake.

When he regained consciousness a second time, he pain was less intense, enough so that he could move slightly without blacking out. At first he was disoriented, confused, uncertain of where he was or how he had gotten there. But as the minutes passed he began to remember; the trial, the prison bus, the shotgun blast, everything.

The moon was high in the sky and nearly full. By its silvery light he could see that he was trapped in a narrow opening formed when the roof of the bus had collapsed down upon the seats around him. The tightness at his midsection let him know that he was still chained to the floor beneath him by his restraints.

He was resting in a pool of something sticky and viscous; it sucked at his skin as he braced himself up on his right arm and pulled his face away from the floor. His thoughts were slow, jumbled, as if he was seeing everything from behind a veil of thick fog, and it took him several moments to realize that his left arm was hanging limply at his side.

He could barely feel the pain emanating from his dislocated shoulder.

It took him even longer to realize that he couldn't feel his legs at all, but he wasn't able move his head enough to see them beneath all of the wreckage.

He wasn't going anywhere.

His heart sank at the realization.

A sound caught his attention.

It was a familiar sound, yet one he couldn't place.

A rhythmic thumping, like sheets snapping in the wind.

The sound grew louder, closer.

Something's coming.

The sound nagged at him, teasing him with its identity.

He turned his head to the left, so that he was looking out the window of the bus to the desert landscape beyond, searching for the source. The floor of the arroyo in which they had landed was dotted with outcroppings of rock and the occasional piece of wreckage from the accident.

Martin barely had eyes for the landscape, however.

He was too busy staring at the seven white crosses arrayed in a semi-circle just a few feet away from where he was trapped, their shadows stretching across the desert sand behind them in the stark moonlight.

One cross for each of the other men that had been traveling in the bus with him.

Martin's scream was drowned out as the thumping sound grew near, louder.

Abruptly, silence descended.

The night seemed to hold its breath.

Out of the shadows behind the crosses a lone figure emerged.

Darkness seemed to cling to the newcomer, hugging him, like a large cloak draped about his form, preventing Martin from getting a good look. All he could tell was that it was a man.

For a moment Martin even wondered if the figure was simply a figment of his imagination, a phantom brought on by the shock and blood loss he knew he must be experiencing, but then the figure began to walk toward him. As he did the shadows surrounding him slowly dripped away, pooling at his feet.

Now Martin could see the newcomer more clearly. The stranger was tall, somewhere over six feet, and dressed in a pair of dark jeans and a matching shirt. Despite the summer heat he wore a long trenchcoat over his clothing. Perhaps it was the sound of the trenchcoat flapping behind him that he had heard, Martin thought. Maybe he would be getting out of this after all.

Then the shadows at the feet of the stranger reformed into man-sized shapes dressed in loosing flowing robes and wearing featureless faces.

The dam inside Martin's mind burst and the memories flowed like sudden rain.

Any hope of rescue swiftly fled.

The stranger spoke. "My, my, my. What a predicament you've gotten yourself into, Martin. Stuck like a rabbit in a hole. What a damn shame, that." The man's voice oozed with sarcasm and the threat of violence. Behind him, the creature's tittered and swayed, predators waiting to rush their prey.

Martin couldn't speak. His lips trembled, his mouth gaped, but no sound came out. The fear he felt at the others presence had swept the fog away from his mind, however. His heart beat faster, harder. The blood around his body flowed anew.

"What's the matter?" the stranger asked. "Cat got your tongue? You had to know we would be coming for you, didn't you?"

At last, Martin found his voice.

"Who are you? What do you want?"

The stranger cocked his head to one side. "Who am I? What do I want," he mimicked. "I'm surprised you haven't figured it out yet. What is the line from that stupid book? 'His tail swept a third of the stars out of the sky and flung them to the earth?' The stranger grinned, a horrible, leering grin that split the night like the rasp of a chainsaw. "I'm nothing more than a fallen star, you stupid monkey. But unfortunate for you, even fallen stars need to feed. And I'm tired of you messing with my dinner."

He snapped his fingers and the creatures rushed forward, charging into the confined space around him. His flesh burned where they touched him and he thought for certain he was finished, but seconds later he found himself dragged free of the wreckage and dumped to the ground in front of the stranger, his chains now severed and loose.

Before he could do more than gather his wits, his arms and legs were quickly seized by several more of the things, holding him down. Another gripped his head in a vice-like grip, preventing him from turning away.

The stranger stepped closer, scooping up a handful of dirt as he did so. He spat into his hands, mixed the saliva in with the dirt, and then smeared the mixture over Martin's eyes.

Cold.

Intense, burning cold, the likes of which he'd never experienced.

Martin clawed at his eyes, wiping the muck off of his skin, relieving the pain.

The sight that met his eyes when he opened them again forced another ragged scream from his already weary vocal chords.

The crosses were gone. In their place were seven wraith-like forms, writhing in pain. Though hazy and indistinct, they were still recognizable as the men who had occupied the bus with him. Their lower bodies were encased in cobweb-like substance that pulsed and glowed with an eerie greenish-purple cast and kept them rooted where they stood. Within its depths, Martin could see hundreds of tiny mouths opening and closing. Each time they did the wraiths would scream in pain.

Horrified, Martin tore his gaze away from the dead, only to find himself looking at the stranger again. The man's shirt was now hanging open. Across the grey skin of his chest were hundreds of similar mouths, open and closing in unison with the others. The stranger's head was thrown back in pleasure and his eyes shown with joy.

Martin's recoiled in fear.

Looking down, the stranger grinned once more. "Should have left things well enough alone."

He reached for something behind him outside of Martin's view. A moment passed and then he thrust the same arm toward the earth with breathtaking force.

When he pulled away, another white wooden roadside cross stood stark in the moonlight, still swaying slightly.

Martin jerked his head back, stunned. "But,..but I'm not dead yet," he sputtered, his mind trying hard to come to grips with the situation as his body continued to bleed out its lifeblood into the desert sands beneath him.

The stranger leaned in close, so that the injured man could smell the stink and feel the heat of his breath on his check. "Don't worry." The grin again. "You will be soon."

The faceless creatures faded into the darkness. The stranger stood and stepped back a few feet from Martin, giving him a good look. The man's coat billowed out behind him like a great sheet caught in the wind and then split in two. Seconds later he leaped up into the moonlit sky and disappeared.

In his wake, a single, dark feather drifted to the earth and came to rest just inches from Martin's face.

Seeing it, Martin finally understood the oddly familiar sound he had heard just before the stranger had appeared.

It had been the sound of wings.

Large, powerful wings.

Angel's wings.

As his life left him and his body went cold and silent, Martin's soul found itself trapped there with the others and it began to scream.

It would continue screaming for a long time to come.

DAT TAY VAO

F. Paul Wilson

1.

Patsy cupped his hands gently over his belly to keep his intestines where they belonged. Weak, wet, and helpless, he lay on his back in the alley and looked up at the stars in the crystal sky, unable to move, afraid to call out. The one time he'd yelled loud enough to be heard all the way to the street, loops of bowel had squirmed against his hands, feeling like a pile of Mom's slippery-slick homemade sausage all gray from boiling and coated with her tomato sauce. Visions of his insides surging from the slit in his abdomen like spring snakes from a novelty can of nuts had kept him from yelling again.

No one had come.

He knew he was dying. Good as dead, in fact. He could feel the blood oozing out of the vertical gash in his belly, seeping around his fingers and trailing down his forearms to the ground. Wet from neck to knees. Probably lying in a pool of blood ... his very own homemade marinara sauce.

Help was maybe fifty feet away and he couldn't call for it. Even if he could stand the sight of his guts jumping out of him, he no longer had the strength to yell. Yet help was out there ... the nightsounds of Quang Ngai streetlife ... so near ...

Nothing ever goes right for me. Nothing. Ever.

It had been such a sweet deal. Six keys of Cambodian brown. He could've got that home to Flatbush no sweat and then he'd have been set up real good. Uncle Tony would've known what to do with the stuff and Patsy would've been made. And he'd never be called Fatman again. Only the grunts over here called him Fatman. He'd be Pasquale to the old boys, and Pat to the younger guys.

And Uncle Tony would've called him Kid, like he always did.

Yeah. Would have. If Uncle Tony could see him now, he'd call him Shit-for-Brains. He could hear him now:

Six keys for ten G's? Whatsamatta witchoo? Din't I always tell you if it seems too good to be true, it usually is? Ay! Gabidose! Din't you smell no rat?

Nope. No rat smell. Because I didn't want to smell a rat. Too eager for the deal. Too anxious for the quick score. Too damn stupid as usual to see how that sleazeball Hung was playing me like a hooked fish.

No Cambodian brown.

No deal.

Just a long, sharp K-bar.

The stars above went fuzzy and swam around, then came into focus again.

The pain had been awful at first, but that was gone now. Except for the cold, it was almost like getting smashed and crashed on scotch and grass and just drifting off. Almost pleasant. Except for the cold. And the fear.

Footsteps ... coming from the left. He managed to turn his head a few degrees. A lone figure approached, silhouetted against the light from the street. A slow, unsteady, almost staggering walk. Whoever it was didn't seem to be in any hurry. Hung? Come to finish him off?

But no. This guy was too skinny to be Hung.

The figure came up and squatted flatfooted on his haunches next to Patsy. In the dim glow of starlight and streetlight he saw a wrinkled face and a silvery goatee. The gook babbled something in Vietnamese.

God, it was Ho Chi Minh himself come to rob him.

Too late. The money's gone. All gone.

No. Wasn't Ho. Couldn't be. Just an old papa-san in the usual black pajamas. They all looked the same, especially the old ones. The only thing different about this one was the big scar across his right eye. Looked as if the lids had been fused closed over the socket.

The old man reached down to where Patsy guarded his intestines and pushed his hands away. Patsy tried to scream in protest but heard only a sigh, tried to put his hands back up on his belly but they'd weakened to limp rubber and wouldn't move.

The old man smiled as he singsonged in gooktalk and pressed his hands against the open wound in Patsy's belly. Patsy screamed then, a hoarse, breathy sound torn from him by the searing pain that shot in all directions from where the old gook's hands lay. The stars really swam around this time, fading as they moved, but they didn't go out.

By the time his vision cleared, the old gook was up and turned around and weaving back toward the street. The pain, too, was sidling away.

Patsy tried again to lift his hands up to his belly, and this time they moved. They seemed stronger. He wiggled his fingers through the wetness of his blood, feeling for the edges of the wound, afraid of finding loops of bowel waiting for him.

He missed the slit on the first pass. And missed it on the second. How could that happen? It had been at least a foot long and had gaped open a good three or four inches, right there to the left of his belly button. He tried again, carefully this time ...

... and found a thin little ridge of flesh.

But no opening.

He raised his head—he hadn't been able to do that before—and looked down at his belly. His shirt and pants were a bloody mess, but he couldn't see any guts sticking out. And he couldn't see any wound, either. Just a dark wet mound of flesh.

If he wasn't so goddamn fat he could see down there! He rolled onto his side—God, he was stronger!—and pushed himself up to his knees to where he could slump his butt onto his heels, all the time keeping at least one hand tight over his belly. But nothing came out, or even pushed against his hand. He pulled his shirt open.

The wound was closed, replaced by a thin, purplish vertical line.

Patsy felt woozy again. What's going on here?

He was in a coma—that had to be it. He was dreaming this.

But everything was so *real*—the rough ground beneath his knees, the congealing red wetness of the blood on his shirt, the sounds from the street, even the smell of the garbage around him. All so real ...

Bracing himself against the wall, he inched his way up to his feet. His knees were wobbly and for a moment he thought they'd give out on him. But they held and now he was standing.

He was afraid to look down, afraid he'd see himself still on the ground. Finally, he took a quick glance. Nothing there but two clotted puddles of blood, one on each side of where he'd been lying.

He tore off the rest of the ruined shirt and began walking—very carefully at first—toward the street. Any moment now he would wake up or die, and this craziness would stop. No doubt bout that. But until then he was going to play out this little fantasy to the end.

2.

By the time he made it to his bunk—after giving the barracks guards and a few wandering night owls a story about an attempted robbery and a fight—Patsy had begun to believe that he was really awake and walking around.

It was so easy to say it had all been a dream, or maybe hallucinations brought on by acid slipped into his after-dinner coffee by some wise-ass. He managed to convince himself of that scenario a good half dozen times. And then he would look down at the scar on his belly, and at the blood on his pants ...

Patsy sat on his rack in a daze.

It really happened! He just touched me and closed me up!

A hushed voice in the dark snapped him out of it.

"Hey! Fatman! Got any weed?"

It sounded like Donner from two bunks over, a steady customer.

"Not tonight, Hank,"

"What? Fatman's never out of stock!"

"He is tonight"

"You shittin' me?"

"Good night, Hank."

Actually, he had a bunch of bags stashed in his mattress, but Patsy didn't feel like dealing tonight. His mind was too numb to make change. He couldn't even mourn the loss of all his cash—every red cent he'd saved up from almost a year's worth of chickenshit deals with guys like Donner. All he could think about, all he could see, was that old one-eyed gook leaning over him, smiling, babbling, and touching him.

He'd talk to Tram tomorrow. Tram knew everything that went on in this goddamn country. Maybe he'd heard something about the old gook. Maybe he could be persuaded to look for him.

One way or another, Patsy was going to find that old gook. He had plans for him. Big plans.

3.

Somehow he managed to make it through breakfast without perking the powdered eggs and scrambling the coffee.

It hadn't been easy. He'd been late getting to the mess hall kitchen. He'd got up on time but had stood in the shower staring at that purple line up and down his belly for he didn't know how long, remembering the cut of Hung's knife, the feel of his intestines in his hands.

Did it really happen?

He knew it had. Accepting it and living with it was going to be the problem.

Finally he'd pulled on his fatigues and hustled over to the kitchen. Rising long before sunup was the only bad thing about being an army cook. The guys up front might call him a pogue but it sure beat hell out of being a stupid grunt in the field. *Anything* was better than getting shot at. Look what happened in Hue last month, and the whispers about My Lai. Only gavones got sent into the field. Smart guys got mess assignments in nice safe towns like Quang Ngai.

At least smart guys with an Uncle Tony did.

Patsy smiled as he scraped hardened scrambled egg off the griddle. He'd always liked to cook. Good thing too. Because in a way, the cooking he'd done for Christmas last year had kept him out of the fight this year.

As always, Uncle Tony had come for Christmas dinner. At the table Pop edged around to the big question: What to do about Patsy and the draft. To everyone's surprise, he'd passed his induction physical ...

... another example of how nothing ever went right for him. Patsy had learned that a weight of 225 pounds would keep a guy his height out on medical deferment. Since he wasn't too many pounds short of that, he gorged on everything in sight for weeks. It would've been fun if he hadn't been so desperate. But he made the weight: On the morning of his induction physical the bathroom scale read 229.

But the scale they used downtown at the Federal Building read 224.

He was in and set to go to boot camp after the first of the year.

Pop finally came to the point: Could Uncle Tony maybe ...?

Patsy could still hear the disdain in Uncle Tony's voice as he spoke around a mouthful of bread.

"You some kinda peacenik or somethin'?"

No, no, Pop had said, and went on to explain how he was afraid that Patsy, being so fat and so clumsy and all, would get killed in boot camp or step on a mine his first day in the field. You know how he is.

Uncle Tony knew. Everybody knew Patsy's fugazi reputa¬tion. Uncle Tony had said nothing as he poured the thick red gravy over his lasagna, gravy Patsy had spent all morning cooking. He took a bite and pointed his fork at Patsy.

"Y'gotta do your duty, kid. I fought in the big one. You gotta fight in this here little one." He swallowed. "Say, you made this gravy, dincha? It's good. It's real good. And it gives me an idea of how we can keep you alive so you can go on making this stuff every Christmas."

So Uncle Tony pulled some strings and Patsy wound up an army cook.

He finished with the cleanup and headed downtown to the central market area, looking for Tram. He smelled the market before he got to it—the odors of live hens, *thit heo*, and roasting dog meat mingled in the air.

He found Tram in his usual spot by his cousin's vegetable stand, wearing his old ARVN fatigue jacket. He'd removed his right foot at the ankle and was polishing its shoe.

"Nice shine, yes, Fatman?" he said as he looked up and saw Patsy.

"Beautiful." He knew Tram liked to shock passersby with his plastic lower leg and foot. Patsy should have been used to the gag by now, but every time he saw that foot he thought of having his leg blown off ...

"I want to find someone."

"American or gook?" He crossed his right lower leg over his left and snapped his foot back into place at the ankle. Patsy couldn't help feeling uncomfortable about a guy who called his own kind gooks.

"Gook."

"What name?"

"Uh, that's the problem. I don't know."

Tram squinted up at him. "How I supposed to find somebody without a name?"

"Old papa-san. Looks like Uncle Ho."

Tram laughed. "All you guys think old gooks look like Ho!"

"And he has a scar across his eye"—Patsy put his index finger over his right eye—"that seals it closed like this."

4.

Tram froze for a heartbeat, then snapped his eyes back down to his prosthetic foot. He composed his expression while he calmed his whirling mind.

Trinh ... Trinh was in town last night! And Fatman saw him!

He tried to change the subject. Keeping his eyes down, he said, "I am glad to see you still walking around this morning. Did Hung not show up last night? I warned you—he number ten bad gook."

After waiting and hearing no reply, Tram looked up and saw that Fatman's eyes had changed. They looked glazed.

"Yes," Fatman finally said, shaking himself. "You warned me." He cleared his throat. "But about the guy I asked you about—"

"Why you want find this old gook?"

"I want to help him."

"How?"

"I want to do something for him."

"You want do something for old gook?"

Fatman's gaze wandered away as he spoke. "You might say I owe him a favor."

Tram's first thought was that Fatman was lying. He doubted this young American knew the meaning of returning a favor.

"Can you find him for me?" Fatman said.

Tram thought about that. And as he did, he saw Hung saunter out of a side street into the central market. He watched Hung's jaw drop when he spotted Fatman, watched his amber skin pale to the color of boiled bean curd as he spun and hurriedly stumbled away.

Tram knew in that instant that Hung had betrayed Fatman last night in a most vicious manner, and that Trinh had happened by and saved Fatman with the *Dat-tay-vao*.

It was all clear now.

On impulse, Tram said, "He lives in my cousin's village. I can take you to him."

"Great" Fatman said, grinning and clapping him on the shoulder. "I'll get us a jeep!"

"No jeep," Tram said. "We walk."

"Walk?" Fatman's face lost much of its enthusiasm. "Is it far?"

"Not far. Just a few klicks on the way to Mo Due. A fishing village. We leave now."

"Now? But—"

"Could be he not there if we wait."

This wasn't exactly true, but he didn't want to give Fatman too much time to think. Tram watched reluctance and eagerness battle their way back and forth across the American's face. Finally ...

"All right. Let's go. Long as it's not too far."

"If not too far for man with one foot, not too far for man with two."

5.

As Tram led Fatman south toward the tiny fishing village where Trinh had been living for the past year, he wondered why he'd agreed to bring the two of them together. His instincts were against it, yet he'd agreed to lead the American to Trinh.

Why?

Why was a word too often on his mind, it seemed. Especially where Americans were concerned. Why did they send so many of their young men over here? Most of them were either too frightened or too disinterested to make good soldiers. And the few who were eager for the fight hadn't the experience to make them truly valuable. They did not last long.

He wanted to shout across the sea: Send us seasoned soldiers, not your children!

But who would listen?

And did age really matter? After all, hadn't he been even younger than these American boys in the fight against the French at Dien Bien Phu fifteen years ago? But he and his fellow Vietminh had had a special advantage on their side. They had all burned with a fiery zeal to drive the French from their land.

Tram had been a communist then. He smiled at the thought as he limped along on the artificial foot, a replacement for the real one he'd lost to a Cong booby trap last year. Communist ... he had been young at Dien Bien Phu and the constant talk from his fellow Vietminh about the glories of class war and revolution had drawn him into their ideological camp. But after the fighting was over, after the partition, what he saw of the birth pangs of the glorious new social order almost made him long for French rule again.

He'd come south then and had remained here ever since. He'd willingly fought for the South until the finger-charge booby trap had caught him at the knee; after that he found that his verve for any sort of fight had departed with his leg.

He glanced at Fatman, sweating so profusely as he walked beside him along the twisting jungle trail. He'd come to like the boy, but he could not say why. Fatman was greedy, cowardly, and selfish, and he cared for no one other than himself. Yet Tram had found himself responding to the boy's vulnerability. Something tragic behind the bluff and bravado. With Tram's aid, Fatman had gone from the butt of many of the jokes around the American barracks to their favored supplier of marijuana. Tram could not deny that he'd profited well by helping him gain that position. He'd needed the money to supplement his meager pension from the ARVN, but that had not been his only motivation. He'd felt a need to help the boy.

And he *was* a boy, no mistake about that. Young enough to be Tram's son. But Tram knew he could never raise such a son as this.

So many of the Americans he'd met here were like Fatman. No values, no traditions, no heritage. Empty. Hollow creatures who had grown up with nothing expected of them. And now, despite all the money and all the speeches, they knew in their hearts that they were not expected to win this war.

What sort of parents provided nothing for their children to believe in, and then sent them halfway around the world to fight for a country they had never heard of?

And that last was certainly a humbling experience—to learn that until a few years ago most of these boys had been blithely unaware of the existence of the land that had been the center of Tram's life since he'd been a teenager.

"How much farther now?" Fatman said.

Tram could tell from the American's expression that he was uneasy being so far from town. Perhaps now was the time to ask.

"Where did Hung stab you?" he said.

Fatman staggered as if Tram had struck him a blow. He stopped and gaped at Tram with a gray face.

"How ...?"

"There is little that goes on in Quang Ngai that I do not know," he said, unable to resist an opportunity to enhance his stature. "Now, show me where."

Tram withheld a gasp as Fatman pulled up his sweat-soaked shirt to reveal the purple seam running up and down to the left of his navel. Hung had gut cut him, not only to cause an agonizing death, but to show his contempt.

"I warned you ..."

Fatman pulled down his shirt. "I know, I know. But after Hung left me in the alley, this old guy came along and touched me and sealed it up like magic. Can he do that all the time?"

"Not all the time. He has lived in the village for one year. He can do it some of the time every day. He will do it many more years."

Fatman's voice was a breathy whisper. "Years! But how? Is it some drug he takes? He looked like he was drunk."

"Oh, no. *Dat-tay-vao* not work if you drunk."

"What won't work?"

"*Dat-tay-vao* ... Trinh has the touch that heals."

"Heals what? Just knife wounds and stuff?"

"Anything."

Fatman's eyes bulged. "You've got to get me to him!" He glanced quickly at Tram. "So I can thank him ... reward him."

"He requires no reward."

"I've got to find him. How far to go?"

"Not much." He could smell the sea now. "We turn here."

As he guided Fatman left into thicker brush that clawed at their faces and snagged their clothes, he wondered again if he'd done the right thing by bringing him here. But it was too late to turn back.

Besides, Fatman had been touched by the *Dat-tay-vao*. Surely that worked some healing changes on the spirit as well as the body. Perhaps the young American truly wanted to pay his respects to Trinh.

6.

He will do it many more years!

The words echoed in Patsy's ears and once again he began counting the millions he'd make off the old gook. God, it was going to be so great! And so easy! Uncle Tony's contacts would help get the guy into the states where Patsy would set him up in a "clinic." Then he would begin to cure the incurable.

And oh God the prices he'd charge.

How much to cure someone of cancer? Who could say what price was too high? He could ask anything—*anything!*

But Patsy wasn't going to be greedy. He'd be fair. He wouldn't strip the patients bare. He'd just ask for half—half of everything they owned.

He almost laughed out loud. This was going to be *so* sweet! All he had to do was—

Just ahead of him, Tram shouted something in Vietnamese. Patsy didn't recognize the word, but he knew a curse when he heard one. Tram started running. They had broken free of the suffocating jungle atop a small sandy rise. Out ahead, the sun rippled off a calm sea. A breeze off the water brought blessed relief from the heat. Below lay a miserable ville—a jumble of huts made of odd bits of wood, sheet metal, palm fronds, and mud.,

One of the huts was burning. Frantic villagers were hurling sand and water at it.

Patsy followed Tram's headlong downhill run at a cautious walk. He didn't like this. He was far from town and doubted he could find his way back; he was surrounded by gooks and something bad was going down.

He didn't like this at all.

As he approached, the burning hut collapsed in a shower of sparks. To the side, a cluster of black pajama-clad women stood around a supine figure. Tram had pushed his way through to the center of the babbling group and now knelt beside the figure. Patsy followed him in.

"Aw, shit!"

He recognized the guy on the ground. Wasn't easy. He'd been burned bad and somebody had busted caps all over him, but his face was fairly undamaged and the scarred eye left no doubt that it was the same old gook who'd healed him up last night. His good eye was closed and he looked dead, but his chest still moved with shallow respirations. Patsy's stomach lurched at the sight of all the blood and charred flesh. What was keeping him alive?

Suddenly weak and dizzy, Patsy dropped to his knees beside Tram. His millions ... all those sweet dreams of millions and millions of easy dollars were fading away.

Nothing ever goes right for me!

"I share your grief," Tram said, looking at him with sorrowful dark eyes.

"Yeah. What happened?"

Tram glanced around at the frightened, grieving villagers. "They say the Cong bring one of their sick officers here and demand that Trinh heal him. Trinh couldn't. He try to explain that the time not right yet but they grow angry and tie him up and shoot him and set his hut on fire."

"Can't he heal himself?"

Tram shook his head slowly, sadly. "No. *Dat-tay-vao* does not help the one who has it. Only others."

Patsy wanted to cry. All his plans ... it wasn't *fair!*

"Those shitbums!"

"Worse than shitbums," Tram said. "These Charlie say they come back soon and destroy whole village."

Patsy's anger and self-pity vanished in a cold blast of fear. He peered at the trees and bushes, feeling naked with a thousand eyes watching him.

... *they come back soon* ...

His knees suddenly felt stronger.

"Let's get back to town." He began to rise to his feet, but Tram held him back.

"Wait. He looking at you."

Sure enough, the old gook's good eye was open and staring directly into his. Slowly, with obvious effort, he raised his charred right hand toward Patsy. His voice rasped some-thing.

Tram translated: "He say, 'You the one.' "

"What's that supposed to mean?"

Patsy didn't have time for this dramatic bullshit. He wanted out of here. But he also wanted to stay tight with Tram because Tram was the only one who could lead him back to Quang Ngai.

"I don't know. Maybe he mean that you the one he fix last night."

Patsy was aware of Tram and the villagers watching him, as if they expected something of him. Then he realized what it was: He was supposed to be grateful, show respect to the old gook. Fine. If it was what Tram wanted him to do, he'd do it. Anything to get them on their way out of here. He took a deep breath and gripped the hand, wincing at the feel of the fire-crisped skin—

Electricity shot up his arm.

His whole body spasmed with the searing bolt. He felt himself flopping around like a fish on a hook, and then he was falling. The air went out of him in a rush as his back slammed against the ground. It was a moment before he could open his eyes, and when he did he saw Tram and the villagers staring down at him with gaping mouths and wide, astonished eyes. He glanced at the old gook.

"What the hell did he do to me?"

The old gook was staring back, but it was a glassy, un¬focused, sightless stare. He was dead.

The villagers must have noticed this too because some of the women began to weep.

Patsy staggered to his feet.

"What happened?"

"Don't know," Tram said with a puzzled shake of his head. "Why you fall? He not strong enough push you down."

Patsy opened his mouth to explain, then closed it. Nothing he could say would make sense.

He shrugged. "Let's go."

He felt like hell and just wanted to be gone. It wasn't only the threat of Charlie returning; he was tired and discouraged and so bitterly disappointed he could have sat down on the ground right then and there and cried like a wimp.

"Okay. But first I help bury Trinh. You help, too."

"What? You kidding me? Forget it!"

Tram said nothing, but the look he gave Patsy said it all: It called him fat, lazy, and ungrateful.

Screw you! Patsy thought.

Who cared what Tram or anybody else in this stinking sewer of a country thought. It held nothing for him anymore. All his money was gone, and his one chance for the brass ring lay dead and fried on the ground before him.

7.

As he helped dig a grave for Trinh, Tram glanced over at Fatman where he sat in the elephant grass staring morosely out to sea. Tram could sense that he was not grief-stricken over Trinh's fate. He was unhappy for himself.

So ... he had been right about Fatman from the first: The American had come here with something in mind other than paying his respects to Trinh. Tram didn't know what it was, but he was sure Fatman had not had the best interests of Trinh or the village at heart.

He sighed. He was sick of foreigners. When would the wars end? Wars could be measured in languages here. He knew numerous Vietnamese dialects,

Pidgin, French, and now English. If the North won, would he then have to learn Russian? Perhaps he would have been better off if the booby trap had taken his life instead of just his leg. Then, like Trinh, the endless wars would be over for him.

He looked down into the empty hole where Trinh's body soon would lie. Were they burying the *Dat-tay-vao* with him? Or would it rise and find its way to another? So strange and mysterious, the *Dat-tay-vao* ... so many conflicting tales. Some said it came here with the Buddha himself, some said it had always been here. Some said it was as capricious as the wind in the choice of its instruments, while others said it followed a definite plan.

Who was to say truly? The *Dat-tay-vao* was a rule unto itself, full of mysteries not meant to be plumbed.

As he turned back to his digging, Tram's attention was caught by a dark blot in the water's glare. He squinted to make it out, then heard the chatter of one machine gun, then others, saw villagers begin to run and fall, felt sand kick up around him.

A Cong gunboat!

He ran for the tree where Fatman half sat, half crouched with a slack, terrified expression. He was almost there when something hit him in the chest and right shoulder with the force of a sledgehammer, and then he was flying through the air, spinning, screaming with pain.

He landed with his face in the sand and rolled. He couldn't breathe! Panic swept over him. Every time he tried to take a breath, he heard a sucking sound from the wound in his chest wall, but no air reached his lungs. His chest felt ready to explode. Black clouds encroached on his dimming vision.

Suddenly, Fatman was leaning over him, shouting through the typhoon roaring in his ears.

"Tram! Tram! Jesus God get up! You gotta get me outta here! Stop bleeding f'Christsake and get me out of here!"

Tram's vision clouded to total darkness and the roaring grew until it drowned out the voice.

8.

Patsy dug his fingers into his scalp.

How was he going to get back to town? Tram was dying, turning blue right here in front of him, and he didn't know enough Vietnamese to use with anyone else and didn't know the way back to Quang Ngai and the whole area was lousy with Charlie.

What am I gonna do?

As suddenly as they started, the AKs stopped. The cries of the wounded and the terrified filled the air in their place.

Now was the time to get out.

Patsy looked at Tram's mottled, dusky face. If he could stopper up that sucking chest wound, maybe Tram could hang on, and maybe tell him the way back to town. He slapped the heel of his hand over it and pressed.

Tram's body arched in seeming agony. Patsy felt something too—electric ecstasy shot up his arm and spread through his body like subliminal fire. He fell back, confused, weak, dizzy.

What the hell—?

He heard raspy breathing and looked up. Air was gushing in and out of Tram's wide-open mouth in hungry gasps; his eyes opened and his color began to lighten.

Tram's chest wasn't sucking anymore. As Patsy leaned forward to check the wound, he felt something in his hand and looked. A bloody lead slug sat in his palm. He looked at the chest where he'd laid that hand and what he saw made the walls of his stomach ripple and compress as if looking for something to throw up.

Tram's wound wasn't *there* anymore! Only a purplish blotch remained.

Tram raised his head and looked down at where the bullet had torn into him.

"The *Dat-tay-vao!* You have it now! Trinh passed it on to you! You have the *Dat-tay-vao!*"

I do? he thought, staring at the bullet rolling in his palm. Holy shit, I do!

He wouldn't have to get some gook back to the States to make his mint—all he had to do was get himself home in one piece.

Which made it all the more important to get the hell out of this village. Now.

"Let's go!"

"Fatman, you can't go. Not now. You must help. They—"

Patsy threw himself flat as something exploded in the jungle a hundred yards behind them, hurling a brown and green geyser of dirt and underbrush high into the air.

Mortar!

Another explosion followed close on the heels of the first, but this one was down by the waterline south of the village.

Tram was pointing out to sea.

"Look! They firing from boat." He laughed. "Can't aim mortar from boat!"

Patsy stayed hunkered down with his arms wrapped tight around his head, quaking with terror as the ground jittered with each of the next three explosions. Then they stopped.

"See?" Tram said, sitting boldly in the clearing and looking out to sea. "Even *they* know it foolish! They leaving. They only use for terror. Cong very good at terror."

No argument there, Patsy thought as he climbed once more to his feet.

"Get me out of here now, Tram. You owe me!"

Tram's eyes caught Patsy's and pinned him to the spot like an insect on a board. "Look at them, Fatman."

Patsy tore his gaze away and looked at the ville. He saw the villagers—the maimed and bleeding ones and their friends and families—looking back at him. Waiting. They said nothing, but their eyes ...

He ripped his gaze loose. "Those Cong'll be back!"

"They need you, Fatman," Tram said. "You are only one who can help them now."

Patsy looked again, unwillingly. Their eyes ... calling him. He could almost feel their hurt, their need.

"No way!"

He turned and began walking toward the brush. He'd find his own way back if Tram wouldn't lead him. Better than waiting around here to get caught and tortured by Charlie. It might take him all day, but—

"Fatman!" Tram shouted. "For once in your life!"

That stung. Patsy turned and looked at the villagers once more, feeling their need like a taut rope around his chest, pulling him toward them. He ground his teeth. It was idiotic to stay, but ...

One more. Just one, to see if I still have it.

He could spare a couple of minutes for that, then be on his way. At least that way he'd be sure what had happened with Tram wasn't some sort of crazy freak accident.

Just one.

As he stepped toward the villagers, he heard their voices begin to murmur excitedly. He didn't know what they were saying but felt their grateful welcome like a warm current through the draw of their need.

He stopped at the nearest wounded villager, a woman holding a bloody, unconscious child in her arms. His stomach lurched as he saw the wound—a slug had nearly torn the kid's arm off at the shoulder. Blood oozed steadily between the fingers of the hand the woman kept clenched over the wound. Swallowing the revulsion that welled up in him, he slipped his hands under the mother's to touch the wound—

—and his knees almost buckled with the ecstasy that shot through him.

The child whimpered and opened his eyes. The mother removed her hand from the wound.

Make that *former* wound. It was gone, just like Tram's.

She cried out with joy and fell to her knees beside Patsy, clutching his leg as she wept.

Patsy swayed. He had it! No doubt about it—he had the goddamn *Dat-tay-vao!* And it felt so good! Not just the pleasure it caused, but how that little gook kid was looking up at him now with his bottomless black eyes and flashing him a shy smile. He felt high, like he'd been smoking some of his best merchandise.

One more. Just one more.

He disengaged his leg from the mother and moved over to where an old woman writhed in agony on the ground, clutching her abdomen.

Belly wound ... I know the feeling, mama-san.

He knelt and wormed his hand under hers. That burst of pleasure surged again as she stiffened and two slugs popped into his hand. Her breathing eased and she looked up at him with gratitude beaming from her eyes.

Another!

On it went. Patsy could have stopped at any time, but found he didn't want to. The villagers seemed to have no doubt that he would stay and heal them all. They knew he could do it and *expected* him to do it. It was so new, such a unique feeling, he didn't want it to end. Ever. He felt a sense of belonging he'd never known before. He felt protective of the villagers. But it went beyond them, beyond this little ville, seemed to take in the whole world.

Finally, it was over.

Patsy stood in the clearing before the huts, looking for another wounded body. He checked his watch—he'd been at it only thirty minutes and there were no more villagers left to heal. They all clustered around him at a respectful distance, watching silently. He gave himself up to the euphoria enveloping him, blending with the sound of the waves, the wind in the trees, the cries of the gulls. He hadn't realized what a beautiful place this was. If only—

A new sound intruded—the drone of a boat engine. Patsy looked out at the water and saw the Cong gunboat returning. Fear knifed through the pleasurable haze as the villagers scattered for the trees. Were the Cong going to land?

No. Patsy saw a couple of the crew crouched on the deck, heard the familiar *choonk!* of a mortar shell shooting out of its tube. An explosion quickly followed somewhere back in the jungle. Tram had been right. No way they could get any accuracy with a mortar on the rocking deck of a gunboat. Just terror tactics.

Damn those bastards! Why'd they have to come back and wreck his mood. Just when he'd been feeling good for the first time since leaving home. Matter of fact, he'd been feeling better than he could ever remember, home or anywhere else. For once, everything seemed right.

For once, something was going Patsy's way, and the Cong had to ruin it.

Two more wild mortar shots, then he heard gunfire start from the south and saw three new gunboats roaring up toward the first. But these were flying the old red, white, and blue. Patsy laughed and raised his fist.

"Get 'em!"

The Cong let one more shell go choonk! before pouring on the gas and slewing away.

Safe!

Then he heard a whine from above and the world exploded under him.

9.

... a voice from far away ... Tram's ...

"... *chopper coming, Fatman ... get you away soon ... hear it? ... almost here ...*"

Patsy opened his eyes and saw the sky, then saw Tram's face poke into view. He looked sick.

"Fatman!' You hear me?"

"How bad?" Patsy asked.

"You be okay."

Patsy turned his head and saw a ring of weeping villagers who were looking everywhere and anywhere but at him. He realized he couldn't feel anything below his neck. He tried to lift his head for a look at himself but didn't have the strength.

"I wanna see."

"You rest," Tram said.

"Get my head up, dammit!"

With obvious reluctance, Tram gently lifted his head. As Patsy looked down at what was left of him, he heard a high, keening wail. His vision swam, mercifully blotting out sight of the bloody ruin that had once been the lower half of his body. He realized that the wail was his own voice.

Tram lowered his head and the wail stopped.

I shouldn't even be alive!

Then he knew. He was waiting for someone. Not just anyone would do. A certain someone.

A hazy peace came. He drifted into it and stayed there until the chopping thrum of a slick brought him out; then he heard an American voice.

"I thought you said he was alive!"

Tram's voice: "He is."

Patsy opened his eyes and saw the shocked face of an American soldier.

"Who are you?" Patsy asked.

"Walt Erskine. Medic. I'm gonna—"

"You're the one," Patsy said. Somehow, he bent his arm at the elbow and lifted his hand. "Shake."

The medic looked confused. "Yeah. Okay. Sure."

He grabbed Patsy's hand and Patsy felt the searing electric charge.

Erskine jerked back and fell on his ass, clutching his hand. "What the *hell?*"

The peace closed in on Patsy again. He'd held on as long as he could. Now he could embrace it. One final thought arced through his mind like a lone meteorite in a starless sky. The *Dat-tay-vao* was going to America after all.

CONSTITUTION
Scott Nicholson

On the third day, he felt the flesh loosening around his fingerbones. He slipped into the bedroom and pulled on a pair of white silk gloves. Demora wouldn't notice, at least not right away. And he could always tell her that he was practicing a mime routine. She'd fall for that. She'd fall for anything, as long as the lie came from his lips.

"Randall, honey," Demora called from downstairs. She would be in the kitchen, pouring him a drink. Scotch with a half-pound of ice cubes. He could already picture the glass beaded with grotesque sweat.

He wished he himself could sweat. The summer heat had made his condition worse. The thunderstorm that afternoon had provided a brief respite. It rolled in at three just like clockwork. But time really had no meaning anymore, not since he had died. His wife called to him again.

"Yes, dear?" he answered, struggling to make his throat work smoothly. He touched his Adam's apple with one gloved hand.

"I've got a drinky-poo for you."

"I'll be right down."

He stopped at the bathroom on the way. He stood in front of the mirror and lifted his eyelids. No *tache noir* yet. Black eyes would be a dead giveaway.

He went into the living room. The drink rested on the coffee table. He gingerly settled into his easy chair. Demora had loaded his pipe so that it would be at his elbow, awaiting the touch of fire.

She came out of the kitchen, her gown disguising her huggable roundness. Her hair was up in a severe bun. It wasn't her best look. The bareness of her neck made her chins more noticeable. But she was still beautiful. She smiled.

"Hard day at work, dear?" Her voice was sparrow-light and cheerful.

"Not really."

Because he hadn't done anything. He went down to the theater and made sure he was visible, so that everyone would know that reliable old Randall was on the job. Then he sat in his office with the lights off, listening to the banging as the set designers prepped for "My Fair Lady." It was another world, out there between the curtains, a world that he could no longer have a part in. He would have cried if he could've summoned the necessary fluids.

"Dear?"

Demora's voice snapped him out of his reverie.

"Yes, my sweet?" he said, with a steady delivery. He had been a decent actor, once. He saw no reason why he couldn't pull off his greatest performance. The deceased Randall, starring as the living Randall, for a limited run only.

"Are you okay? You seem a little ... I don't know."

Her eyes darkened with worry. It made her eyebrows vee on her forehead.

"I'm fine, dear. Right as rain, dandy as a doodle."

"Hmm. If you say so."

"I say so."

He lifted his drink. It was difficult. His strength was ebbing.

He sipped, then gulped. No taste. He wished he could feel the burn, the tingle, the glow, the cold, anything.

"Is it just right, my little honey-pot smooch?" Demora asked. She held one hand in front of her ample bosom, eager to please.

"Perfect," he said, forcing a smile. His lips were too dry. They felt as if they were about to split. He let the smile fade.

Randall fumbled for the pipe. All his little routines were now Herculean tasks. He stuck the pipe stem in his mouth and felt it against his wooden tongue. Demora pulled a lighter out of nowhere and thumbed a bright flame.

Heat. He sucked, lost for feeling, lost for pain, lost for comfort. He swallowed and didn't cough. Smoking was difficult now that he no longer breathed.

Demora hovered, flitting around his elbows like a rotund hummingbird, her speed belying her size. She unrolled the newspaper and draped it across his lap, then knelt to remove his shoes.

"No, darling," he said. She looked up, disappointed.

He was afraid that the stench would be overpowering.

"I may go for a walk later," he said.

She nodded and grinned.

It was only when she was handing him the television remote that she mentioned the gloves.

"Just a little change, my sweet," he said. He flexed his fingers. They felt like sausages encased in plastic sheaths.

The evening passed in the world outside. The sun made its weary trek down the sky. The crickets began their nightly complaining from the alleys. Streetlights hummed. Demora hummed, too. She was a mezzo-soprano.

They readied for bed. This was the worst time of all, the most awkward moment. Randall snuck to the bathroom and put on his pajamas, careful not to look at his flesh.

The soft parts would go first. The ones without bones. But which ones? His earlobes? The tip of his nose? His lips? Or ...

He believed he could put her off for another night. But two nights in a row? She would be suspicious.

Still, he couldn't risk betraying himself in a fit of passion. That would be too sudden. He wanted the moment to be right. He wanted to break the news gently.

He rolled antiperspirant under his arms. Hairs came loose and clung to the deodorant ball. He splashed cologne on his neck. He was afraid to comb his hair.

"Randall?"

She was under the covers.

"Coming, dear," he answered.

He turned out the lights, not looking at the bed. He still had the gloves on. Silly boy.

"Silly boy," she said, feeling the gloves on her shoulders as he hugged her.

She was wearing lingerie, silk lace and frills. He rubbed the fabric against his cheek, lightly, so that his skin wouldn't slough. He missed having a sense of touch.

"Playing games tonight?" she whispered, a giggle in her nose.

"Not tonight, dear, I've ..."

You've what?, he thought. Got a headache? Used that last night. Suffering the heartbreak of psoriasis? This morning's excuse.

"Honey?" she said, her voice husky with desire and disappointment.

"Tomorrow night, I promise," he said, in his most gentlemanly tone. It was the voice he used doing Laurence Olivier doing Hamlet.

He brushed his parched lips carefully against Demora's cheek. He nudged his nose against her ear. He tried to give her butterfly kisses, but his eyelids were too stiff.

Randall lay back on the pillows and pretended to sleep. He hoped she wouldn't put her head on his chest and notice the lack of a heartbeat. But soon she was snoring lightly, managing to turn even that into a song. His eyes remained open the entire night.

His blood had settled overnight as he lay in unsleep. The liver mortis mottled his skin. Getting out of bed was a chore. He just wanted to rest, rest, in peace.

But Demora needed him. This was no time to be selfish.

He dared not take the bus to work. He was drawing too many flies. His hands were too slow to brush them away. So he walked to work, his feet like mud in his shoes.

He looked at the sky, wide and blue over the tops of the buildings. He had never before noticed the breadth and depth of reality. The gray-chested pigeons hopping on the ledges, barren flagpoles erect in the air, awnings drooping like damp parachutes, shrubs rising from concrete boxes with cigarette butts for mulch. So much detail, every bit of mica in the sidewalk glistening in the sun, every flake of drab paint on the windowsills curling, all glass standing clear and thick and brittle and bold.

And the people, fat men with umbrellas, stalactite ladies with faux pearls, boys with big shoes, weasel women and pony girls. So many people, flush with health, cheeks blushed with blood, all hearts racing, pounding, pouring, pumping life. So alive. Such a treasure it was to breathe. The living knew not their wealth.

Randall pulled his derby lower over his face. He'd had to lighten the skin under his eyes with makeup. He had a kit at home. He'd done his own makeup for years, painting himself a hundred times to become someone else. He never thought he'd have to recreate his own face.

He entered the theater, his coat collar high around his ears even though the mercury was in the eighties. He had doused his clothes with a half-bottle of aftershave, but he didn't want to chance any personal encounters.

He waved at the stage director and went into his office. He took off his coat and sat in the chair. He tugged at the fingertip of his glove and heard a wet tearing sound. Probably the fingermeat was separating at his wedding band. He left the glove alone.

He stank. He knew that. Demora had not said a word. She would never criticize.

Randall sat. After a long eternity of hours that were all the same, the clock on the wall moved around. Time to go home, to Demora. He tried to rise.

He couldn't move. Rigor mortis had finally set in.

He had been wondering how long he could continue, how long he could pretend, how long he could fool himself and his Makers. Too many decades of smoking and lack of exercise.

Last Monday. Oh, what pain in his chest, a swollen river of fire, a smothering silence, a great white pillow of pressure on his head. That final sensation had been rich, screaming with the juice of nerves, as raw as birth and as bittersweet as the last day of autumn.

He winced at the memory. He had felt something lifting from his body, a powder, a fairy-dust, a star whisper. And he had resisted the pull.

Because of her.

And because of her, he could not sit locked in his chair, his muscles frozen around his skeleton, his face a tense mask, his eyes dry and bulging. He would not be found like this.

He summoned his willpower. He strained against invisible bonds. Finally, his jaw yanked downward.

He flexed his fingers, hearing his knuckles crack. He stood, his bones snapping like old sticks. He walked, his legs a daisy chain of calcite.

On the way home, he avoided looking into human eyes. He no longer envied their moistness. He no longer ached for tears. He had lost the desire to breathe, to live, to be normal. Living was just a state of mind.

Demora looked affectionately at him as she set the table. She tilted her head.

"Are you gaining weight, sweetheart?" she asked.

"No, dear."

He wasn't gaining. He was bloating.

Randall wore his hat while eating dinner. He wondered what was happening to the food now that his organs no longer digested. His gloves were stained with the cherry jubilee. Demora's lips were red, probably his as well.

He felt an urge to kiss her.

"Tonight, my love?" she said, looking deeply into his eyes.

"Yes," he answered. He lifted a toast in her direction. The Bourdeaux pooled in his dead stomach.

Did she suspect? He was pallid. He stank of loam and rancid meat. His skin was gelatin. His cheeks sagged from his skull. Flies orbited his head.

But he didn't think she minded. She loved him as he was, however he was. He saw it in her eyes.

Those fools had it wrong. All the great tragedies were based on a lie. Romeo and Juliet, hah.

Anybody could die for love. That was easy. The true test was living for love, afterwards.

Later, in bed, under sheets and midnight's rainbow, as candles flickered.

"I love you," Demora whispered.

"I love you, " Randall said, and he had never meant it so completely.

"Forever and for true?"

"Forever and a day."

He kissed her.

His mouth found new vigor.

His eyes moistened, as if brimming for weeping.

He felt stirrings below his belly.

His tongue writhed and squirmed in passion.

No, not his tongue.

Maggots.

Demora returned his kiss. Their limbs entwined, their flesh joined in a squishy, beautiful swapping of the juices of love. They drove their bodies toward satisfaction, but for Randall, the only fulfillment was in pleasing his wife.

By the time Randall had pulled away, bits of him were clinging to Demora. She endured without complaint. He hugged her into sleep. He stared unblinking at the ceiling, listening to the slow tick of the bedside clock and the gases expelling from his body. In the still air of dark night, the whole world was a coffin. Randall wondered if being dead would always be so endlessly, endlessly boring.

Finally, the sun reddened the window. Another day of being dead. Randall went to the bathroom and studied himself in the mirror. His eyes writhed with larvae. The softer meat of his face, the area around his eyes and lips, was dark as coal. The rest was shaded green, faintly moldy and mossy, down to his chest. He dared not look lower.

He turned on the shower, and the steam curled around him as he stepped under the nozzle. He welcomed the cleansing. The forceful jets of water dented his mottled skin, but he felt nothing. The flies spun in confused circles, their host lost in the scent of soap.

Bits of skin and flesh rained from his body. He stared between his rotted feet at the pieces of himself collecting in the drain. He spun the spigots until the water stopped. More of him fell away as he toweled himself dry.

"Honey?" Demora knocked on the bathroom door.

"I'm almost done." His voice was muffled by the insects that had spawned in his mouth.

"Coffee and toast, or would you rather have hot cereal?"

Randall couldn't face stuffing more tasteless food into his body. All he wanted was to pull his own eyelids down, to sleep, sleep. But Demora. She needed. He couldn't leave her all alone. He'd promised love eternal.

"I'm not hungry," he said, trying his best to sound cheerful. After all, they had made love last night. He ought to be in a good mood.

"Are you sure, dear?"

"Yes, I'm sure."

He reached for his bathrobe as her footsteps faded down the hall. He wrapped the terry cloth around him. Once the soft fabric would have comforted him. Now, it only reminded him of all he couldn't feel. He decided he would call in sick to work that day.

He went down the stairs, his feet slogging damply on the oak treads. The gloves, the makeup, the illusions were all useless now. The flesh under his jowls drooped in surrender to gravity and swung from side to side as he walked to the dinette. Demora whistled in the kitchen, an adagio operetta, her music accompanied by the percussion of cooking utensils. Randall slumped into a chair, beyond hope. If only he could die, finally and for real.

He straightened as Demora entered the room. Death wishes were selfish. He had made a promise. No force, from Beyond or otherwise, would make him yield before his duty was met.

Demora sat at the table across from him. Steam curled from her cup of coffee, a spirit of heat.

"We have to talk," she said, leaning forward. Her eyes narrowed and her lips tightened, the look she got when she was serious about something. He looked out the window at the green living world.

"It's a beautiful day," he said, "and I have a beautiful wife."

She almost smiled. "That's sweet, but you're changing the subject."

"What subject?" A piece of his lip plopped onto the table. A maggot writhed in the black meat.

"You're keeping something from me."

"Me?" He tried to open his eyes in feigned innocence, but he had no eyelids.

"We've always been honest with each other ..."

"Of course, dear."

"... and I can tell when something's bothering you."

"Nothing's bothering me." Newly-born flies spilled from his mouth along with his words. The flies' wings were shiny in the morning light.

"Don't lie to me, honey."

Yes, lying was futile. She could always read him like a book.

"I can tell you're unhappy," she continued. He raised his hand to protest. The white bones of his fingers showed through in places.

222

"And nothing would pain me more than for you to be unhappy," Demora said. Those lips, those kind, serious eyes. He was never more sure of anything than he was of her undying love.

"Is it selfish of me?" he asked. "To refuse to let go?"

"No, I'm the selfish one. I'm holding you here when your heart is leading you in another direction."

"For better or worse. That was my vow to you."

"Till death do us part. That was also your vow."

Her eyes welled with tears. So he had hurt her, despite all his effort and will, despite his defiance of nature. He couldn't bear to hurt her.

She nodded at him. He understood. She was releasing him, granting him permission to die for her. He had been wrong. The supreme sacrifice was hers, not his.

"I'm so very tired," he whispered.

She reached across the table, gripping his decaying hands in hers. His wedding ring clacked against bone.

"I love you," he said, feeling his soul lifting and leaking away, wafting from his putrid corpse to mingle with the sky.

"I know," she answered, her voice breaking. "Forever and a day."

Even the day after forever had to end. His heart was light, buoyant with relief and freed now from the cages of the flesh. His last sensation was of Demora's hands squeezing good-bye, urging him onward, giving her blessing to his departure. He had fulfilled his vows, and all that remained was to find peace.

And wait for Demora.

MR. AICKMAN'S AIR RIFLE
Peter Straub

1

On the twenty-first, or "Concierge," floor of New York's Governor General Hospital, located just south of midtown on Seventh Avenue, a glow of recessed lighting and a rank of framed, eye-level graphics (Twombley, Shapiro, Marden, Warhol) escort visitors from a brace of express elevators to the reassuring spectacle of a graceful cherry wood desk occupied by a red-jacketed gatekeeper named Mr. Singh. Like a hand cupped beneath a waiting elbow, this gentleman's enquiring yet deferential appraisal and his stupendous display of fresh flowers nudge the visitor over hushed beige carpeting and into the wood-paneled realm of Floor 21 itself.

First to appear is the nursing station, where in a flattering chiaroscuro efficient women occupy themselves with charts, telephones, and the ever-changing patterns traversing their computer monitors; directly ahead lies the first of the great, half-open doors of the residents' rooms or suites, each with its brass numeral and discreet nameplate. The great hallway extends some sixty yards, passing seven named and numbered doors on its way to a bright window with an uptown view. To the left, the hallway passes the front of the nurses' station and the four doors directly opposite, then divides The shorter portion continues on to a large, south-facing window with a good prospect of the Hudson River, the longer defines the southern boundary of the station. Hung with an Elizabeth Murray lithograph and a Robert Mapplethorpe calla lily, an ochre wall then rises up to guide the hallway over another carpeted fifty feet to a long, narrow room. The small brass sign beside its wide, pebble-glass doors reads *Salon*.

The Salon is not a salon but a lounge, and a rather makeshift lounge at that. At one end sits a good-sized television set; at the other, a green fabric sofa with two matching chairs. Midpoint in the room, which was intended for the comfort of stricken relatives and other visitors but has always been patronized chiefly by Floor 21's more ambulatory patients, stands a white-draped table equipped with coffee dispensers, stacks of cups and saucers, and cut-glass containers for sugar and artificial sweeteners. In the hours from four to six in the afternoon, platters laden with pastries and chocolates from the neighborhood's gourmet specialty shops appear, as if delivered by unseen hands, upon the table.

On an afternoon early in April, when during the hours in question the long window behind the table of goodies registered swift, unpredictable alternations of light and dark, the male patients who constituted four-fifths of the residents of Floor 21, all of them recent victims of atrial fibrillation or atrial flutter, which is to say sufferers from that dire annoyance in the life of a busy American male, non-fatal heart failure, the youngest a man of fifty-eight and the most senior twenty-two years older, found themselves once again partaking of the cream cakes and petit fours and reminding themselves that they had not, after all, undergone heart attacks. Their recent adventures had aroused in them an indulgent fatalism. After all, should the worst happen, which of course it would not, they were already at the epi-center of a swarm of cardiologists!

To varying degrees, these were men of accomplishment and achievement in their common profession, that of letters.

In descending order of age, the four men enjoying the amenities of the Salon were Max Baccarat, the much respected former president of Gladstone Books, the acquisition of which by a German conglomerate had lately precipitated his retirement; Anthony Flax, a self-described "critic" who had spent the past twenty years as a full-time book reviewer for a variety of periodicals and journals, a leisurely occupation he could afford due to his having been the husband, now for three years the widower, of a sugar-substitute heiress; William Messinger, a writer whose lengthy backlist of horror/mystery/suspense novels had been kept continuously in print for twenty-five years by the bi-annual appearance of yet another new astonishment; and Charles Chipp Traynor, child of a wealthy New England family, Harvard graduate, self-declared veteran of the Vietnam conflict, and author of four non-fiction books, also (alas) a notorious plagiarist.

The connections between these four men, no less complex and multi-layered than one would gather from their professional circumstances, had inspired some initial awkwardness on their first few encounters in the Salon, but a shared desire for the treats on offer had encouraged these gentlemen to reach the accommodation displayed on the afternoon in question. By silent agreement, Max Baccarat arrived first, a few minutes after opening, to avail himself of the greatest possible range of selection and the most comfortable seating position, which was on that end side of the sofa nearest the pebble-glass doors, where the cushion was a touch more yielding than its mate. Once the great publisher had installed himself to his satisfaction, Bill Messinger and Tony Flax happened in to browse over the day's bounty before seating themselves at a comfortable distance from each other. Invariably the last to arrive, Traynor edged around the door sometime around 4:15, his manner suggesting that he had wandered in by accident, probably in search of another room altogether. The loose, patterned hospital gown he wore fastened at neck and backside added to his air of inoffensiveness, and his round glasses and stooped shoulders gave him a generic resemblance to a creature from *The Wind in the Willows*.

Of the four, the plagiarist alone had surrendered to the hospital's tacit wishes concerning patients' in-house mode of dress. Over silk pajamas of a glaring, Greek-village white, Max Baccarat wore a dark, dashing navy blue dressing gown, reputedly a Christmas present from Graham Greene, which fell nearly to the tops of his velvet fox-head slippers. Over his own pajamas, of fine-combed baby-blue cotton instead of white silk, Tony Flax had buttoned a lightweight tan trench coat, complete with epaulettes and grenade rings. Wth his extra chins and florid complexion, it made him look like a correspondent from a war conducted well within striking distance of hotel bars. Bill Messenger had taken one look at the flimsy shift offered him by the hospital staff and decided to stick, for as long as he could get away with it, to the pin-striped Armani suit and black loafers he had worn into the ER. His favorite men's stores delivered fresh shirts, socks and underwear.

When Messenger's early, less successful books had been published by Max's firm, Tony Flax had given him consistently positive reviews; after Bill's defection to a better house and larger advances for more ambitious books, Tony's increasingly bored and dismissive reviews accused him of hubris, then ceased altogether. Messenger's last three novels had not been reviewed anywhere in the *Times*, an insult he attributed to Tony's malign influence over its current editors. Likewise, Max had published Chippie Traynor's first two anecdotal histories of World War I, the second of which had been considered for a Pulitzer Prize, then lost him to a more prominent publisher whose shrewd publicists had placed him on NPR, *The Today Show*, and—after the film deal for his third book—*Charlie Rose*. Bill had given blurbs to Traynor's first two books, and Tony Flax had hailed him as a great vernacular historian. Then, two decades later, a stunned graduate student in Texas discovered lengthy, painstakingly altered parallels between Traynor's books and the contents of several Ph.D. dissertations containing oral histories taken in the 1930s. Beyond that, the student found that perhaps a third of the personal histories had been invented, simply made up, like fiction.

Within days, the graduate student had detonated Chippie's reputation. One week after the detonation, his university placed him "on leave," a status assumed to be permanent. He had vanished into a his family's Lincoln-Log compound in Maine, not to be seen or heard from until the moment when Bill Messenger and Tony Flax, who had left open the Salon's doors the better to avoid conversation, had witnessed his sorry, supine figure being wheeled past. Max Baccarat was immediately informed of the scoundrel's arrival, and before the end of the day the legendary dressing gown, the trench coat, and the pin-striped suit had overcome their mutual resentments to form an alliance against the disgraced newcomer. There was nothing, they found, like a common enemy to smooth over complicated, even difficult relationships.

Chippie Traynor had not found his way to the lounge until the following day, and he had been accompanied by a tremulous elderly woman who with equal plausibility could have passed for either his mother or his wife. Sidling around the door at 4:15, he had taken in the trio watching him from the green sofa and chairs, blinked in disbelief and recognition, ducked his head even closer to his chest, and permitted his companion to lead him to a chair located a few feet from the television set. It was clear that he was struggling with the impulse to scuttle out of the room, never to reappear. Once deposited in the chair, he tilted his head upward and whispered a few words into the woman's ear. She moved toward the pastries, and at last he eyed his former compatriots.

"Well, well," he said. "Max, Tony, and Bill. What are you in for, anyway? Me, I passed out on the street in Boothbay Harbor and had to be air-lifted in. Medevaced, like back in the day."

"These days, a lot of things must remind you of Vietnam, Chippie," Max said. "We're heart failure. You?"

"Atrial fib. Shortness of breath. Weaker than a baby. Fell down right in the street, boom. As soon as I get regulated, I'm supposed to have some sort of Echo scan."

"Heart failure, all right," Max said. "Go ahead, have a cream cake. You're among friends."

"Somehow, I doubt that," Traynor said. He was breathing hard, and he gulped air as he waved the old woman further down the table, toward the chocolate slabs and puffs. He watched carefully as she selected a number of the little cakes. "Don't forget the decaf, will you, sweetie?"

The others waited for him to introduce his companion, but he sat in silence as she placed a plate of cakes and a cup of coffee on a stand next to the television set, then faded backward into a chair that seemed to have materialized, just for her, from the ether. Traynor lifted a forkful of shiny brown goo to his mouth, sucked it off the fork, and gulped coffee. Because of his long, thick nose and recessed chin, first the fork, then the cup seemed to disappear into the lower half of his face. He twisted his head in the general direction of his companion and said, "Health food, yum yum."

She smiled vaguely at the ceiling. Traynor turned back to face the other three men, who were staring open-eyed, as if at a performance of some kind.

"Thanks for all the cards and letters, guys. I loved getting your phone calls, too. Really meant a lot to me. Oh, sorry, I'm not being very polite, am I?"

"There's no need to be sarcastic," Max said.

"I suppose not. We were never friends, were we?"

"You were looking for a publisher, not a friend," Max said. "And we did quite well together, or so I thought, before you decided you needed greener pastures. Bill did the same thing to me, come to think of it. Of course, Bill actually wrote the books that came out under his name. For a publisher, that's quite a significant difference." (Several descendants of the Ph.D.s from whom Traynor had stolen material had initiated suits against his publishing houses, Gladstone House among them.)

"Do we have to talk about this?' asked Tony Flax. He rammed his hands in the pockets of his trench coat and glanced from side to side. "Ancient history, hmmm?"

"You're just embarrassed by the reviews you gave him," Bill said. "But everybody did the same thing, including me. What did I say about *The Middle of the Trenches?* 'The ...' The what? 'The most truthful, in a way the most visionary book ever written about trench warfare.'"

"Jesus, you remember your *blurbs?*" Tony asked. He laughed and tried to draw the others in.

"I remember everything," said Bill Messenger. "Curse of being a novelist— great memory, lousy sense of direction."

"You always remembered how to get to the bank," Tony said.

"Lucky me, I didn't have to marry it," Bill said.

"Are you accusing me of marrying for money?" Tony said, defending himself by the usual tactic of pretending that what was commonly accepted was altogether unthinkable. "Not that I have any reason to defend myself against you, Messenger. As that famous memory of yours should recall, I was one of the first people to support your work."

From nowhere, a reedy English female voice said, "I did enjoy reading your reviews of Mr. Messenger's early novels, Mr. Flax. I'm sure that's why I went round to our little book shop and purchased them. They weren't at all my usual sort of *thing*, you know, but you made them sound ... I think the word would be *imperative*."

Max, Tony, and Bill peered past Charles Chipp Traynor to get a good look at his companion. For the first time, they took in that she was wearing a long, loose collection of elements that suggested feminine literary garb of the nineteen twenties: a hazy, rather shimmery woolen cardigan over a white, high-buttoned blouse, pearls, an ankle-length heather skirt, and low-heeled black shoes with laces. Her long, sensitive nose pointed up, exposing the clean line of her jaw; her lips twitched in what might have been amusement. Two things struck the men staring at her: that this woman looked a bit familiar, and that in spite of her age and general oddness, she would have to be described as beautiful.

"Well, yes," Tony said. "Thank you. I believe I was trying to express something of the sort. They were books ... well. Bill, you never understood this, I think, but I felt they were books that deserved to be read. For their workmanship, their modesty, what I thought was their actual decency."

"You mean they did what you expected them to do," Bill said.

"Decency is an uncommon literary virtue," said Traynor's companion.

"Thank you, yes," Tony said.

"But not a very interesting one, really," Bill said. "Which probably explains why it isn't all that common."

"I think you are correct, Mr. Messenger, to imply that decency is more valuable in the realm of personal relations. And for the record, I do feel your work since then has undergone a general improvement, Perhaps Mr. Flax's limitations perhaps do not permit him to appreciate your progress." She paused. There was a dangerous smile on her face. "Of course you can hardly be said to have improved to the extent claimed in your latest round of interviews."

In the moment of silence that followed, Max Baccarat looked from one of his new allies to the other and found them in a state too reflective for commentary. He cleared his throat. "Might we have the honor of an introduction, Madame? Chippie seems to have forgotten his manners."

"My name is of no importance," she said, only barely favoring him with the flicker of a glance. "And Mr. Traynor has a thorough knowledge of my feelings on the matter."

"There's two sides to every story," Chippie said. "It may not be grammar, but it's the truth."

229

"Oh, there are many more than that," said his companion, smiling again.

"Darling, would you help me return to my room?"

Chippie extended an arm, and the Englishwoman floated to her feet, cradled his root-like fist against the side of her chest, nodded to the gaping men, and gracefully conducted her charge from the room.

"So who the fuck was *that?*" said Max Baccarat.

2

Certain rituals structured the night-time hours on Floor 21. At 8:30 P.M., blood pressure was taken and evening medications administered by Tess Corrigan, an Irish softie with a saggy gut, an alcoholic, angina-ridden husband, and an understandable tolerance for misbehavior. Tess herself sometimes appeared to be mildly intoxicated. Class resentment caused her to treat Max a touch brusquely, but Tony's trench coat amused her to wheezy laughter. After Bill Messenger had signed two books for her niece, a devoted fan, Tess had allowed him to do anything he cared to, including taking illicit journeys downstairs to the gift shop. "Oh, Mr. Messenger," she had said, "a fella with your gifts, the books you could write about this place." Three hours after Tess's departure, a big, heavily-dreadlocked nurse with an islands accent surged into the patients' rooms to awaken them for the purpose of distributing tranquilizers and knockout pills. Because she resembled a greatly inflated, ever-simmering Whoopi Goldberg, Max, Tony, and Bill referred to this terrifying and implacable figure as "Molly." (Molly's real name, printed on the ID card attached to a sash used as a waistband, was permanently concealed behind beaded swags and little hanging pouches.) At six in the morning, Molly swept in again, wielding the blood-pressure mechanism like an angry deity maintaining a good grip on a sinner. At the end of her shift, she came wrapped in a strong, dark scent, suggestive of forest fires in underground crypts. The three literary gentlemen found this aroma disturbingly erotic.

On the morning after the appearance within the Salon of Charles Chipp Traynor and his disconcerting muse, Molly raked Bill with a look of pity and scorn as she trussed his upper arm and strangled it by pumping a rubber bulb. Her crypt-fire odor seemed particularly smoky.

"What?" he asked.

Molly shook her massive head. "Toddle, toddle, toddle, you must believe you're the new postman in this beautiful neighborhood of ours."

Terror seized his gut. "I don't think I know what you're talking about."

Molly chuckled and gave the bulb a final squeeze, causing his arm to go numb from bicep to his fingertips. "Of course not. But you do know that we have no limitations on visiting hours up here in our paradise, don't you?"

"Um," he said.

"Then let me tell you something you do not know, Mr. Postman. Miz LaValley in 21R-12 passed away last night. I do not imagine you ever took it upon yourself to pay the poor woman a social call. And *that*, Mr. Postman, means that you, Mr. Baccarat, Mr. Flax, and our new addition, Mr. Traynor, are now the only patients on Floor 21."

"Ah," he said.

As soon as she left his room, he showered and dressed in the previous day's clothing, eager to get out into the corridor and check on the conditions in 21R-14, Chippie Traynor's room, for it was what he had seen there in the hours between Tess Corrigan's florid departure and Molly Goldberg's first drive-by shooting that had led to his becoming the floor's postman.

It had been just before nine in the evening, and something had urged him to take a final turn around the floor before surrendering himself to the hateful "gown" and turning off his lights. His route took him past the command center, where the Night Visitor, scowling over a desk too small for her, made grim notations on a chart, and down the corridor toward the window looking out toward the Hudson river and the great harbor. Along the way he passed 21R-14, where muffled noises had caused him to look in. From the corridor, he could see the bottom third of the plagiarist's bed, on which the sheets and blanket appeared to be writhing, or at least shifting about in a conspicuous manner. Messenger noticed a pair of black, lace-up women's shoes on the floor near the bottom of the bed. An untidy heap of clothing lay beside the in-turned shoes. For a few seconds ripe with shock and envy, he had listened to the soft noises coming from the room. Then he whirled around and rushed toward his allies' chambers.

"Who *is* that dame?" Max Baccarat had asked, essentially repeating the question he had asked earlier that day. "*What* is she? That miserable Traynor, God damn him to hell, may he have a heart attack and die. A woman like that, who cares how old she is?"

Tony Flax had groaned in disbelief and said, "I swear, that woman is either the ghost of Virginia Woolf or her direct descendant. All my life, I had the hots for Virginia Woolf, and now she turns up with that ugly crook, Chippie Traynor? Get out of here, Bill, I have to strategize."

3

At 4:15, the three conspirators pretended not to notice the plagiarist's furtive, animal-like entrance to the Salon. Max Baccarat's silvery hair, cleansed, stroked, clipped, buffed, and shaped during an emergency session with a hair therapist named Mr. Keith, seemed to glow with a virile inner light as he settled into the comfortable part of the sofa and organized his decaf cup and plate of chocolates and little cakes as if preparing soldiers for battle. Tony Flax's rubber chins shone a twice-shaved red, and his glasses sparkled. Beneath the hem of the trench coat, which appeared to have been ironed, colorful argyle socks descended from just below his lumpy knees to what seemed to be a pair of nifty two-tone shoes. Beneath the jacket of his pin-striped suit, Bill Messenger sported a brand-new, high-collared black silk T-shirt delivered by courier that morning from 65th and Madison. Thus attired, the longer-term residents of Floor 21 seemed lost as much in self-admiration as in the political discussion under way when at last they allowed themselves to acknowledge Chippie's presence. Max's eye skipped over Traynor and wandered toward the door.

"Will your lady friend be joining us?" he asked. "I thought she made some really very valid points yesterday, and I'd enjoy hearing what she has to say about our situation in Iraq. My two friends here are simple-minded liberals, you can never get anything sensible out of them."

"You wouldn't like what she'd have to say about Iraq," Traynor said. "And neither would they."

"Know her well, do you?" Tony asked.

"You could say that." Traynor's gown slipped as he bent over the table to pump coffee into his cup from the dispenser, and the three other men hastily turned their glances elsewhere.

"Tie that up, Chippie, would you?" Bill asked. "It's like a view of the Euganean Hills."

"Then look somewhere else. I'm getting some coffee, and then I have to pick out a couple of these yum-yums."

"You're alone today, then?" Tony asked.

"Looks like it."

"By the way," Bill said, "you were entirely right to point out that nothing is really as simple as it seems. There *are* more than two sides to every issue. I mean, wasn't that the point of what we were saying about Iraq?"

"To you, maybe," Max said. "You'd accept two sides as long as they were both printed in *The Nation*."

"Anyhow," Bill said, "please tell your friend that the next time she cares to visit this hospital, we'll try to remember what she said about decency."

"What makes you think she's going to come here again?"

"She seemed very fond of you," Tony said.

"The lady mentioned your limitations." Chippie finished assembling his assortment of treats and at last refastened his gaping robe. "I'm surprised you have any interest in seeing her again."

Tony's cheeks turned a deeper red. "All of us have limitations, I'm sure. In fact, I was just remembering ..."

"Oh?' Chippie lifted his snout and peered through his little lenses. "Were you? What, specifically?"

"Nothing," said Tony. "I shouldn't have said anything. Sorry."

"Did any of you know Mrs. LaValley, the lady in 21R-12?" Bill asked. "She died last night. Apart from us, she was the only other person on the floor."

"I knew Edie LaValley," Chippie said. "In fact, my friend and I dropped in and had a nice little chat with her just before dinner-time last night. I'm glad I had a chance to say goodbye to the old girl."

"Edie LaValley?" Max said. "Hold on. I seem to remember ..."

"Wait, I do, too," Bill said. "Only ..."

"I know, she was that girl who work for Nick Wheadle over at Viking, thirty years ago, back when Wheadle was everybody's golden boy," Tony said. "Stupendous girl. She got married to him and was Edith Wheadle for a while, but after the divorce she went back to her old name. We went out for a couple of months in 1983, '84. What happened to her after that?"

"She spent six years doing research for me," Traynor said. "She wasn't my *only* researcher, because I generally had three of them on the payroll, not to mention a couple of graduate students. Edie was very good at the job, though. Extremely conscientious."

"And knockout, drop-dead gorgeous," Tony said. "At least before she fell into Nick Wheadle's clutches."

"I didn't know you used so many researchers," Max said. "Could that be how you wound up quoting all those ...?"

"Deliberately misquoting, I suppose you mean," Chippie said. "But the answer is no." A fat, sugar-coated square of sponge cake disappeared beneath his nose.

"But Edie Wheadle," Max said in a reflective voice. "By God, I think I ..."

"Think nothing of it," Traynor said. "That's what she did."

"Edie must have looked very different toward the end," said Tony. He sounded almost hopeful. "Twenty years, illness, all of that."

"My friend and I thought she looked much the same." Chippie's mild, creaturely face swung toward Tony Flax. "Weren't you about to tell us something?"

Tony flushed again. "No, not really."

"Perhaps an old memory resurfaced. That often happens on a night when someone in the vicinity dies—the death seems to awaken something."

"Edie's death certainly seemed to have awakened you," Bill said. "Didn't you ever hear of closing your door?"

"The nurses waltz right in anyhow, and there are no locks," Traynor said. "Better to be frank about matters, especially on Floor 21. It looks as though Max has something on his mind."

"Yes," Max said. "If Tony doesn't feel like talking, I will. Last night, an old memory of mine resurfaced, as Chippie puts it, and I'd like to get it off my chest, if that's the appropriate term."

"Good man," Traynor said. "Have another of those delicious little yummies and tell us all about it."

"This happened back when I was a little boy," Max said, wiping his lips with a crisp linen handkerchief.

Bill Messenger and Tony Flax seemed to go very still.

"I was raised in Pennsylvania, up in the Susquehanna Valley area. It's strange country, a little wilder and more backward than you'd expect, a little hillbillyish, especially once you get back in the Endless Mountains. My folks had a little store that sold everything under the sun, it seemed to me, and we lived in the building next door, close to the edge of town. Our town was called Manship, not that you can find it on any map. We had a one-room schoolhouse, an Episcopalian church and a Unitarian church, a feed and grain store, a place called The Lunch Counter, a Tract house, and a tavern called the Rusty Dusty, where, I'm sad to say, my father spent far too much of his time.

"When he came home loaded, as happened just about every other night, he was in a foul mood. It was mainly guilt, d'you see, because my mother had been slaving away in the store for hours, plus making dinner, and she was in a rage, which only made him feel worse. All he really wanted to do was to beat himself up, but I was an easy target, so he beat me up instead. Nowadays, we'd call it child abuse, but back then, in a place like Manship, it was just normal parenting, at least for a drunk. I wish I could tell you fellows that everything turned out well, and that my father sobered up, and we reconciled, and I forgave him, but none of that happened. Instead, he got meaner and meaner, and we got poorer and poorer. I learned to hate to the old bastard, and I still hated him when a traveling junk wagon ran over him, right there in front of the Rusty Dusty, when I was eleven years old. 1935, the height of the Great Depression. He was lying passed out in the street, and the junkman never saw him.

"Now, I was determined to get out of that god-forsaken little town, and out of the Susquehanna Valley and the Endless Mountains, and obviously I did, because here I am today, with an excellent place in the world, if I might pat myself on the back a little bit. What I did was, I managed to keep the store going even while I went to the high school in the next town, and then I got a scholarship to U. Penn., where I waited on tables and tended bar and sent money back to my mother. Two days after I graduated, she died of a heart attack. That was her reward.

"I bought a bus ticket to New York. Even though I was never a great reader, I liked the idea of getting into the book business. Everything that happened after that you could read about in old copies of *Publisher's Weekly*. Maybe one day I'll write a book about it all.

"If I do, I'll never put in what I'm about to tell you now. It slipped my mind completely—the whole thing. You'll realize how bizarre that is after I'm done. I forgot all about it! Until about three this morning, that is, when I woke up too scared to breathe, my heart going bump bump, and the sweat pouring out of me. Every little bit of this business just came *back* to me, I mean everything, ever god-damned little tiny detail ..."

He looked at Bill and Tony. "What? You two guys look like you should be back in the ER."

"Every detail?" Tony said. "It'st ..."

"You woke up then, too?" Bill asked him.

"Are you two knotheads going to let me talk, or do you intend to keep interrupting?"

"I just wanted to ask this one thing, but I changed my mind," Tony said. "Sorry, Max. I shouldn't have said anything. It was a crazy idea. Sorry."

"Was your Dad an alcoholic, too?" Bill asked Tony Flax.

Tony squeezed up his face, said, "Aaaah," and waggled one hand in the air. "I don't like the word 'alcoholic.'"

"Yeah," Bill said. "All right."

"I guess the answer is, you're going to keep interrupting."

"No, please, Max, go on," Bill said.

Max frowned at both of them, then gave a dubious glance to Chippie Traynor, who stuffed another tiny cream cake into his maw and smiled around it.

"Fine. I don't know why I want to tell you about this anyhow. It's not like I actually *understand* it, as you'll see, and it's kind of ugly and kind of scary—I guess what amazes me is that I just remembered it all, or that I managed to put it out of my mind for nearly seventy years, one or the other. But you know? It's like, it's real even if it never happened, or even if I dreamed the whole thing."

"This story wouldn't happen to involve a house, would it?" Tony asked.

"Most god-damned stories involve houses," Max said. "Even a lousy book critic ought to know that."

"Tony knows that," Chippie said. "See his ridiculous coat? That's a house. Isn't it, Tony?"

"You know what this is," Tony said. "It's a *trench coat*, a real one. Only from World War II, not World War I. It used to belong to my father. He was a hero in the war."

"As I was about to say," Max said, looking around and continuing only when the other three were paying attention, "when I woke up in the middle of the night I could remember the feel of the old blanket on my bed, the feel of pebbles and earth on my bare feet when I ran to the outhouse, I could remember the way my mother's scrambled eggs tasted. The whole anxious thing I had going on inside me while my mother was making breakfast.

" I was going to go off by myself in the woods. That was all right with my mother. At least it got rid of me for the day. But she didn't know was that I had decided to steal one of the guns in the case at the back of the store.

"And you know what? She didn't pay any attention to the guns. About half of them belonged to people who swapped them for food because guns were all they had left to barter with. My mother hated the whole idea. And my father was in a fog until he could get to the tavern, and after that he couldn't think straight enough to remember how many guns were supposed to be back in that case. Anyhow, for the past few days, I'd had my eye on an over-under shotgun that used to belong to a farmer called Hakewell, and while my mother wasn't watching I nipped in back and took it out of the case. Then I stuffed my pockets with shells, ten of them. There was something going on way back in the woods, and while I wanted to keep my eye on it, I wanted to be able to protect myself, too, in case anything got out of hand."

Bill Messenger jumped to his feet and for a moment seemed preoccupied with brushing what might have been pastry crumbs off the bottom of his suit jacket. Max Baccarat frowned at him, then glanced down at the skirts of his dressing gown in a brief inspection. Bill continued to brush off imaginary particles of food, slowly turning in a circle as he did so.

"There is something you wish to communicate," Max said. "The odd thing, you know, is that for the moment, you see, I thought communication was in my hands."

Bill stopped fiddling with his jacket and regarded the old publisher with his eyebrows tugged toward the bridge of his nose and his mouth a thin, downturned line. He placed his hands on his hips. "I don't know what you're doing, Max, and I don't know where you're getting this. But I certainly wish you'd stop."

"What are you talking about?"

"He's right, Max," said Tony Flax.

"You jumped-up little fop," Max said, ignoring Tony. "You damned little show pony. What's your problem? You haven't told a good story in the past ten years, so listen to mine, you might learn something."

"You know what you are?" Bill asked him. "Twenty years ago, you used to be a decent second-rate publisher. Unfortunately, it's been all downhill from there. Now you're not even a third-rate publisher, you're a sellout. You took the money and went on the lam. Morally, you don't exist at all. You're a fancy dressing gown. And by the way, Graham Greene didn't give it to you, because Graham Greene wouldn't have given you a glass of water on a hot day."

Both of them were panting a bit and trying not to show it. Like a dog trying to choose between masters, Tony Flax swung his head from one to the other. In the end, he settled on Max Baccarat. "I don't really get it either, you know, but I think you should stop, too."

"Nobody cares what you think," Max told him. "Your brain dropped dead the day you swapped your integrity for a mountain of coffee sweetener."

"You did marry for money, Flax," Bill Messinger said. "Let's try being honest, all right? You sure as hell didn't fall in love with her beautiful face."

"And how about you, Traynor?" Max shouted. "I suppose you think I should stop, too."

"Nobody cares what I think," Chippie said. "I'm the lowest of the low. People despise me."

"First of all," Bill said, "if you want to talk about details, Max, you ought to get them *right*. It wasn't an 'over-under shotgun,' whatever the hell that is, it was a —"

"His name wasn't Hakewell," Tony said. "It was Hackman, like the actor.

"It wasn't Hakewell or Hackman," Bill said. "It started with an A."

"But there was a *house*," Tony said. "You know, I think my father probably was an alcoholic. His personality never changed, though. He was always a mean son of a bitch, drunk or sober."

"Mine, too," said Bill. "Where are you from, anyhow, Tony?"

"A little town in Oregon, called Milton. How about you?"

"Rhinelander, Wisconsin. My dad was the Chief of Police. I suppose there were lots of woods around Milton."

"We might as well have been in a forest. You?"

"The same."

"I'm from Boston, but we spent the summers in Maine," Chippie said.

237

"You know what Maine is? Eighty per cent woods. There are places in Maine, the roads don't even have names."

"There was a *house*," Tony Flax insisted. "Back in the woods, and it didn't belong there. Nobody builds houses in the middle of the woods, miles away from everything, without even a road to use, not even a road without a name."

"This can't be real," Bill said. "I had a house, you had a house, and I bet Max had a house, even though he's so long-winded he hasn't gotten to it yet. I had an air rifle, Max had a shotgun, what did you have?"

"My Dad's .22," Tony said. "Just a little thing—around us, nobody took a .22 all that seriously."

Max was looking seriously disgruntled. "What, we all had the same *dream?*"

"You said it wasn't a dream," said Chippie Traynor. "You said it was a memory."

"It felt like a memory, all right," Tony said. "Just the way Max described it—the way the ground felt under my feet, the smell of my mother's cooking."

"I wish your lady friend was here now, Traynor," Max said. "She'd be able to explain what's going on, wouldn't she?"

"I have a number of lady friends," Chippie said, calmly stuffing a little glazed cake into his mouth.

"All right, Max," Bill said. "Let's explore this. You come across this big house, right? And there's someone in it?"

"Eventually, there is," Max said, and Tony Flax nodded.

"Right. And you can't even tell what age he is—or even if it *is* a he, right?"

"It was hiding in the back of a room," Tony says. "When I thought it was a girl, it really scared me. I didn't want it to be a girl."

"I didn't, either," Max said. "Oh—imagine how that would feel, a girl hiding in the shadows at the back of a room."

"Only this never happened," Bill said. "If we all seem to remember this bizarre story, then none of us is really remembering it."

"Okay, but it was a boy," Tony said. "And he got older."

"Right there in that house," said Max. "I thought it was like watching my damnable father grow up right in front of my eyes. In what, six weeks?"

"About that," Tony said.

"And him in there all alone," said Bill. "Without so much as a stick of furniture. I thought that was one of the things that made it so frightening."

"Scared the shit out of me," Tony said. "When my Dad came back from the war, sometimes he put on his uniform and tied us to the chairs. Tied us to the chairs!"

"I didn't think it was really going to injure him," Bill said.

"I didn't even think I'd hit him," Tony said.

"I knew damn well I'd hit him," Max said. "I wanted to blow his head off. But my Dad lived another three years, and then the junkman finally ran him over."

"Max," Tony said, "you mentioned there was a Tract House in Manship. What's a Tract House?"

"It was where they printed the religious tracts, you ignoramus. You could go in there and pick them up for free. All of this was like child abuse, I'm telling you. Spare the Rod stuff."

"It was like his eye exploded," Bill said. Absent-mindedly, he took one of the untouched pastries from Max's plate and bit into it.

Max stared at him.

"They didn't change the goodies this morning, " Bill said. "This thing is a little stale."

"I prefer my pastries stale," said Chippie Traynor.

"I prefer to keep mine for myself, and not have them lifted off my plate," said Max, sounding as though something were caught in his throat.

"The bullet went straight through the left lens of his glasses and right into his head," said Toby. "And when he raised his head, his eye was full of blood."

"Would you look out that window?" Max said in a loud voice.

Bill Messenger and Tony Flax turned to the window, saw nothing special— perhaps a bit more haze in the air than they expected—and looked back at the old publisher.

"Sorry," Max said. He passed a trembling hand over his face. "I think I'll go back to my room."

4

"Nobody visits me," Bill Messenger said to Tess Corrigan. She was taking his blood pressure, and appeared to be having a little trouble getting accurate numbers. "I don't even really remember how long I've been here, but I haven't had a single visitor."

"Haven't you now?" Tess squinted at the blood pressure tube, sighed, and once again pumped the ball and tightened the band around his arm. Her breath contained a pure, razor-sharp whiff of alcohol.

"It makes me wonder, do I have any friends?"

Toss grunted with satisfaction and scribbled numbers on his chart. "Writers lead lonely lives," she told him. "Most of them aren't fit for human company, anyhow." She patted his wrist. "You're a lovely specimen, though."

"Tess, how long have I been here?"

"Oh, it was only a little while ago," she said. "And I believe it was raining at the time."

After she left, Bill watched television for a little while, but television, a frequent and dependable companion in his earlier life, seemed to have become intolerably stupid. He turned it off and for a time flipped through the pages of the latest book by a highly regarded contemporary novelist several decades younger than himself. He had bought the book before going into the hospital, thinking that during his stay he would have enough uninterrupted time to dig into the experience so many others had described as rich, complex, and marvelously nuanced, but he was having problems getting through it. The book bored him. The people were loathsome and the style was gelid. He kept wishing he had brought along some uncomplicated and professional trash he could use as a palate cleanser. By 10:00, he was asleep.

At 11:30, a figure wrapped in cold air appeared in his room, and he woke up as she approached. The woman coming nearer in the darkness must have been Molly, the Jamaican nurse who always charged in at this hour, but she did not give off Molly's arousing scent of fires in underground crypts. She smelled of damp weeds and muddy riverbanks. Bob did not want this version of Molly to get any closer to him than the end of his bed, and with his heart beating so violently that he could feel the limping rhythm of his heart, he commanded her to stop. She instantly obeyed.

He pushed the button to raise the head of his bed and tried to make her out as his body folded upright,. The river-smell had intensified, and cold air streamed toward him. He had no desire at all to turn on any of the three lights at his disposal. Dimly, he could make out a thin, tallish figure with dead hair plastered to her face, wearing what seemed to be a long cardigan sweater, soaked through and (he thought) dripping onto the floor. In this figure's hands was a fat, unjacketed book stained dark by her wet fingers.

"I don't want you here," he said. "And I don't want to read that book, either. I've already read everything you ever wrote, but that was a long time ago."

The drenched figure glided forward and deposited the book between his feet. Terrified that he might recognize her face, Bill clamped his eyes shut and kept them shut until the odors of river-water and mud had vanished from the air.

When Molly burst into the room to gather the new day's information the next morning, Bill Messenger realized that his night's visitation could have occurred only in a dream. Here was the well-known, predictable world around him, and every inch of it was a profound relief to him. Bill took in his bed, the little nest of monitors ready to be called upon should an emergency take place, his television and its remote control device, the door to his spacious bathroom, the door to the hallway, as ever half-open. On the other of his bed lay the long window, now curtained for the sake of the night's sleep. And here, above all, was Molly, a one-woman Reality Principle, exuding the rich odor of burning graves as she tried to cut off his circulation with a blood-pressure machine. The bulk and massivity of her upper arms suggested that Molly's own blood pressure would have to be read by means of some other technology, perhaps steam gauge. The whites of her eyes shone with a faint trace of pink, leading Bill to speculate for a moment of wild improbability if the ferocious night nurse indulged in marijuana.

"You're doing well, Mr. Postman," she said. "Making good progress."

"I'm glad to hear it," he said. "When do you think I'll be able to go home?"

"That is for the doctors to decide, not me. You'll have to bring it up with them." From a pocket hidden beneath her swags and pouches, she produced a white paper cup half-filled with pills and capsules of varying sizes and colors. She thrust it at him. "Morning meds. Gulp them down like a good boy, now." Her other hand held out a small plastic bottle of Poland Spring water, the provenance of which reminded Messenger of what Chippie Traynor had said about Maine. Deep woods, roads without names ...

He upended the cup over his mouth, opened the bottle of water, and managed to get all his pills down at the first try.

Molly whirled around to leave with her usual sense of having had more than enough of her time wasted by the likes of him, and was half way to the door before he remembered something that had been on his mind for the past few days.

"I haven't seen the *Times* since I don't remember when," he said. "Could you please get me a copy? I wouldn't even mind one that's a couple of days old."

Molly gave him a long, measuring look, then nodded her head. "Because many of our people find them so upsetting, we tend not to get the newspapers up here. But I'll see if I can locate one for you." She moved ponderously to the door and paused to look back at him again just before she walked out. "By the way, from now on you and your friends will have to get along without Mr. Traynor's company."

241

"Why?" Bill asked. "What happened to him?"

"Mr. Traynor is ... gone, sir."

"Chippie died, you mean? When did that happen?" With a shudder, he remembered the figure from his dream. The smell of rotting weeds and wet riverbank awakened within him, and he felt as if she were once again standing before him.

"Did I say he was dead? What I said was, he is ... *gone*."

For reasons he could not identify, Bill Messenger did not go through the morning's rituals with his usual impatience. He felt slow-moving, reluctant to engage the day. In the shower, he seemed barely able to raise him arms. The water seemed brackish, and his soap all but refused to lather. The towels were stiff and thin, like the cheap towels he remembered from his youth. After he had succeeded in drying off at least most of the easily reachable parts of his body, he sat on his bed and listened to the breath laboring in and out of his body. Without him noticing, the handsome pin-striped suit had become as wrinkled and tired as he felt himself to be, and besides that he seemed to be out of clean shirts. He pulled a dirty one from the closet. His swollen feet took some time to ram into his black loafers.

Armored at last in the costume of a great worldly success, Bill stepped out into the great corridor with a good measure of his old dispatch. He wished Max Baccarat had not called him a "jumped-up little fop" and a "damned little show pony" the other day, for he genuinely enjoyed good clothing, and it hurt him to think that others might take this simple pleasure, which after all did contain a moral element, as a sign of vanity. On the other hand, he should have thought twice before telling Max that he was a third-rate publisher and a sellout. Everybody knew that robe hadn't been a gift from Graham Greene, though. That myth represented nothing more than Max Baccarat's habit of portraying and presenting himself as an old-line publishing grandee, like Alfred Knopf.

The nursing station—what he liked to think of as "the command center"—was oddly understaffed this morning. In a landscape of empty desks and unattended computer monitors, Molly sat on a pair of stools she had placed side by side, frowning as ever down at some form she was obliged to work through. Bill nodded at her and received the non-response he had anticipated. Instead of turning left toward the Salon as he usually did, Bill decided to stroll over to the elevators and the cherry wood desk where diplomatic, red-jacketed Mr. Singh guided newcomers past his display of Casablanca lilies, tea roses, and lupines. On his perambulations through the halls, he often passed through Mr. Singh's tiny realm, and he found the man a kindly, reassuring presence.

Today, though, Mr. Singh seemed not to be on duty, and the great glass vase had been removed from his desk. OUT OF ORDER signs had been taped to the elevators.

Feeling a vague sense of disquiet, Bill retraced his steps and walked past the side of the nursing station to embark upon the long corridor that led to the north-facing window. Max Baccarat's room lie down this corridor, and Bill thought he might pay a call on the old gent. He could apologize for the insults he had given him, and perhaps receive an apology in return. Twice, Baccarat had thrown the word "little" at him, and Bill's cheeks stung as if he had been slapped. About the story, or the memory, or whatever it had been, however, Bill intended to say nothing. He did not believe that he, Max, and Tony Flax had dreamed of the same bizarre set of events, nor that they had experienced these decidedly dream-like events in youth. The illusion that they had done so had been inspired by proximity and daily contact. The world of Floor 21 was as hermetic as a prison.

He came to Max's room and knocked at the half-open door. There was no reply. "Max?" he called out. "Feel like having a visitor?"

In the absence of a reply, he thought that Max might be asleep. It would do no harm to check on his old acquaintance. How odd, it occurred to him, to think that he and Max had both had relations with little Edie Wheadle. And Tony Flax, too. And that she should have died on this floor, unknown to them! *There* was someone to whom he rightly could have apologized—at the end, he had treated her quite badly. She had been the sort of girl, he thought, who almost expected to be treated badly. But far from being an excuse, that was the opposite, an indictment.

Putting inconvenient Edie Wheadle out of his mind, Bill moved past the bathroom and the "reception" area into the room proper, there to find Max Baccarat not in bed as he had expected, but beyond it and seated in one of the low, slightly cantilevered chairs, which he had turned to face the window.

"Max?"

The old man did not acknowledge is presence in any way. Bill noticed that he was not wearing the splendid blue robe, only his white pajamas, and his feet were bare. Unless he had fallen asleep, he was staring at the window and appeared to have been doing so for some time. His silvery hair was mussed and stringy. As Bill approached, he took in the rigidity of Max's head and neck, the stiff tension in his shoulders. He came around the foot of the bed and at last saw the whole of the old man's body, stationed sideways to him as it faced the window. Max was gripping the arms of the chair and leaning forward. His mouth hung open, and his lips had been drawn back. His eyes, too, were open, hugely, as they stared straight ahead.

With a little thrill of anticipatory fear, Bill glanced at the window. What he saw, haze shot through with streaks of light, could hardly have brought Max Baccarat to this pitch. His face seemed rigid with terror. Then Bill realized that this had nothing to do with terror, and Max had suffered a great, paralyzing stroke. That was the explanation for the pathetic scene before him. He jumped to the side of the bed and pushed the call button for the nurse. When he did not get an immediate response, he pushed it again, twice, and held the button down for several seconds. Still no soft footsteps came from the corridor.

A folded copy of the *Times* lay on Max's bed, and with a sharp, almost painful sense of hunger for the million vast and minuscule dramas taking place outside Governor General, he realized that what he had said to Molly was no more than the literal truth: it seemed weeks since he had seen a newspaper. With the justification that Max would have no use for it, Bill snatched up the paper and felt, deep in the core of his being, a real greed for its contents—devouring the columns of print would be akin to gobbling up great bits of the world. He tucked the neat, folded package of the *Times* under his arm and left the room.

"Nurse," he called. It came to him that he had never learned the real name of the woman they called Molly Goldberg. "Hello? There's a man in trouble down here!"

He walked quickly down the hallway in what he perceived as a deep, unsettling silence. "Hello, nurse!" he called, at least in part to hear at least the sound of his own voice.

When Bill reached the deserted nurses' station, he rejected the impulse to say, "Where is everybody?" The Night Visitor no longer occupied her pair of stools, and the usual chiaroscuro had deepened into a murky darkness. It was though they had pulled the plugs and stolen away.

"I don't get this," Bill said. "*Doctors* might bail, but nurses don't."

He looked up and down the corridor and saw only a gray carpet and a row of half-open doors. Behind one of those doors sat Max Baccarat, who had once been something a friend. Max was destroyed, Bill thought; damage so severe could not be repaired. Like a film of greasy dust, the sense descended upon him that he was wasting his time. If the doctors and nurses were elsewhere, as seemed the case, nothing could be done for Max until their return. Even after that, in all likelihood very little could be done for poor old Max. His heart failure had been a symptom of a wider systemic problem.

But still. He could not just walk away and ignore Max's plight. Messenger turned around and paced down the corridor to the door where the nameplate read Anthony Flax. "Tony," he said. "Are you in there? I think Max had a stroke."

He rapped on the door and pushed it all the way open. Dreading what he might find, he walked into the room. "Tony?" He already knew the room was empty, and when he was able to see the bed, all was as he had expected: an empty bed, an empty chair, a blank television screen, and blinds pulled down to keep the day from entering.

Bill left Tony's room, turned left, then took the hallway that led past the Salon. A man in an unclean janitor's uniform, his back to Bill, was removing the Mapplethorpe photographs from the wall and loading them face-down onto a wheeled cart.

"What are you doing?" he asked.

The man in the janitor uniform looked over his shoulder and said, "I'm doing my job, that's what I'm doing." He had greasy hair, a low forehead, and an acne-scarred face with deep furrows in the cheeks.

"But why are you taking down those pictures?"

The man turned around to face him. He was strikingly ugly, and his ugliness seemed part of his intention, as if he had chosen it. "Gee, buddy, why do you suppose I'd do something like that? To upset *you?* Well, I'm sorry if you're upset, but you had nothing to do with this. They tell me to do stuff like this, I do it. End of story." He pushed his face forward, ready for the next step.

"Sorry," Bill said. "I understand completely. Have you seen a doctor or a nurse up here in the past few minutes? A man on the other side of the floor just had a stroke. He needs medical attention."

"Too bad, but I don't have anything to do with doctors. The man I deal with is my supervisor, and supervisors don't wear white coats, and they don't carry stethoscopes. Now if you'll excuse me, I'll be on my way."

"But I need a doctor!"

"You look okay to me," the man said, turning away. He took the last photograph from the wall and pushed his cart through the metal doors that marked the boundary of the realm ruled by Tess Corrigan, Molly Goldberg, and their colleagues. Bill followed him through, and instantly found himself in a functional, green-painted corridor lit by fluorescent lighting and lined with locked doors. The janitor pushed his trolley around a corner and disappeared.

"Is anybody here?" Bill's voice carried through the empty hallways. "A man here needs a doctor!"

The corridor he was in led to another, which led to another, which went past a small, deserted nurses' station and ended at a huge, flat door with a sign that said MEDICAL PERSONNEL ONLY. Bill pushed at the door, but it was locked. He had the feeling that he could wander through these corridors for hours and find nothing but blank walls and locked doors. When he returned to the metal doors and pushed through to the private wing, relief flooded through him, making him feel light-headed.

The Salon invited him in—he wanted to sit down, he wanted to catch his breath and see if any of the little cakes had been set out yet. He had forgotten to order breakfast, and hunger was making him weak. Bill put his hand on one of the pebble-glass doors and saw an indistinct figure seated near the table. For a moment, his heart felt cold, and he hesitated before he opened the door.

Tony Flax was bent over in his chair, and what Bill Messenger noticed first was that the critic was wearing one of the thin hospital gowns that tied at the neck and the back. His trench coat lay puddled on the floor. Then he saw that Flax appeared to be weeping. His hands were clasped to his face, and his back rose and fell with jerky, uncontrolled movements.

"Tony?" he said. "What happened to you?"

Flax continued to weep silently, with the concentration and selfishness of a small child.

"Can I help you, Tony?" Bill asked.

When Flax did not respond, Bill looked around the room for the source of his distress. Half-filled coffee cups stood on the little tables, and petits fours lay jumbled and scattered over the plates and the white table. As he watched, a cockroach nearly two inches long burrowed out of a little square of white chocolate and disappeared around the back of a Battenburg cake. The cockroach looked as shiny and polished as a new pair of black shoes.

Something was moving on the other side of the window, but Bill Messenger wanted nothing to do with it. "Tony," he said, "I'll be in my room."

Down the corridor he went, the tails of his suit jacket flapping behind him. A heavy, liquid pressure built up in his chest, and the lights seemed to darken, then grow brighter again. He remembered Max, his mind gone, staring open-mouthed at his window: what had he seen?

Bill thought of Chippie Traynor, one of his mole-like eyes bloodied behind the shattered lens of his glasses.

At the entrance to his room, he hesitated once again as he had outside the Salon, fearing that if he went in, he might not be alone. But of course he would be alone, for apart from the janitor no one else on Floor 21 was capable of movement. Slowly, making as little noise as possible, he slipped around his door and entered his room. It looked exactly as it had when he had awakened that morning. The younger author's book lay discarded on his bed, the monitors awaited an emergency, the blinds covered the long window. Bill thought the wildly alternating pattern of light and dark that moved across the blinds proved nothing. Freaky New York weather, you never knew what it was going to do. He did not hear odd noises, like half-remembered voices, calling to him from the other side of the glass.

As he moved nearer to the foot of the bed, he saw on the floor the bright jacket of the book he had decided not to read, and knew that in the night it had fallen from his moveable tray. The book on his bed had no jacket, and at first he had no idea where it came from. When he remembered the circumstances under which he had seen this book—or one a great deal like it—he felt revulsion, as though it were a great slug.

Bill turned his back on the bed, swung his chair around, and plucked the newspaper from under his arm. After he had scanned the headlines without making much effort to take them in, habit led him to the obituaries on the last two pages of the financial section. As soon as he had folded the pages back, a photograph of a sly, mild face with a recessed chin and tiny spectacles lurking above an overgrown nose levitated up from the columns of newsprint. The header announced CHARLES CHIPP TRAYNOR, POPULAR WAR HISTORIAN TARRED BY SCANDAL.

Helplessly, Bill read the first paragraph of Chippie's obituary. Four days past, this once-renowned historian whose career had been destroyed by charges of plagiarism and fraud had committed suicide by leaping from the window of his fifteenth-story apartment on the Upper West Side.

Four days ago? Bill thought. It seemed to him that was when Chippie Traynor had first appeared in the Salon. He dropped the paper, with the effect that Traynor's fleshy nose and mild eyes peered up at him from the floor. The terrible little man seemed to be everywhere, despite having *gone*. He could sense Chippie Traynor floating outside his window like a small, inoffensive balloon from Macy's Thanksgiving Day Parade. Children would say, "Who's that?', and their parents would look up, shield their eyes, shrug, and say, "I don't know, hone. Wasn't he in a Disney cartoon?" Only he was not in a Disney cartoon, and the children and their parents could not see him, and he wasn't at all cute. One of his eyes had been injured. This Chippie Traynor, not the one that had given them a view of his backside in the Salon, hovered outside Bill Messenger's window, whispering the wretched and insinuating secrets of the despised, the contemptible, the rejected and fallen from grace.

Bill turned from the window and took a single step into the nowhere that awaited him. He had nowhere to go, he knew, so nowhere had to be where he was going. It would probably going to be a lot like this place, only less comfortable. Much, *much* less comfortable. With nowhere to go, he reached out his hand and picked up the dull brown book lying at the foot of his bed. Bringing it toward his body felt like reeling in some monstrous fish that struggled against the line. There were faint water marks on the front cover, and it bore a faint, familiar smell. When he had it within reading distance, Bill turned the spine up and read the title and author's name: *In the Middle of the Trenches*, by Charles Chipp Traynor. It was the book he had blurbed. Max Baccarat had published it, and Tony Flax had rhapsodized over it in the *Sunday Times* book review section. About a hundred pages from the end, a bookmark in the shape of a thin silver cord with a hook at one end protruded from the top of the book.

Bill opened the book at the place indicated, and the slender bookmark slithered downwards like a living thing. Then the hook caught the top of the pages, and its length hung shining and swaying over the bottom edge. No longer able to resist, Bill read some random sentences, then two long paragraphs. This section undoubtedly had been lifted from the oral histories, and it recounted an odd event in the life of a young man who, years before his induction into the Armed Forces, had come upon a strange house deep in the piney woods of East Texas and been so unsettled by what he had seen through its windows that he brought a rifle with him on his next visit. Bill realized that he had never read this part of the book. In fact, he had written his blurb after merely skimming through the first two chapters. He thought Max had read even less of the book than he had. In a hurry to meet his deadline, Tony Flax had probably read the first half.

At the end of his account, the former soldier said, "In the many times over the years when I thought about this incident, it always seemed to me that the man I shot was myself. It seemed my own eye I had destroyed, my own socket that bled."

AGATHA'S GHOST

Ramsey Campbell

He'd done his best to hide her radio, but he'd forgotten to switch it off. That was the voice like someone speaking with a hand over their mouth she heard as she awoke. She was seated at the dining-table, on which he'd turned all four plates over and crossed the knives and forks on top of them to show that crosses were no use against him. She didn't know if it was daytime or the middle of the night, what with the glare of the overhead bulb and the grime on the windows, until she recognised the voice somewhere upstairs. It was Barbara Day, presenter of the lunchtime phone-in show.

Agatha eased her aching joints off the chair and lifted her handbag from between her ankles so that she could stalk into the hall. Was he lurking under the stairs? That had been his favourite hiding-place when he was little, and now, with most of the doors shut, it was darker than ever. She stamped hard on every tread as she made her slow way up to find the radio.

It was in the bathroom, next to a bath full almost to the brim. When she poked the water, a chill cramped her arm. Now she remembered: she'd been about to have her bath when the phone had rung, and she'd laboured downstairs just in time to miss the call, after which she'd had to sit down for a rest and dozed off. He'd got her into that state with his pranks—what might he try next? Then she heard Barbara Day repeat the phone number, and at once Agatha knew why he was so anxious to distract her. He was trying not to let her realise where she could find help.

She clutched her bag and the radio to her with both hands all the way downstairs. She sat on the next to bottom stair and trapped the bag between her thighs and the radio between her ankles before she leaned forward, dragging agony up her spine, to topple the phone off its rickety bow-legged table onto her lap. She pronounced each digit as she lugged the holes around the dial, but she was beginning to wonder if he'd distracted her so much she had dialled the wrong number when the bell in her ear became a woman's voice. "Daytime with Day," it announced.

"Barbara Day?"

"No, madam, just her researcher. Barbara is—"

"I'm quite aware you aren't she. I can hear her at this moment on the radio. May I speak to her, please?"

"Have you a story for us?"

"Not a story, no. The truth."

"I get you, and it's about ..."

"I prefer to explain that to Miss Day herself."

"It's Ms, or you can call her Barbara if you like, but I need to have an idea what you want to talk about so I know if I can put you through."

Agatha had dealt with many secretaries when she was selling advertising for the newspaper, but never one like this. "I'm being haunted. Haunted by a wicked spirit. Is that sufficient? Is that worthy of your superior's time?"

"We'll always go for the unusual. Anything that makes people special. Can I take your name and number?"

"Agatha Derwent," Agatha began, then shook her fist. The paper disc had been removed from the centre of the dial. "My number," she cried, not having given it to anyone since she could remember, "my number," and grinned so violently the teeth almost came loose from her gums. "It's may I please go to the party."

"I'm sorry, I'm lost. Did you just say—"

"My number is may I please—" Since even talking at half speed seemed unlikely to communicate the message, Agatha made the effort to translate it. "It's three one six—"

"Double two three five. Got you. If you put your phone down now, Agatha, and switch your radio off we'll call you back."

Agatha planted the receiver on its stand and held them together. She wasn't about to switch off the radio when it might refer to her. She was listening to Barbara Day's conversation with a retired policeman who built dinosaur skeletons out of used toothbrushes, and staring at the darkest corner of the hall in case the twitch of spindly legs she'd glimpsed there meant that her persecutor was about to show himself, when the phone rang, almost flinging itself out of her startled grasp. "Agatha Derwent," she called at the top of her voice as she grappled with the receiver and found her cheek with it. "Agatha—"

"Agatha. We're putting you on air now, so can you switch us off and not say anything till Barbara speaks to you."

The minion's voice gave way to the policeman's, requesting listeners to send him all their old toothbrushes, and Agatha's sense of his being in two places simultaneously was so disconcerting that she nearly kicked the radio over in her haste to toe its switch. Then Barbara Day said in her ear "Next we have Agatha, and I believe you want to tell us about a ghost, don't you, Agatha?"

"I want everyone who's listening to know about him."

"I'm holding my breath. I'm sure we all are. Where did you have this experience, Agatha?"

"Here in my house. He's always here. I'm sure he'll be somewhere close to me at this very moment," Agatha said, raising her voice and watching the corner next to the hinges of the front door grow secretively darker, "to make certain he hears everything I say about him."

"You sound a brave lady, Agatha. You aren't afraid of him, are you? Can you tell us what he looks like?"

"I could, but there'd be no point. He never lets me see him."

"He doesn't. Then excuse me for asking, only I know the listeners would expect me to, but how do you know it's a he?"

"Because I know who it is. It's my nephew Kenneth that died last year."

"Did you see a lot of him? That's to say, were you fond of each other?"

"I'd have liked him a great deal more if he'd acted even half his age."

"Will he now, do you think? I've often thought if there's life after death it ought to be our last stage of growing up."

"There's life after death all right, don't you wonder about that, but it's done him no good. It's more like a second childhood. He always liked to joke and play the fool with me, but then he started stealing from me, and now I can't see him he does it all the time."

"That must be awful for you. What sort of—"

"Clothes and jewellery and photographs and old letters that wouldn't mean a sausage to anyone but me. He had my keys more than once till I made certain my bag never left me, and now he's started putting things in it that aren't mine to show me it isn't safe."

"How old is he, Agatha? I mean, how old was—"

"Far too old to behave as he's behaving," Agatha said loud enough to be heard throughout the house. "Forty-seven next month."

"And forgive me for asking, but as one lady to another, how old would that make—"

"I'm retired from a very responsible job, maybe even more responsible than yours if you'll forgive my saying so. What are you trying to imply, that

I'm growing forgetful? I'd know if I owned a brass candlestick, wouldn't I? Do you think anybody would be in the habit of keeping one of those in their bag? Or a mousetrap, or a tin of dog food when I've never owned an animal in my life because my father told me how you caught diseases from them, or a plastic harmonica, or a tin of lighter fuel when all I ever use are matches?"

"I was only wondering if you might have picked up any of these items somewhere and—"

"That would be a clever trick for me to play, cleverer than any of his, since I haven't stirred out of this house for weeks. I bought enough tins to last me the rest of the year, and I've been waiting to catch him at his wickedness, but he thinks it's a fine game keeping me on edge every moment of the day and night. Do you know he whispers in my ear when I'm trying to get to sleep? I thought I could deal with him all by myself, but I won't have him wearing me down. One thing I'll tell you he's wishing I wouldn't: he doesn't want me to get help. He hid the phone directory, and he even tried to take away my radio so I wouldn't have your number. He doesn't want anyone to know about him."

"Well, all of us certainly do now, so I hope you feel less alone, Agatha. What kind of help—"

"Whatever has to be done to send him away."

"Do you think you ought to have a priest in?"

"I went to the one up the road, and shall I tell you what he said?"

"Do share it with us, please."

"He told me they don't"—Agatha made her voice high-pitched and supercilious—"believe in such things as ghosts any more."

"Good heavens, Agatha, I'd have thought that was what they were supposed to be all about, wouldn't you? I'm sure some of our listeners must believe, and I hope they'll phone in with ideas. That was Agatha from the city centre, and let me just remind you if you need reminding of our number ..."

At the start of this sentence Barbara Day's voice had recoiled from Agatha, who felt abandoned until the researcher came between them. "Thanks for calling. You can turn your radio on now," she said.

Agatha found the switch on the radio with one of the toes poking out of her winter tights before she fumbled the receiver into place. She returned the phone to its table as she levered herself to her feet with the arm that wasn't hugging her bag, in which she rummaged for her keys to unlock the front room. None of them fitted the lock, he'd stolen her keys and substituted someone else's—and then she saw that she was trying to use them upside down. He'd nearly succeeded in confusing her, but she threw the door triumphantly wide and grabbed the radio to carry it to her armchair.

When she lowered herself into the depression shaped like herself the chair emitted a piteous creak. It was the only one he hadn't damaged so that her friends would have nowhere to sit. He'd made the television cease to work, and she suspected he'd rendered the windows the same colour as the dead screen, to put into her head the notion that the world outside had been switched off. She knew that wasn't the case, because people who were on her side had started talking about her on the radio. Ben, who sounded like a black man, wanted Agatha to keep stirring a tablespoonful of salt in a glass of water while she walked through the entire house—that ought to get rid of any ghosts, he said. Then there was a lady of about her age who sounded the type she would have liked to have had for a friend and who advised her to keep candles burning for a night and a day in every room and corridor. That sounded just the ticket to Agatha, not least because she'd bought dozens of candles the last time she'd felt safe to leave the house. She'd stored them in—She'd bought them in case he started making lights go out again and pulling at the kitchen chair she had to stand on to replace the bulbs. She'd put them—The candlestick he'd planted in her bag would come in useful after all. The candles, they were in, they were in the kitchen cupboard where she'd hidden them, unless he'd moved them, unless he'd heard the lady tell her how to use them and was moving them at that very moment. Agatha grasped the arm of her chair, avoiding holes her nails had gouged in the upholstery, and was about to heave herself to her feet when Barbara Day said in a tone she hadn't previously employed "I hope Agatha is still listening. Go ahead. You're—"

"Kenneth Derwent. The nephew of Agatha Derwent who you had on."

The kick Agatha gave the radio sent it sprawling on its back as she did in the chair. Was there nowhere he couldn't go, no trick he was incapable of playing? He'd clearly fooled Barbara Day, who responded "We can take it you aren't dead."

"Not according to my wife. Just my aunt, and that's the kind of thing she's been making out lately. I must say I think—"

"Just to interrupt for a moment, does that mean everything your aunt said was happening to her—"

"She's doing it to herself."

Only Agatha's determination to be aware of whatever lies he told kept her from stamping on the radio. "I did wonder," Barbara Day said, "only she seemed so clear about it, so sure of herself."

"She always has been. That's part of her problem, that she can't bear not to be. And I'm sorry, but you didn't help by talking to her as though it was all real, never mind letting your callers encourage her."

"We don't censor people unless they say something that's against the law. I expect you'll be going to see your aunt, will you, to try and put things right?"

"She hasn't let me in since she started accusing me of stealing all the stuff she hides herself. She won't let anybody in, and now you've had someone telling her to put lighted candles all round the place, for God's sake."

"I can see that mightn't be such a good idea, so Agatha, if you're listening—"

Agatha wasn't about to, not for another second. She threw herself out of the chair, kicking the radio across the room. It smashed against the wall, under the mirror he'd draped at some point with an antimacassar, and fell silent. She stalked at it and trampled on the fragments before snatching the cloth off the mirror in case he was spying on her from beneath it. She was glaring at the wild spectacle he'd driven her to make of herself when the phone rang.

She marched into the hall and seized the receiver, not letting go of her bag. "Who is it now? What do you want?"

"Agatha Derwent? This is the producer of Daytime with Day. I don't know if you heard some of our listeners who phoned in with suggestions for you."

"I heard them all right, and they aren't all I heard."

"Yes, well, I just wanted to say we don't think it would be such a good idea to put candles in your house. It could be very dangerous, and I'd hate to think we were in any way responsible, so if I could ask you—"

"I'm perfectly responsible for myself, thank you, whatever impression somebody has been trying to give. I hope you'll agree as one professional lady to another that's how I sound," Agatha said in a voice that tasted like syrup thick with sugar, and cut her off. She pinched the receiver between finger and thumb and replaced it delicately as a way of controlling her rage at the way she'd been made to appear. No sooner had she let go of it than the phone rang again.

She knew before she lifted the receiver who it had to be. The only trick he hadn't played so far was this. She ground the receiver against her cheekbone and held her breath to discover how long he could stand to pretend not to be there. In almost no time he said "Aunt Agatha?"

"Are you afraid it mightn't be? Afraid I might have got someone in to listen to you?"

"I wish you would have people in. I wish you wouldn't stay all by yourself.

Look, I'm going to come round as soon as the bank shuts, so will you let me in?"

"There's nobody but me to hear your lies now, so stop pretending. Haven't you done enough for one day, making everybody think—" Suddenly, as if she had already lit the candles, the house seemed to brighten with the realisation she'd had. "You are clever, aren't you? You've excelled yourself. All the things you've been doing are meant to make me look mad if I tell anyone about them."

"Listen to what you've just said, Aunt Agatha. Can't you see—"

"Don't waste your energy. You've confused me for the last time, Kenneth," she said, and immediately knew what he was attempting to distract her from. "You got out by going on the radio, and now you can't come back in unless I let you, is that it? You won't get in through my phone, I promise you," she cried, pounding the receiver against the wall. She heard him start to panic, and then his voice was in black fragments that she pulverised under her heel.

She knew he hadn't finished trying to return. She drew all the downstairs curtains in case he might peer in, she hauled herself upstairs along the banister to fetch a blanket that she managed to stuff into the tops of the sashes of the kitchen windows. Once the glass was covered she crouched to the cupboard under the sink.

He hadn't got back in yet—the candles were still there. She had to put her bag down and grip it between her wobbly legs each time she lit a candle with a match from the box that wasn't going to rattle her no matter how much it did so to itself. She stuck a candle on a saucer on the kitchen table, and found another saucer on which to bear a lit candle into the dining-room. The candle for the front room had to make do with a cup, because he'd hidden the rest of her dozens of saucers. Her resourcefulness must be angering him, she thought, for as she carried another cup with a flickering candle in it along the hall he began to ring the bell and pound the front door with the rusty knocker.

"Aunt Agatha," he called, "Aunt Agatha," in a voice that didn't stay coaxing for long. He tried sounding apologetic, plaintive, commanding, worse of all concerned, but she gritted her teeth until he started prowling around the outside of the house and thumping on the windows. "Go away," she cried at the blotch that dragged itself over the curtains, searching for a crack between them. "You won't get in."

He did his best to distress her by shaking the handle of the back door while he made his knuckles sound so hard against the wood that she was afraid he might punch his way through. The illusion must have been his latest trick, because all at once she heard his footsteps growing childishly small on the front path, and the clang of the garden gate.

She held on to the banisters for a few moments, enjoying the peace, though not once she became aware of his having made her smash the phone. If she hadn't, might he have been trapped in it for ever? Suppose he'd angered her so as to trick her into releasing him? She hugged the bag while she stooped painfully to retrieve the cup with the candle in it from the floor.

She was less than halfway up the stairs when the flame began to flutter. She took another laborious step and knew he was in the house. All his play-acting outside had been nothing but an attempt to befuddle her. "Stop your puffing," she cried as the flame dipped and jittered, "don't you puff me." It shook, it bent double and set the wax flaring, and now she was in no doubt that he wasn't just in the house; he'd crept up behind her—he was waiting for her to be unable to bear not to look. She swung around without warning and thrust the candle into his face. "See how you like—"

But he'd snatched his face away as though it had never been there. Nothing was in front of her except the air into which the cup and its candle thrust, too far. The shock loosened her grip on her bag. She tried to catch it and keep hold of the cup as the latter pulled her off her feet. The bag fell, then the candle, and she could only follow them.

She didn't know if the candle went out as she did. She didn't know anything for she didn't know how long. When she grew aware of darkness, she found she was afraid to discover how much pain she might be in. Then she understood that she was fully conscious, and there was no pain, nor anything to feel it. He'd got the best of her in every way he could. He'd stolen her bag, and her house, and her body as well.

She was in the midst of the remains of the house, a few charred fragments of wall protruding from the sodden earth. All around her were houses, but she couldn't go to her neighbours; she wouldn't have them see her like this, if they could see her at all. None of them had believed her when she'd tried to tell them about Kenneth. For a moment she thought he'd left her with nowhere to go, and then she realised who would believe in her: those who already had.

She heard their voices as they'd sounded on the radio. They weren't just memories, they were more like beacons of sound, and her sense of them reached across the night, urging her to venture out and find them. She felt as she had when she was very young and on the edge of sleep—that she could go anywhere and do anything. She was free of Kenneth at last, that was why, and yet now that he was gone she was tempted to play a few of his tricks, in memory of him and to prove she still existed. Maybe this was her second childhood, she thought as she scurried like the shadow of a spider across the city to seek out her new friends.

BLUE HEELER

Weston Ochse

Doobie Banks pedaled furiously well aware that he was already late getting home. If he wanted to see his friend, he needed to hurry. No way could his parents find out where he was going. Not now. Not ever. If they did, he'd probably be grounded for life.

His neon-green Schwinn rattled down the hard-packed clay path, spinning wheels whipping through the tops of the weeds. Only deer, stray dogs and the occasional kid with dreams of glory ever made it down this lonely way. Doobie reached the final downhill slant and coasted, standing high on the pedals letting the wind rush through his hair, feeling like Lance Armstrong racing down the French Alps on his way to another Tour de France victory. The oaks and elms crouching along the sides of the road became his audience, watching in silent awe as he broke the world record and won the race. When Doobie hit the bottom of the slope, he slowed, pumping his arms into the air. He imagined the cheers of a thousand fans.

His smile lasted a full minute before it faded.

What he'd give for a thousand friends. Heck. What he'd give for just one.

Brett Brady had been his best friend until they'd sent him away to the nut house two months ago. Doobie remembered the moment clearly—his best friend cutting his own hair out in huge chunks and screaming at the top of his lungs about dogs and kids and fire and how he couldn't breathe.

What else could Brett be but crazy?

And now everyone avoided Doobie as if crazy was contagious. People were stupid. Crazy wasn't contagious. Crazy was just crazy.

At least Doobie had the Blue Heeler as a friend. Doobie and the Blue Heeler didn't play any games together and they didn't do things that normal friends did, but that was okay with Doobie. They talked a lot—of sorts. Blue Heeler showed Doobie things that he never even thought existed. More than anything, Doobie felt a need to be friends with the Blue Heeler. After all, if there was anyone in the universe who needed friends more than Doobie Banks, it was the Blue Heeler.

The path dead-ended at a squat building made entirely of cement blocks. The windowless one-story structure had been stained by years of neglect. Built with no doors, the only possible entrance seemed to be an empty space near the bottom of the wall where a cement block had once been. Like the first day he'd seen it, the empty space yawned with as much mystery as a black hole.

Doobie Banks skidded to a stop in front of the building. He dropped his bike and plopped down in front of the empty space in the wall. He removed his backpack and pulled out a pack of red licorice, a portable radio, and a full bottle of water. He spent several seconds tuning the radio until he found the right station. Then he adjusted the volume and sat it beside him. He ripped open the package of licorice and pulled two pieces of the long thin candy out. He began chewing on one as he stuck the other inside of the small opening. Within seconds it disappeared.

Doobie grinned as he opened the water bottle and took a deep drought. When he'd finished, he passed the bottle through. This time a whitish-blue hand grabbed it before Doobie had pushed it all the way into the darkness.

"I bet you're thirsty," said Doobie. "There hasn't been much rain lately. My Dad says it's because of all the pollution. He says that by the time I'm in college, we'll all have to wear gas masks."

The hand appeared again. This time it was empty, palm up. Doobie didn't miss a beat as he pressed a piece of licorice into it. The hand disappeared back into the hole and Doobie began telling the occupant of the concrete cube about his day at school, especially when Mrs. Wheaton caught Johnnie Beamer and Eddie Gowan putting superglue on Missy Pucket's chair. It wasn't until the package was empty, that he stopped talking.

"Enough about me. What about you? How was your day?" asked Doobie, placing his hand in the opening.

The hand appeared and grasped Doobie's in a soft embrace.

Doobie closed his eyes and allowed the images to flow. After a few minutes he opened his eyes and exclaimed, "That's where it is."

Ten minutes later Doobie swung down Beatrice Boulevard, sweat and worry twisting away in the wind. Jumping the bike over the curb, he took a short-cut through the yard, barely missing his mother's rose bushes. He spied her through the dining room window sitting down at the table with his dad. For a single moment, their gazes met, and Doobie knew he was in trouble.

Skidding to a stop by his dad's pick-up, he let the bike flop and winged his book bag over his shoulder as he leapt clear, all in one smooth move. Breathlessly, he burst into the dining room and took his chair. He grabbed a serving bowl filled with peas and began to spoon them on his plate before his mother could say a word.

The next morning during breakfast, he remembered what the Blue Heeler told him. He finished his cereal and placed the bowl in the sink. His mother leaned against the counter drinking a cup of coffee. Doobie glanced at her, then looked away.

What if she didn't believe him? What if she found out about the Blue Heeler? No way would she allow him to keep visiting, and if he couldn't go, then how would the poor man get fed?

"Out with it, young man." His mother had her patented arched eyebrow-devious smile *you aren't going to fool me* look.

"I've been thinking," Doobie began.

"That's a start," she said.

"Really, Mom. I've been thinking about your wedding ring."

Her smile disappeared as she gazed at the sink. "Thinking about it won't bring it back, Doobie," she sighed. "Trust me. I've tried."

"Maybe. But let me ask you this. What if the plumber actually found the ring and didn't tell you? What if he took it to a pawn shop and got money for it?"

His mother stared at him for a moment. "You thought all of that yourself?"

"Sure," he said.

"Which pawn shop would it be in, do you think?"

"Probably the one over in Henryville. Trading it here in Providence would be too close to home."

His mother's lips tightened the way they did right before she yelled at him. Doobie braced himself. But instead of yelling, she took a sip of her coffee. Doobie noticed her hands shaking slightly.

"What do you think?" he asked.

"I think you're going to be late for school," she said evenly.

Doobie noticed the clock. If he didn't hurry, he *was* going to be late. Grabbing his books, he hugged his mom and leapt out the door and onto the porch. His bike lay where he'd dropped it the night before. Soon, he was speeding down the street, channeling Lance Armstrong as best he could.

The day went quickly. Besides Vin Montgomery puking in the hallway and Monray Simpson getting caught cheating in algebra, the day was like any other. As soon as the final bell rang releasing everyone for the weekend, Doobie was out the door and on his bike, pedaling madly for the quick mart and then onto the Blue Heeler's.

In the Quick Mart he bought two bottles of soda, two sticks of beef jerky and a package of licorice. As he slid onto his bike, his dad pulled up in his Bonneville with the words *Warren County Sheriff* circling a black star on the door. His father pushed the brim of his tan cowboy hat up a little and gave Doobie a pointed look.

Doobie walked his bike over.

"What'd you buy in the store?" asked his dad.

"Some candy and soda."

"That all?"

"Some jerky too."

"Where'd you get the money, son?"

"Left over from grandma's visit," said Doobie, suddenly feeling like his dad's interest was a little more than normal.

"Ah."

"Where you going?" asked Doobie, trying to change the subject.

"Over to Henryville."

"Ah," said Doobie, knowing exactly why his father was going.

His father stared at him for several long moments, then nodded sharply. "You best be getting on home then. No lolly-gaggling, ya hear?"

"Yes sir," said Doobie.

Ten minutes later, Doobie dropped his bike and threw himself down before the dark opening in the concrete building. He passed a soda inside. Right after he opened his soda, he heard the *phlit* of Blue Heeler opening the other. They drank together for a moment. Then as they shared the licorice, Doobie described the events of the day, especially how Monray had tried to run away after she got caught cheating. She'd actually jumped out the window and was halfway across the parking lot before the teacher had time to react.

After the tale, Doobie became more serious. He laid his hand in the opening. "Why is it that you won't tell me why you're in here? You know I'm your best friend, right?"

The Blue Heeler's hand appeared and Doobie grasped it. His mind filled with images of fifty blue heeler dogs chasing, cavorting and dancing among the weeds, their lips peeled back in pure joy. Doobie recognized the emotion as the same joy he felt when he rode his bike. Rabbits and fowl and butterflies fled in panic. The dogs ignored them, their attention only on the impossibly angled turn.

Doobie jerked his hand away. "No. That's not the reason. You're in here for a reason."

He placed his hand back in the opening. The Blue Heeler touched him, the contact immediately filling his mind with the image of a blue heeler licking him on the face, eyes hopeful and pleading. The image was so real that Doobie brought his hands up to ward off the dog. But without the contact, the image disappeared.

"Come on," said Doobie.

The hand pulled back into the darkness. Doobie waited for several minutes, but it didn't appear again.

"Come on," said Doobie, trying another strategy. "Maybe I can help you get out of here."

He placed his hand in the opening and waited.

"Come on," he said.

Like a spider, the hand walked across the earth, fingers tentatively moving onto Doobie's hand. Then the fingers closed and gripped. Tighter and tighter they gripped, until Doobie cried out. Instead of releasing him, the Blue Heeler's hand gripped even tighter and then the images flowed. Images of dogs and men and children and police cars flashed in his mind too fast for him to understand. It was as if the Blue Heeler was trying to find something to say, searching through his own memories. Finally, the images slowed then halted until only one single image filled him.

A newspaper banner from June of 1985.

Then the image and the hand were gone. Doobie heard the sound of a car on the old dirt path behind him. He stared longingly into the hole a moment deciding whether to stay or not to stay, but the sound of tree limbs scratching the sides of the car convinced him of the driver's determination. Doobie didn't need to be discovered here. The last kid they'd found wandering on the path had been Brett Brady and that was the day he'd gone insane. Without a word of goodbye, Doobie tossed the two sticks of beef jerky inside, jumped on his bike, and picked his way through the trees.

After a dozen yards, he dropped his bike and dove among the ferns. Although partially obscured by finger-thick branches and sassafras leaves, he had a window of foliage were he could see the front of the cement building. Rocks and dirt crunched as the car pulled to a stop and idled. Doobie sucked in air as he recognized the star on the door.

His dad sat behind the wheel staring at the building. Occasionally he'd sip from a metal travel mug that Doobie had given him last Father's Day. Doobie couldn't have been more surprised. He'd never thought that his dad would know about the man, but then his dad was a deputy sheriff in Providence, so he really should know about everything. Funny how his dad had never mentioned the Blue Heeler.

That night his father spent the dinner staring silently at him. Through the salad, the main course, even during the ice cream dessert, Doobie tried to ignore his father's stares. Even his mother barely spoke. Doobie couldn't have been happier when the dinner was over. He made himself scarce and watched television in his room until midnight.

Doobie woke up late the next morning. He heard his mom banging around downstairs. His dad's Bonneville wasn't in the driveway which was strange. His dad hardly ever worked on the weekends, unless there was some big *case* going on.

Doobie waited until he heard his mom go into the laundry room before he ran through the kitchen and out the back door. By the time she screamed his name from the front door, he'd made it halfway down the block. Instead of acknowledging her, he pedaled harder, knowing that he was far enough away to deny that he'd heard her. He didn't like lying, but he had to in this case. As sure as he knew that Peggy Washoe's hair was red, he knew his mother would have a list of chores for him and he didn't have the time.

While watching Charlie's Angels last night, he'd thought of an idea. He'd never known that the library kept copies of old newspapers. Now, he'd go check to see if they could help him. He'd find a way to make it up to his mother later. She'd understand. He was sure of it.

When he arrived at the library, he discovered that the place didn't open for ten more minutes. Doobie parked his bike in the empty rack and waited on the steps. In his haste to get by his mother, he'd forgotten to eat breakfast. Now, his stomach protested. Then he thought of the Blue Heeler and toughened up. As far as Doobie knew, the man only ate what Doobie brought him. The back of his neck tickled as he remembered a movie he'd once seen where an imprisoned man ate spiders and beetles and the occasional rodent. Doobie shuddered and promised himself that he'd bring the Blue Heeler something more substantial to eat next time they met.

Brett Brady, back before he went crazy and was still his best friend, was the one who'd introduced Doobie to the Blue Heeler. Brett had always brought food when he visited the man so Doobie had continued the tradition.

Doobie remembered how scared he'd been when he'd first seen the building and been told of its lone occupant. After all, what would a person have to do that was bad enough to have a prison built around them? But Brett had dispelled his fears with implacable logic.

"They arrest all sorts of innocent people. My dad talks about it all of the time. He says it's a conspiracy to get rid of people the government don't like," Brett said.

"My dad wouldn't arrest anyone unless they were guilty," said Doobie.

"Sure he would," argued Brett. "Remember the law, *innocent 'til proved guilty.* Everyone's innocent, then the lawyers show up and make them guilty."

Doobie remembered how he'd stared at his friend, recognizing that parts of the argument were patently wrong. Before he'd been able to argue, Brent had continued.

"That don't matter anyway. There are plenty of reasons that Old Blue could be locked up in there," Brett said pointing at the building. "I've talked to him, though, and he wouldn't harm a soul."

"You talk to him?"

"Of course," said Brett. "Kind of," he added. "I mean, Old Blue don't speak like you and me."

"What do you mean?"

"Magic," said Brett grinning. "Just stick your hand in there and you'll see what I mean. Stick your hand in the hole and feel the magic."

Doobie had stared at the hole imagining all of the things that could lie inside. All the world's boogiemen, a thousand spiders, an army of fire ants, a desiccated raccoon crawling with maggots ... and his best friend wanted him to stick his hand in the hole. Never had a hole so dark and low, yawned so greatly.

The rattle of keys brought him back to the present. He stood and turned as the library door creaked open. A white-haired woman that he'd met once or twice before smiled as she held the door for him.

Once inside, Doobie explained what he wanted. The woman took him to a special computer and explained how they'd archived the newspapers all the way back to 1978 and were waiting on some money from the government so that they could archive all the way back to 1950. She keyed up 1985 for Doobie and showed him how to scroll through each issue. Confident that he understood the operations, she returned to her desk near the front door.

Doobie found June. He didn't know what he was looking for, but figured that it would jump out. At least he hoped so, because for such a small town, there was an awful lot of news. He scrolled past reports of houses burning, car accidents, crop cultivation, births, deaths, weddings, divorces and everything under the sun.

A report of some dogs destroyed because they'd been killing sheep and chickens all over the county held his interest briefly. Doobie checked the article and found that they were blue heelers. Coincidence? According to the report, three dozen were placed inside a fence then shot. The bodies were burned *in the event any had rabies.*

A report of a robbery over in Henryville made him pause, but when it said that no one was caught, he knew it couldn't be the Blue Heeler. Doobie couldn't believe that his friend would rob a bank. No way!

When Doobie reached the headlines for June 20th, he stopped and stared at the screen. The headline read *ANOTHER ONE GONE!* Doobie scanned the article and read about the missing boys. Since October of the previous year six boys had disappeared from Providence. Other than the boy's all being ten years old, the police were *dumbfounded* and had *no leads.* The bodies of the other five boys had turned up along the county roads naked, dead, and wearing a dog collar.

Doobie felt slightly queasy. Is that what the Blue Heeler did? Is that why he was locked up in the private prison? Doobie stared at the word *dog collar* and thought of the blue heelers dancing in the meadow. It just couldn't be.

He forced himself to read further, wondering why such a huge event had gone unmentioned. With all of the rumors, something like this would have been perfect fodder for the gossipers. Parents would have loved to use the threat of who the newspaper called the *Kennel Master* as a boogieman to keep the kids in line. So why hadn't they? What would keep an entire town quiet about such an awful event?

Doobie read on. The newspaper reported nothing but speculation and worry until June 25th. A *mailman delivering mail along Route 16 found the boy*—naked, dead and wearing a dog collar. *The investigation was at a standstill.* Doobie stared at the word *dog collar* again. His hands went to his own neck. He couldn't help but wonder about the Blue Heeler.

On June 27th they arrested Milner Mines, age 54, for the murders of six young boys. The sheriff admitted that *Mr. Mines had been a suspect* and that his answers during questioning were unsatisfactory. A picture of a small man dressed in dungarees being led into the county courthouse in handcuffs filled the front page. Doobie read through the associated reports. *He let kids play with the dogs all of the time. I thought it was wrong for a man his age to like kids. I knew it was him all along. They should have known right from the start.* It seemed like everyone had an opinion.

Then Doobie saw a familiar name. *The Banks Family will be holding a memorial at their home on Beatrice Boulevard.* The Banks family? Beatrice Boulevard? Doobie felt dizzy as he read the words *Freddie Banks, only son of Martin and Susan Banks.* Those were his parents' names. That was the street he lived on. Who was Freddie? The words swam before his eyes. Who was Freddie?

Freddie Banks, only son of Martin and Susan Banks.

... only son of Martin and Susan Banks.

... only son ...

Doobie staggered to his feet. He reached out for balance and knocked over a magazine display. The librarian stood, but Doobie was already past her. By the time she made it out from behind her desk, he had shot out the door and onto the sidewalk. The world swam before his eyes.

Susan Banks hung up the telephone. He held her hands to keep them from shaking.

"She said it wasn't until she returned to her desk that she realized what year he'd asked for. Then she'd been unable to get back to him in time before he saw—"

"We should have destroyed it all," said Martin. He sat at the table with a drink in his hand. "We should have—"

"We couldn't hide it forever, Martin. One day we'd have to tell him anyway. Something like this is just too big to hide."

"Nothing's too big to hide," he sneered, gulping half the amber liquid.

Susan Banks carried a cold glass of milk over and placed it beside the plate of cookies on the kitchen table. She put her hand on Doobie's shoulder, but he shrugged it off.

The temperature outside raged. Although they had air-conditioning, they barely used it. Instead, they opened the windows and turned out the lights. Air seeped in from the screen door to the porch. Light pushed through the gauzy white curtain over the sink. Although it was cooler, a gloom captured everything.

"Good thing I was driving by and saw his bike. No telling what he would've done," said Martin.

"I'm sitting right here. You can talk to me."

Susan leaned across the table and kissed her husband on the forehead. "Yes, it was a good thing. Thank you honey."

"Mom. I'm sitting right here."

She placed her hand on Doobie's cheek and stared lovingly at him. "I know. I know you're sitting here. It's just been a stressful day."

All three of them sat around a small circular kitchen table. Susan sat between Doobie and his dad.

Martin pulled a thin cigar from his breast pocket.

"Not inside," said his mother.

Martin grumbled and shoved it back into his shirt pocket.

"Why didn't you tell me about my brother?" asked Doobie in a small voice.

"Aw, Hell." His dad finished the rest of the amber liquid in the glass. He stood, walked to the counter and poured himself another.

His mother grabbed Doobie's left hand and held it in her own. Large slow tears tracked gently down her cheeks. "Oh, Doobie. We were going to tell you. I promise we were."

"Does everyone know about him?"

"Those were crazy times back then. Nothing like that *man* had ever happened to our town, you know? All those kids killed. My—" her voice choked "—son killed."

"I just don't understand why you wouldn't tell me about him. Why no one ever talks about him."

She shook her head and stared into space. "We didn't want to remember. We didn't want to have to relive all the things that were done, especially when—"

"Susan!" Doobie's dad strode across the room and placed his hand on her shoulder. "That's enough, now." He sat down in his chair and placed the glass in front of him. "Doobie, don't take what I'm about to say as me being mad at you," began his dad, "But this has nothing to do with you."

He lifted the glass to drink from it then decided not to. He placed it on the table and wrapped both of his hands around it as if to keep them busy. "This business of your brother happened years before you were born. You didn't even know him. It was our loss. Remember that he was our son. We loved him like we love you."

Susan stared at her hands as they held Doobie's hand in a firm grip. She nodded as her husband spoke. When he finished, she added, her voice husky, "Just because you weren't the first doesn't mean we love you any less. Truth be told, we probably love you more. After all, we have love enough for two sons and only one son to give it too."

A truck with a bad muffler cruised down the street in front of the house. A dog barked in the neighbor's back yard. No one spoke for a long minute.

Doobie's dad was the first to break the silence. He reached into his front pant's pocket and came out with a gold wedding band. "Seems like we're ready for some good news. Look, darling." He held the ring in the palm of his hand and held it out to her.

Doobie's mother released her grip around her son's hands, grabbed the ring and threw her arms around her husband's neck. "Oh honey. Thank you so much."

Martin chuckled. "Don't thank me. Thank the kid. He's the one pointed it out."

"What?" She stared at Doobie wide-eyed. "You mean he was right?"

"One-hundred percent. I was coming back from the county lock-up when I saw him run out of the library. Thanks to Doobie, our plumber, one Herman Moore, now has an all expense paid vacation behind bars for a while. I bet with a little digging, we'll find out that he's done this before."

Doobie smiled as feelings began to filter back. He grabbed a cookie and took a small bite. He couldn't help but think about his brother. He wanted to ask so many questions. Crumbs rained down on the Formica tabletop. He licked a finger and scooped them up.

"And the pawnshop over in Henryville?" she asked.

"Yep. I have to admit, I couldn't help wonder how Doobie knew, but it was the pawnshop owner who ID'd Herman Moore."

"Doobie. How did you know? How did you figure it out?"

Doobie thought about stalling, but the question had been inevitable. Although he'd probably get into trouble, he didn't want things hanging over his head anymore. To many lies had been passed between them. "The prisoner told me."

His dad smiled. "What prisoner would that be?"

"You know," said Doobie.

"No. I don't know," said his dad, his smile faltering a little.

"I didn't know at first that he'd been the one. I mean, no one ever told me, so I had no idea that boys had gone missing."

"Doobie? What are you talking about?" asked his mother.

"I'm talking about the man they arrested. Milner Mines," he said. As the words left his mouth, his parents' eyes widened. "I didn't know he'd killed them. I thought he was—"

"Doobie Banks. Where'd you hear that name?" asked his mother.

His father choked down the contents of the glass, a morose smile taking shape.

"Where'd you hear that name?" she shouted, shaking Doobie by the shoulders.

"It was in the newspaper. I read the name in the newspaper. Stop it. You're hurting me, mom."

She released her grip and hugged herself. "I never wanted to hear that name again."

"Neither did I," said his dad.

"We called him Blue Heeler," said Doobie. Guilt settled along his small shoulders. "We thought he was nice. We didn't know about the murders.

We just didn't know."

Susan stared at her son. "We?"

"He didn't commit the murders, son," said his dad.

"What?" asked Doobie.

"Oh, we sure thought he did, but he never did anything. He was an innocent man."

"But the newspapers. Then who—"

"The next month another kid went missing and we found out it was this drifter living in an old abandoned tobacco silo over near the county line."

"*He* told you?" asked Susan.

"Yeah. He knew all about the ring. He knows lots of stuff that no one else knows. Then when I asked him why he was locked up, he told me to look in the newspaper for the answer." Doobie felt more relieved than he'd expected. Not only had he told his parents what he'd been hiding from them, but he'd also discovered that his only friend in the world wasn't guilty of anything. "Wait. If he's not guilty, then why is he still locked up?"

"Who are you talking about?" asked Susan, her voice rising.

"Milner Mines," said Doobie. "The Blue Heeler. Why do you have him still locked up in that building?"

Doobie's dad stared back at him.

Doobie's mother's eyes were impossibly wide. "But Doobie, Milner Mines died in 1985," she said.

Doobie looked from his mother to his dad and back again. "Then who is the prisoner?" Doobie felt a moment of panic mixed with elation. If the Blue Heeler wasn't guilty of anything then he could go free. Doobie could finally see what he looks like. They had the chance to be real friends.

Doobie stood.

"Where are you going?" asked his mother.

"To tell him that he's free," said Doobie. Then he ran out the door. He jerked his bike out of the open trunk of his father's Bonneville, righted it on the driveway, and sped off.

He heard the screen door open behind him. "Doobie Banks, get back here."

He ignored the call and pedaled harder. When he reached the end of the block, he glanced once over his shoulder and saw his dad's Bonneville backing out of the driveway.

Doobie swerved off the road and down a steep marshy embankment to the creek bed below. Within minutes he was pedaling down the well-known path towards the Blue Heeler. He remembered promising to bring the man some food, but then realized that the Blue Heeler was going to go free tonight.

They could go to a restaurant together. Maybe his mother would fix them some pork chops and macaroni and cheese.

Doobie skidded to a stop. He heard a vehicle turn onto the road from the highway far up the lane, followed by the sounds of branches scraping metal.

"Blue Heeler. Hey," shouted Doobie breathlessly. "Hey Blue, you can go free."

His dad started honking the horn.

Doobie placed his hand in the opening. "Come on. Talk to me."

A blue hand slowly appeared. Doobie reached out and grasped it. Images immediately flooded his mind. Blue heelers running through a meadow. Blue heelers penned into a stable ringed by chicken wire. Laughter as drunken men shot each blue heeler. A gasoline can was emptied on the still twitching corpses of blue heelers. The smell of burning blue heelers.

His dad's car was almost upon them. The honking sounded like a long ugly peal.

The images continued. He saw his dad and mother, but younger. He saw the faces of many men and women of Providence that he recognized. He saw walls being bricked around him until nothing was left. No door. No window. No light. No air. No way to breathe.

The Bonneville hit the clearing too fast. His dad struggled for control and almost struck a tree, but at the last minute, managed to stop. Before the engine died, his dad leaped out of the car. His mother jumped out of the other side.

Doobie stood and smiled.

His mother ran up and smacked him across the cheek. "You come when I call you," she yelled.

"But I wanted to tell him that he could go free."

Doobie's dad knelt and inspected the hole. He glanced inside then stood. "We should have torn this thing down years ago. We just couldn't bring ourselves to do it."

"I saw both of you there. Here, I mean. I saw you when he was being imprisoned." Doobie felt his cheek. "If you knew he was innocent, then why didn't you let him go?"

"Because it was too late," said his dad, coming back from the truck with a flashlight. "What we'd done couldn't be undone." He knelt on the ground and poked the flashlight into the hole.

"He can't be dead. I've talked to him. Brett talked to him."

"That's the kid who went crazy?" asked his dad.

"Yeah, but I'm not crazy. How did I know where your ring was, mom?

How'd I know to look in the newspaper for that exact year? I was talking to him when you arrived."

Doobie's dad stood and held out the flashlight. "Here," he said. "Take a look for yourself."

Doobie's mother put a hand on his shoulder and held him fast.

"Susan, he needs to see for himself," countered his dad.

Doobie stared into his parents' eyes unable to understand what was happening. His logic was impervious, so why were they acting this way?

She released her grip. Doobie took the flashlight and knelt at the same opening he'd knelt at for the past several months. He stared intently as the light plumbed the darkness.

Near the opening he spied empty wrappers. Licorice, gum, potato chips and other sorts of snack food wrappers lay open and empty. Soda cans lay empty and scattered.

"Blue Heeler? Where are you? Come into the light so I can see you."

He scanned the whole room and didn't see anyone. He shone the light on the ceiling and on the walls. From his vantage point he couldn't see into the near right hand corner. He wedged his arm and his head into the hole and angled for a better view.

"This was our shame, Doobie," said his dad.

"We were so angry," said his mother.

"So damned angry," said his dad.

Doobie angled far enough so that he could sweep the light into the corner. When he did, his breathing stopped. A dead man wearing work boots and dungarees lay in repose, skeletal legs and arms splayed at odd angles. A skeletal hand grasped an empty beef jerky wrapper.

Doobie screamed and crawled out of the opening back into the light.

"When we caught the real killer, we argued about opening this place up," said his dad. "No one was brave enough to do it, though."

Doobie stared wild-eyed at his parents, unable to grasp the events that had transpired. He'd spoken to someone. He'd spoken to something. So where was he now? Where was *it* now? Doobie dropped the flashlight and placed his hand in the opening.

"So we left him there for us to remember. The building was here to remind us of how nasty life can become."

"Blue Heeler? Where are you? Come to me, Blue Heeler?"

His dad reached down to grab him, but Doobie shrugged him off. "We left him here to remind us of how awful we can become."

"Blue Heeler! Where are you, darn it?"

His mother began to weep.

"Blue Heeler?"
Nothing.
"Blue Heeler, where are you?"

SARAH'S VISIONS
Chelsea Quinn Yarbro

"I see here you're thirty-eight years and four months," said the occupational counselor, his twenty-six-year-old face turning grave. "Getting on, all things considered. It's high time you reviewed your options." The two men were talking in the most common language on earth, a combination of Chinese, neo-Hindi, Spanish, and English, the language of electronics and downloaded knowledge, as well as commerce and diplomacy.

Edaltran Roolsto—Tig to his friends—did his best not to be irked. He sat straighter in his chair and kept himself from fussing with his cuffs. "I've kept up my skills, and my record is quite satisfactory."

"Yes," said the counselor. "I see two post-PhD"—he pronounced it *phid*— "degrees; in 1378 and '81; from Ecumal Intellectual Training Center—not bad, but hardly enough for an exemption, is it. So unless you have some project that will continue beyond three years, your retirement will commence in the month you turn forty. You can't expect to continue as you have done, not with your employment history. I'm sorry, but you know our regulations don't allow it." He tapped the scanner on the wall of his office approvingly, his fingers sliding along a column of figures that were taken by his main peripheral from his brain and made a holographic display of them. "You've been a diligent engineer, but your basic training is a decade out of date, and you know how electronics goes—two years and even the best machines are obsolete, and your education along with them."

"I've kept up," Roolsto insisted. "You can see that I've taken cerebral downloads regularly, and I have spent ten percent of my work time in updating classes. I've participated in all major demonstrations against government agencies that have any hint of democratic liberalism. I have the credentials that go with them." He made himself calm down, thinking that not so very long from today, the counselor would be sitting where he was now, and would be facing the same sinking panic. "Still, I realize the position you're in—you have new PhDs coming along every six months, and they need work as much as the rest of us, but that doesn't mean that—"

The counselor cut him off. "Have you given any thought to retirement? Considering your age, I should think—"

"Of course I have," Roolsto said indignantly. "We have courses in it at Ecurnal—required courses."

"And if that's the case, what have you considered? Forty is coming up quickly. You need to be ready." The counselor touched the implant on the side of his head and the display on the screen changed to show a long list of retirement activities. "Water horticulture is always a popular choice."

"I don't think so," said Roosto. "I don't want to spend my days wading among plants, useful as they are to all of us."

"Then what about genetic comparisons? That's not only popular, it's extremely useful, and with your background, your modification to the process should be approved without a hitch."

"Actually, my partner and I were thinking about joining a re-creation colony." Now that he said it, he felt much better.

"A re-creation colony?" The counselor looked shocked. "What made you think of that? With your skills, you should consider becoming an input monitor, or a genetic one, not trying to live as people lived in the distant past. That's for people who can't cope, and I wouldn't have thought you had such a problem, not yet, in any case."

"I don't think I have the temperament for input monitoring, or genetic monitoring, for that matter; I think the peripherals would be too intrusive," said Roolsto quietly. "I did a secondary course in Pre-Collapse history in my training- twenty, and I think it would be interesting to participate in the re-creation of those long-ago days."

"Are you certain?" the counselor asked. "It's a major step, not one to be taken on impulse. All your peripherals and augmentations will have to be removed, and all your download ports as well. You have to raise your own food, and hunt for meat. You'd have to give up all the amenities that make modern life liveable. Do you really want to give this up for primitive settlements and having to learn everything from the ground up, no downloads, no enhancements?"

"No, I don't particularly want to, but I think it would be good for me." Roosto sighed. "I want to do things I've never done before I die. I want to know what my ancestors knew. I don't expect you to understand."

"Good," said the counselor, trying to sound sympathetic and failing. "Because I don't."

"Tig. Oh, Tig; it's good you're home. I've been thinking all afternoon that I should have gone with you to the appointment, but you know how things have been at the Center and I couldn't really spare the time away, not with the way things are going and—" She stopped herself as her enhancement peripheral alerted her to his state of mind; she adjusted the timbre of her voice. "How did it go? What did the counselor say?" Randar Demilo made a gesture of familiar welcome as Roosto stepped into their spacious flat on the sixty-third floor of Block 196 at the south end of Plateau D11, above the vast expanse of hydroponic greenery of Nursery 57 sometimes called the Green Lagoon; he looked a bit flustered, and Randar noticed at once, and understood that all was not well with Roolsto. She decided not to mention anything more about her own trouble at work just now; there would be time for that later, when she could command his full attention. "Did you say anything about the re-creation—"

"He isn't interested in re-creation colonies, and he didn't think I should be, either," he replied dejectedly. "He wanted to interest me in water horticulture and genetic comparisons or input monitoring—the usual boring retirement routine. Even half a day doing any of those tasks would be stultifying."

"Oh, dear," said Randar. She, like Roosto, was nearing forty, the age of compulsory retirement for nearly everyone on earth except those rare few who qualified for extensions. "Do you think they'll deny your request?"

"Who knows?" asked Roosto. He went to sit down, an exasperated expression in his bronze-colored eyes. "He's a youngster, hardly more than twenty, and I suspect he thinks only madmen want to live in re-creation colonies. The hardships outweigh the advantages for him."

"Did you tell the counselor what era interested you?" She sounded nervous, and managed a little cough to cover it.

"Not yet," he said, getting up again to go and make a stuffed bread for both of them, selecting a small, oblong cabbage from the hydroponic unit in the window. "If he doesn't understand re-creation, then the time period won't make much difference." He decided upon a dough and set about preparing their meal.

"Did you tell him you cook?" She held up her hands nervously then lowered them again. She did her best to encourage him. "They'll want to know this if they're going to allow us in a re-creation colony."

"We didn't get that far," said Roosto, as he plugged his kitchen equipment into the port on the side of his skull; all his appliances began to hum as he considered what ingredients to choose. Gradually three of the machines shut down and he concentrated his attention on the vegetable compounder into which he put the cabbage and programmed it for onions and the standard mix, the poultry extruder, and the cereal preparation unit for the dough. He had done this so often that he supposed he could now manage it in his sleep. As he ran the recipe through his mind, the three machines thunked, whirred, and macerated their various elements finally resulting in wheat-like shells stuffed with a slurry of six vegetables and a chickeny goo, then put the shells into warming coils.

"Oh, Roosto, I'm sorry it didn't go well," she said as she brought him a glass of chilled plum wine. "This should help take the edge off."

"I have an appointment next week. I'm going to take my information in my peripheral and that might work better, it'll be clearer in any case. He can see what we're considering. If he'll try the down-load he'll probably get a better idea of what I'm trying to accomplish." He drank the plum wine, not too quickly, and wandered back into their great room. "Randar, I'm sorry this is turning out to be such a hard time for you." He had a persistent stimulus from his enhancement peripheral, warning him of her dissatisfaction; his vocal modifier kicked in, adding soothing bass notes to the sound of his voice.

"I'm sorry, too, Roolsto. I'd like to be as sure of myself and my future as you are, but for now, I'm still wondering what's best for me to do."

"You'll need to make up your mind in the next six months." He pressed his lips together, trying to organize his thoughts. He had resolved not to put pressure on hr, but now that he was facing the actual retirement assignment, he couldn't keep from saying "If you don't decide to come with me, they probably won't let me go, either."

She pulled away from him a little. "Why would they do that?"

"They say there's an increase incident of regret among those who're part of a pair but don't go to the colony as a pair. If you think you'd really rather stay here, that makes it more likely that I'll try to return, but the contract is ironclad. No return from re-creation. That's why singles are so often refused as colonists."

"I know, Roolsto. And I want to be with you, but I'm not as convinced as you are that re-creation colonies are the way."

He launched into the same argument he had been using for the last year, as if repetition would change her mind. "Re-creations are going to help us reclaim the land now that water levels are beginning to drop. In another two hundred years, we should have significantly more land above high tide, and in two hundred more years, still more land. If people spread out again, they'll need to expand their farming back to the fields, not just to the nurseries—it won't all be hydroponic. The skills of the ancients can help us break away from our protected cities, establish centers in the drying marshes, and work toward rebuilding the kind of—"

"I know, Tig; I know. We've been over this so many times. And I'm with you, at least philosophically. I have some doubts about the reality." She poured more plum wine into his glass and filled her own for the first time.

"And we get to live longer," he added, saying the one thing that they had studiously avoided over the last months. "No compulsory departure at sixty as we have here on the Plateau."

Randar turned pale. "That hasn't anything to do with it."

"Because the chance of living past fifty in the re-creation colonies is about fifty percent?" He picked up his glass and held it up to the light from the window-screen that just at present was showing the westering sun, although the window faced south. "Those are better odds than what we have here, where the chance of extension beyond sixty is not quite ten percent."

"True enough," she conceded. "But they say it's a hard life in the re-creation colonies. You said yourself that farming takes strength, and so do the other forms of employment offered there. Physical labor as difficult as hydroponic horticulture can be is ordinary and expected, and has to be done in unshielded weather, as well. I know it shouldn't bother me, but it does. I like my conveniences. I like my peripherals. I'm still not sure I can give them up. I'm not even convinced that I want to. I'm certain I don't want to raise livestock and vegetables, and do primitive preservation of all that to keep from starving in the winter. I'm used to how we live, and I don't know that I can change."

"Of course—life without peripherals is hard to imagine, but humanity managed without them for tens of thousands of years, and I'd like to think we can still do so." He took a deep breath, trying not to make this disagreement into a ritual. "We don't have to decide now. We still have six months to register for our retirement activities."

"I just can't help wondering what will become of us, doing direct farming without hydroponics, or building in wood or stone, or trying to actually make clothes or—" She set her glass of wine down. "Let's not argue, Tig. Let's have a pleasant evening, and tomorrow we can continue our research."

"You're right. We've been over this before, Randar." He touched her shoulder and smiled in a perfunctory way, accepting her offer of a truce. "Dinner's ready."

The counselor this time was about thirty, a good-looking woman in fashionable clothes and a full array of peripheries. She regarded Roolsto with a kind of condescension that bordered on pity. "It says here you're considering a re-creation colony."

"I am," he said forcefully.

"What are you hoping to achieve? You may think you know enough to live in one, but you haven't got the whole picture. The colonies don't usually turn out to be what's expected." She smiled without any sign of the smile in her eyes.

"How do you mean?"

"Well, as you know, the life is hard. Without peripherals, many aspects of everyday life take up much more time and attention than they do here. You have to milk your cows and goats by hand, you have to cook with pots and pans and knives, you have to make your own beds and do your own washing. You will have to rely on your neighbors and be available to assist them when needed. You won't be able to be in touch except through letters and direct conversation. You'll have to rely on physicians, not your body monitor, to keep you healthy. That all sounds minor, but it isn't." She tapped the screen and showed one of the re-creation colonies where men and animals were farming, while women made cloth and tended vegetables. "This is the Eighteenth Century Colony. There are two large villages—the colonists call them cities though the larger of the two is barely fifteen thousand residents—and all entertainment is live performance which has to be attended personally. Again, that is something you're unaccustomed to. And you may find it inconvenient to have to travel for entertainment. Information is distributed through printed matter—which has to be prepared, printed, and distributed—and that is one of the reasons for the paper mill. You will have to read—and by that, it means you must read everything—not simply download."

"The mining is done by robots at that colony, and so is the smelting of ores." Roolsto wanted to show her he had done his research. "I'm interested in the Nineteenth Century Colony, myself."

"Steam engines and nothing more sophisticated that rail travel?" She sneered. "Well, if you think that would be satisfactory—"

"Not just steam engines. Steam ships. Paddlewheelers on the rivers. I have an idea for a safer, more efficient boiler, one that is in accord with the technology of the time, an improvement that would mean faster travel, which would speed trade. Rail is all very well in its way, but steamships mean more extensive trade, even on the limited scale permitted for the colonies. It could mean that many of the farmers could expand their markets, and many manufacturers could reach more of the farmers. That could be the beginning of another kind of Industrial Revolution, one that would benefit all of us in the next few hundred years. The Nineteenth Century Colony has four navigable rivers, and a large salt-water bay as part of its territory, which is a good range for paddlewheelers." For the first time there was real animation in his face. "The region allocated to the Nineteenth Century Colony allows for trading in four other colonies reachable by water. I think that this can be developed for everyone's advantage. This could mean that ocean travel—on a limited basis—is possible, and that is the most exciting prospect I can think of."

"Twenty years of education, twenty years of work, and twenty for retirement," said the woman, repeating the formula everyone knew. "It's been an effective formula ever since the Recovery. Why do you find the lure of a re-creation colony so attractive, when it goes against the very basis of our civilization." It was not a question.

"I don't want to go against civilization, I want to change its limitations; we've accepted them for too long," said Roolsto in an unguarded response; he had never dared to express himself so blatantly, not even to Randar.

"Order creates limits for the benefit of us all. There would be chaos without it." The woman's face was blank with ire.

"I don't debate that," said Roolsto. "I think all of the ways the Recovery has shaped civilization is beneficial for all of us. But I also think we may be permitting the Recovery to limit us, and itself." He held up his hands to silence her protests. "We won't know if we don't test it, which is what I believe the point of the re-creation colonies is."

"And you think you can deal with the hardships for the last twenty years of your life—if you last that long?"

"I hope I can. I'd certainly like the chance to find out," he said. "I'd rather struggle in a re-creation colony than waste away in a nursery pod."

The woman stared hard at him. "In that case, you'd better go to one," she said at last, and tapped something into her peripherals. "There. You'll begin your processing next week. And ten days after your retirement, you'll have to leave the Plateau."

"Just like that?" Roolsto asked.

"Yes—why?—do you want to change your mind?" Her smile was predatory.

"No," he said promptly. "I just didn't think it would be so easy."

The woman laughed as she pointed toward her office door.

Randar looked pale as Roolsto described his meeting to her. At the end of it, she pressed her lips together until she had garnered all the impressions she could from her enhancement peripheral and ordered her thoughts. "Then it's settled. You've decided."

"For me, yes. You don't have to go—unless you want to."

"But you said they wouldn't allow you to go without me," she said.

"Apparently that's not as fixed a policy as they claim. My application will go through; I hope you'll send yours in with mine," said Roolsto, and went on abashedly, "I mean it, Randar. I hope you will decide to join me, but I think they'll take me, no matter what. I don't want to have to go alone, Randar. I'd miss you too much." He gave his clothes to the wardrobe-minder and went on to the bathroom, Randar following behind. "I'll have the application tomorrow, and then I can start planning for forty. The counselor said she'd submit my application to the Colony Board at once."

She stared at him. "I haven't made up my mind yet."

"I understand that," said Roolsto.

"I might decide to remain here." She lifted her chin a little.

"I understand that," he repeated, and held up his hands in mock submission. "I'll honor your decision, whatever it may be." He kept himself from adding that he hoped she would come with him: he had made that clear so many times that it wouldn't be fair to pressure her with that now.

For some inexplicable reason, his compliance offended her more than his efforts at persuasion. "Then leaving here is more important to you than I am?"

"It's not that." He considered his response carefully. "I don't want to lose you, Randar, but I know that I have to be part of the Nineteenth Century Colony. I am certain of it."

"What about Mimmeu?" she asked suddenly. "Don't you want to be here when she is awarded her first PhD when she turns twenty?"

"We've talked about her before, and you know she understands. I'll make a download for her peripherals, so she'll know how proud I am of her, what a fine daughter she is, and she can keep the download in her peripherals, so she can view it whenever she wants to," said Roolsto. "She'll be able to see for herself how pleased I am whether I can attend her end-of-matriculation ceremony or not."

"Do you really think so?" There was a note of injury in her voice that had not been there before.

"Our daughter is a reasonable person. She knows the requirements of planning for forty. She knows that I've been considering a re-creation colony for a long time, and she knows what that will demand of me." He held out his hand to Randar. "Don't worry; I won't do anything that will slight Mimmeu, or you."

"Just being gone will be a slight, and you know it." Randar turned sulky eyes on him. "Why disappoint her?"

"The ceremony is less than a day, and retirement is twenty years," said Roolsto, sighing as he made an attempt to embrace her. "Mimmeu understands that. And she understands my intention to join a re-creation colony."

"Twenty years here, assured, barring fatal accidents—it could be only a few years in the re-creation colony, whatever century you choose. There'll be no more physical monitors to protect you, no advanced medicine to care for any sickness or injury you may have to contend with." She moved away from him and deliberately changed the subject. "I had trouble at work today. I'm training my replacement—"

"I remember," said Roolsto. "You said yesterday that he wasn't as attentive as he should be. He hasn't got better?"

"So you *have* been listening," she marveled. "No, he hasn't. He's complained to the supervisor that I'm too strict and I don't answer his questions clearly."

"That doesn't sound encouraging," said Roolsto.

"That's what he said—that I haven't explained his duties clearly." She flung up her hands in exasperation. "I don't know how much clearer I can be. I've used everything my peripherals can produce to help him understand, but he doesn't seem to pay any attention." Suddenly her aggravation deserted her. "Maybe I should go with you. At least the colonies are full of used people who do more than tend root-stock, run scans, and fill our peripherals with monitored data. Making clothes can't be worse than those."

"Perhaps not," he said. "But you've told me many times that you aren't sure you want to live as colonists do, that you don't want to lose your peripherals."

"I don't," she declared. "But I don't want to do nothing but the same dull thing half a day, every day, day in and day out, and that's what retirement requires of us so long as we're on a Plateau."

"That's what I've been trying to tell you for the last year-and-a-half," said Roolsto. "That you don't want twenty years of endless repetition with an occasional short journey to another Plateau for variety."

"But the colonies sound so *slow.* Everything has to be done without augmentation. Everything. I researched it all and it was endless. You have to gather everything, prepare everything, attend to everything with nothing to alleviate the work—" She tapped her frontal peripheral and said, "This is playing a download of last night's gala on Plateau J9, half a world away, and I'll be able to experience it any time I like from any point of view that suits me, not at all like having to go there and sit and listen. That troubles me—how intrusive life can be when there're no peripherals. And that's all you can do in the colonies—work from the beginning. Or sit and read. Or—"

"Or what?" he asked when she did not go on.

"Or ... all the rest of it," she said, resentment flashing in her eyes. "The work doesn't sound very interesting to me, and the society is too disorganized."

"But it could be better than staying here. Weigh the inconvenience of the colonies against the boredom here." He folded his hands. "We can argue about this for the next eighteen months, if you like, but in the end, you have to decide what you want more: the convenience of this life with peripherals, or the adventure of the colony with me." His face was deeply sad.

"I know, Tig, I know," she said, feeling shamed by her own doubts.

"When you've made up your mind, we can make whatever arrangements you want. I'll try not to pressure you, but I do want you to come with me."

"When will you turn in your final contract?" Randar asked, afraid that she might have gone too far.

"Five months. The Colony Board has to be sure that the colony has room for me. They'll look at my plan for my participation and decide if it serves the colony's purpose. And you'll have to present your proposal as well." He took a deep breath.

"I'm sorry to delay so much," said Randar, annoyed that she had to say this at all. "This is what I mean—you can encompass my reservations because of your enhancement peripherals, and still we argue. Without the peripherals, who knows how we'll manage?"

He bit back a sharp rejoinder and only said, "You need to be certain, whatever you decide."

Randar rounded on him. "The colonies aren't utopias!"

"Neither is this," said Roolsto, and went to change clothes.

The download was long and complicated, requiring a number of written answers as well as entries on Roolsto's peripherals. He understood this was to make sure that his reading and writing skills were sufficient to the work he would have to do, since he would no longer have the instruction of software programs to guide him. He wrote enough at his job to have a fairly fluid hand; his responses on the page were legible and he found he could express himself fairly well in the clumsy medium of the unaugmented written word. His state of mind seemed at once clearer and less comprehensive, yet he persevered.

The counselor he saw next was a man only a few years younger than he.

He welcomed Roolsto to his office, saying, "I'm Vingi Yusla, of the Colonial Board. Please sit down."

Roolsto stared at him, shocked to see anyone with so few peripherals. He managed to regain his composure as he sat. "I'm—"

"—Edaltran Roolsto, called Tig. Yes, I know." He indicated the stacks of paper on his desk. "Applicant responses. We're considering nine this week alone. The re-creation colonies are becoming more popular. We may soon open another Nineteenth Century Colony, or a Twentieth Century one."

"May I ask what traits you're looking for in your applicants?" Roolsto asked, suddenly worried.

"Certainly—I'd worry if you didn't ask." He sat down again. "Our primary concern is to find those applicants who can communicate without peripherals, because that is the single most necessary requirement of colonists: that they can communicate with one another." He smiled. "If everything goes well, you'll start your peripheral withdrawal in six months. You've shown the kind of skills we're looking for, and the inclination to join a colony. You'll begin your conversation lessons soon after that, and the month that you depart, your last peripherals will be withdrawn, so you can become accustomed to dealing without them before you arrive in the Nineteenth Century Colony." He tapped his input peripheral. "You'll keep this the longest. The enhancing peripheral will be removed as soon as we can schedule the procedure."

For the first time, Roolsto felt a niggle of doubt. He had assumed all along that he would be able to manage without peripherals, but now that he was confronting the reality of losing them, he faltered. "How is it, without an enhancing peripheral? How do you manage to get along without it?"

"Well," said Yusla, "it takes some getting used to. You have to learn to pay close attention to those around you, to watch their behavior as well as listen to them. You need to ask more questions and to listen to the answers carefully."

"I understand that," said Roolsto. "But how can you tell if you really understand one another? There's no real feed-back function like an enhancement peripheral. Isn't it a handicap not to have enhanced peripherals? Without one, how will I know that I truly comprehend what anyone else means? Even something so minor as seeing the color they mean when they say *red* won't be possible. And that's nothing compared to more difficult concepts."

"You're right about the difficulties you can face without the enhancing peripheral," said Yusla. "That's why we put so much emphasis on colonists' ability to communicate. We've seen over the last fifty years that communication is the key to colonial success."

Roolsto looked uneasy. "So the enhancement peripheral goes first. Then which one?"

"The body monitor goes next. You have to learn to recognize the way your body functions without the monitors to keep you going. I should warn you that you're likely to have trouble with sore muscles and insomnia while you're adjusting to its absence." Yusla chuckled. "Something else you'll need to pay attention to—your immediate environment."

"In what way?" Roolsto asked.

"In every way," said Yusla. "Keep in mind that if you decide against becoming a colonist, the peripherals that have been removed can't be replaced."

"I realize that," said Roolsto testily.

"It's a good idea to think about it, just in case."

It was unnerving not to have enhanced information to elucidate Yusla's meaning, so Roolsto asked, "How do you mean that?" As he asked, he wondered if this were some kind of test.

"I mean that you will need to consider your commitment before you start losing peripherals. Life here on the Plateau can become awkward without a full complement of peripherals." He tried, unsuccessfully, to laugh.

"What would become of me if I decide to remain here after my peripherals are gone?" He could see the irony in Yusla's expression, and it puzzled him until Yusla answered.

"Oh, that's easy—you go to work for the Colonial Board, assessing applicants for the colonies."

Everyone in the conversation group was approaching forty, and there was an undercurrent of anxiety that clung to them. There were nine of them; all of them had a tentativeness about them, for they had recently had their enhancement peripheral removed and were trying to learn to manage without the constant stream of information the peripheral had provided.

"Let's all sit down, shall we?" said the group leader, a woman in her mid-forties who lacked the enhancement peripheral and the body monitor, but otherwise had the usual peripherals; she had not ended up going to a colony and Roolsto was curious as to why she had not. "I know this is off-putting, but it is essential that you get used to coping without your enhancement peripherals."

One of the potential colonists frowned. "What should I say to you?"

"Whatever you think is most appropriate," the leader answered, and, indicating that she was offering important information, continued, "I'm Gieli Nir, by the way, for those of you who forgot to read the placard on the door." It was the sort of information their enhancement peripherals would have provided.

Feeling embarrassed, Roolsto said, "I'm going to have to learn to read all the signs for myself, aren't I."

"Yes," said Nir. "And talking about it will help retrain your mind to make the change."

One of the group said, "My peripheral will—"

"—be gone," Nir reminded him. "Shall we begin with learning to make introductions?" She pointed to a straight-backed woman sitting across from her. "If you will?"

The woman coughed and fidgeted. Finally she said, "I'm Aem Plagin. Who are you?"

"That's a good beginning," Nir approved. "Who'd like to answer her?"

Another woman spoke up. "I'm Lentso Toruig." She remembered to smile.

Gradually they worked their way all around the group; by the end of it, all of them were feeling a little less awkward. Nir looked at them one by one. "Without your peripherals, you will have to learn how to remember names and other information. So I want each of you to make a point of reviewing all you've learned about one another, and to write it down so you'll know next time we meet; I'll do my best to get all your names right, so you can have an example to follow. Some of you will be losing your enhancement peripheral shortly, and you'll want to have made a start at this kind of remembering."

"I see you don't have an enhancement peripheral," Roolsto pointed out, relieved to have had her provide the opportunity to inquire.

"And the body monitor is gone, too." She sounded comfortable saying this, far more so than those listening to her. "I was going to be a colonist in the Eighteenth Century Colony when someone on their Board rejected me because I had said I wouldn't want to wear petticoats and skirts, which is required for re-creation. There was a conference and I appealed their decision, but as it turned out, I was refused again. So now I help you and applicants like you to prepare for your lives in the re-creation colonies."

Toruig spoke up. "Doesn't this all seem a little artificial to you—this slavish dedication to authentic re-creation, including social forms and standards of education?"

"As much as we know of such things," Roolsto interjected.

"Yes," said Toruig. "Assuming we have an accurate understanding of such things, which isn't always the case." She gave Roolsto a sharp look before continuing. "If we do leave the Plateaus when the water level is lower, surely we'll have our technology to support us, and all of this will turn out to be unnecessary."

"You may be right, Toruig," said Nir. "But what if there are problems as the seas drop and the climate changes—for surely it will change. Then the ability to manage without peripherals and within the limits of the period being re-created may be crucial to keeping us from being reduced to barbarism. It happened before, more than once. This way, the colonists will make it possible for all of us to be able to cope." She was about to add something more, but went silent.

"Don't the colonies depend upon the Plateaus to keep them functioning?" asked a fellow called Ong Hapsta.

"Not as much as they used to," said Nir. "Every decade sees them more self-sufficient. If things go as planned, in another hundred years, there will be only minimal support needed from the Plateaus."

"That's what all the research says." Toruig was heavily sarcastic. "But it's our research saying what we expect it to say. What if the colonies never become self-sustaining? What if the colonies are always dependent on the Plateaus? I can't find any download that deals with that possibility."

"You're wise to question the research," said Nir while the others in the group did their best not to squirm. "But given the information at hand, and the variables we've tried to anticipate, at least three of the colonies have an excellent chance to perform at expectations. The rest have too many possibilities to be able to place them on a scale."

"Have you factored in weather? Earthquakes? Tsunamis? Droughts? Floods?" Toruig's voice rose steadily.

"Most of those possibilities have been considered, along with blights, diseases, and meteor strikes," said Nir, a bit more stiffly. "As far as we can tell, our expectations are realistic, given what we know and what our projections reveal. You may challenge them if you feel it necessary, but I am working from the most recent data available." She paused, looking each member of the group in the unaugmented eye. "We can't guarantee that the colonies will all thrive all the time. No one can make such a claim. The Plateaus aren't completely safe from disasters: Plateau G4 had a severe windstorm two years ago, more powerful than anything the shields could handle, yet now the city is largely rebuilt. The colonies have had problems, of course, but so far they've come through them and were restored to—"

"Why isn't that in the research downloads?" asked Roolsto.

"Because it isn't important unless you're going to a colony; as prospective colonists, you can see far more information than most others can , or want to," said Nir. "You can ask for access to all the records of the colonies and you'll get download authorizations."

Roolsto decided he would get that access. "Where do I apply for access?"

Nir took a small notepad and wrote down a contact code; she handed the paper to him and regarded the rest. "Do any of the rest of you want to research this?"

"I do," said Toruig. "I'm scheduled to lose my enhancement peripheral in two days, so I'll want to see this information tonight or tomorrow."

She handed over another piece of paper. "I recommend reviewing all the download." Nir's face was somber. "This is a huge change you're all undertaking, and the more prepared you are, the likelier you are to adapt to colonial life."

"What do you think we should do?" asked Hopsta.

Nir sighed. "You'll probably benefit from research—that much is obvious. But as your peripherals are removed, you'll have to learn to function without them. If I were going to ... to go to a colony, I would do my best to live as the colonists live as much as you can. Don't use your peripherals for daily activities if you can avoid them. Don't rely on your body monitor. Don't try to deal with anyone who insists on using peripherals. If your partners are staying on the Plateau—"

"Don't partners have to come with us?" asked Plagin, sounding shocked.

"Most of the time, but not always."

The group exchanged uneasy glances, and the stream from their enhancement peripherals picked up dramatically.

"Is that why we aren't allowed to bring our partners to this group?" Hopsta inquired, an edge in his voice.

"One of the reasons," said Nir. "You need assessments from Colonial Board reviewers that show your actions apart from your partners. This allows us to give you information while we gather important data." She shook her head slowly. "Usually it takes three meetings for the training group to figure that out."

"You could download all the behavior modifications to our peripherals," said Toruig.

"But you wouldn't have to practice," said Nir. "And we're drifting away from the training you will require." She pulled her tunic fussily. "So, now, how do you ask for directions—without using your peripherals."

Hopsta frowned. "There should be location screens at major intersections."

"No," said Nir. "There may be signposts, but no location screens. You may need to purchase a map. They're usually available at booksellers' establishments."

Toruig slapped down her hands. "How do we find anything?"

"That's why you buy maps," said Nir patiently. "And you can ask for directions."

"Who do I ask?" Toruig asked.

"Local merchants," Plagin suggested.

"Law officers," said Roolsto.

"Both very good suggestions," said Nir, relieved that they were now back on topic for their meeting. "How would you do that—ask for directions?"

"Postmen," Roolsto added, then said, "I'd walk up to the person, introduce myself, and then ask how I might find my way to the place I was seeking. That's what the old texts report was the custom."

A frown flickered over Nir's face, but she said, "Very good. Yes. That should succeed in most cases."

"But why should they tell you anything?" asked Dothle Kura, who had been sitting in silence since he spoke his name.

"Because that is the custom among early societies," said Nir. "Without peripherals, it's a necessity for the community to offer such help. Personal communication is essential."

"Oh." Kura went silent again.

"We will see you have money enough to last you for a year," Nir went on, changing instructional direction. "Next time we'll concentrate on money, but today I want you to think about what you will have to pay for once you leave the Plateau. Most transactions may require some bargaining, and this is usually done face-to-face. You will speak directly with the person providing you goods or services, and will agree on a price before any good or services are made available to you."

"And won't we have to do the same with goods and services, when we seek employment?" Roolsto asked.

"Yes. You will. But you will be purchasing before you are selling, and so you will need to know how to evaluate the charges made, and your readiness to pay them." Nir paused. "And you will have to give a token payment to anyone who does you a service. The person you ask for directions might expect you to offer a small payment for the information."

"So that's why you mentioned money," exclaimed Plagin.

"It was one of the reasons," said Nir. "You will want to show proper appreciation for what they have provided. When you leave for your colony, your manual will tell you the range of payment considered appropriate for various kinds of services and information." She pointed to the table across the room where newly baked mixed-berry compote was being spread on a variety of breads. "Have something to eat and we'll resume our discussion in half an hour." She pointed to an old-fashioned round clock with a moving second hand. "You'll have to get used to these. No timing-and-location peripherals in the colonies, remember."

"That's the last peripheral to go, isn't it?" Roolsto asked.

"For most of you, yes." Nir put her hand on the back of her chair. "If you want to practice keeping time with clocks, you can requisition a watch now. I'd recommend it, though you'll be issued one when you reach your colony. You'll manage the transition more easily if you start using one now."

"I'd like that," said Roolsto, and heard four others join him.

"You'll have to fill the form out in pen, and I'll have to submit it as paper." Nir smiled a little.

"Tell me something," Plagin asked. "Is it true that all our paper here on the Plateau comes from paper mills in the colonies?"

"Well, yes, that's true," said Nir.

"Then the colonies do trade beyond their colonial limits," said Plagin as if claiming a prize.

"Yes, they do. But only with the Plateaus, not among st themselves. That would compromise the exercise." Nir looked nervous now, and she changed her tone of voice. "You can see why we want to evaluate what the colonies can produce. They need to be self-sufficient and self-sustaining of course, but over time as the water levels drop, more Plateaus will need to trade with the colonies, which means that we need to see which of them can create the greatest surpluses. In the next two centuries, we'll have a greater interaction with the colonies, and both they and we need to prepare for that."

There was an odd quiet that came upon the group. Finally, when a few of them had become restive, Kura spoke up. "Good to know."

The others seconded him with their peripherals, leaving Nir to guess at their interchange.

"How do you feel?" asked Randar as she came up to the side of their bed; her question sounded strange, the voice flat without his peripherals to enhance it.

"A little disoriented," he admitted, resisting the impulse to sit up; he was still trying to assess himself now that his enhancement peripheral had been removed.

"That's normal, I'm told," she said, her doubt obvious even to Roolsto.

It struck him that he had never heard her voice—or anyone's voice—as it was, without enhancement and modification to clarify and define intentions. He looked directly at her. "Say something else."

"Something else?" She looked puzzled. "What do you want me to talk about?"

"Anything!" He levered himself onto his elbow and took stock of the room. "Tell me what you see."

"Our room, of course."

"Yes. I know. But what color is it?" He was staring in shock at the light-taupe shade of the walls.

"It's a soft, vibrant lilac," she said as if speaking to a child. "You've seen it every day for almost twenty years."

"Um-hum," he responded as he managed to sit up. He glanced toward the window and saw the other housing towers rising around them, and the vast, green swath of the hydroponic installations in the middle of them. He had never realized the sameness of the Plateau before, and it struck him most unpleasantly now. "Is there anything to drink? I'm feeling a bit parched."

"I have the melon tea you like," said Randar, sounding nervous. "I'll get it for you."

"Thanks. That's nice of you." He swung his legs off the bed and sat for a long moment staring at his feet and noticing the texture of the flooring, which was strangely flimsy under his soles, not at all like the substantial stone he recalled; he found this disconcerting, and hoped he would soon get over it. He was about to try to stand when Randar came back with a large mug of tea on a small tray. "Thanks," he said again as he reached to take it.

"I have the kitchen making an omelette for you—with mushrooms and cheese, the way you like it." She watch him in a dissatisfied way, anxious to see him drink. "It'll be ready shortly."

He took a sip of the tea and put the mug down. The stuff was almost tasteless. He knew he had to say something to reassure Randar, so he said, "That'll be nice. I hope you're making something for yourself as well."

She nodded too eagerly. "Yes. Oh, yes."

"Then we can have breakfast together. We can take up to half an hour, what do you say?" He achieved a kind of smile, and wondered if her enhancement peripheral compensated for his disingenuousness. There was no way to be certain. How many times had he encountered friends and associates whose greetings and conversation had seemed enthusiastic and genial but was more because of his peripherals improving their remarks instead of a reliable dulcifying of their actual speech? How often had that been true of him?

"Uncomfortable?" Randar asked.

"Nothing to trouble yourself with," said Roolsto, and managed to get to his feet. "There. You see?"

"You look ... odd," she said.

"The peripheral is gone," he told her. "That must make a difference."

"And it's just the first change." She frowned. "What's it like?"

"It's hard to describe," he answered slowly. "You'll see for yourself when you have yours removed. I'll do what I can to help you."

She shifted unhappily. "I don't know if I can go through with it."

He was tempted to argue with her, but knew he would not be able to deal with his altered perceptions. "Well, keep an eye on how things go with me before you make up your mind."

She was surprised that he hadn't railed at her, or tried some other means to persuade her. "All right," she said, and bolted for the kitchen.

Roolsto drank some more of the disappointing tea as he began to make his way about the room. It seemed smaller than he remembered, and the furniture looked more ordinary. He stopped at his armoire and opened it, let down by the clothes he saw within it. They seemed so much the same, and their colors weren't as vivid as he had thought they were. Sighing a little, he selected a tailored woolen tunic in a color like dust, then trousers that were two shades darker. His underwear was off-white and completely unremarkable. He had just finished securing the patches on the tunic when Randar called from the kitchen. "I'm coming," he assured her, and made his way there.

"Your omelette," said Randar, pushing the plate toward him along the counter. "Will you want the basil puree for it?"

"Let me taste it first," he said, wondering if he would find the food as lackluster as he was beginning to fear everything else would be; he steeled himself for disappointment as he accepted the fork she handed him and took a small wedge of the folded, creamy egg. He was surprised at how salty it was, and so he said, "Yes. I'll have some of the basil puree."

"Isn't it the way you like?" Randar asked.

"It isn't enhanced. It'll take some getting used to."

"Don't bother," she snapped. "You'll be in the colony before you need to adjust. Save it for then." Getting up from her stool, she left him alone to eat.

"I don't think I can do without my peripherals," said Randar as she climbed the steps to the adult health center; she couldn't quite look at him as she spoke. "I think colony life would be interesting, but I can't stand the thought of doing without enhancement and monitors. Not even a location chip—how do you find your way in strange territory?"

"But you can't go to the colonies with your peripherals," Roolsto pointed out, stopping his upward progress to look directly at her."

"I know," she said miserably. "I look at you and I see you struggling, being clumsy, getting tired, not being able to enjoy anythi—"

"It's just my transition," said Roolsto hastily, trying to ignore the stares of other men and women passing in and out of the building. "I'll be used to doing without them by the time I leave, and so will you." This last was more of a plea than an assertion.

Randar shook her head. "No, Tig. I don't think I can do it."

He regarded her steadily. "Then you won't be allowed to go with me."

"I know, I know, and it makes me feel awful, but living without peripherals in a colony sounds like punishment, not retirement. I'd rather be bored than frightened, and that's what I'll be if I lose my peripherals." She turned and started down the stairs.

Roolsto followed her reluctantly. "All right, but promise me you'll think about it. Don't rule it out completely. Randar: promise me."

She didn't answer him until she was on the walkway, and then she held up her hands in protest. "I don't think I can do it, no matter how much I try to believe I can. The colony is *your* dream, Tig, not mine. I know whatever I end up doing, it'll be boring, but I'll have my peripherals, and that will make things a lot easier. I like my peripherals, Tig. I'm used to them. I don't want to lose them." She sounded annoyed and fatigued, and she couldn't look at him. "I don't want to lose you, either."

He felt a tightness in his throat that surprised him. "What do you want me to say? That I won't leave? That—"

"You can't change your mind now, not with your enhancement peripheral removed. It isn't the same as it used to be, with you having no enhancement." She was doing her utmost not to cry, and almost succeeded.

"Randar, Randar, " Roolsto said as he tried to console her; his voice dropped almost to a whisper. "If you really don't want me to go, tell me now. I'll get a retirement position training potential colonists. Other people have done it. I can do it, too."

"Why? You want to go to the Nineteenth Century Colony. That's what all this has been about, isn't it?"

"Yes, I do, and yes, it is," he said with emotion that her peripherals made eloquent for him. "But not without you."

"I don't think I can do it. It's interesting, the thought of living the way people did all those centuries ago, but it isn't as important to me as to you. I don't think you'll be the same in that colony. Steam engines and telegraphs!" She took a long, shaky breath. "You will have to decide what is more important to you—staying here with me, or going to the colony. I don't like to issue an ultimatum, but I've been watching you go through your preparation, and

I've realized I just can't do it. All the training and discussion in the world won't make any difference." She took his hand. "I'm sorry, Roolsto. I wish I could embrace the change as you do, but I can't, and so you'll have to decide what matters most to you."

He listened in silence, realizing that he had been anticipating something like this for the last month; much to his chagrin, he was relieved that Randar had finally spoken out. Slowly he pulled his hand away. "I'll think about it." Even as he said it, he knew his mind was made up. "Nineteen years together is a long time. It's hard to imagine life without you."

"I will miss you terribly if you choose to go."

"You feel cheated that I would put a colony ahead of you?" Roolsto guessed aloud.

"Wouldn't you?" she challenged.

"I do—you've put your peripherals ahead of me."

After that, neither of them could think of anything to say.

By the time all of his peripherals had been removed, Randar was barely talking to him. Roolsto accepted this with as much grace as he could summon; he made sure they spent little time together, and he convinced himself that this was out of kindness to her. Gradually he developed a sense of inevitability about their alienation, and without his peripherals to enhance her responses, he soon became convinced of the correctness of his conclusion.

On the day he was to depart, he dressed in the unfamiliar clothes he had been issued the week before, hefted his packed suitcase and steamer trunk, loaded them on a reproduction of an ancient hand-truck, and started out of the apartment he and Randar had shared for so long. He was still smarting from the terse good-bye his daughter had condescended to give him; she had sided with her mother and was unwilling to concede anything good could come of going to the re-creation colonies.

Randar was at the door, looking forlorn but with an admixture of superiority. "I wish you'd change your mind," she said to him.

"And I wish you would," he said ruefully.

"You know why I can't," she reminded him.

"I know." He leaned over and kissed her, wondering as he did what her peripherals helped her to feel that he could no longer share.

"Well," she said when the kiss was over. "I'm going to miss you."

"And I you."

She regarded him silently for more than a minute, then said, "I hope you find what you're looking for in the colony."

"And I hope you remain happy with your decision to remain here," he said with a depth of sincerity that surprised him. "I have to get to the transportation center, Randar."

She shrugged as if her shoulders were controlled by wires. "Then go," she said, and moved aside so that he could maneuver his hand-truck out into the corridor. As soon as he was clear of the door, she closed it and leaned on it, as if to ensure it remained shut.

Roolsto stood still for a few heartbeats, then turned and trudged off toward the elevator and the first step on his last and best adventure.

Author's note:

As a lifetime leftist, when the former Governor of Alaska was out on the stump for the presidential elections, I found her remarks about the evils of the Democrats, filtered through her Fundamentalist Christian perspectives and her own rugged life philosophy wonderfully surreal, and I decided to try to put something together reflecting her various takes on the future. This, for good or ill, was the result.

MORE THAN WORDS

David Niall Wilson

The lines shifted as his fingers walked the page. The symbols, so familiar after long hours of study, blurred, dancing across the ancient scroll and evading translation. Cyrus knew he would have to stop soon. He was doing no good by pushing so hard, and he'd have to go over anything accomplished in such a state for errors. Wasted time. Better to start fresh.

But the symbols would not be still. Patterns shifted. Cyrus blinked.

Stick-footed birds and dog-headed Anubis swirled over reeds and crocodiles; the names of kings long dead shifted and blended, creating new names—new sounds and words. Cyrus' eyelids drooped, and he fought to remain upright. He cursed his own lack of common sense. No coffee. Not enough light. Not enough sleep.

He shifted in his seat, trying to use the motion and the discomfort of sitting in one position for too long to fight off the fog stealing over his thoughts. In his left hand he held a coin formed of hand-beaten gold. It was very old, and the front was emblazoned with the likeness of Mark Antony. Roman. Like a Centurion, he sent it marching across the tops of his fingers, flipping it along with a solemn dexterity. The gold caught the dim light, flashing rhythmically.

Cyrus was a sight. His hair stood out at odd angles, half the product of heat, the other of humidity. Too many sliding fingers where a comb would fear to tread. His glasses were fogged around the edges and his eyes burned at the corners from the sweat. It was hot. It was late. He needed to sleep.

The scroll beckoned like a long lost lover.

His thoughts shifted from the present, and he drifted. Three years back, in a tent in a fly-by-night carnival just outside Chicago, Illinois, he'd had a "past lives" reading. Wax dripping into a bowl of tepid water and too-long, gaudily-painted fingernails tracing the shapes. Eyes lined in every color of the rainbow—melting ghost-like to pale, white cheeks. Long, dark hair that might have been real—or not.

The interior of the tent had been draped in deep colors. Royal Blue. Scarlet. Gold. Imperial Purple. Tapestries depicted scenes from the worlds behind the world. The past. Temples and kings, Pharaohs and queens. Cards had lined the edge of that table, untouched. The Fool. The Universe. Crystals of all shapes and sizes glittered and spun on chains and leather thongs, catching the candle-light and flinging it about the room.

"Old." The voice was powerful—quiet—insidious. Old. "You are old. Your flesh is of this time, but your soul has walked before."

"What do you mean?" His own words drifting back to him, stinking of the inanity he'd felt.

"Old is what it is. Nothing more to be said." Long nails swirled wax droplets. The silence reverberated with those sounds that are only present in the absence of other sound. Breathing. Heartbeats. Soft, better-left-un-defined skittering in the corners of the tent.

"Words." she breathed softly. "Words were your life. Words and life. Bound. You brought life to the words—words to the life and they took it. All gone. Took it away and burned."

Cyrus shook his head and glanced to the side. The light of the lantern flickered. He was momentarily trapped in the vision of flames. Within those flames hieroglyphs danced and screamed. Sound that should have been silence—sound in a moment that was all silence—surfaced, and he shook his head. Enough.

Rising carefully, he stepped back and drew the plastic shield down over the surface of the table. He worked on the scroll directly, but when he was not working, it was sealed from the environment by a clear acrylic cover. He knew he should keep the shield in place at all times. That was the rule, but the feel of the parchment helped his concentration. It felt—right. When it was late enough that the others would not see, he always drew aside the protective cover.

The light flickered, and he stepped away from the table, turning to grab the nearest lantern. He moved about the tent, dousing the rest quickly. Outside, wind whispered across the dunes. Sand danced and shifted. Insects whirred. At night, the desert lived.

Cyrus closed his eyes and leaned against the table, catching his breath. The old woman's words flickered through his mind and he shook his head, trying to dislodge them. Why now, he wondered. Why now, after all these years, *that* voice? The words continued to buzz in his ears like flies.

Words.

He staggered away from the table and lurched through the flap of the tent into the darkness beyond.

Cyrus' own quarters were down several rows of nondescript tents, just past the mess tent. No one stirred at that late hour. No one but Cyrus, caught up in the histories and mysteries of years so long fallen to dust that it could take days just to bring a single sentence to light. The others cared, each in his or her own way, but they didn't *feel* it the way Cyrus felt it. They didn't share his dreams—or his nightmares.

Something moved in the shadows to his left and Cyrus flinched, staggering into the wall of a tent three away from his own. Cursing, he righted himself, extricating his foot from the cables and stakes. He stopped and waited, but no one had noticed.

Again the motion to his left. Metal banged on metal, the tone echoing. Cyrus grew very still. His breath slid slowly in and out of his lungs, and he fought to slow it further. Who else was awake? What were they doing?

Sound. Nothing was clear, no words, but the whispered rasp of low-toned voices carried on the breeze. They came from the direction of the ruins. Lovers, slipping off into the dunes at night? Cyrus' mind sifted quickly through those who shared his days and evenings. There were couples, but it was difficult to imagine any of them carrying on so late, or so openly. In the world of academics and science, appearances were often the key to success. It wasn't what you knew, but how it was presented, to whom, and how it was received that could make the difference.

Who else, though? The sound repeated—and again. The echoes were loud enough that Cyrus began to wonder why no one else was up to investigate. The voices, while not loud, were constant—crying out one to another in the darkness. The sound of footsteps joined that of metal on metal, and Cyrus pressed himself against the canvas of one of the tents, staring off through the shadows.

Nothing. He saw nothing. There was a slight darkening of the skyline where the pyramid rose above the sand. Beyond that, not even the stars shone in the sky. No moon illuminated the sky. A complete void.

Cyrus' heartbeat slammed in his chest. His breath grew short, and his eyes closed tight against the nothingness that confronted him. There was nothing there. Nothing *could* be there. Nothing.

Flames licked at walls of wood, flickering upward and crackling. The snap of sparks reverberated through his mind.

Cyrus turned and pressed between the last two tents, found the flap to his own and stumbled through. He brought two fingers to his cheek. His skin was hot—damp from sweat. Too hot for just the heat of the desert at night. Now he felt the chill as the damp sweat met the cooler air of his tent, and he shivered. The fan in the corner spun lazily in an arc, turning his skin clammy.

Cyrus turned, lit the lantern beside his cot and turned up the wick. Long shadows danced along the canvas walls, but they were all born of the internal workings of his life—the fly strips whirling and reflecting light. The fan, endlessly panning the tent's interior. Each was a familiar shadow. They didn't join with the sounds beyond his tent—beyond the camp. They were a part of Cyrus' own world.

Lying back on the firm cot, his pillow tucked beneath his neck, he closed his eyes and drifted. Nothing felt right, but fatigue would not be denied. His temples ached. His eyes burned from too many hours spent scrutinizing words that were written for people so long dead he could be treading on their bones, the dust beneath his feet, and never know it. A dull throb numbed the back of his head.

The voices in the distance grew clearer as he drifted. He could make out a word here, another there. For some reason he couldn't follow the conversation. Something was a little off, the echo of the sound, or maybe they were just too distant.

Cyrus blinked sleepily. The words focused more clearly. Something about fire. Orders cried out into the darkness. Burning. He heard what sounded like flames lapping at wooden walls. His memories shifted and re-arranged. He saw the apartment building down the street from where he'd grown up, charring steadily, the white-washed walls blackening as orange and yellow flames licked their way up the side. Destroying.

Canvas tents flapping in the wind. Nothing but canvas.

The words faded. Softened.

Cyrus dreamed.

The scrolls were stacked haphazardly—forming a small mountain of papyrus and vellum that stretched toward the sky, tube-shaped fingers of words wound upon words. Cyrus stared upward from where they'd bound him, kneeling in the sand. His heartbeat was a dull, thudding drone.

Blood trickled down his forehead, gift of the heavy butt of a Roman sword. The sand was losing the heat of the day, and the wind held a chill driven from the heart of despair. Voices called out all around him. Torches flickered, dim echoes of the deeper flames from the city. So much destruction. So much waste.

The words would have preserved it, he knew. The words would have painted the city in her glory, the history and the inventories, the finances and the great loves. *All in the words. All in a mangled heap, circled in stones and reduced to flapping bits of tinder, awaiting the torch.*

Cyrus could see the Queen's eyes, filled with reproach. That was the last expression he'd seen on her beautiful face, and as he remembered, tears trickled from the corners of his eyes to etch lines in the grime coating his face. He could not reach up to brush them away, so they tortured him as he remembered. The words had been his to protect. His to preserve. Hers for eternity. She was Queen, but she was Isis Walking, as well, and he had failed her. He had failed them all.

All around him, booted feet clattered. The sound of more boxes and bundles being dragged from the libraries and from the temples echoed and twined with the cries of warriors, the sobs of young women and boys, the snorting of impatient animals left too long without care—and the moaning wails of death. Cyrus lowered his eyes from the pyre and softly mumbled prayers to Anubis—prayers of death—if not for those destroying his world, then for himself. Swiftly.

Footsteps grew nearer and suddenly Cyrus was sent sprawling as a huge hand slapped flat to the back of his head. Roaring laughter punctuated the pain, and with no hands to break the fall, Cyrus hit the sand so swiftly he barely had time to turn his head. His cheek burned where the grit bit deep.

"You are the scribe." It was not a question. The voice behind the words dripped contempt.

Cyrus said nothing. He lay in the sand, eyes closed, trying not to think of the pain in his cheek, or the flames drawing nearer to the pyre. Trying not to think of the Queen and her deep, disappointed eyes.

A boot crashed into his ribs. The words were repeated in Greek, and this time the inflection made them a question.

Unable even to breathe, Cyrus nodded. His head wore a rut in the sand, and the pain nearly blacked out the world. Salt blinded him, and he could not brush it away, nor the sand. His lips were crusted with it, thick with blood.

A huge, powerful hand gripped him by his hair and lifted. Cyrus struggled weakly, but there was no way to get purchase with his wrists bound, and he had no strength to match his tormentor. His gaze was turned inexorably up, following the rising mountain of paper. Wind whipped the loose sheets of papyrus about in crazy whirling forms that, through the haze of sweat and pain, looked almost like ghosts.

Cyrus closed his eyes, but moments later a fist slammed into the side of his head, and he felt the flesh of his ear expanding—ballooning out to impossible dimensions. His head throbbed hotly and he gagged, held from the ground only by the fist tight in his hair.

"You will watch." That voice was close in his ear, the breath hot and tepid—stinking of rotted meat and mead. The stench of the man's sweat was horrifying,

and the sting at the roots of Cyrus' hair was unbearable. He was shamed by his weakness, but he did not close his eyes again.

Moments later, a short, swarthy Roman swaggered from the shadows, torch held high, and moved to the pyre. The scrolls seemed to stretch forever. Cyrus could not see the top of the mountain—could not bear to see it. Though his tongue was thick as a sausage and his throat parched to the point of cutting off his breath, he watched, tears streaming from the corners of his eyes and running down through the blood-soaked sand caked on his cheeks.

The torch dipped—hesitated. A wide, half-toothed grin slipped over the soldier's face, and he turned, staring straight into Cyrus' eyes. The torch dropped and the flames leapt to the sky like birds startled from the rushes. The darkness parted and a wave of heat and light seared Cyrus's skin—blinded him

"No," he tried to whisper but the sound was so much sand drifting across the dry and rocky ground. "No."

Cyrus woke. The flapping of the tents was louder. A wind had risen from the desert, and sand hissed between the tents. The stakes holding the canvas tightly in place strained, and Cyrus could feel the tension on the ropes. He was bathed in sweat. His scalp tingled with the memory of another's pain, and his eyes would not adjust to the darkness immediately. Strobed images of licking flames and crooked, yellowed teeth filled his mind.

Slowly, he released his grip on the sheets. He hadn't noticed, at first, that he was clutching his hands tightly at his sides, as though anchoring himself in place. As though he might be carried away.

What was that SOUND?

The voices were loud and insistent, and he heard the distinct ring of metal on metal, a grating sound that could only come from equipment being moved—and roughly. Or ...

The vision of short, broad swords glinting in the searing brilliance of firelight too-close—too-hot—shifted across his vision. The scuff of sandals on sand. Stones falling.

He shook his head and sat up, sliding his legs off the side of his cot.

"Jesus," he muttered. He could feel the exhaustion that must show in his eyes, but there was no way to sleep. His sheets felt like hot sand.

He rose quickly and moved back to the flap of his tent. The lantern hung on a hook at one side of the door, but he ignored it. The moon would be enough to see by, and he only wanted a glance—a single stabilizing sight of some idiot dragging a crate of equipment between the tents in the middle of the night, to calm his nerves. Whoever it was had questions to answer, that much was certain. Cyrus would see to it. Sleep was a valuable commodity to the obsessed, and he couldn't afford any lost without good cause.

He couldn't afford the dreams.

The sand danced its lonely dance, whipping into the tents to either side of the narrow path between. There was no one. There was nothing to see. In the not-so-distance the sounds echoed. Cyrus glanced in the direction of the city, ancient and modern, not even a soft glow of light at this hour, though not so distant.

Alexandria. He stared into the distance, as if he could melt the miles with his mind and draw her closer. The city had been a Mecca of learning, a haven for words in a world filled with the imminence of action. So long ago.

Cleopatra had walked there. Proud queen, one of a hundred by that same name, walking the footsteps of a Goddess and living the life of an aristocratic nightmare world where intelligence fell to brute strength. A world where the learning of Greece and the dreams of even Alexander had fallen to dust. Or been burned.

The wind picked up suddenly, and sand wisped around his feet. The sound was the voice of asps. Slithering. Hissing against the tent. Cyrus shuddered involuntarily and took half a step back toward his tent.

—He heard a shout—a wild, wailing cry of pain. He heard footsteps, some rushing as if propelled by madness, some slower, methodical and steady.

—He heard only the sand, felt it sliding over his ankles and slipping up under the cuffs of his pants.

—He heard the clatter of steel on steel, deep guttural voices that made no sense, words that whirled in his mind, echoed at the edge of consciousness— then—cleared.

Roman. He was hearing voices crying out in Latin so archaic, so off-kilter from any he'd spoken or heard spoken, in school or on the site, that it jarred his senses loose from their moorings. The pronunciations and inflections were unfamiliar. Wrong. No ... he staggered back toward his tent again, tripping over his own feet and falling heavily toward the sand. Not wrong. Jesus, not wrong at all.

Cyrus didn't break his fall. His hands never moved to catch against the floor of his tent. The words had startled something out of him, something deep and resonant, and he was unable to concentrate on anything but the sound. The pure, "correct" sound. Latin. The absolute. The reality. Not an exercise in pronunciation and history being bandied about by foppish professors, but gut-true speech.

The hard smack of his head on the ground sent stars spinning through the words, confusing them again. Darkness coalesced before his eyes, blocking the dim light of the stars, then dropped over his mind and eyes like a shroud. Cyrus passed into that darkness, and he dreamed. *The heat was tremendous.*

Cyrus knew he was too close to the fire, but he didn't care. His eyes were closed again. The soldiers seemed to have temporarily lost interest in their captive as the fire leaped to the sky, dancing up the pyre of scrolls and parchment like a band of howling demons. It was so quick to give in, that pile of words. So many lives and loves, hours and dreams had gone into the compiling and transcribing that it was beyond simple comprehension, except in a moment like this. Except when it was all a single spark, blazing toward ash. Except when the words condensed to a single roar and spewed to the heavens, dispersed with no more thought or reason than could be found in the swirling of the sand.

As if snapping free of a dream, one of the soldiers turned, noted Cyrus' closed eyelids, and cuffed him hard on the side of the head.

"Open your eyes, scribe. Watch. You will see, and you will remember."

Cyrus would remember. He would see, even when his eyes were closed. He would know the sound of a thousand thousand words screaming at once until the thread that was his own in the tapestry of fate wound to its end and faded into oblivion. His eyes watered, then poured salty tears. The tears formed a rainbow-esque halo around the soaring flames, and the pain at the roots of his hair kept his nerves taut and screaming in time with the crackle and pop from the fire.

Cyrus', hands scraped roughly across the sand, tearing at his flesh and imbedding the grit in the new cuts. His head was pounding, and his eyes streamed with the tears from his dream. Dream? How could he have been dreaming? A vision?

Cyrus shook his head, regretted the action, then shook it again anyway. He had to get control. The moon was bright overhead, and the wind tossed sand into his face with every gust, threatening to blind him. The tears were drying on his cheeks, leaving them cold and clammy. His armpits were clammy, as well, and his thighs. Sweat coated him in a thin veil of ice.

Cyrus rose, aware that he flinched, expecting somehow the tight grip of strong fingers in his hair. Nobody else moved in the camp. Nobody was ever moving in the camp at that hour, but Cyrus glanced first one way, then the other, shivering. He rose to a kneeling position and wrapped his arms across his chest.

"Christ," he whispered.

He glanced up, and over the line of tents directly ahead, he saw a bright, flickering glow. Too bright to be a lantern, too distant. Alexandria was the other direction, so it could not be the city. Had the people of the city gone up in arms against their digging? Were there hundreds of torch bearing Egyptians descending on the camp?

Cyrus rose. He tried to paint that picture in his mind, bringing up memories of Frankenstein movies and angry villagers. He couldn't make the leap. His mind echoed with the sounds of swords sliding in and out of scabbards, the roar of flames, and the hoarse Latin words grated in his ear.

Stumbling to his feet, Cyrus turned and moved through the tents. He had to see. He had to know where the light was coming from, had to know who and what was making those sounds. His throat was so dry he could scarcely breathe. His eyes were filled with salt water and grit, but he squinted and continued on, not bothering to wipe them clean.

Cyrus kept his gaze pointed straight ahead, into the desert, but he couldn't quite clear his sight. Images itched at his thoughts, begging for attention. The scrolls. Behind him, beneath their protective covering, held safe from wind and rain, oxygen and groping fingers. So many hours—too many hours—brow drenched in sweat and fingers brushing that parchment. As if the words and symbols could be fathomed by touch, ancient Braille reaching out to him across the centuries. Braille was an apt description—he felt blind.

After all their efforts, uncovering the ruins, painstakingly sifting through sand and grit, stone chambers and pots, the scrolls were all they had. The answers they needed to complete their work were tangled in the scrawled symbols, enigmatic and dense. They had found a huge, underground vault of a ruin. They had found evidence of civilization from the era of Elizabeth Taylor's Cleopatra, and Hollywood's Caesar, but they had found no reason—not even a scrap of a reason, as a matter of fact—for the place's existence.

Too far from the city to be part of the city. Too far from the Nile for tilling or growing. Too deeply buried for anything but a secret, and the secrets of the ancients were that much more difficult to unravel, buried as they were in sand and years.

Cyrus believed he'd find the answer. He believed the words would speak to him, and the belief was an odd one. It was more a remembering, an act of reacquainting himself with facts long known, but buried deep in his mind. Deeper than he was comfortable delving. Deeper than he knew how to reach, but still there.

The wind grew stronger. Sand swirled around his ankles, tore into his arms, and his legs, stung his neck and slipped in through every opening in his clothing. He walked steadily on, ignoring the whirling cloud of desert that rose to escort him. A minute? Ten? He turned for just an instant, but the camp—the tents and the scrolls, professors and students—might as well not have existed. It didn't matter. The whirling sand formed hieroglyphs, spinning madly—out of control. Indecipherable. Lost.

303

Cyrus tripped, stumbling forward with his arms stretched out before him. He couldn't see where he was going, what he was falling toward. He closed his eyes and braced himself, almost prepared when his hands brushed the ground. Almost, but not quite. His forehead struck hard, and bright pinpoints of light scattered the sand into diamond-flashes of pain. He lay still for a moment, sand whirling around and over him, into his mouth and against the lids of his eyes. He knew he had to get up, but his head was pounding, and he couldn't order his thoughts. He kept his eyes closed tightly, pressed his palms to the sand, and gathered his strength.

Before he could push upright, something gripped his hair so tightly he could feel the roots screaming for release from his scalp. Cyrus cried out, but this allowed the sand to whip between his lips and he bit it off. He was dragged to his knees and held, though he raised his hands over his head and tried desperately to rip that hellish grip away and free himself.

The wind died down perceptibly. Cyrus felt a pounding in his forehead, and knew there was a nasty knot there from his fall. He tried again to tear free, only managing to send a second wave of searing pain through his scalp. The roar of wind and sand was shifting. It didn't grow any quieter, but shifted in tone—in rhythm. Cyrus felt sweat dripping down his cheeks and reached to brush it away. The sand had stopped whipping against his face, but he did not open his eyes.

Then something struck him, hard, on the side of the head. The bright spots of pain returned, spreading down from his forehead toward his ear. He heard a voice, guttural and incomprehensible, grating near his ear. Cyrus shook himself violently, trying to rise, but a second rocking blow to the head brought him up short. The voice grew louder and more commanding, and Cyrus forced himself to listen. If he didn't figure this one out quickly, he had the feeling his days of figuring things out would come to an abrupt halt.

The voice sounded again, and Cyrus caught a single word (Latin for eyes). He opened his eyes quickly, and a flash of his dream passed through his mind.

"Open your eyes, scribe."

The roar suddenly took a shape in his mind's eye, and Cyrus forced himself to look up. It could not be there, but it was, the pyre, flames leaping to the sky with fingers that groped and tongues of destruction that leaped and danced. He could make out the shapes beneath the flames, through the billowing smoke and the shimmering heat. Even the sweat dripping into his eyes and forcing him to bite back tears that would blur things more completely couldn't fully disguise the scrolls. Thousands of scrolls, and not like those so carefully pinned beneath the protective covers in the tents behind him, but full scrolls, rolled and yanked from the ornate canisters that had housed them.

Soot and ash rose from the fire and shot to the sky, and each one seemed to form a letter, or a word, darting away forever.

Thoughts crowded in on him. Cyrus recognized the thoughts, and yet, he didn't. He tried to twist his head, to get a glimpse of the man gripping his hair, but this won him a hard shake that nearly made him pass out, and he gave it up. The fire blazed.

More voices sounded to his right, loud and insistent, and there was a flurry of motion and sound. Cyrus couldn't see what it was, but he sensed that whatever it was, it was important. Those around him scuttled in all directions. Only his captor stood firm and silent.

A face haunted him. A woman's face, foreign and unfamiliar, yet not. As close to his heart as the image of his mother, or the first girl he'd ever loved. Perhaps closer. She was frowning at him, disapproving. Tears rolled from his eyes to trickle down his cheeks, and Cyrus cursed silently because he knew they'd see the weeping as weakness. They would believe it was because of the hand in his hair and the sand grinding into his knees. In his mind, the woman wept with him.

"Release him."

The words snapped from Cyrus' right side. For a long moment, the grip in his hair tightened, as if willing the words away. With a quick snap downward that forced Cyrus' eyes to the ground, the hand was gone, and though he knelt in the sand, tears running down his cheeks and his head pounding from the falls and the cuffs of those he could not see, he was free. He did not move.

Footsteps drew near—slow, odd steps. Uneven and not too heavy. Cyrus could just make out the sound over the crackling of the flames. He wanted to scream, but no sound would come. Nothing. His chest had constricted so tightly with pain, frustration, and sorrow that he could scarcely believe it was possible to breathe. The emotions were off-kilter, some his own, some those of another—or not exactly another, but another Cyrus. The pain he understood. The sorrow he felt more deeply, and the frustration, but he could not assign them a place in his mind. He did not understand the fire—not exactly. He knew that it hurt to watch it, and that he should stop it, should fling himself on it and burn with the words, leaving the nightmares behind.

"They burn well."

The voice was the same that had demanded his release. The words came so suddenly that Cyrus nearly missed them in the sound and well of emotion.

"It is almost as if," the voice continued—in Latin, Cyrus understood that much by now—"the demons trapped in those scrolls were screaming for release."

"Demons?" Cyrus' voice cracked. His dry throat proved unfit for the task of translating his thoughts, and beside the smooth, articulate voice of whoever stood beside him, he knew he sounded crude. His face burned with indignation, and anger.

"Oh yes," the voice continued. Cyrus stole a quick glance to the side. He caught sight of one sandaled foot and the hem of a robe—toga? It was ornate, decorated in gold. Elegant. "The demons are banished with the words, scribe. They flee before us, as your armies fled—as your queen would have fled, given the chance. They flee us because they are evil, warping the minds of good Roman citizens and reaching out to ensnare even our leader, and because we are strong."

Words floated up from somewhere deep within Cyrus' mind. Not his own, he knew, not his own because the words weren't in his own tongue. He did not reply in Latin, but in Greek, fluid, easy speech that belied the difficulty of the translation. Greek because it was what the man beside him hated, symbolizing things beyond his grasp.

"The words aren't evil," he spat. "Their destruction—that is evil. The burning of history, one page at a time, one scroll after the other. You can't kill the past by destroying its records, you only deny yourself the chance to experience it."

The guard drew back his arm and smashed a fist hard into the side of Cyrus' head. He nearly bit his tongue as the pain shot through his temple, exploding in a thousand sparks that flew up to join the flames in his vision. He heard voices from far away, but he could no longer quite make out what they were saying. He would have fallen, but again, the rough hand of the guard gripped his hair, and sagging, Cyrus leaned forward, letting his full weight hang from that grip.

He felt a shift, and knew the guard was drawing back to strike again, but the blow never fell.

"Take him away." The words filtered through it all, and Cyrus staggered to his feet as the guard turned without a word and started walking, never loosening his grip. "Keep him alive. He has seen, and he will remember. When we return to Alexandria, he will write of our conquest. He will preserve our deeds—or die."

Cyrus shook his head, regretted it as the tear on his hair screamed through his brain with stabbing lances of pain.

"No," he whispered. He couldn't tell what language, but he knew what he was thinking—what they were thinking—what must be said and done and NOT done. "No," he repeated.

And then there was darkness. Blessed, complete darkness. He dreamed of letters that streamed from spiraling smoke into a papyrus sky. He dreamed of her face—a woman he didn't know—a queen he loved. He dreamed of asps and through it all, a voice whispered to his mind of Rome and conquest, war and always in Latin. He knew the voice now, knew it could be none other, and he tried to silence the words, but there was a power in them he could not deny. A destiny. Octavian was mad, but he was Imperator. He was conqueror. He would take the queen to his homeland in chains and parade her like an animal if he could, but this did not frighten Cyrus. He dreamed of asps, and his joined mind, then and now, gone and back again, knew the simple truth. Cleopatra would die. Cyrus would not.

The great library was a ruin. Ashes blended with sand on the hot wind, no more a record of history than the sand itself. Lost. The second library, the hidden place that was to have preserved so much, was a ruin as well. An urn for the cremation of history. They had found it, and they had found him—and he had not died. The life he should have taken had been taken from him, instead, and the words he'd learned—the words he'd sworn to protect—had been taken as well, replaced by lies, and deceit, histories that were not and never had been, and yet endured. Endured because he, Cyrus, had carefully recorded them, as he was told, a dog on a leash with quill in hand. The final betrayal. Though he slept, he wept. The silence dragged him in and down, and the world swirled away into accusing silence. Her eyes glared from the depths of shadow, accusing and dark.

Cyrus woke to hands shaking him by his shoulder. He jerked back, smacking his head solidly into whoever was behind him. There was a cry and the sound of stumbling footsteps.

"Christ, what the hell is wrong with you?" He knew the voice, but it took him a moment to place it, to clear the Greek and the Latin from his mind and focus. Professor Rosenman.

Cyrus spun, nearly falling from his seat as his stiff arms and legs ignored the commands he sent them, stiff from being too long in one position. His head pounded.

"Where are they?" he asked, catching himself on the edge of the table. "Where did they go? The fire ... I"

"Take it easy, Cyrus," Rosenman snapped. "Jesus, you fell asleep on the god damned table. Who are you talking about? And what is all ... that?"

Cyrus started to ask more questions, bit off the words, and spun back to the table. He was seated in the work tent—somehow—impossibly—and the table was covered with scribbled notes. Page after page of notes littered every inch of the work surface. The cover was open, and his pen lay dangerously close to the scroll—too close—close enough to damage, or stain—for ink to blot. He grabbed the offending pen and gripped it tightly, grabbing a page off the desk at the same time and staring at it—reading what had been written. What *he* had written.

He mouthed the words, hearing that voice in his head that was so close to his own.

His mind spun again, the tent—the carnival—so many years before, and so few in the scope of the moment.

"Words." the old woman breathed softly. "Words were your life. Words and life. Bound. You brought life to the words—words to the life and they took it. All gone. Took it away and burned it."

He let his hand fall to the table and he stared at the wall across from him. He was shaking. His heartbeat was out of control, and his breath was short and harsh. Behind him, he felt Rosenman's eyes boring into the back of his head.

"You'd better have a damned good reason for this," the older man said at last. "You've broken every rule we have, worked too long, too late, let alone took the cover off the scroll."

Cyrus turned, and he spoke, his voice seeming to drift in from the distance. "I'm finished," he said softly. "It is done."

"What is done?" Rosenman growled, stepping suddenly forward and grabbing at one of the sheets in irritation. "What in the hell do you think you've done?"

Rosenman started to read, but Cyrus was already standing, staggering toward the door. He knew what he'd done. He knew what was written on those sheets, because he'd written the words, once and again—one language, one world, to the next. His words. He'd betrayed his queen, and he'd warped the passage of time into a romanticized version of Roman glory—but he'd written the truth, as well.

Without a backward glance, Cyrus staggered into the bright sunlight of morning.

Rosenman read, eyes growing wide, then sat down before his knees could give way.

"They stole the words and set them free. The queen was strong, and she escaped through the portals of time, but I am left behind to record. The words were my responsibility, and I betrayed her trust. I did not join her, I cowered, and I served those who burned time. In the hours between midnight and the dawn, I have set myself the task of atonement. I leave these words with a prayer to the Goddess Isis that they will be found, and that they will be understood. In time, perhaps, time can right itself. This is my story."

Rosenman set the paper aside carefully and leaned hurriedly to the beginning of the scroll. He worked slowly, meticulously, and somehow—symbols that had seemed obscure became clearer. Things he had not seen, or had ignored, became truth. Hands trembling, he began to gather the papers, not bothering to cover the scroll, or to reach for the gloves he knew he should wear. Not daring to read further.

He felt the sudden weight of eyes on his shoulder, standing the hairs on his neck on end. The image of a woman's face flashed through his mind, then was gone. Gathering the papers, he hurried after Cyrus.

Behind them, left alone, the scroll flapped gently in the breeze, as if waving in approval

CHILLERS

Lisa Morton

Los Angeles used to be nice. Before it froze.

I hope you know that; I hope it's back to being the way it was. Warm, sunny. Streets of mansions beneath nodding palm trees. Restaurants with outdoor patios that didn't even need heaters. Beaches covered with sand that burned the bottoms of your feet.

As I write this, that's all just a memory.

Maybe you're reading this because I gave it to you, but that's probably not the case. I can admit that to myself these days.

Do you know how it started? When everything turned cold, and *they* came? Even if you do, you haven't heard my version.

Of how everything changed in a week.

A single, frozen week that became forever.

"There's ice in the gutter."

That was my first inclination that something was wrong. It was January in L.A., about 7:30 in the morning. Tim and I left the house the same time every day, heading off to our respective jobs.

It had already been a chilly winter, but it was still startling to find the gutters frozen solid. It was odd enough just to find water at the edge of Southern California's streets; but I'd been born in the San Fernando Valley 32 years ago, had spent my entire life there, and I'd *never* awakened to find solid blocks of ice where puddles had stood twelve hours earlier.

Tim joined me, looking down. "Yep, Laura," he said, smirking, "you may not know this, but that's what happens to water when it gets really cold."

Tim was from Michigan.

"But it doesn't happen in L.A.," I protested.

Tim ignored the ice and went around to the driver's side of his Toyota pick-up. "Hothouse flower," he taunted me, before waving and climbing behind the wheel.

Tim drove off, and I headed to my own Honda. There was a light sheet of frost covering the windshield. I was wearing my heaviest jacket—which was really just a blazer with a lining—and I shivered as I climbed into my car.

I didn't know it then, but I was about to start shivering a lot.

The next day it snowed.

We'd had snow before; my mom's house, where we were living then, was in Burbank, not far from the San Gabriel mountains, and once every few years, we'd see the tops whitened after winter storms. Once, when I'd still believed in Santa, we'd even awoken on a morning during the Christmas season to find a fine dusting of the white stuff on our cacti and yucca.

But this was no fine dusting—this was a solid four inches of honest-to-god-of-winter snow.

Tim had laughed as he'd kicked out a path to his truck. "Fucking snow!"

"Yeah," I'd answered him, not nearly as ebullient. "Snow. Cold."

Tim had suddenly hurled a snowball at me. The icy mass hit me in the side of the head and broke apart, misting me in moist chill. "Tim!"

He'd thrown up his hands in mock surrender, then grabbed me and pulled me into a bearhug.

We'd only been married two years, and even though my mom's stroke had forced us to move into my childhood home to help her out, we still acted like newlyweds. Besides, the house was a nice three-bedroom/two-bath that my folks had bought when they'd first moved to the Valley back in the '60s, and it was better than the one-bedroom apartment we'd had. Since a heart attack had killed my dad a year ago, the house had somehow seemed to magically expand to near-mansion proportions. If mom occasionally heard us, in our bedroom down at the end of the hallway ... well, she just smiled at me in the mornings, as I finished her sponge bath and welcomed Rosario, who watched her during the days.

Tim was chuckling as he hugged me, but I wasn't amused. "Hey, c'mon," he said, giving my cheek little pecks, "snow in L.A. It's kind of fun, isn't it?"

"No, it's not. We shouldn't have snow here. Is this some weird off-shoot of global warming or something?"

He laughed again, kissed me, and turned me loose. "Anybody ever tell you you worry too much?"

"Funny. When I married you, some of my friends told me I didn't worry enough."

The next morning—it was a Friday, for some reason, I remember that—Rosario didn't show up.

It was the first time she'd been late in the year that she'd worked for me. Her English (which was about as good as my Spanish) may not have been perfect, but she was unfailingly polite, hardworking, and punctual.

I waited until I was late to my own job, then called Rosario's number. It had snowed again overnight, and there were a lot of traffic snarl-ups on the freeways; no one in L.A. knew how to drive in snow.

Rosario didn't answer. There wasn't even a voice-mail.

"Shit," I said, hanging up, then turned to my mom, who had just been re-learning how to walk and talk after the stroke. "Rosario's not answering."

"I think I can manage ..." Mom said, with more resolution than I thought she actually felt.

"Absolutely not. Especially not with this freaky weather."

In the end, I called in sick to my office, figuring I could call the agency I'd used to find Rosario and get someone else by tomorrow. But the agency didn't answer, either.

Mom had turned on the TV, and while I decided what to do, the news reports started.

They were on every channel: Record numbers of people were disappearing in L.A. The same thing seemed to be happening in other major U.S. cities, too. All over the country, unusually low temperatures were sharing emergency broadcasts with thousands of reports of missing persons.

"Laura ..." Mom started.

"I know."

I got my phone and called Tim.

He answered from his car. He was stuck on the 5 freeway, which was backed up solid from accidents and snow banks. Los Angeles, it seemed, had no supply of snow ploughs.

"Have you been listening to the news?" I asked.

"Yeah," he said. "Weird, huh?"

"I think you should come home, Tim." I glanced back, and saw Mom watching me anxiously.

"I may not have much choice. I don't know that surface streets are going to be much better."

"Come home, Tim."

"Yeah, okay. I'll get off and turn around as soon as I can."

Tim made it home, and we spent the rest of that day in a state of sort of bemused anxiety. It wasn't until the next day that things really got bad.

When the bodies started to show up.

I found the first one when I went outside to see if I could start my car. It was sitting next to what had been a rosemary bush in the front yard. I saw the hand first, the fingers blue and frozen stone-like into a claw. I stared at it in disbelief, then walked around the snow drift to where I could see the rest.

Or at least as much as there was. It was little more than a torso, with the legs missing just below the hips, most of the stomach torn away, and one arm gone. But the head was intact, and I recognized the face. It was our next-door neighbor, an older man named Sammy Inoue who'd shared gardening tips and coffee with my mom.

I must have made some kind of sound, because suddenly Tim was there beside me, his arms around me, holding me up. "Oh shit," he breathed, his words turning to vapor in the freezing air. "Let's go in, Laura."

I let him lead me away. We tried to call 911, but kept getting busy signals.

Suddenly I realized I hadn't seen mom yet today. I ran back to her bedroom, opened the door ...

... and saw her bed was empty.

"Tim!"

We searched the whole house, but there was no trace of her.

"Where the fuck would she have gone?" Tim asked, once we'd even checked the garage.

"She couldn't have gone anywhere on her own, not in this snow."

"Well, she did *go* somewhere."

"Or was taken," I answered.

Tim stared at me for a few seconds, then barked a single nervous laugh. "Taken? By who? Little gray aliens who want to probe her?"

I think I panicked then. "Mom!" I screamed.

I ran to the front door, threw it open, and ran into the street, my legs sinking in snow up to the knees. "Mom! MOM!"

Tim came after me and tugged on my arm. "Laura, you said it yourself—she couldn't be out here!"

"She has to be! Mom—"

My shout suddenly died as I slipped on something, looked down—and saw another frozen arm.

"Jesus, no ..." Tim muttered.

I began flailing at the snow, trying to uncover the corpse I'd stumbled on.

It wasn't mom. But that wasn't much relief ...

... because there were a lot of them.

When I'd uncovered the third severed arm, I staggered back and looked around. I knew then why the snow around me was mounded in strange shapes.

"Come back to the house," Tim said behind me, and he sounded scared.

"What if she's one of them out here—"

I broke off at a sound: a strange noise coming from somewhere to my left, from the entrance to an apartment building's underground garage. It wasn't like anything I'd ever heard—a sort of buzzing hum, almost like a summer insect but faster and more ... *unearthly.*

"What the hell ..." Tim said, and I knew he'd heard it, too.

Something was in the parking garage. It was too dark to see, but we caught glimpses of movement, a darker form shifting in the blackness and making that sound.

Tim grabbed my arm and started pulling. "Back to the house. NOW!"

I let him drag me, but I kept looking back at the black hole of the garage entrance. Whatever was in there ... I could feel its eyes on me. Watching me.

Somehow, I knew it was still hungry.

The power went out later that day.

We had a stash of emergency supplies—every house in Southern California had its earthquake preparedness kit, I think—and I discovered a little hand-crank radio. We powered it up and found a station still broadcasting.

Over the single tinny speaker, we struggled to make out words often spoken in a feverish rush, in anxious, terrified tones. From what anyone could tell, the missing people had been taken, frozen, partially consumed, and their remains left behind like fast food wrappers. Someone with a love of movies and a morbid sense of humor had re-named L.A. "The Big Chill", and the things that we were now sharing our city with were called "chillers".

No one had exactly seen a chiller yet, but there were a few things about them that had already been learned or guessed. They couldn't operate at any temperature over forty degrees. They stuck to shadowy places in the day. They could apparently enter a house or building regardless of barred doors or locked windows. Warmth was the only protection.

Where they'd come from was anybody's guess. One middle-aged man shouted out his theory that they were invaders and this was a war. A younger, calmer woman suggested they were a by-product of a secret government project gone awry. A well-known writer thought that perhaps global warming had broken down a barrier between dimensions, allowing the chillers to cross over and convert our world into one big meat locker.

Tim moved into action. He ran to the kitchen and started pawing through cupboards. "How much food do we have?" he demanded.

I joined him, taking stock. "We went shopping on Tuesday. And we don't have to worry about the stuff in the refrigerator spoiling if we just put it outside. I think we're okay for a week."

Tim nodded, then looked around. "Okay, we need to figure the gas will probably go off soon, so we'll need to think about heat." He ran into the living room and eyed the fireplace.

"Thank god your parents never had this converted over to one of those gas-log things," he said.

I agreed, then we started thinking about wood.

"We'll need to stay just in this room. We barricade ourselves in here with plenty of fuel. We can bust up some of the furniture for firewood."

I didn't like that. There were pieces here—dressers, chairs, tables—I'd grown up with and that had belonged to my grandmother. "I don't think Mom will like that."

Tim came to me and put his hands on my shoulders, with just enough force to make me focus on him. "Laura ... your mom's probably dead."

"No, she's just—"

"Just NOTHING, Laura. Her room got cold last night, and those things came in here and got her—"

"No!"

I broke down for a while after that. I think I cried a long time. I don't really remember. All I can recall is that at some point I looked up as Tim came into the house, carrying a bundle of wood that I thought used to be part of Mr. Inoue's garage door.

I think what I asked him was, "How long do you think this'll last?"

We both knew the answer; summer was a long way away. Tim set down the wood, pulled me to him, and stroked my hair. "We'll get through this, baby. We will."

Then he held me while we watched the sun sink, taking the last of the day's shelter with it.

Mom had put a thermometer out on the patio, a cheerful little instrument in a terracotta sunburst, so we brought that into the living room, along with clothing and grooming supplies and books and anything else we might need. Then we sealed off the hallway, and hunkered down for the night.

We figured we'd take turns, feeding the fire and keeping an eye on the thermometer. As long as we kept things at forty degrees throughout the night, we'd be fine.

As long as we did that every night.

The first night was okay. It was my turn, about four in the morning, when I heard that buzzing coming from the other side of the barricade we'd put up at the entrance to the hallway.

Tim had fashioned a torch from a branch and some old sheets dipped in gasoline, and we'd decided we'd keep it by us, a last resort weapon. As I listened to that terrible sound, straining to hear it over the snare drum of my own heart, my hand reached for the torch ...

... but the sound faded out. The chiller that had been in my house had left.

At least for tonight.

"We need to find other people."

It was the next day, and Tim and I were enjoying a fine meal of rice cakes (only slightly stale) and canned peaches.

"A sled dog team would be nice, too," I added.

"I'm serious. Even if we can come up with enough fuel to keep us warm through winter, what about food? We're almost out now."

I tried to imagine a trip to the local supermarket; it'd probably already been picked over, and certainly was completely cold and dark inside.

A nice home for a group of hungry chillers.

I nodded. "I know. But ... well, we can't drive in the snow."

Tim laughed and spluttered around a mouthful of crunchy rice. "God, that's one of the things I love about you, Laura: You're *so* L.A. Believe it or not, we'll have to walk."

I think I started to shake. "It's not safe. Not with ..."

Tim had obviously thought about this. "We'll go early in the day. We stick to the middle of the street, stay away from buildings and shade. We'll take torches. We've even got that kitchen torch thing. You know, the one your mom used to make crème brulee with."

I had to smile at that. I wondered if a chiller would get a tasty burnt crust.

"So where would we go, armed with our deadly kitchen torch?" I asked.

"I heard something on the radio last night—just before it went off the air—they were telling people to go to their nearest school, preferably a larger one like a high school. We're only about two miles from the high school."

I tried to imagine walking two miles through the knee-high snow. Hell, I didn't even like skiing. "Are you sure we can manage two miles?"

Tim leaned across the table and took my hand. "I think we have to try. Let's go now."

"Really?"

"Really."

We each filled a backpack, stuffed our pockets with matches, and carried two torches.

Tim had actually found a set of ancient snowshoes in Mr. Inoue's garage, and he insisted on making me wear them. I laughed as he tied them around my feet, but it did make walking on the snow much easier. For himself, Tim found my folks' old tennis rackets, and they worked pretty well.

It was about 8:30 as we set off. The day was clear and bright, and under other circumstances it would have been a gorgeous Southern California winter day, complete with smog-free blue sky that hurt your eyes to look at.

Unfortunately, it was only about forty degrees in the full sun.

"Remember: middle of the street," Tim reminded me.

"Okay," I said, feeling none too sure.

I also didn't want to leave the house.

That house was a big part of who I was. Its walls and rooms had formed me as much as anything. I knew every inch of it, from the blue-and-yellow tile in the bathroom to the big old magnolia tree in the backyard, the one that dropped its waxy white blossoms all over everything in the spring. Those blossoms had made daddy curse like mad every year as he'd cleaned them up, and ...

"Laura, honey ... let's go." It was Tim, his voice soft, his grip gently but steadily turning me away from the house.

From home. And even though we were only going a few miles, somehow, I thought I was leaving it forever.

We only got a block before we heard the chillers.

We were trudging down the middle of my street, and I was reciting the names of all the neighbors I knew:the Daltons. The Juarez family. Mrs. Anouryan. There was Danny Washington's place, the one that'd always had a least two Harleys parked in the driveway; I remembered how Danny'd always bitched about the jets from the Burbank Airport that took off right over our neighborhood.

I realized I hadn't heard a jet—or a plane, or a helicopter, or in fact, even a bird—in several days. There was no constant roar from the freeways, no sound of gardeners' leaf blowers and lawn mowers, no hiphop music from a passing lowrider with its windows down. In fact, the only sounds were our breathing, and the occasional sound of snow falling from a withered tree.

I'd never wanted noise so badly. I'd probably never spent a truly quiet day in my entire suburban life, and it left me feeling unanchored and terrified now.

I tried to go back to mentally naming my neighbors (even though they were probably all dead by now, their half-eaten remains buried under the same snow I was plodding across). There was old Mr. Cheung's place, with the banana tree he'd been so proud of, now dead and shriveled, never meant to withstand L.A.'s new low temperatures.

And the buzzing was coming from inside Mr. Cheung's house.

"Just keep going," Tim whispered to me. "They can't get us as long as we stay in the sun where it's warm."

The only problem was that the rest of the street was older and completely overgrown with tall trees. Even though they'd shed their foliage with the cold, they still made a shady patchwork we'd be moving through.

"Tim ..." I started.

We both stopped, peering ahead. "I know," Tim said.

Now there was buzzing on either side of the street around us. We still couldn't see the chillers, but we knew they were there, waiting for us.

"So we go another way," Tim said, and started back the way we'd come.

It wasn't easy. Walking on the big snowshoes was tiring, and trying to find a path through the urban maze of tall apartment buildings and trees was nearly impossible. We had to rest every fifteen minutes, feeling our feet and ankles grow numb from the work and the cold.

By noon we'd gone six blocks.

"This isn't going to work," I gasped out during the latest break. "We have to go back ..."

"We're not going back." Tim's tone made argument futile.

"We won't make the high school before dark, not at this rate."

He looked around, gesturing. "Then we'll hole up in one of these houses overnight and start again in the morning."

But that wasn't how it went down.

By four that afternoon, we were close; I figured maybe another three blocks to reach the school. But the shadows were already lengthening, and we could feel the air around us growing colder by the minute.

And the buzzing sounds were growing closer.

Tim's eyes were darting around like pebbles in a cyclone. He suddenly dug a hand into his pockets. "Light the torches."

My fingers were slow in responding, but I finally got a disposable lighter out, lit it after a few tries, and held its flame to the torches.

One didn't catch. It was frozen solid.

The other did. I cast the useless one aside, and glanced at Tim. Both of his were blazing, and he held them before him like shields.

"Can you move any faster?" he asked me.

"I'll try," was the best I could manage.

We started forward. The sound of the torches sputtering was welcome, and I knew our goal was within our reach. I was moving faster over the snow, energized by hope—

Then a chiller grabbed me.

It was a strange sensation, and at first I had no idea what had happened. It was my left ankle; it suddenly refused to obey me, and I felt myself tottering. I looked back, and what I saw ...

There was a shadow stretched across the snow, a dark patch without real humanoid shape; it was roughly oval, but surrounded by tendrils that writhed out from the central mass. One of those tendrils was wrapped around my leg.

Pulling me towards the larger mass.

I screamed out as I went down. I tried to turn, to hurl my torch towards the thing, but I'd forgotten about the huge, clumsy snowshoes, which kept me planted firmly in place. Instead, my torch was buried in snow, going out with a plume of steam and a final wet gasp.

Tim was there, though, and as I twisted in the chiller's grasp, I saw my husband, my savior, thrust a flame into the dark patch that held me. There was a sound like steam escaping the edges of a pressure cooker—almost a scream—followed by a pop, and the chiller vanished.

Literally. It didn't flee, or fade out, or lap-dissolve like a decaying vampire in an old film. It just popped out of existence. Suddenly, I believed the man on the radio who'd suggested the chillers might be extra-dimensional because surely nothing from our universe would look or sound or die like that.

Tim pushed one of his torches into my hand, then pulled me to my feet. "We have to stay close!"

I didn't have the breath to agree.

The sun had set now, and even though the sky overhead glowed a soothing indigo, we were plunged into shadow.

The noise of the chillers around us was almost deafening. Everywhere I looked, I saw the squirming shadows skating over the snow towards us.

"Go!" Tim yelled in my ear, and my legs started moving forward almost against my will.

We instinctively placed ourselves side by side, Tim sweeping his torch to the left, me to the right. At least we no longer had to worry about finding a sunlit path among the shadows.

We advanced one block, and could now see the bulk of the high school, silhouetted two blocks away against the blue horizon.

"We're almost there!" Tim shouted.

But there were so many chillers.

I'd heard that "pop" sound dozens of times now, and hoped that meant I'd killed a small army of these goddamned things.

But there were so many massed around us now, we could only move forward by inches at a time.

Then Tim's torch went out.

It happened so quickly, I didn't really see any of it. One minute he was beside me, his strength reassuring, his warmth keeping me going. Then he was *cold*, and I turned, and saw he was already freezing, dozens of whips of black wrapped around his arms and legs and torso, his voice already dying in frozen gasps.

Later, they told me I was just screaming, incoherent, waving my torch like a madwoman.

What really happened: There were people in the high school, and they'd heard me scream when I'd fallen. They'd run into the street (they had flamethrowers, not just torches), and although it was too late for Tim, they'd been able to turn the tide of chillers back from me.

It'd taken two of them to subdue me.

Now I live here, in the high school. There are about two-hundred of us, living mainly in the former gymnasium. Privacy is a thing of the past; we spend most of our time huddling together to create a few extra, precious degrees of warmth.

I'm stronger now than I used to be. I've learned how to get around well on skis, and I can use a flamethrower. I'm good on the scavenging crews—when we go out to find supplies in stores or homes—and I stopped being afraid of the chillers a while ago. Now I just take a grim satisfaction in the number of "pops" I can rack up on each of our excursions.

It's April, and there's no sign of spring yet. A lot of us keep hoping things will change soon; if we can just hold out until August (when L.A.'s summer always truly set in), surely even the chillers won't be able to beat back the heat.

We still don't know exactly where they came from, or what they are. The religious people here like to think they're demons, that we're in the Rapture. I guess they think Hell has finally frozen over.

I don't really care. All I care about these days is missing mom, and Tim, and smog and freeways and endless mindless chatter about movies and fresh food and hot days.

Oh, and one other thing you should know:

I'm pregnant.

So now you know who I hope you are, you who're reading this. I hope you're strong and healthy and living in a world with too many hot days that leave your temples throbbing and your clothes soaked. I hope you and I have shared iced drinks under an umbrella, served by a beautiful young waitperson in shorts. I hope we've sat together in an air-conditioned movie theater and laughed ourselves silly, or sprawled on a living room couch reading the same book, dropping ice cubes on ourselves to stay cool.

"*That's what happens to water when it gets really cold,*" Tim once chided me.

If instead your world is still cold, and you've never known a day without snow and struggle ...

... then I hope you'll at least try to remember me, and the city I once loved, with each chiller you send back to Hell.

Do that much for me, and I'll rest easier.

CHANGED

Nancy Holder

The vampires invaded New York the night Jilly turned sixteen. She was pacing in front of a club called Watami, waiting for Eli to show, eager to see what he had bought her. He was late, and she knew it was Sean's fault. Sean wouldn't want to come, because it was Jilly's birthday and Sean hated her. But Eli would make him do it, and they would show and she would wonder all over again why Eli couldn't love her like that ... and how he could love someone who didn't like her.

Then, out of nowhere, the place was swarming with white-faced, bone-haired, blood-eyed monsters. They just started *attacking*, grabbing people and ripping open their throats—dancers, drinkers, bartenders, and her three best straight friends, Torrance, Miles, and Diego.

She still had no idea how she'd gotten out of there, but she called Eli first and then her parents. *No service, no service, beepbeepbeep* ... no texting, no net; no one could freakin' communicate.

She was Jilly Stepanek, lately of the Bronx, a semi-slacker who wanted to go to film school at NYU once she got her grades back up. She had been a neo-goth, into Victorian/Edwardian clothes and pale makeup without the Marilyn Manson vibe, loved steampunk—but now all she was, was another terrified chick on the run from the monsters. Used to be the monsters were in her head; now they were breathing down her neck in real time.

No one stepped forward to represent the vampires or explain why they had taken over the five boroughs like the world's worst gang. There were no demands, no negotiations, just lots of dying. In less than a week, drained corpses—the homeless, first—littered the streets of Manhattan, SoHo, and the Village. As far as Jilly could tell, none of them rose to become vampires themselves. Maybe all the movies weren't true; maybe once they killed you, you were just dead.

The vampires had hunting animals like falcons that dug into their white arms. The little monsters were all head and wings, with huge white faces and bloodshot eyes and teeth that clack-clack-clacked like windup toys. Blood dripped and splattered onto the ground from the places the bird-suckers gouged their claws into their masters' arms, but—she observed from as far away as possible—either the vampires couldn't feel it or they liked it. Maybe it was their version of cutting.

The bird-suckers swooped and pirouetted across the night clouds, tearing the city pigeons to pieces. A few nights of slaughter and they owned the skies. A few nights more, and there were no wild dogs on the island of Manhattan.

Three nights after her birthday, a vampire attacked and killed her father; its vampire-bird ran her mother to ground while they were running out of their house. Jilly screamed for her mom to run faster, run faster, oh, god, but it swooped down on the back of her mother's head and started pecking and tearing. Her mother fell; her eyes were open but she wasn't seeing a thing. Blood from her neck gushed onto the sidewalk beneath a lamp post, and it looked like her shadow was seeping out of her body.

Hiding in the bushes, heaving, Jilly waited it out. Then she ran the other way, in nothing but a black chemise, some petticoats, her boots, and a long black coat she had bought at a garage sale.

She tried to get to Eli's row house but whole blocks exploded right in front of her, and others whooshed up in flames like paper lanterns. Weeping and gasping, she phoned him over and over; she texted with shaking hands. *No service no service beep beep beep.*

She raced in circles to get past the fires as the smoke boiled up into the dotted clouds of clack-clack-clacking birds.

By four days after her birthday, the streets were a real jungle. The survivors were as vicious as the street dogs the vampires-birds had eaten: hoarding food, and threatening to kill each other over water bottles and safe places to sleep. She had some experience with hostility, from when she had gone drug-mad. Rehab and a lot of love had redeemed her, but the old lessons were not forgotten.

Dodging fiends and madmen, she stole tons of phones—or maybe she only took them, since there was no one left alive in the stores to ring up the sales—but there was really, really, really no service. Trying to find one that worked became an addiction. At least it gave her something to do—other than hide, and run.

Her therapist, Dr. Robles, used to caution her to ease up, not use her busy brain quite so much. He said she had to let go of loving Eli because people who were gay were gay; there wasn't going to be a change of heart no matter how much she wanted one.

She tried to find a cybercafé that the vampires hadn't gutted, but there were none to be found. She broke into office buildings and hacked their computers, but they were fried. She wondered how the vampires did it. She was sure it was part of their plot to take over the world.

Just like the vampires, she slept during the day, in the brightest sunlight she could find, her black coat covering her like a shroud. Even though she had never been a Catholic, she prayed to the God of the crucifix, because crucifixes could hold the vampires at bay. She wanted to pray in St. Patrick's Cathedral but it was too dark and enclosed; she could almost hear the vampires hissing in the chapels lining the sanctuary. Her lips were cracked and chapped. She was filthy. But maybe God would help her anyway.

Please, God, please, God, please, God, please God, please please please don't let Eli get burned to death or sucked dry by the demons amen.

High rises burned down to ash; cars exploded, and the vampires capered on stacks of the dead. And Jilly staggered through it like the last victim of the Apocalypse. No one hooked up with her and she didn't make any effort to take on a sidekick or become one. She had to get to Eli; at least she could die with him.

So she kept skirting the crazily burning buildings in her tattered bad-fairy gear, the indigo in her hair bleached by the sun and coated with dirt. She showed people the photograph of him she always carried in her coat pocket. *No, Jilly, no, Jilly, no, Jilly, no Jilly, no Jilly, no no no sorry, loser.*

She kept waiting for the fires to burn down, burn out. The smoke took a toll on her; the air smelled like someone barbecuing rotten hot dogs; she felt it congealing in her lungs and coating her skin. Five days after her birthday, she was so tired she could hardly breathe anyway, which was a sort of blessing because maybe she would die and then she could stop everything. Escaping the bad was also one of her habits. She was empty, outside and in, just a husk. If a vampire tried to suck her blood, it would probably find nothing but red powder.

She really thought that the time had come for her to die. She thought about her parents, and her friends, but mostly she thought about Eli Stein. He had been her first and only love, before he had realized he was gay. She still loved him; she would always love him, no matter what form his love for her would take. *Brainbrain, go away, obsess again some other day ...*

He was crazy-mad for Sean instead and she hoped ...

No, she couldn't even think that. If she went anywhere near praying for something to happen to Sean ...

You are evil, Jilly, and you deserve to die.

Beneath her coat, she fell asleep and dreamed of Eli, and Sean; because in the summer after tenth grade that was who they were, Eliandsean, like one person, like the person she had hoped to become with him. Once Eli had found his other half, they had come to her house almost every day, because they could hold hands there.

They could brag about their slammin' skillz on their skateboards and video games like any other teenage boys, and they could flirt with each other and sit on the couch with their arms around each other while Jilly's mom brought them sodas and grilled cheese sandwiches. They were amazed and delighted by the acceptance in Jilly's house. Tolerance for their hostess in her own house, came after a hard struggle, won by determined parents who never let go of Jilly, even after she ran away with a biker, shaved her head, and told her shrink there were no bones in her hands.

It was all crazy in a new way; taggers wrote VAMPIRES SUCK over every surface there was, and people tried to share whatever information they'd learned about them: they were mindless, they were super-smart; they had a leader, it was all random. They lured you in with dark sexuality. They attacked you like animals without a plan. It had something to do with global warming; they were terrorists. They were a plague created by the government.

She saw plenty of them. White-faced and leering, they darted down streets and stared out of windows, like terrible Will Smith CGI effects. She didn't know how she hadn't been killed yet, with all the near misses. One thing she did know, they were more like people than beasts. Just very evil people. Their birds were mindless attackers, but the vampires themselves listened to music and went joyriding on motorcycles and kept the subway people alive so they could go on rides; *it's a dead world after all.*

After another near miss—a vampire turned a corner just ahead of her, and she flew around on her heel and ran, hard—she broke down weeping, her thin stomach contracting; and then God must have taken the hint, or felt guilty, or whatever, but He/She/It/They did something miraculous:

It began to rain. Hard. Buckets poured down from heaven like old lady angels washing their doorstoops; gallons and rivers tumbled onto rooftops and treetops like all the tears of all the New Yorkers, like all the blood that had gushed out of the necks of the dead.

And the rain toned down the fires just enough that she soaked her coat and then raced through the fire line, arriving on the other side into some kind of hellish otherworld; everything was covered with gray and white-bone ash: trees, buildings, abandoned cars, rubble. She shuffled through layers of powdery death.

And there it was. *There it was.*

Eli's row house. With the formerly turquoise paint and the American flags and some kid's ash-colored tricycle overturned in a pile of ash like strange granular leaves. Then she thought she saw a shadow move across the window, and she stared at it for a long time, because she had actually made it, and in her heart she'd expected there to be no signs of life. There were no more shadows and she wondered if she had gone crazy or died and imagined the whole thing. By then, Jilly was certain the dead could be as crazy as the living. She staggered up the stoop stairs, kicking up layers of death that made her gag and choke.

She knocked on the door, but no one answered, and she pushed it open.

Eli and his father faced each other in the living room with the old tapestry of the Jews at Masada hanging over the upright piano. Eli looked taller and thinner, his dark hair long as ever, and he had a semi-beard. He looked like a leftist rabbi in the NYU sweatshirt she had given him. Mr. Stein was still Mr. Stein, in a navy blue sweater and dark trousers.

Mr. Stein was shouting. "You stupid faggot, you're going to die out there."

"Just shut up!" Eli shrieked. "Stop calling me that!"

"Eli," she whispered from the doorway. "Eli, it's me."

They both turned.

"Jilly!"

Eli whooped, gathered her up, and hugged her against himself. She felt as light as a desiccated leaf, unbelievably dizzy, and reeling with happiness. Eli was alive. He was safe. And he was still here, in his old house, living indoors, with his parents.

"Oh, my God, are you okay?" he asked; and then, before she could answer, he said, "Have you seen Sean?"

"No," she said, and he deflated. She saw the misery on his face, felt it in the way he nearly crushed her.

In the kitchen, his gaunt, black-haired witchmother was *cooking*, as if nothing had changed. They had electricity, and gas, and as Jilly smelled the hot food—onions, meat—her mouth began to salivate. She burst into tears and he held her tightly, swaddling her in himself. He smelled so good. So clean. Almost virginal.

His father's eyes bulged like an insect's and he stared at Jilly, as if she were an intruder.

"I've been trying to get here," she said. "Everything was on fire. And then the rain came."

"The rain," Mr. Stein said reverently, glancing at the tapestry.

"Now we can look for Sean." Eli said.

"Don't speak that name." Mr. Stein snapped.

For God's sake, what do you care about that now? she wanted to snap back at him. But she took Eli's hand and folded it under her chin. She saw the layer of ash-mud on her hands and wondered what she looked like. A zombie, probably.

"I was just about to leave, to search for him," he said, bringing her knuckles to his mouth. He kissed them, then laid her hand against his cheek. His tears dampened her skin, like more rain. "He called just before it happened, from midtown. I don't know what he was doing there. We had a fight. I was lying down."

Weren't you going to meet me at the club?

Eli searched Jilly's face with his fingers and she felt each brush of his fingertips close a wound the long days and nights had cut into her soul. There was no one she loved more. She would go to her grave loving Eli Stein.

"Of course you're not leaving now. Look at her. She looks like she's dead." Mr. Stein had never liked her. Not only was she formerly a mad slut, she wasn't Jewish, and her family had given Eli and Sean safe harbor to commit their carnal atrocities.

"You need to fix the door," Jilly said. "Or at least to lock it."

"I thought it was locked," Mr. Stein said. He looked at Eli. "Did you unlock it?" He walked to the door to check it, passing close by Jilly so that she had to take a step out of his way. He grabbed the door; she heard a click, and then he turned the knob.

"It's broken." He glared at Eli. "Did you break it?"

"Dad, why would I do that?" Eli asked.

"Maybe vampires tried to get in last night," Jilly ventured. "You need to put up some crucifixes. They really do work."

Mr. Stein crossed his arms over his chest. "Not normal," he muttered.

"Dinner is almost ready," Mrs. Stein announced from the kitchen, smiling weakly. Jilly wondered where on earth she had found a brisket. In the still-working refrigerator of their house, she supposed.

Eli gave her a look that said, *My parents have lost their minds, obviously.* He had some experience with mental illness, since he was her best friend.

She didn't smile, even though, as usual, they were thinking the same thing. It wasn't funny. She didn't know who was crazy and who wasn't.

"You could take a shower, Jilly," Mrs. Stein continued.

Jilly was too weak and exhausted to take a shower. But Mrs. Stein gave her some mashed potatoes and a piece of cheese and they energized her enough to stagger into the bathroom. For the first time in weeks, she was a few degrees less afraid to be enclosed in a small room; to take off her clothes; to stand vulnerable underneath water …

... and then Eli was in the bathroom, taking off his clothes too. He climbed into the shower and wrapped his arms around her, sobbing. She started to cry, too, naked with her best friend who did not want her the way she wanted him; they clung to each other and mourned.

"He's out there," he said. "I know he is."

She turned around and leaned her back against his chest. It was so unreal that she was here. To just walk through their door ...

"Your parents are probably out there having a fit," she said, her eyes closed as she savored the pleasure of mist, and warmth, and Eli.

"Are you crazy? They're probably dancing in circles. 'He's in there with a girl! He's not gay! He's not a faggot!'" He mimicked his father's voice perfectly. Then he added softly, "What about your parents?"

She raised her chin so the water would sluice over her face. Her silence was all he needed.

"Oh, Jilly. Jilly, God, what happened?"

"I can't talk about it. Don't say anything. I'll never stop crying."

He laid his hand over her forehead. "I'll only say that they were so good to me. And in Judaism, goodness is a living thing," he whispered.

"Thanks." She licked her stinging lips again.

Head dipped, he turned off the water. Then he toweled her off and retrieved some neatly folded clothes set out by his mother in the hall. A pair of sweat pants swam on her and belled around her ankles. There was a black sweater, no bra. Not that it mattered.

He put back on his clothes, laced his fingers with hers, and took her into his room. There were pictures of her everywhere—at school, at their first Broadway play, holding hands in Central Park. The ones of Sean outnumbered them, though. First there were a lot of pictures of just the two of them, Eli and Sean, the brand new boyfriends; and then, of Eli, Sean, *and* Jilly, as Eli brought the two "together"—mugging for the camera, practicing for a drama skit, their very silly trip to a book signing at Forbidden Planet. Sean looked pissed off in any picture she was in. Didn't Eli notice?

She stretched out on the blue velour bedspread, feeling as if she had just set down a heavy load of books. It was incredible to her that he had been sleeping on this wonderful bed, in his own room. She didn't even know if her building was still standing. She could go back, get more clothes, get her valuables and money.

Eli would go with her. They could look for Sean on the way.

She dozed. Eli spooned her, holding her; each time she inhaled, he exhaled. It had been that way in the early days, for them. When Sean came along, he added something new; he was a literal breath of fresh air. Even Jilly had been charmed by the surfer dude who had lived in L.A. and knew movie people who might be able to help her. He talked about working as a stand-in. He hung around stunt men. His uncle had rented out his surf shop as a movie set.

But once he was sure of Eli's love, he changed. She saw it happen. Eli didn't. Maybe changed was the wrong word; around her, he became chilly and disinterested, and she knew he was never going to introduce her to anyone in the industry. But Eli didn't see it.

Sean had actually been a kind of vampire. He sucked up anything he wanted; he drained Eli's friends and classmates by using them to advance up the social ladder, then blindsided them with his snotty I-am-mean-and-because-I-deserve-to-be-you-must-permit-it attitude. She could almost predict each time he'd finally show his other face. Jilly's mom used to say they should give Sean the benefit of the doubt because he had been through a lot. Any guy who was gay had suffered. So they had to be nice to him, even though he a jerk. She knew what her mom was not saying: *We put up with your bad behavior. Welcome to the real world—the one that does not revolve around you.*

Her mom would never say anything like that, of course.

Because she was dead.

But she had never talked like that, not even when Jilly was the most drug-crazy; she had said Jilly was hurting.

But even when Jilly was at her worst, she still would have done anything to help Eli become more, and more, and more of all the wonderful things Eli was.

"God, I'm glad you're here," he whispered, nuzzling the back of her head. She cried some more, and he held her.

There was a soft knock on the door. Mrs. Stein whispered, "It's dinner time."

Jilly was very hungry, and the smell of food was making her clench and unclench her hands. But Eli had fallen asleep with his arm over her. She tried to figure out a way to slide out from underneath him without waking him up. She couldn't manage it, so she stayed beside him. Her arm began to ache. Her stomach growled.

As she contracted and released her muscles, trying to keep the blood circulating, she heard Mrs. Stein crying. It was a high-pitched, irritating kind of weeping, and it set Jilly on edge.

"No one is helping us!" Mrs. Stein cried. "No one."

Jilly, hungry and despairing and exhausted, listened to the rain, and imagined New York City going up in steam. Then she let herself go fully to sleep for the first time since she had turned sixteen.

The yelling jerked Jilly awake.

"You will die!" Mr. Stein shouted downstairs.

"Stop yelling!" Mrs. Stein was crying again. "You'll drive him away, the way you always have."

"What, drive away? Didn't you hear what he just said? He's leaving anyway!"

Jilly groaned, feeling in the bed for Eli, realizing he'd gotten up. His parents were trying, in their way, to tell him that they loved him and didn't want him to risk his life by leaving their home. She felt the same way. She didn't want to get out of bed. She knew Eli so well, knew they were going to leave as soon as she emerged from the bedroom—*maybe we can eat first*—and it wasn't going to be a graceful exit.

"It's because they blame you for not fixing me," Eli told her as they left his parents' house. It was still raining; Mrs. Stein had given them parkas with hoods and umbrellas. The rain seemed to have cleared the sky of the vampire birds of prey. Another miracle.

At least they had gotten to have some breakfast first—last night's brisket, and pancakes. And blessed coffee. While she'd been on the street, she'd heard a story that one man had knifed another over the last cup of coffee in a pot in a diner.

She didn't say anything. She couldn't forgive Eli's parents for being so narrow-minded as to pick a fight with their son and his best friend, when they might never see either of them alive again.

She adjusted the heavy backpack, filled with extra clothes, shampoo, toothbrushes, and toothpaste. Eli was carrying the heavier one, packed with food. He had a small satchel over his shoulder too, packed with photographs of Sean, seven of them, as if someone might not recognize him in the first six. Sean was weird-looking, with almond-shaped eyes and a long, hooked nose in a long, narrow face. So he wasn't handsome, he wasn't nice, and there were other gay guys in their school if Eli wanted a boyfriend. Gay guys who liked Jilly a lot. Unfortunately, Sean was the guy for him.

Eli groaned when they reached the pocket park, site of their first make-out session, after her birthday party in the eighth grade. She'd been so excited and happy she hadn't slept all night.

"Even the trees got burned up," he said. They walked close together, holding hands. She had a strange floating sensation; if he hadn't held onto her, she thought she might have floated away from sheer fear.

They passed dozens of burning buildings, sizzling and steaming in the rain. The subway station split the sidewalk; by mutual unspoken consent, they gave it a wide berth. Darkness and seclusion—perfect vampire territory.

Shadows and shapes moved in the alleyways; they walked down the center of the street, gripping each other's hand. It was strange, but Jilly was more afraid with Eli there than she had been by herself. She didn't think she could stand it if something happened to him. He was so nervous; he was broadcasting "come and get me" to anyone interested in easy pickings.

He pulled a cell phone out of his parka and dialed numbers, listening each time. Finally he grunted and put it back in his pocket, and moved his bangs out of his eyes. Her heart stirred, and she touched his cheek. He smiled distractedly; she knew he was glad she was there, but it was Sean he most wanted to see.

She used to have these long conversations with her girl friends about if Eli would ever come back to her. Eli had been her actual boyfriend for two years. They had made out all the time, but never gone any father than that. They'd been too young. Then he and Sean had found each other ... or rather, Sean had found him. Sean had moved to New York and zeroed in on Eli, even before Sean was sure Eli was gay. So Eli had given Jilly the "we can still be friends" speech.

Only in their case, it was true. They were excellent friends. They thought alike, read alike. He thought NYU was a great goal. He talked about going there too. They both hated sports. And Sean, who was a jock, hated that.

He never said a word about it to Eli. As far as Eli was concerned, Sean loved Jilly like a sister. Had used those exact words, in fact, the one time Jilly tried to discuss it with him. But when Eli wasn't paying attention, Sean zinged her out with vast amounts of passive-aggressive BS—veiled threats and lots of snark. He picked fights just before they were supposed to meet her somewhere—like Watami. Being somewhere in midtown when he was supposed to celebrate with her was classic Sean, King of Bitter Homosexuality.

Eli brushed it off, refused to agree to her reality. So she didn't bring it up again, ever. She didn't want to give Sean the ammunition for an "It's either her or me" speech.

As they walked out of the burn zone, the sky began to darken, and a rush of resentment roared through Jilly. Her tired body was aching for Eli's soft, clean bed. She wanted to take another shower, and brush her teeth for a year. She didn't want to be risking her life, or Eli's, for someone who hated her.

Her mind was trying to figure out what life would be like if they found Sean. And then, before she knew what she was doing, she said, "Watami. The club. Maybe he went there."

He looked at her. "He wasn't going to go. And he'd come to my house first, or try to get to me through our friends." And they did have other friends, gay friends, who envied them for having Jilly's family to hang with.

"Okay, never mind. Maybe he went to school."

Eli raised his brows. "Maybe." He smiled. "It's big. Maybe they're doing like a Red Cross shelter there." He hugged her. "You're a genius, Jilly."

Too smart for my own good, she thought. The old Jilly, pre-rehab—the one without the boundaries—might not have suggested places to look for Sean. But Jilly was a good, nice person now. Maybe that was why he didn't love her. She wasn't edgy enough. She could change ...

But he can't. He is gay, she reminded herself.

It was nearly dark. It was so dangerous to be out like this; she'd seen vampires leap from the shadows and drag people away. Sometimes they growled; sometimes they were silent. Jilly had been sleeping next to an old lady in a store one afternoon. When she woke at dusk, all that was left of the lady were her shoes. Jilly had no idea why she herself had been left alive. Maybe the old lady had been enough.

They met a man on the street a few blocks from the school named Bo. He staggered when he walked and he talked very slowly. There was a scar across his face from the slice of vampire fangs.

"They have to feed as soon as they change," he told them. "The vampire who tried to kill me was brand new. There was another one with him, the one who made him into a vampire. He was laughing. My friends staked him. They don't change to dust."

Then he staggered on.

"Wait!" Jilly cried. "Tell us everything you know."

"The new ones are the worst," he said. "They're the most lethal. Just like baby snakes."

Now, as the gloom gathered around them in the rain, they hurried to their old high school. There were lights on and shadows moving in the windows. Neither spoke as they crossed the street and walked past the marquee. The letters had been stolen; there was no school news.

Rose bushes lined the entrance. She couldn't smell their fragrance but the sight of them, drenched by the downpour, gave her a lift. The double doors were painted with crosses; so were the walls and the windows. The taggers had written VAMPIRES SUCK GO TO HELL VAMPIRES on the walls.

There were two guards at the doors—a male teacher named Mr. Vernia and her English teacher, Mary Ann Francis. They hugged both Eli and Jilly hard, asked for news—asked how it was—then ushered them in.

It smelled, and the noise was unbelievable. Students, adults, little kids, and teachers—everyone was milling around; the noise was deafening. People who hated her ran up and hugged her, crying and saying how glad they were that she was alive. She realized she and Eli should have eaten a good meal before they'd come in. If they opened up their pack now, they would have to share.

Is that so bad, sharing?

"Jilly. Eli," their principal, Ms. Howison, said when she spotted them. There were circles under her eyes and deep lines in her forehead. She looked like a skeleton. "Thank God."

Ms. Howison had tried to keep her from coming back to school after rehab. But crises did strange things to people.

Eli skipped the pleasantries and pulled out all his pictures of Sean. Men and women, computer nerds and cheerleaders, carefully examined each one, even if they knew exactly who Sean was, before passing it on. No one had seen him.

Jilly got too tired to stay awake any longer. Principal Howison promised her that all the doors and windows had been covered with crosses and the ground was dotted with garlic bulbs and communion wafers. Jilly wondered if the rain had dissolved the wafers. How many molecules of holiness did you have to have to keep the monsters at bay?

Bazillions of cots were set up in the gym and sure enough, there were Red Cross volunteers. Eli and Jilly pulled two cots together, stashed their packs underneath, and lay down in their clothes. It was better than what she'd been sleeping on before she found Eli, at least.

Eli touched her face with his hands. "I'm so glad you're here."

"Me, too," she said, but what she meant was, *I'm so glad you're with me.*

Eli fell asleep. She looked at the diffused light drifting across his face, making him glow. She wanted to kiss him but she didn't want to wake him; correction, she didn't want him to wake up and remind her that he didn't love her that way.

Then she heard someone crying. It was muffled, as if they were trying not to make any noise. She raised her head slightly, and realized it was Ms. Howison.

Jilly disentangled herself from Eli slowly. Then she rocked quietly onto her side, planted her feet underneath herself, and sat up. She walked over to where the woman was sitting in a chair, facing the rows and rows of cots. She looked as if she'd just thrown up.

"Hey," Jilly said uncertainly, "Ms. Howison."

"Oh, God," she whispered, lowering her gaze to her hands. "Oh, God. Jilly. You're still here. I was hoping ..." She turned her head away.

"What?" Jilly asked.

She took a deep breath and let it out. She was shaking like crazy. "I need you to come with me for a second."

"What's wrong?"

"Just ... come." The principal wouldn't look at her. Jilly shifted. "Please."

Ms. Howison got up out of her chair and walked out of the gym. The overhead fluorescents were on. Jilly followed her past the coaches' offices and then into the girls' locker room, past the rows upon rows of lockers, and then through another door into the shower area.

Ms. Howison cleared her throat and said, "She's here." Then she stepped back and slammed the door between herself and Jilly.

Jilly tried to bolt.

Sean was there, and he was a vampire. All the color in his long, narrow face was gone. His eyes looked glazed, as if he was on drugs. And she should know.

He grabbed her, wrapping his arms around her like a boyfriend; she smelled his breath, like garbage. He wasn't cold; he was room temperature. She was completely numb. Her heart was skipping beats.

She wet her pants.

"I'm glad to see you, too," he said, grinning at her.

She set me up. She gave me to him. That bitch.

He wrapped his hand around her bicep and dragged her forward. She burst into tears and started wailing. He clamped his other dead hand still over her mouth so hard she was afraid her front teeth were going to break off.

"Shut up," he hissed, chuckling. "I've wanted to say that to you forever. Shut up, shut up, shut up."

She kept whimpering. She couldn't stop. Maybe he knew that; he dragged her along with his hand over her mouth. His fingernails dug into her arm and she knew he had broken the skin, but she didn't feel it.

He walked her into storage room where they kept cleaning supplies— brooms, mops, big jugs of cleaner. She started screaming behind his hand, and he slapped her, hard. Then he slammed her against the wall. With a gasp, she bounced back off and fell on her butt.

He slammed the door, leaving her in darkness. With a sob, she crawled to it and started to pound on it.

"*Don't*," he hissed on the other side.

He's going to get Eli, she thought. *Oh, God, he's going to vampirize him. That's what he's here for.*

Maybe he will let me go.

But why would he? He was the King of Bitter. And she would never leave without Eli.

She fumbled around for a light switch, found one, and turned on the blessed, wonderful light. Her arm was bleeding and it finally began to sting. She didn't know if she wanted to feel anything. She wondered what it would be like when he—

The door burst open, and Sean came back inside. His eyes were glittering. He looked crazy. "Eli says hi."

"No," she begged. "Don't do it. Please, Sean. Don't change him."

Sean blinked at her. Then he laughed. "Honey, that's what love is all about, don't you know?"

She doubled up her fists and bit her knuckles. He lifted a brow.

"I smell fresh bloo-ood," he sang. "Yours. It smells *great*. If you were alone in the ocean, the sharks would come and chew you up. Alone in the forest, it would be the wolves. Alone in the city, and it's us."

Vampires. "How ... how did this happen to you?"

He ignored her. "I'm going to give you a choice, girlfriend. The choice is this: You can change, or he can change. The other one of you ... is the blood in the water." He moved his shoulders. "I'll let you pick."

She stared at him. "What are you saying?"

"God, you are so stupid. So incredibly, moronically stupid. I could never figure out why he loved you." He shook his head.

Why did it matter, she wondered, when Eli still loved him more?

"Does it even matter which way I choose?" she said. "You don't even like me," Of course he would change Eli and let her die.

"Maybe it doesn't. Maybe I just want to see what you'd say," he told her. "I'm giving him the same choice."

She stared at him in mute terror.

"I told him that I would change you if he asked me to." He folded his arms across his chest and leaned against the back of the door. He didn't look different at all—he was the same surf-charmer Sean.

"You know I'll say to change him," she said. What did she have to live for, after all? Only Eli. And if he were gone ...

"Be right back," he said, turning to go.

"Why are you doing this?" she asked.

He didn't turn back around, just looked at her over his shoulder, as if she was being a nuisance.

"I don't know why he's so loyal to you. He doesn't love you the way he loves me."

"But he loves me," she said, as she realized. "That's why ..."

He turned around and stared at her. The expression on his face was the most frightening thing she had ever seen. She took another step back, and another. She bumped into the wall.

He raised his chin, opened the door, and left.

She paced. She thought about drinking the cleaner. She tried to break the mops and brooms to make a wooden stake. She couldn't so much as crack one of them.

She fell to her knees and prayed to He/She/It/Them *Get us out of here get us out of here come in, God, come in, over ...*

The door opened, and Sean came back in, grinning like someone who had finally, really, totally gotten what he wanted. Triumph was written all over his face. He looked taller. Meaner.

Ready to kill her.

"Eli will be changing," he said. "GMTA; you both made the same choice. Eli."

She jerked. *No, he wouldn't.*

"And you'll be his first meal. Have you ever seen a newly changed vampire? All they want to do is suck someone's blood. That's all I wanted to do."

"You're lying," she said. "Eli would never ..."

But Eli *would*. He hadn't even asked her if she wanted to leave his parents' house to help him look for Sean. He had put her in harm's way, for Sean. He didn't love her the way he loved Sean. Lovers did things differently than friends.

"If it makes you feel any better, he feels terrible about it." Sean sneered at her.

"He's going to hate you for making him do this," she said. "He'll never forgive you." She was talking to a vampire. To a vampire that was going to kill her. To a gay vampire who was going to turn Eli into a gay vampire.

She felt reality begin to slip away. This wasn't happening.

"I'm going to get him now," he said, going for a smile, not quite pulling it off. Irritated, he slammed the door.

She stood as still as one of the mops she couldn't turn into a vampire stake. Her heart hammered in her chest and she had no idea how she could hear all that thumping and pumping because she was

at the door
at the door
at the door
pounding and screaming, begging to be let out.

Ms. Howison was going to have a change of heart and rally all the people in the gym and rescue her.

Sean was going to open the door and take her in his arms, and tell her that he'd been so mean to her because he actually loved *her*, not Eli. That he had only pretended to love Eli so he could stay close to her. And that he wouldn't kill either of them, not if Jilly didn't want him to.

Sean was going to tell her that he was sorry, both of them could be changed, and they would go on as they were, as a trio, only nicer, like Dorothy, the Tin Woodsman, and the Scarecrow.

Sean was going to see some other hot guy on the way back to Eli and fall in love with him instead, change him, and leave.

Eli was going to escape, and find her, and they would get out of New York together.

She pounded on the door as she remembered the night Eli had confessed that he had met someone else ... a guy someone else ... and he had cried because he didn't want to hurt her, his best friend.

"I will always love you totally and forever, I promise," he had said.

The door opened, and she scrambled backwards away from it as fast as she could. Her elbow rammed into a container of cleaner. *Throw it at them. Do something. Save yourself.*

Sean and Eli stood close together. Sean had his arm around Eli, and Eli had on his baggy parka. Eli, as far as she could tell, was still human. His bangs were in his eyes.

He was looking at the floor, as if he couldn't stand to look at her.

"No," she whispered. But it must have been yes, he must have told Sean to change him. Sean was going to change him, and then he was going to kill her.

Her heart broke. She was on the verge of going completely crazy, all over again.

Sean took a step toward her. "If it makes you feel any better, it's going to hurt when I change him," he promised her. He sounded bizarrely sincere.

He shut the door. The three of them stood inside the cramped space. She was only two feet away.

Sean placed both hands on Eli's shoulders and turned Eli toward him. Tears were streaming down Eli's cheeks. He looked young and scared.

Sean threw back his head and hissed. Fangs extended from his mouth.

And Eli whipped his hand into the pocket of his parka; pulling out a jagged strip of wood—

—*Yes!*—

—and he glanced at Jilly—

—*Yes!*—

—and as Sean prepared to sing his fangs into Eli's neck, Jilly rammed Sean as hard as she could. He must have seen it coming, must have guessed—but Eli got the stake into him, dead center in his unbeating heart.

Sean stared down at it, and then at Eli, as blood began to pour down the front of him. Then he laughed, once, and blew Eli a kiss.

He looked at Jilly—gargled, "Bitch," his throat full of his own blood— then slid to the floor like a sack of garbage, inert, harmless.

Eli and Jilly stared at him. Neither spoke. She heard Eli panting.

Then Eli gathered her up. Kissed her.

Kissed her.

They clung to each other beside the dead vampire. And Eli threw himself over Sean, holding *him*, kissing *him*.

"Oh, my God, Sean," he keened. "Oh, God, oh, God. *Jilly.*" He reached for her hand. She gave it to him, wrapping herself around him as he started to wail.

After he wore himself out, she tried to get up, thinking to see if there were more vampires, to check on Ms. Howison and the others, but he held her too tightly, and she wouldn't have moved away from him for the world.

He held Sean tightly too. "I can't believe it. How evil he was." Eli's voice was hoarse from all the sobbing.

"I know," she said. "He was always—"

"Sean wasn't even in there. When you're changed, the vampirism infects you and steals your soul," Eli went on. "You're not there. You're gone."

Tears clung to the tip of his nose.

"Sean loved you, Jilly. He told me that a million times every day. He was so glad you're my best friend."

She started to say, "No, he hated me," but suddenly she realized: that was going to be his coping mechanism. He was going to believe from now on that the Sean he knew and loved would have never made him kill his best friend.

She put her hand on the crown of his head and found herself thinking of the tapestry of the Jews at Masada in his parents' living room. It was a pivotal moment in Jewish history, when cornered Jewish soldiers chose to commit mass suicide rather than submit to Roman rule. Mr. Stein talked about it now and then, and sometimes Jilly had wondered if what he was saying was that Eli should take his own life, rather than be gay. She couldn't believe that, though, couldn't stand even to suspect it. The rigidity of the adult world was what had made her crazy. The unbelievable insanity of Mr. Stein, who condemned his own son just because Eli couldn't change into a heterosexual Jewish warrior and defy the invading sin of misplaced lust. At least, that was what her therapist had told her.

"You are brilliant, and you're so ... *much*," Dr. Robles had declared. Dr. Robles, her savior. "People don't change, Jilly. They just see things differently than they used to, and respond according to the way they already are. It's all context. Reality. Is. Context."

Dr. Robles had saved her because he didn't try to change her. So she had never tried to change Eli.

She took a deep breath and thought about her hopeless love for him. And something shifted.

Her love was *not* hopeless. She loved him. It didn't have to break her heart. It didn't have to do anything but be there. Be there.

So she said, "Sean loved you so much." Because that would help him the most.

"Thank you," he whispered. "He loved you too. And I love you, Jilly." He looked up at her, broken and crumpled like a rag—the boy she kissed in the eighth grade, a thousand million times, almost until her lips bled.

"And I love you," she replied. "I love you more than my own life. I always have." It was right to say that now. People didn't change, and love didn't, either. Where Eli was concerned, there was no context.

"Thank you," he said. No embarrassment, no apologies; their love was what it was. Alone in a closet, with a dead vampire, hiding in a school because the rest of the city was overrun by vampires ...

She laid her head on his shoulder, and he laced his fingers with hers.

"Happy birthday, sweet sixteen," he whispered. "My Jilly girl."

"Thank you," she whispered. It was the best present ever.

After a while, they opened the door. The sun was out, and for one instant, she thought she heard the trilling of a lark.

Then she realized that it was Eli's cell phone.

Beepbeepbeepbeep. This is God, Jilly. I'm back on the job amen.

DEAD AIR

Gary Kemble

Tom's eyes flicked open. Beige. Why were passenger jet interiors always mostly beige? On the screen in front of him, bad actors delivered predictable lines. He pulled the headphone buds from his ears. He rubbed his eyes, trying to rid himself of the gritty feeling. He tried to stretch and the bar of the magazine holder on the back of the seat in front dug into his shins. It was obscene—such a huge plane, such limited leg-room.

His eyes scanned to the right of the cabin, drawn by the noise of excited people trying to be quiet. It reminded him of the soundstage tours directors sometimes organised for investors: rich, boring people hoping some of that Hollywood glitz would rub off on them. Occasionally, a word or phrase rose above the general hubbub: "Amazing!" "Never seen anything like it!" "Beautiful!"

Only the emergency lights were on, but Tom could make out the shapes of fellow travellers jostling for position by the windows. A flight attendant tried to shepherd them back to their seats, without much luck. One of the group reviewed footage on their camcorder's LCD screen. They pivoted and Tom caught a glimpse of green flashes on black.

He tried to give a shit but couldn't. The past two weeks had been hell and, quite frankly, so long as the wing wasn't falling off, he didn't care if he missed the Four Horsemen of the Apocalypse, galloping down to deliver End Times on the good, green Earth. He turned his attention to the corny action movie playing on the screen in front of him, but didn't bother with the headphones. In minutes was asleep again.

His mind played one of those crappy montage sequences the studio kept insisting he write. Answering the phone; his agent telling him to get his arse over to LA, Universal wanted to buy his screenplay. Cross-fade to Barbara at

Brisbane airport, telling him he had three months to make them all rich, wry smile telling him she was only half joking. Stephen making him solemnly swear to bring him back the new Xbox 360 and an unrated version of *Left 4 Dead.* Jump-cut to a shitty apartment in LA filled with cardboard boxes; jetlag and loneliness tearing at the backs of his eyes. Then words, hundreds of thousands of them. Drafts, re-writes, pitches, final drafts that were never final, emails home, apologies, a credit card order for an Xbox, more re-writes. Extreme close-up: a bright-eyed Starbucks barista with teeth and tits too good to be true. A dozen roses and where the fuck did that Kenny G shit come from? An empty fuck, stained sheets, and wasn't this supposed to be where we run through the park in slo-mo? Guilt. Cross-fade to a cab out to LAX. Cross-fade to a circus in a field by the freeway, fire-breathers sending plumes of orange and yellow into the polluted mauve sky. Fade to black.

Tom's gasped as the plane dropped through a patch of dead air. His eyes flitted open. The movie was over, the screen in front of him showing a dark reflection of his own visage. Mussed up hair, bushy handlebar moustache. People sometimes mistook him for a biker. A bland chime trilled and the Fasten Seatbelt sign lit up. He glanced to his right, expecting to see sleeping people covered in thin blankets and, beyond them, dark sky through the windows. But the windows were obscured by bodies, people still jostling for position. But now they were silent. Maybe he hadn't been asleep that long. Goosebumps rose on Tom's arms and he pulled the blanket up to his chest.

The plane hit another patch of turbulence, this one far worse than the last, and Tom clutched the armrests. He looked around the plane. Other than the watchers, and the flight attendants, everyone seemed to be either sleeping or pretending to sleep.

A flight attendant strode down the aisle, gripping headrests on either side to steady herself. She stopped a couple of rows in front of Tom, and leant over towards the crowd by the window. Further up, another flight attendant did the same.

"Excuse me everyone, you'll really have to go back to your seats now," she said.

No-one moved. A low rumbling permeated the mass of still flesh.

"Excuse me, sir."

The flight attendant reached over, and tapped a thick-set man on the shoulder.

"Sir?"

The man turned. Tom meant to scream but he was frozen, just as she was. There was nothing outwardly wrong with the man but the expression; dead eyes staring out of the slack face told Tom more than red skin and pointy horns. He knew evil when he saw it. The man swivelled in slow motion, and then his head darted forward, latching onto the flight attendant's arm.

Blood came quickly, screams followed. A strip of flesh tore loose as the flight attendant tried to escape. She fell into the aisle. Tom finally screamed, surprised at the sound of it. His numb hands fumbled with his blanket. The woman shuffled backwards on her arse, blood pulsing onto the royal blue carpet. The heavy-set man jumped into the aisle, gore slipping down his chin and dripping onto his Haunted Mansion t-shirt.

Tom tore the blanket free. The cabin came to life, people rubbing their faces and looking around to see what all the fuss was about. Somewhere up front, another scream. Tom wanted to grab these people and shove their faces in the blood, just to get them moving. *Why the fuck do I have to deal with this?*

Haunted Mansion fell on the flight attendant, winding her. His head snapped forwards again, this time latching onto her neck. Tom reached for the seatbelt buckle as the 747 hit more turbulence, this time strong enough to lift him out of the seat. His fingers caught on the buckle and he realised he hadn't decided whether he was going to run towards the woman, or in the other direction.

In the end, it was an easy decision.

Haunted Mansion wasn't alone. The smell of blood had roused them from their night sky vigil. Half a dozen pale faces turned towards him, vacant stares assessing the situation.

As he squeezed out of his seat a long-haired girl in a Bratz nightie launched herself at him. He dropped his shoulder into her gut and carried her into the aisle, pinning her down with his body. The flight attendant had stopped screaming. One foot twitched idly as Haunted Mansion guzzled blood out of her neck.

As Tom pressed down on Bratz her teeth snapped together inches from his face. He looked around and saw her slack-faced soul-mates trying to negotiate their way out of the narrow rows of seating. They seemed unable to figure out the mess of blankets, seatbelts and bags.

The PA system chimed.

"We have an emergency situation, could all ..."

The message ended with a piercing, then gurgling, scream.

Tom reached behind him, grabbing the first thing he could lay his hands on. The glossy magazine almost slipped from his grasp and he realised he had blood on his hands. He slapped it down on the girl's face. For a moment she stopped biting, giving him time to roll it into a tight cylinder.

Tom climbed up, kneeing the girl in the face. He looked down the aisle towards the front of the plane. From here, in the near dark, it looked as if everyone on board was one of "them". Towards the back it looked just as bad, but he was closer to the back of the plane than the front. He had an idea. The toilets.

He ran, using his rolled up magazine as a baton, fending off the grasping hands and searching maws. The green "Vacant" lights beckoned. He could hole up in the toilet, wait until things calmed down. Hey, he'd even have a magazine to read.

A man dressed in a grey suit stepped into his path. Tom raised his magazine, and the man raised a gun in reply.

"Get down! Get the fuck down!" the man yelled in a thick Brooklyn accent. "Air Marshal. The situation is under control."

With his free hand he pulled out a gold badge, sheathed in a leather wallet.

God bless America!

"Sir, return to your seat."

He lowered the gun. Tom's eyes darted to his left, where dark forms groaned. The plane was starting to stink of blood.

The plane plummeted. Tom dropped his magazine and grabbed hold of the nearest armrest. His body rose and then slammed down onto the floor. He watched, shocked, as the momentum threw the Air Marshal against the ceiling. Above the screams, Tom heard the sickening sound of breaking bones. The Air Marshal fell back to the floor, a rag doll clutching an automatic pistol. Tom scurried to his side, feeling for a pulse despite the unnatural angle of his neck and the blood bubbling from his mouth. Dead.

Tom picked up the gun and ran. He could see the doors to the toilets now, one directly ahead at the very back of the plane and the other to its left. The plane was mostly empty back here. He slowed and risked a look behind him. Most of the crazies had shuffled into the aisle and were making their way across the plane, towards the normal people. They moved slowly, although he had seen their capacity for haste. It reminded him of the way birds nonchalantly edged out of the way of cars, just in time to avoid being squashed. Why rush? The norms, for their part, were showing the stuff that had made United States the nation it was today. Screaming, begging, that whole deal. Although, he guessed there must have been a few fellow Aussies in there as well. What happened to the Anzac spirit, he wondered, as he turned for his hiding place.

Hands snaked around his ankles and locked tight. He looked down as a head of shaggy black hair inched forwards, then turned, revealing a white face and mouthful of bloody teeth. Tom lowered the gun and pulled the trigger.

Gore splattered across his shoes and his ears filled with ringing. Down the cabin, tens of pairs of eyes turned his way. They advanced, ghouls with a strange, shuffling gait, while the norms screamed for help.

As Tom reached for the toilet door, a flit of movement caught his eye. A hand grabbed his, pulling it away from the handle.

"This one's mine, arsehole," the flight attendant said. She blew a wisp of black hair from her face and shouldered him out of the way. Behind him, the groans and screams drew closer.

"Wait!"

He forced his way into the toilet, then slammed the door. She flicked the lock across and the light came on. Intense brown eyes so dark they were almost black. Crisp white blouse, splotched with red. Gaylen, her name tag read. Tom threw his arm out to steady himself, leaving a bloody hand print on the mirror. They stood there, both gasping for air, bodies so close he could smell her sweat and perfume, overpowering and the sinister tang of blood. She spat out a curse, breaking the moment.

"Fucking maniacs!"

"Zombies."

"*What?*"

"Zombies."

Gaylen rolled her eyes. "They're not *zombies.*"

"They lurch. They crave flesh. They're zombies."

"This isn't some tacky Z-grade movie. They're ... does it really matter what they are? Zombies? Maniacs? Terrorists? What matters is they're in control of this plane, while we're trapped in here. Here's what I was thinking ..."

"I'm not going back out there."

"Listen to me ..."

"I'm not going back out there. I've got a wife. A kid." Tom's mind helpfully threw up an image of Maria the barista's brown legs wrapped around him, Barbara's portrait lying hidden in the bedside drawer.

"Okay, you're not going back out there. Jeez, I thought you Aussies were supposed to be tough guys. You know, Crocodile Dundee, Steve Irwin ..."

She stopped; Tom figured she'd exhausted her list of notable Australians, or maybe she remembered Irwin's fateful encounter with a stingray. She was clearly too young to recall Mel Gibson's turn as Mad Max. Although, technically, he was a Yank, anyway.

"Do you know who's flying the plane?" Gaylen said.

Tom laughed. "I would've thought you would know."

"It's probably on auto-pilot. I think some of the passengers saw something ..."

"You don't know that."

"They were crowded around the windows. I think they saw something and it turned them into ..."

Something thumped against the door, hard enough to rattle it in its frame.

"Zombies?" Tom offered.

"... it made them crazy. If the flight crew saw the same thing, then they've got about as much chance of landing the plane as you do. You don't, by any chance, know how to land a plane?"

Tom stared down at the gun in his hands. Barbara thought he was coming home because he couldn't bear to be without her, regardless of what it meant for his career. She didn't know about Maria. Tom put it down to a mid-life crisis. It was a cop-out, but now death hovered over him, he thought he could live with that. He shook his head.

"You?"

Gaylen checked her face in the mirror, and wiped a spot of blood off her cheek.

"I know enough for someone in a control tower to talk me down."

She ran her fingers through her hair.

"I don't even know your name," she said.

"Tom."

"Hi, Tom. I'm Gaylen. Here's what I'm going to do. I'm going to make my way to the front of the plane. I'm going to let myself into the cockpit and put this baby down on the nearest runway that can handle her. I'd really appreciate your help. Are you in?"

Tom laughed, and this time went with it until the tears rolled down his face. *Make my way, put this baby down*—shit, it was getting more and more like a tacky Z-grade movie every minute. Outside, something uttered a gurgling groan.

"You Americans," he said.

"Come on. Let's roll."

Gaylen pulled the lock open. The light went out. Tom moved behind her. He expected her to count three but she didn't, she just pushed the door open. A hand immediately shot through the gap, and Gaylen fell back onto him, pushing them both down onto the toilet seat. Tom pressed the gun into the hand grabbing for them and pulled the trigger, sending a bloom of blood and fingers splashing onto the walls and mirror. The zombie, or whatever it was, staggered backwards. Gaylen and Tom pushed out of the toilet.

A woman held the bloody stump in front of her blank face, trying to figure out what had just happened, groaning slightly under her breath. Tom put her out of her misery with a shot to the head, and the two of them ventured back out into the cabin.

While they Gaylen and Tom were exchanging life stories, the ghouls had been busy. The walls were smeared with blood. Bodies lay strewn across seats, some with obvious wounds and others as though they'd just decided to drop dead rather than have to face this horror. Tom knew how they felt. The crazies were feeding. Survivors had formed into bands now, but hysteria still ruled the day. Tom watched, stunned, as an elderly woman inflated her life jacket and ran for the nearest exit. She clutched the hefty steel handle.

"She'll never get it open," Gaylen said. "Air pressure. You'd snap the handle before the door opened."

A pack of the infected fell on the woman. Her screams were mercifully short-lived.

The way forward was blocked by a hulking form hunched over a body. Black t-shirt, with place names stencilled on the back. Slowly, the man on the floor turned, face dripping with gore. Intestines slipped out of the Air Marshal's torn body, as more of the monsters feasted.

Tom squeezed his finger on the trigger, screaming. Low velocity rounds whizzed through the air, adding a cordite tang to the heady fug. Tom expected to see a brace of zombies fall. Instead, the freak in the Megadeth t-shirt climbed to his feet, growling deep in his chest.

"Give that to me," Gaylen said, snatching the gun off him.

She snapped a round into Megadeth's head, barely waited for him to drop before she acquired new targets, making them dead—*really dead*, this time—SWAT-training-video-dead. She moved down the walkway, dispatching psychos, as Tom followed, bathed in a cloud of gun smoke.

"You don't grow up in LA without learning to shoot a gun," she said, over her shoulder.

When the hammer fell on an empty chamber, Gaylen discarded the weapon and ran for the galley up ahead. Beyond that bodies—both the traditional type and the new fangled lurching, groaning type—massed.

"The way is thick with those motherfuckers," Tom muttered.

The plane lurched to one side. An overhead locker burst open and luggage tumbled out. Tom threw his hands up to protect his head, then found himself clutching a bottle clad in a plastic bag. He turned it over in his hands, then ripped the Speyside single malt out of the bag. He spun the lid off.

"You realise it's illegal to open that before you reach your destination?" Gaylen said.

Tom grinned and took a swig, then offered it to her. She reached for it. A flicker of movement caught Tom's eye. A large man in a tweed jacket and bloodstained yellow tie shambled out of the galley. Gaylen dropped. Tom pitched the bottle. It sailed through the air, trailing a tail of pungent whisky, before smacking the man in the middle of his moustachioed face. He staggered backwards, then tripped over a set of headphones.

Gaylen snatched up a plastic knife, leapt on the flailing undead businessman and rammed the blade into his eye socket. Tom's stomach rolled at the sickening squelch. Gaylen drove it down until it was buried to the hilt, then gave it one final wham with her palm. The monster kicked one shoe off, then was still.

"I prefer bourbon anyway," she said.

Ahead, Tom could see nothing resembling a survivor. He guessed they could be holed up in the toilets, but if so they were of no use to them.

"C'mon," Gaylen said, and handed him a beige plastic tray.

They dodged more zombies than they killed, using their trays as bludgeons and shields. The undead seemed capable of bursts of speed, but in general they milled about, not paying much attention to themselves or others. The air stank of shit, piss and blood. Through coach class, then into business and first, until they reached a staircase that spiralled up to the top deck.

There was a series of solid thumps, and a man clad in blue pinstripe pyjamas landed face-first at the bottom of the stairs.

They ran over the top of him, and didn't look back. The lights were low on the top deck, and most of the seats were reclined into beds. Lucky bastards, Tom thought. Then he saw what had become of one of the passengers. She was lying on her bed, guts torn open, intestines spilling out of the cavity and onto the floor.

"Where is everyone?" he whispered.

Gaylen shrugged.

They crept down the aisle until they reached a solid-looking door with a peephole at eye level and a keypad halfway down. Gaylen punched in a five-digit code and was rewarded with a low-pitched buzz.

She turned, brow furrowed. Her eyes widened. "Shit."

Tom looked back into the cabin. "Shit is right."

Like a choreographed dance move, zombies sat up in the four nearest beds. As they shambled to their feet the blankets fell off their bodies.

Gaylen stabbed her finger at the keypad. Bzzzzz!

"Gaylen?"

She tried another sequence. Bzzzzz! "Fuck!"

The zombies shuffled towards them. None of these ones looked injured. There was a middle-aged woman in tight tracksuit pants and an over-large tee that reminded Tom of the 80s. A naked man with too much body hair, wedding tackle dangling in the frosty air. A teenage boy with spiky hair, wallet dangling from its chain. And a fat man, business shirt straining for dear life to stay closed over his ample belly. As they moved into the aisle they jostled for position, and the fat man's shirt popped open.

"What's wrong?" Tom said.

"Code. Can't remember if it's five-one-one-eight-seven or five-one-one-seven-eight."

"Try both."

"I have."

Tom picked up a real knife—only the finest stainless steel in first class—and wielded it like a rapier.

"Come on, you braindead fucks."

The teen lurched first, making his move far too early. As his face dropped, Tom brought his knee up and around, surprised he remembered any of his old taekwon-do moves—even more surprised his groin muscles allowed him to perform the manoeuvre with only a twinge of pain. His knee connected with the side of the kid's head, sending him sprawling over another bed.

"Any time now would be good," Tom said over his shoulder. He was chastened with another buzz. He wondered if the door would open at all. His PC at the studio had a "three strikes and you're in IT helpdesk hell" policy, and he imagined airliner security would have to be at least one notch up.

The fat man broke into a trot, blubber bouncing up and down, arms out-stretched. Tom lashed out with the knife, jabbing it straight through the eyeball and into the brain. He winced as a gout of semi-coagulated blood splashed over his hand and ran down his arm. The fat man twisted and fell, taking the knife with him.

Behind him, a high-pitched alarm sounded. The naked man and tracksuit woman paused, unsure. Was he just imagining it, or were first class zombies more intelligent than their coach compatriots?

"That doesn't sound too good," he said.

"No, it is good. It means I got the code right."

"Oh yeah, then why the hell are we still out here?"

"The alarm sounds for thirty seconds before the door opens."

"Great," Tom said and, right on queue, tracksuit woman and the streaker launched themselves. Tom had time to wonder how the man came to be naked in the first place, and then they were on them.

Tom caught tracksuit woman's wrists, expecting to hold her and surprised when he was driven back into the flight deck door, hard enough to send sparks flying across his vision.

Gaylen feinted left then darted right, getting in behind the naked man

348

and pummelling his head into the door. There was a solid crack as something broke—Tom didn't know what—and the zombie fell to the floor.

Tracksuit woman had her mouth open, hissing, inches from his face. She was dead, there was no mistaking it. She wasn't outwardly injured but her fetid breath left no room for misinterpretation. Only something dead could smell that bad. She twisted her wrists against his sweaty palms and he thought he saw a glint of victory in her eyes. He felt her teeth against his neck. Would she just kill him, he wondered, or was what they had infectious?

The alarm cut out, so at least he would die without that racket in his head. He tried to imagine Cat Stevens singing "Moonshadow", but couldn't quite manage it. Then Gaylen was there, over tracksuit woman's shoulder. Her hand flew down in a blur, hitting the side of the zombie woman's head. The ghoul's mouth closed against his exposed neck, then fell away. As she slumped to the floor, Tom saw the pen sticking out of her ear.

"Mightier than the sword," Gaylen said.

"Give me a sword any day. No, a chainsaw."

To their right, the teen zombie stirred. And at the back of the cabin, shapes shifted in the shadows. The zombies had found the spiral staircase.

Gaylen pulled the door open.

They slid into the cockpit, slammed the door shut, and sat back against it, panting. Tom's breath caught in his throat. Through the windows he could see moonlight glistening off the ocean. It was beautiful.

Then other things intruded on his vision. Dark forms hunched over the control panels.

The pilot groaned, then pushed himself to his feet. Behind them, something slammed against the cockpit door. The pilot turned; a flap of flesh hung open on his neck, his shirt was stained maroon. In his peripheral vision Tom caught movement. His head snapped to one side and saw the other flight crew were moving. Had they been in zombie hibernation?

Gaylen pulled open a narrow cupboard, revealing a line of jackets on coat hangers. She pulled one out, let the coat fall to the floor and untwisted the metal.

"What ..." Tom started, but didn't have time to finish.

The navigator leapt at him. Tom snatched the coat off the floor and threw it over the zombie's head, then pushed him away. It worked surprisingly well. The zombie careened across the cabin before sprawling over the control panel.

Behind them there was another bone-rattling thump, and the door dented in slightly.

"Will that thing hold?"

"Yeah," Gaylen said.

She darted forwards with her untwisted coat hanger, aiming for the eyes. She missed, jabbing the pilot in the cheek then the mouth. The pilot tried to catch her between his hairy arms, the action expelling fetid air from his dead lungs. Gaylen ducked under his arms and jumped on his back, wrapping the hanger around his neck. The pilot spun, swinging Gaylen's feet off the ground.

Tom grabbed a hanger out of the cupboard. As he turned, someone caught him from behind. He felt hot breath on his neck, spun his head and caught a glimpse of bloody epaulettes. Tom drove himself backwards, into the wall, smashing the zombie between himself and the control panel.

The zombie writhed on the control panel. Suddenly, klaxons sounded and the plane dipped towards the sea.

"What have I done?" Tom yelled.

"Autopilot!" Gaylen managed, before the pilot threw her off his back. She smashed against the back of the cockpit, then slumped to the floor.

Tom jammed his forearm against the thing's neck. He untwisted the coat hanger as the zombie's groans vibrated against his arm. He stared into the creature's dead eyes, feeling a pang of pity before thrusting the coat hanger home. The zombie screamed, jittered, then stopped moving.

He pulled the coat hanger free. The ocean loomed large in the cockpit windows. Suddenly the moon glistening off the waves didn't seem so beautiful.

From First Class came another crash, followed by the splintering of wood and twisting of metal. A head burst through the door, which buckled then popped open. Tom saw the misshapen head, black jacket and gore-soaked white collar and thought the preacher had bashed the door down with his head. Then he saw the horde pressing in behind him and realised the churchman had been used as a battering ram. The zombies were growing smarter, and fast.

The warning sound from the speakers became more urgent, and was joined by a female voice saying "Pull up" over and over again. Gaylen shook her head and ran for the joystick. Tom steeled himself for the zombie onslaught, gore-stained coat hanger at the ready.

Time slowed. For a moment it seemed there were so many zombies trying to get through the doorway at once that they would wedge themselves there. Then a woman wearing a floral print dress and inflated life jacket squeezed through. Her dress caught on the jagged edge of the mangled door and tore, revealing a sun-tanned shoulder that in death had lost some of its glow.

Gaylen pulled back on the joystick. Sky gradually filled the windows, but they were so close to the ocean now Tom could see white caps on the waves. The zombie pilot jumped on Gaylen. The 747 lurched Earthwards again, the momentum throwing the sundress-clad zombie into Tom's arms.

Gaylen yanked at the pilot's hands. She looked through the windscreen and her eyes widened.

"It's too ..."

When Tom came to he thought his adulterous ways had landed him in Hell. His body rose and fell on the icy waves. All around him, luggage and bodies filled the ocean. Some of the corpses floated still, others thrashed around sluggishly. Fog gave the scene an otherworldly appearance. Arms clutched his torso.

"Gaylen?"

He traced the arms back to their shoulders, then felt for where the head should have been. *Should* have been.

"Gaylen?"

He crested a wave. The fog lifted slightly. Shreds of floral print. A life jacket. Tanned shoulders. And a ragged, bloody stump where the neck and head should have been.

Tom screamed and kicked away from the corpse. He slipped under the waves and came up coughing, cursing, gagging. Dead arms stretched out for his embrace. As he kicked away the dead woman turned, and he saw her head floating behind the body, hanging by its spinal cord.

"Holy shit. Holy fucking *Christing* shit!"

Tom floundered in the cold sea, then found a loose life jacket and pulled it under his arms. He cried, screamed for Gaylen, and all the other dead people. He howled for his wife and son.

Around him, he could hear the undead survivors groaning. The stench of burnt flesh hung in the fog.

Tom greyed out. He dreamt of family holidays, of his son calling to him from the beach. Of his own father and their fishing trips on Moreton Bay.

Tom's eyes snapped open. The putt-putt-putt of the diesel engine was unmistakable. A wave dropped away and he saw the fishing trawler cutting through the flotsam and jetsam, twin spotlights aimed straight at him, lighting up the full horror of the crash scene. Suitcases, backpacks, shoes with the feet still in them, twitching, mutilated bodies with dead, staring eyes.

"Hey! Heeeey!"

Tom set out for the trawler, leaving his dreams behind, swimming for his life, his son, his wife. He considered for a moment that he really had the zombie in the floral dress to thank for the fact he was alive at all. She must have absorbed the force of the impact somehow. He pushed the thought away and concentrated on swimming.

The trawler batted aside a sizeable chunk of wreckage with a solid thump. Gantries on either side trailed nets through the debris.

"Heeey!"

Tom grabbed hold of the net, crying out in pain as the rough twine sliced into his numb hands. Blood splashed into the water.

He pulled himself up, hand over hand, clumsy, tingling legs slipping against the netting. He grabbed the red railing running around the deck and hauled himself over the side, collapsing in a heap. For a while he just lay there, panting, staring up at the sky. Stars burned bright.

Tom sat up and looked around. His stomach knotted at the sight of what looked like blood on the deck, black in the moonlight. *Fish bleed, don't they?* To his right the menacing hook of a gaffer hang in its holder, screwed to the railing. In the bridge, a dark figure stood hunched over the wheel.

"Thank Christ!" Tom yelled. "Thank fucking Christ! Thank you! Where the hell are we? Tonga? New Zealand?"

Something solid slapped against the hull.

"Were there any other survivors?"

The zombie turned and shuffled out into the moonlight, revealing gore-stained overalls and an all-too-familiar stare.

The hope Tom had nurtured withered, and it took every ounce of energy he possessed to get his aching body moving. He shuffled sideways, back against the railing, eyes locked on the fisher-zombie. He slid his arse against the old deck, dragging his throbbing legs behind him as the zombie followed in its economical, mechanical gait. It knew there was no escape.

Wind tickled his face and he could smell the stench of death coming from the hold. Tom's hand snaked up behind him, reaching for the gaffer. It was gone.

"No! No, no, no!"

Tom slumped against the side of the boat, defeated. He'd come so close, he'd started to believe that somewhere up there there was a God, and that God, for whatever reason, had decided to give him another go at it.

The zombie loomed over him now. It groaned. Tom didn't know if it was a groan of victory, or just a random exhalation of breath. It didn't matter. It was over. No second chances. No God above. Just Tom, the zombie, and ocean stretching to the horizon in every direction. He considered throwing himself back into the ocean—the one that got away—then realised he didn't have the strength. He had spent most of his waking hours sitting in front of a computer, letting his muscles wither, and now he would pay for his sloth.

"Come on then, you piece of shit," Tom said. "What are you waiting for?"

The sound of a watermelon splitting cut through the night air. The zombie staggered sideways, blood gushing down its neck as it tried in vain to pull the gaffer from its skull. The boat crested a wave and the zombie again lurched for Tom. He ducked and the ghoul pitched over the side of the boat, splashing into the water.

Standing in the moonlight, wet, panting, barely able to stand, was Gaylen.

"I hope you know how to drive a boat," she said, "because you sure as shit can't fly a plane."

TWO FISH TO FEED THE MASSES

Daniel G. Keohane

"They stared at you and did not blink. They showed you what lust and greed would give if only you looked deeper into their deception! If only you tore open your souls and let them lick you clean like ravenous harlots. They damned you!"

The last two words echoed off the buildings, then carried back over Dinneck. He paused, listening to God's words drift behind the abandoned Federal Reserve building towards the Atlantic. Words were food, to be diluted, perhaps, in water. Two fish could feed millions, the book said. Now the seas overflowed with manna that no one would eat.

"No one to eat of God's bounty," he whispered, then remembered his place, his role in this final safe hour of afternoon. He raised his arms, his voice. The Boston skyline reached up to the abandoned heavens with him.

"It's not too late to salvage your souls, stolen by the Face! That which is taken can always be regained." As he spoke, Dinneck walked slowly from South Station, knowing his words echoed in the vast halls of the subway below. He hoped they did not fall on barren ground.

Christ the King church was a good half hour walk. Best to be cautious since his watch battery died. Time did not matter, only the setting of the sun. The Shufflers' pack mentality could corner any living person too foolish to properly plan an escape route away from their slow, methodical snares. Even overcast days were spent indoors. The Runners dared not risk such gloom, but the Shufflers were too stupid to know the difference between the murk of twilight and a thick-clouded storm blowing past. This fact made the Shufflers no less dangerous, unless the sun broke through. Then, Dinneck would walk among the fallen shells of their bodies, eyes smoking, contrails of their captive souls burned free into the air.

Dinneck would avoid these unfortunates if he came across them. They were dead, of course, insides decaying slowly in crusted shells that once were skin. They were dead *before* the sun broke through the clouds. But the demons within them, stupid, growling slugs never quite adapting to their new forms might linger still, looking for a new host. These victims of the sun were always gone in the morning. The Runners were efficient that way, as if leaving their lost brethren to lay in the street might make the New Race look bad.

Shufflers. Runners. New Race.

That night Dinneck reviewed the names in his notebook as he sat in the church pew. Candlelight licked across his *New Race Dictum* as if to consecrate the work. He preached by day, begging Hell-imprisoned souls to fight back, reclaim what had been stolen from them. By night, he documented the world as it was, after the Face reached into every house and stole so many away.

"Dad, Dad! Come on, hurry! You can't miss the first five minutes or nothing will make sense! Everyone says that! Hurry!"

"That's OK. I'm recording it. I really have to finish this or Bert'll have my butt. You and Mom watch it tonight. If you want to watch it again with me tomorrow night you can tell me when the good parts are coming."

Nicky's expression passed from sorrowful hurt to hopeful expectation. "You promise? Really promise?"

At that moment Albert Dinneck almost—almost—said to hell with Bert and his deadlines. He'd get the galley revisions in a day later. Still, they were already a *month* late, and tomorrow was "Do or die, Buddy Boy" if *Eyes Closed* was to make Christmas. After tonight, the novel would be done and Albert could focus all of himself on Nicky and Mira.

"I really promise."

The silence in the apartment had been constant for a long time when Albert finally noticed. He reluctantly clicked *save* and rose from his desk, stretching his arms above and behind him. In the living room, a clown face glowed from the television screen. Wide, filling the glass, grinning. Albert had trouble looking too long at it, felt an itch on his fingers and neck. Nicky was gone, perhaps to bed after waiting too long for his father to change his mind. Albert reached down and turned off the television, looked at the clock. Almost two hours since Nicky had come in to beg that he join them.

With the screen dark, he wondered if that really had been a clown on the screen.

Mira was asleep on the couch. No, that wasn't right. She was bent backward, twisted in contorted pain. Streams of blood dried in tributaries from her nose and eyes, smeared in places where they had wiped against the off-white cushions.

"Mira?" He should have run to his wife, held her, called 911. But nothing felt real. The air was thick, an after-image of a massive explosion which he did not see nor smell. A quiet sense of abandonment.

He looked away from Mira—*just sleeping*—and walked across the room, down the hall towards Nicky's bedroom. He was calm, his pulse accelerating only when he opened the door and clicked the light to an empty room, sheets tightly tucked by Mira that morning. Albert checked the bathroom, his own room, the kitchen. His son was gone. Only when certain of this did he return to the living room, lay two fingers to his wife's throat as he'd seen them do on television, not certain what he was searching for. Finally, and for a long while, he screamed and wailed over his dead wife and missing son.

Everyone on their floor was dead. All had been watching television, either *The Show* or something else equally mundane. In the few apartments he'd checked, having to kick in the loosely-bolted doors after minutes of unanswered knocking, he saw the clown face on the television and looked away as soon as his fingers and neck began to itch. Once he tried changing the channel. In the corner of his eye he saw more faces on the screen, sometimes the same, sometimes narrower and dark.

Never once did he feel like a trespasser, though he did wonder if this was simply a dream and he was sleepwalking into his neighbors' homes. Two floors down Albert broke into the McGovern place and drifted slowly through their rooms. Two boys in elementary school, the youngest a year older than his own, and a daughter a freshman in high school. He found none of them. Only the unmoving, dry-blood adults on the couch.

No one answered 911 when, at last, he tried to call. Not knowing what to do, he went back to his own apartment and slept on the living room floor beside his dead wife. Part of him expected to wake from the dream any moment.

Two hours before sunrise, Mira rose up and tried to kill him. Closed her mouth around his bicep and tried to rip the skin free. Eyes bloody and unfocused, teeth closing tighter over her husband's arm, biting down hard and hard and hard—

Dinneck woke shouting and flailing against the pews. *Bang. Bang* against the wood, as if to dislodge the woman's mouth from his arm again. That first night Dinneck had been forced to slam Mira's head against the coffee table to make her let go. Seeing later how the New Race's teeth were so effectively pointed, sharpened either by their own hand or the same metamorphosis which made their skin hard and crusty, Dinneck knew he'd been lucky. Mira's teeth ... but he couldn't finish the thought. He'd gone too far just now in classifying his wife with no more concern that the millions of other Shufflers who came up from Below when the sun fell away.

The rhythmic pad-pad-pad of running outside, along the alley, flirting shapes barely visible past the stained glass windows. The sound followed the Passion of Christ, depicted in wood panels along the church walls, heading for the nave. The main church doors were closed, but never locked. No need. Not this soon.

The running steps scrabbled at the door, lingering longer than last night. Curled fist/claw on the wood. Bang. Bang. Bang. Running away in new pursuit, or simple fleeing the building's lingering power. Silence. Candles hissed across the church. They'd pounded on the door, he realized, not merely banged once for effect as they usually did.

The strength of the church was weakening quickly. Dinneck had felt, almost *tasted*, its power when he first arrived three days ago, It wasn't surprising that first night when the Shufflers dared not even the lowest steps leading from the street. Runners stayed their advances, never daring to run as close as they apparently had tonight.

Like the previous church, Saint Agnes, his refuge was weakening to the point Dinneck felt his security melt whisky-ice thin. Wedged between the Monroe Financial building and a nameless, behemoth brick office, Christ the King church would last him perhaps only this final night.

When God gathered everyone's children in his arms and left the world for the demons to run slipshod across the globe, the churches seemed to remain filled with the Lord's love and protection. Doors carefully closed to prevent spilling. Once Dinneck moved in, the seal was broken and God's power leaked slowly into the stale air outside, drained like a flashlight left on under a child's pillow.

He took up residence in Saint Agnes after fleeing his apartment, four weeks and an eternity ago. The *Holy Light* shone into the eyes of the New Race when they pursued, blinding them, keeping them at a respectful distance. It faded a little every day, until three nights ago when a Runner turned the knob and opened the door, exposing Saint Agnes to the cool night air. Dinneck saw only the arm, long and moorish brown in the afterglow of the wind-flickered candles. The Runner never entered, though for a moment Dinneck had felt a horrible thrill that he might at last see these creatures whose night-shrouded footsteps marked their presence, but of whom he'd seen only flashing glimpses through colored glass.

The Shufflers, however, had come in that night, uncertain and wary. Dinneck huddled on the altar, watching the candles sputter in death, hearing the slow, uncertain steps of the walking dead, the *stolen* dead, moving up the center aisle. He'd curled into a ball behind the altar, squeezing whatever remained of God's love from the narthex, sucking the last of the holiness from the air and praying it would last until daylight.

It had.

When he dared look up the next morning, a single sun-stricken body, its captive soul burned free in the light, lay crumpled in the aisle beside the front pew. The man's face peeled in thick lines at the cheeks, as if someone's fingers had once been drawn down into them. Probably so. A person could not fight these creatures once in their grip, except to flail uselessly at whatever dead flesh they could before being rent and torn into their own death.

Those were good deaths, however. The victim who made the marks on that dead thing's cheeks would not be coming back as a vessel for another demon. There would be nothing left.

Now, Dinneck looked about the dim interior of Christ the King. It was happening here, the fading of the protection, sooner than Dinneck would have thought. Cracks in the walls, maybe, windows never quite closed. Heaven's heat dissipating. He needed a new haven—church or synagogue or Hindu temple—once the sun returned. He'd had been lucky in Saint Agnes. Not again, not if he stayed here past morning.

How long before he ran out of sanctified ground and became trapped in the middle of Route One as daylight winked out and night fell on him like a net? If he made it out of downtown, maybe north into Somerville or Medford, he might find a haven for a night. Maybe bide his time until he reached the suburbs. How many churches were there in Burlington that hadn't already been sucked dry by some other desperate survivor?

Maybe the waterfront held the answer. Steal a boat, sail away. Until his food ran out, and he died slowly, to have his body raped by a grinning imp from Hell, riding back to shore to join the swarming hive of hard shell corpses in the darkness of the MBTA subway tunnels.

Dinneck picked up the notebook. His *New Race Dictum* had grown one page at a time, hurried scrawls of Bic pen on sweat-dropped paper. One of his earliest thoughts was that he'd been spared to chronicle these times. Later, to pay God for the continued stay of his execution, he preached in the deserted streets, trying to bring the people back with his words.

They weren't listening. God was gone. He and the children were on some far away planet, green grass, fields and clouds, Nicky and the McGovern boys laughing and running down hills, swimming in clear, clear lakes. Not for the first time Dinneck appreciated the irony of the true Rapture. All those well-dressed Jehovah's Witnesses, now walking slack among the neighborhoods, ripping warm flesh off shoulders and bellies. The Rapture came, but only the children could ride.

Dinneck drained the last of his canteen. The water was sour, had been when first poured from the plastic jug in the convenience store at the end of the block. Everything more sour each day, more meaningless. He rose from the bench and walked towards the main doors of the church. His steps were silenced by the carpet, but any Dead waiting outside the door would feel his heat, the ripples in the air of a living, beating heart. Blood not yet cold and sagging in unused veins.

The vessel containing the holy water was half full. He lifted the plastic bowl from its wall-mounted base and removed the square of sponge from the center. He squeezed what water he could back into the bowl and drank, stopping only at the sucking of his mouth on dry plastic. The water spread through him, clean, fresh and powerful. It reached his furthest corners, set his fingers and toes to curl involuntarily.

Dinneck felt alive in this brief moment, as if he was still a true child of God. Orphaned, yes, but still His Child. Perhaps Dinneck's body was now the sole vessel of this building's power. The thought set him on edge. He stared at the outer doors, waiting for them to burst open.

His body, his blood now the vessel.

Dinneck looked away from the doors, and understood.

His preaching was not in vain. It simply was not enough. The body and blood of redemption was needed. The realization frightened him. But since walking into the living room and finding his wife on the couch, his son gone, something evil and horrible on the television screen, this decision felt right. The missing ingredient in what remained of his Mission.

He would die, yes. But he would die *well*, unlike those who fell to the street clutching their heart, or stumbled from a ledge to the sidewalk three stories below. When Dinneck died, there would be nothing left of his body. Nothing left of his soul for the demons to infest and manipulate. He would become diluted, nonexistent, cleansing energy coursing through the guts of the Demon World below him. And perhaps, Dinneck might gather some souls for God along the way.

He returned to the bench and the open notebook. Why had he bothered? Soon there would be no one left to read the Dictum. Still, he sat and raised the pen. One final chapter to explain for anyone finding these words what they needed to do, to serve God, to be free at last.

It took most of the next morning in Christ the King's sacristy to locate the reserves of holy water. He held the glass jar in his hand, feeling the weight of his mission. Did they bless the water only when they poured it into the receiving bowls? He broke the seal, unscrewed the cap. No smell, save the sensation of dampness around the lid. Glass to his lips.

He drank in heavy, wanting gulps. The Power was immense, heavy, *too much*, filling the bag of his stomach, reaching through his veins with the electric fingers of God Himself. He wanted to stop, wanted to drop the jar and spew the water. *This is wrong, I am wrong.* Still he drank, until he could hold no more.

The interior of the church was too bright, too much sun through the stained glass. He swallowed air, forcing the water down. Albert Dinneck was now the vessel, and must not break. He stumbled, rocking like a boat in a storm, down the aisle. Near the back of the church his Work lay discarded. He felt it crying out to him in a silent wail of abandonment.

Along the streets, feeling shards of sunlight cut through his skin, tunnel vision in his new state of Grace, to the entrance to the subway's Red Line. Concrete stairs fell into darkness. Down there lurked the monsters. Blood and other unknowable fluids stained the sidewalk, more so near the mouth of this New Hell. That was where he now traveled—Hell. Preach among its denizens a sermon of hope and redemption. Reach into their mouths and free the souls trapped within.

Down the steps, slowly, his stomach stretched painfully. He needed to pee, but knew he could not. *Must* not.

The smell of decomposition, garbage too long in the sun, scent of rotting banana peels and vinegar. At the bottom of the steps he stared into deep pockets of darkness broken only by secondary light streaming from the stairwell behind him, or through various ventilation slats overhead. Still, he saw well enough, the Light in him shining through his eyes into the murk. Maybe it was just his memory of the station's layout playing out in his mind, a mental map translated to vision.

The turnstile clicked as he passed through. Spackled blood dried below the red-painted stripe denoting the MBTA subway line. Both blood and stripe were dark gray shades in this lightless world. He stepped onto the platform. Empty. No lights, the twin open mouths of the tunnel on either side. He would stay here. They would come to him.

Dinneck considered preaching some more, as he used to do in the safety of the light above. His bladder ached. So much power running through him, he dared not break its spell.

Shuffling feet from the tunnel mouths, worn shoes on dust, dry feet whispering. Soon the shapes. Shufflers, too many to count, following his heat and blood scent, emerging from both sides. Dinneck moved to the center of the platform, heart racing. His instincts screamed for him to run back through the turnstiles and into the sun. One more day, one more week, the Power protecting him at night might last *that* long.

Perhaps this was how Jesus felt seeing the soldiers marching up the hill to arrest him. Dinneck could not leave. He must die today. He was now the two fish with which God would feed the masses. The two walls of lumbering bodies merged together, silent save their steps. They stopped. A sound like a police siren, organic and wet, sent them into uncertain hesitancy.

A Runner came up the abandoned tracks, so fast Dinneck thought for a moment it was a train. It scrabbled onto the platform. The Shufflers moved aside, a demonic Moses parting them like the sea. The creature reared up. Tall, with strong, muscular legs bent nearly ninety-degrees to prevent it from hitting the ceiling. Its segmented body glistened as if adorned with flakes of mica. Dinneck could not make out many details, but could see its *shape* clearly enough. Large growths, like many heads along the front and sides of its body, four arms, two where one would expect them, two more reaching from behind like the bones of old wings. The Runner's head sloped small and narrow, bird-like. The overall effect was utterly alien. Dinneck fought an instant revulsion—like looking too closely at the surreal features of a wasp, magnified a hundredfold. He wanted to run. *It* wanted him to run, if only to catch him again for sport.

The legs bent further, the body leaned forward, arms supporting the awkward bulk by slapping onto the concrete floor. He was being studied. The Shufflers, those for whom he'd come, moved closer. The Runner hissed/screamed its siren call. The others stopped, uncertain, wanting to devour the man standing before them but apparently not at the expense of this demon's ire.

Dinneck suddenly thought he understood the nature of these Runners. They were shepherds, former wolves who now, after stealing the sheep, protect their captives from their own ignorance and blind wanderings. *Dinneck* was now the wolf, and the beast before him stared through dull red-glowing slits, deciding if he was a threat.

"I am here to die," Dinneck whispered. His tongue stuck to the roof of his dry mouth. He forced himself to swallow, then added in a louder voice, "I am an offering from God who has left this world to your devices."

The Runner hissed. On either side, its flock moved forward and were allowed to pass. The Runner, slowly, moved back onto the tracks to wait, and watch.

A dozen arms grabbed Dinneck's shirt, pulled him forward. He closed his eyes. He tried not to think, tried to send himself back to his old apartment, when Mira and Nicky were alive. An overwhelming need to run and survive gripped him as tight as the dead, hard-crusted fingers. The mass of Shufflers poured over him like a wave, pressed him to the floor. No hot breath on his neck, only the icy feel of teeth pressing down, splitting his flesh, the warmth of his own blood. Fire, ice, screaming pain through his body. Clothes and skin were torn away. A chunk of his leg pulled free, the stale air racing across his exposed arteries and muscle burned like acid. *Was* acid. So many on him, he couldn't thrash or try to fight.

Dinneck was turned onto his back. Eyes still closed he managed one final scream before a mouth bit down on his chin, throat. Fingers peeled back his cheeks and eyelids, but he saw nothing.

The Runner on the tracks watched the feeding with relieved contentment. There were more Shufflers far back in the tunnels, pushing forward, pressing against those in front of them in their need to consume, to taste even a drop of this new blood. The heat of the victim bathed the platform with an intoxicating glow in their eyes.

Something changed. Where once a pulsing mound of Shuffler bodies heaved and writhed atop Dinneck's body, the Runner now noticed many of its kin no longer moved. Others, impatient, shoved them aside, scrounged with dry lips what might be left, shards of bones, bloody rivulets squeezed away from the feeding.

The mound of bodies grew.

The demon on the tracks noticed too late what was happening. It howled and leapt onto the platform, shoving its way through, tossing Shufflers, both moving and still, aside.

There was little left of Dinneck's body. Wads of flesh, fluid spilled across the floor only to be covered by a desperate black tongue. A long white bone protruding from the mouth of another, though the mouth no longer moved. The Runner swatted at a piece of intestine and felt its preternatural flesh burn.

It backed away, screamed again. Still the horde pressed past it, not just in hunger, now driven by something awakening inside them, desperate for the communion being offered.

Eventually there was nothing left of the man but multi-hued stains on the concrete, heavy lumps of Dinneck's flesh buried within the unmoving Shuffler bodies. When the smell and heat dissipated the mob moved back into the tunnel, leaving the Runner to shove the empty husks of its lost flock off the platform and onto the tracks. It didn't know what else to do for the moment. Its hand still burned where it had touched the victim's flesh.

Dinneck moved through the clouds into the vastness of space. He sensed others with him but could not look to see who they were. He waited for the Light of God to appear from the star-filled dark and embrace him.

Further, further into the cold of the universe he traveled, always waiting for the ethereal doors of heaven to open and swallow him into the Light. Somewhere there was the green grass and fields where his son played. He wanted to believe Mira was one of the freed souls traveling with him. Had she been there, in the subway? Maybe. He had to believe, have faith.

They traveled out, out, into the black void, calling with silent voices. Waiting for the embrace. Waiting for an answer.

FENSTAD'S END

Sarah Langan

Fenstad jogged down the dark hall, hoping to lose her. She'd started off peeking around corners, but now she'd grown bold: her bare feet slapped against the tiles twenty feet behind him. She had big brown eyes, knobby knees, and sores around her mouth from either herpes or scurvy. She was the size of a seven year-old kid, but he'd seen enough anorexics to know better. She was probably in her teens.

He turned left, then right. This hospital was a maze. The slapping got further away, and he decided that she wasn't a girl. Like all the rest, she was a ghost. To reassure himself he started humming The Beach Boys "Feeling Flows," and then stopped when the sound echoed through the hall.

You'll wake the dead, he thought.

The fourth steel door on the right was locked, but he had a key. He opened it, and for a moment didn't move. August light shone through the window and illuminated the room. The place looked smaller than he remembered. A fine layer of dust blanketed the brown leather couch. Mounted on the walls were Salvador Dali's "Birth of Liquid Desires" and "Persistence of Memory." He'd hung them to put his patients in the mind of dreams. Bookcases sheltered the journals and texts he'd spent half his life collecting. In the far corner his wilted fern had turned crispy from neglect. A patient had given that to him, hadn't she? He couldn't remember which one. Carla? Whitney? Gail? No matter. These days the world was a wasteland of forgotten names.

He reached into the lower right hand of his desk and pulled out the bottle of OxyContin. He'd kept the pills here for emergencies after his back surgery once upon a time. He popped one in his mouth, and the chalky taste warmed his blood. *Okay*, he thought. *Okay.*

Like the rest of the world, the hospital was a fucking mess. Flies collected along the windows where blood had been smeared. Empty gurneys and scrubs clogged the halls. As far as he could tell, there weren't any bodies. It was high summer, and he would have been able to smell them. He remembered hearing on the radio that right before the Long Island hospitals closed their doors, self-appointed militiamen had piled the dead and even some of the living into dump trucks and burned them in a pyre at the Jones' Beach sump.

Below the hospital kitchen, the basement was cool and wet. It reminded him of air conditioning and he took a moment to appreciate the luxury of it. He should have come here long ago, but it was only after the night people picked clean the pharmacies and grocery stores had he remembered the hospital this morning. Either the hospital, or he started breaking into the houses of the dead.

As he'd hoped, the walk-in freezer was hooked-up to the auxiliary generator and it still had a little juice left. His stomach growled at the knowledge that he'd have a meal better than cold oatmeal and water tonight. He propped open the metal door with a milk-crate and began filling his backpack with whatever he could carry. He found himself humming again, this time a tune about Brian Wilson. With the opiate threading its way through his blood, he didn't bother, this time, to stop.

The girl was on his mind. There was something about her that he should remember. But why would he want to do that?

Even if she wasn't a ghost, most of the survivors had gone mad. With fire and their bare hands they'd leveled every vestige of the old world that remained. A few had even ornamented their forts along Dune Road with the bodies of the dead. He'd shared camp with a man when it first happened, thinking it would be good to have the company, only to wake during the night to find the man strangling a feral dog that had come begging for scraps. He left peacefully at Fenstad's request, but came back later that night looking for trouble. Fenstad yelled "stop" only once before shooting him in the chest with a flare gun and carrying his body out to sea. The human species: not so nearly as resilient as the psychoanalysts liked to think.

He turned just in time to see the freezer door slam shut. It was too heavy for the milk carton he'd propped against it. The room went black. He was trapped. He leaned against the ice cold wall, and closed his eyes. What a way to go. Frozen solid in the last functional meat locker in the aftermath of the apocalypse. He popped another pill, and imagined that if he wasn't high right now, he might be upset.

That's when someone turned the handle, and the door sprung open. He caught it before it closed again, and looked into the hall, but no one was there.

"Hello?" he called. His voice echoed in the air, alongside the sound of bare feet slapping against cold cement. The girl? *The ghost?*

His breathing came fast even though he wasn't tired. He picked up his bag and jogged to the exit. When he got there, something tugged on his shirt and he jumped. Always, the dead were watching him. They lived in the crevices of his memories like peripheral vision, and populated his dreams.

The girl was brunette, and just under five feet tall. She wore a short denim skirt and thin t-shirt that read, "Super Sex Kitten."

"Dr. Wintrob?" she asked. Purplish circles stained the skin under her eyes like she'd rubbed berries there. A physical pain ran in a line down his chest to his groin. He knew this ghost. Not for the first time since he woke this morning, he wondered if it was time to take a few extra OxyContin:

Can I die yet, God? I think I'd like that.

Not long ago, Deannie Caterino had been his patient at The Schneider's Children Eating Disorder Clinic. Back when people had cared about such things he'd fucked her twice. It was for this reason that he'd been suspended without pay, his colleagues had turned on him, and he'd been sitting safely at home when the shit hit the fan, and the world came to an end.

She let go of his shirt. He set down his backpack. Amidst the frozen steaks and vegetables, he found the preserved lemons. He opened the jar and handed it to her. She dug her hands into the brine and began to chew. The lemons were full of ascorbic acid, and by tomorrow her scurvy sores would probably close. She ate greedily, and he thought it was funny that a few months ago, she'd refused anything but hot tea and an intravenous glucose drip. Funny that as recently as the criminal hearing in January, she'd screamed at the sight of him. Funny how life worked out. He fingered the pills in his pocket to reassure himself that they were there.

Are you there, God? Because I'd like to die, but I want to make sure I never have to see your face.

The fire crackled, and Deannie was so still that he could see the red reflected in her eyes. Without shelter, nights on the beach got cold. He slept under the stars because houses had become mausoleums. He didn't like the dreams other peoples' framed photos and old furniture gave him, and the way lately he'd started to believe in the persistence of the dead.

Deannie took a bite of the shell steak he'd cooked for her. She wasn't talking yet, but he knew her well enough to guess what had happened. She'd somehow survived after the rest had died. Like him, she'd wanted to leave the houses behind, and the hospital was familiar. She'd probably been living there, sleeping in her old Craftmatic Adjustable Bed, ever since. But the girl was near starving, and the freezer was hidden beneath the kitchen, so she'd finished off what canned food in the pantry had remained, and then she'd been so weak she'd hardly been able to walk. When he came along, she'd probably been terrified. But she'd followed him, because he was her only chance.

Now, she picked at her teeth, satisfied by the meal. Despite her affliction, she'd always been a cheerful girl. When she first arrived at the hospital, she strong-armed two fellow patients into a prison break. In their open-backed gowns they'd raced down Baycrest Avenue to hear Wilco play at the town square. They scared the hell out of the summer people, who'd assumed they were escaped lunatics. Fenstad sighed. He'd liked those girls. Genuinely, he'd cared about every one of them.

He thought of his wife suddenly. Bottle blonde and vain as a prom queen. The idea of her had always been more compelling than the woman. But that was hardly her fault; she'd never pretended to be a humanitarian.

Deannie splayed her fingers over the fire. They were too close, and he guessed she was burning them. A winking kitten with its panties around its ankles was perched on her t-shirt. Classic behavior: victims had a habit of fashioning emblems of their trauma. They wanted others to know what they'd been through. With these emblems they tried to exert control over what had happened to them. Cuts on the insides of thighs, tattoos, piercings, gas guzzling SUVs, t-shirts that attracted all the wrong kinds of attention, pills full of opium that dissolved on the tongue like honey, the bodies of the dead nailed to posts in Sag Harbor, these were signs victims used, and in using them they became their own oppressors.

Deannie looked up, and smiled at him like the two of them were at a dance. This was irony; an ironic situation. *I made it across the end of the world, and guess who I met when I got there?*

A seagull swooped down into the water and tugged a muscle free, then smashed it open against a jetty and began to eat. The bird was rarity, like the two of them. The infection that killed the humans got almost everything else, too. A few were immune, and a handful less than that got sick and then recovered. At night he didn't even hear crickets.

Dear God. Are we starting over? Because you've got to kill all the ghosts first, you know.

The end happened slowly, and then really fast. The pollution got bad, which everyone had talked about for so long that when it happened they'd already accepted it as inevitable. He'd worn a mask on his way to work. Ran a Heppa Air Purifier in his office and at home. Stopped eating fresh food and bought the regulation canned variety. Not ideal, but livable. He'd learned this studying prisoners of war at Penn State: men get used to intolerable conditions when there's nothing they can do to improve them.

A few years into his practice, it became evident that women over thirty were no longer able to bear children, and the ones in their twenties were about half as fertile as the decade before. In addition, the parents of several hundred thousand boys across the country reported that their sons' testicles never descended. "The Washington Post" broke the story: the Chinese antibiotic factories that peppered the rust coast of New England were dumping their waste materials into wells and aquifers where Poland Spring water was bottled. One of these waste products mimicked estrogen on the molecular level. Lawsuits flew in every direction. Everybody got rich, and no one collected because the corporations declared bankruptcy.

Then came the wasting woman. When he finished his residency, Fenstad's original specialties had been seasonal affective disorder, bipolar disorder, depression, and obsessive-compulsive disorder. The saddies. But the epidemic changed that. Starving women and girls were admitted into emergency rooms by the thousands. When it reached pandemic proportions, in good conscience the people in his profession had necessarily switched their specialties.

What differed from all previous incarnations of the illness was that the girls and woman didn't refuse food for attention or increased bargaining power. They didn't want anything, except to die. In session they told him what he wanted to hear: I was abused. I'm afraid of becoming a woman. My mother wishes I was perfect. Before I got skinny, the boys at school called me Orca. They'd confess these things without a single tear or hint of genuine emotion. They'd promise to change, and then, after session they'd stick their fingers down their throats because they'd sucked the sugar off a stick of Big Red and he'd wonder: if these girls aren't crazy, who is?

Over the course of a year, the birth rate plummeted to .2 children per couple. He'd been smart about the changing world even though he hadn't liked it. He invested in video game futures in Beijing, and bought into water rights in Nepal. Their house on the ocean in Westhampton was a dream, even if he'd learned too late that it wasn't his dream. It wasn't just Caroline, it was the whole thing: the English Tudor, the Benz C55, the working hard so you can work harder, and in the end what did it get you? He hadn't read a novel since college, and his patients were dying like flies.

Then Caroline got pregnant. In his mind he'd called the lump Rose, and it was only recently that he'd connected the name to a girl from elementary school who'd tossed wads of wet toilet paper at the classroom ceiling when the nuns weren't looking, so that it had thudded unexpectedly to the earth all year long. This was the nature of unrequited love; it endured in regions where nothing else dared.

His daughter was born with a fully formed skull cap, but no brain or spinal cord. By then the graveyards were full, so he buried her in the backyard and said a prayer over her body, unsure whether he should wish an eternal soul upon a thing so wretched. Caroline took to her bed after that. He would have had a harder time with her withdrawal if he'd cared about her. But that wasn't fair. Who knows how he'd really felt back then? It's easy to make things ugly when you stew them, like a pot of broth that boils for hours, into thick, black oil. And besides, like everyone else he'd started going mad.

Things got worse. The papers reported murder like it was barometric pressure, a death toll constantly on the rise. There were too many men in the jails to feed, let alone public lawyers to try them. With each day more women came to the hospital. Too many to treat, not that the treatment ever worked. They died of wasting in their beds. Breathing in the morning, their husbands and fathers and brothers would come home that night to find silent sacks of bones. It happened with Caroline. What haunted him was that he'd seen the disease every day, but never suspected she was sick with it. Caroline haunted him, too.

Not long after Caroline's death, the thing with Deannie happened.

The scientists finally admitted the problem: There was something in the air not compatible with the human nervous system. It acted like a hormone, and changed the way the brain worked. In women it engendered thoughts of death, and out of men it made murderers. Things started to make sense. The rapes, the bloody emergency rooms, the black eyes given and received behind closed doors, the eating and purging, the consumption. There was, it turned out, an explanation for America, only nobody liked it very much.

At his hearing, Fenstad's defense was that the air had diminished his ability to reason. He'd forgotten to change the filter in the purifier in his office for a few days, and temporarily lost his mind. He was indicted, but he probably would have been acquitted. About three months ago, the stuff in the air hit a record high. Scientists isolated the chemical, which it turned out was a byproduct of pressurized rubber recycling. At the height of absurdity, the federal government declared a freeze on all domestic recycling, but by then it was too late. People interviewed on the street said they could feel it, and the rage it created, like acid in their throats. They contained it for as long as they could, and then they acted. The riots began. The armed forces returned from foreign shores. The president declared a state of national emergency. Every night on the news were stories of fires, razed buildings, mass shootings of innocents, suicide, the rotting bodies of forgotten or abandoned women.

369

Everything changed. No one went to work, or collected curbside trash, or fed the coma patients. For a week all Fenstad heard were gunshots and explosions. All he smelled was smoke from mile-wide pyres. And then power went out, and everything got quiet. And then whatever had been pumped it into the air dissipated, and those who remained began to recover.

Sort of.

Deannie smacked her lips now. Her fingers were still too close to the fire, and he saw that the pads of her palms were red. He wanted to stop her, but he didn't want to touch her. So he popped a pill, and let it sit like a melting chocolate on his tongue.

She turned, and it terrified him suddenly that she might speak. "Are you glad?" Deannie asked.

"Sorry?"

Deannie smiled. It wasn't a nice smile. Not at all liked he'd remembered. A lump of clay shaped in all the wrong ways. "That it's all gone. Are you glad, because you won't have to go to jail?"

"That's one way of looking at it."

"I think you're happy. You like this. You don't have to pretend you're a nice guy anymore."

In the distance the gull dropped another muscle. The breeze died down, and everything was still. "What happened wasn't my fault, Deannie. It was the air," Fenstad said.

Deannie pulled her hands out of the fire. She took off her shirt, and he saw her pale skin and small, white bra. In some countries seventeen is legal. In this country, now that there was no law. She saw his reaction and smiled, as if she'd proven her point. "What if the air was fine, do you ever think about that? What if the air was just fine, but they needed a reason for what happened so they told us a story on the news," she said.

"I'm not following you," he told her in the most dispassionate way he knew how, a reflex from years as a therapist. But of course he'd wondered this, too.

She took off her bra, and watched carefully for his reaction. Her nipples were more orange than pink. She lay back on her elbows, and the fire cast shadows against her skin. The night was cool, though, and after a while her downy hairs stood erect over goose bumps. She pulled on her t-shirt. His disappointment was immense. "Forget it," she said.

He was unaccustomed to having a companion, and it made time go slowly.

They been together for a few days now, and she'd gotten her strength back. After breakfast, he wrapped what remained of the food he'd taken from the hospital into a net and buried it in the sand to keep it cool. Behind him, Deannie skimmed rocks. A slip of quartz bounced off a floating fish's eye and then sank. The sound was sludgy.

He turned to see if she flinched, but her face was stony. She was unrecognizable from the happy girl she'd once been. Then again, the same could be said for him. He hadn't shaved in months, nor combed his hair. Sand and salt had polished and then pruned his skin. And then there was his newfound drug habit.

"Hey, Wintrob," Deannie said. Her tone was a command. No longer a girl seeking approval (*Did I do it right?* She'd once asked, and he cringed at the memory).

He came down from the jetty. "Yeah?"

"I want to go to town."

"It's not safe," he said. "We've got plenty of food."

She shrugged. "You're low on your pills, aren't you?"

It was true. They hadn't lasted as long as he'd hoped. Last night he'd lay awake sweating, and the nightmares had started again. They were the reason he'd started this little habit a few months ago, to bandage the ghosts' mouths mute. Last night Caroline had been holding a skeleton wrapped in rags, and he'd realized it was their daughter. Rose was dead. *Which Rose?* he'd remembered thinking in his dream, and then the skeleton grew flesh with scabby lips, and became Deannie.

"True," he said to Deannie, and he knew he should be ashamed. He should be thinking about protecting this girl, and finding shelter for the fall. He should be looking for other people, and trying to rebuild. But he didn't want to start over. He wanted to sit by the water and watch the waves and take his medicine because his bones ached, and the ghosts wouldn't let him sleep.

Town wasn't far. The crazies came out at night, which made day time travel the only option. On their trip she might see some things not fit for a young woman, but that was hardly a consideration anymore. This time instead of the hospital, he'd break into a house. These were rich people in Westhampton, and most had a Disneyland of pharmaceuticals in their medicine cabinets.

He and Deannie began walking up the shore. She stood close to him, like they were friends. Maybe they were. He found himself thinking about the old life. The food mostly, but also the air conditioning. He was humming again. This time it was "God Only Knows".

Shop windows were all shattered, and most of the stores had been picked clean and then burned out by looters. Deannie's bare feet slapped against the hot asphalt, but she didn't seem to notice. Her head bobbled in every direction. She looked at the overturned fire truck, and the rotting body so bloated and full of bacteria that its feet had snapped the plastic on its sandals. "This too, is vanity," was written on the concrete in either paint or blood. She was crying. He didn't know what to say to comfort her, so he didn't say anything.

When they got to the end of Baycrest Avenue, she announced, "I hate this place. Let's go back."

"Wait one second," he said, and jogged around the side of the nearest house, a French colonial with chipped white columns. He had to hold his breath when he broke through the back door. The smell was wretched, and all the shades had been drawn so that the rooms were dark. There was something under the covers in the master bedroom, and it didn't move but in his mind it was alive. Save for some Bayer aspirin, a few band aids, and a prescription for Advair, the medicine cabinet was empty. He turned and started out again, but stopped.

This place was familiar. He walked toward the bed. His stomach lurched and he spit yellow bile. It wasn't the smell; he was accustomed to the smell. He knew this place. In the old days, he'd played cards here, gotten drunk here, watched ball games on the big screen television downstairs. He lifted the brown sheet. The man's skin was pressed tightly against bone. Mummified, with a long slit across his throat. His red hair and middle part were familiar. This was James Clougherty, his best friend.

Fenstad sat down on the corner. He'd seen this so many times before that he'd grown numb. Immune. Exhausted. Fucked up. Agnostic. Bitter. Enraged. Insane.

The dead, they were everywhere.

For the first time since the shit hit the fan, he cried. Blubbered. Shouted. Lost everything to it, even his breath. And then a hand slipped around his fingers, and Deannie was there with him. Together, they wept.

Before they left the house he took some baking items and powdered milk. If he lit a fire tonight he could make bread. It would be tough and dry and after all this time it would taste like heaven. Then he handed Deannie a pink oxford shirt from the spare bedroom and she put it on. They walked back without speaking. They cooked in silence, and then ate in silence, too.

When the dark came she lay down next to him, curled close as a spoon. Something in his heart turned with hope, maybe, and he wanted very much a taste of morphine. She turned so that they were facing each other, and he could have been her father. She closed her eyes and tried to kiss him. Her lips were cold. Out here alone, she needed him. "Stop it," he said. Then he pulled the spare blanket over her shoulders and turned away. She sighed with what he knew was relief. She began to cry, only this time, it was not about the end of the world.

They fell asleep that way, and for the first time in a long time, the dead did not call to him in his dreams.

In the morning she was gone. At first he thought she had run away. Good for her. But he looked down to the edge of the beach, and saw two more people had set up camp. They were better at it than him, and he could see they'd fashioned a tent and were already starting a fire over which to cook breakfast. There was a sound they were making, laughter, and it resounded strangely in his ears.

Deannie turned and beckoned him, her arm like a pale, fluttering flag.

He considered walking in the opposite direction. But there was Deannie, and he did not know these people to trust them, and so he would not leave her. In this way he knew she would be his family in the new world, just as Rose should have been. But for a moment he stood and watched the horizon. Taking a pause between when one breath let out, and the next filled his lungs.

He saw in the horizon what the dead had been whispering all along: The survivors soon would crawl out from houses and dunes. They would meet, and coalesce, and they would rebuild. They would try to learn something from what had happened, but it was not their nature. Like victims who wear their scars, they would relive their histories over and over again. But at least, when they looked to the heavens, they would imagine the possibility of breaking these bonds of their own creation, and reaching the stars.

FAIR EXTENSION
Stephen King

Streeter only saw the sign because he had to pull over and puke. He puked a lot now, and there was very little warning—sometimes a flutter of nausea, sometimes a brassy taste in the back of his mouth, and sometimes nothing at all; just urk and out it came, howdy-do. It made driving a risky proposition, yet he also drove a lot now, partly because he wouldn't be able to by late fall and partly because he had a lot to think about. He had always done his best thinking behind the wheel.

He was out on the Harris Avenue Extension, a broad thoroughfare that ran for two miles beside the Derry County Airport and the attendant businesses: mostly motels and warehouses. The Extension was busy during the daytime, because it connected Derry's west and east sides as well as servicing the airport, but in the evening it was nearly deserted. Streeter pulled over into the bike lane, snatched one of his plastic barf-bags from the pile of them on the passenger seat, dropped his face into it, and let fly. Dinner made an encore appearance. Or would have, if he'd had his eyes open. He didn't. Once you'd seen one bellyful of puke, you'd seen them all.

When the puking phase started, there hadn't been pain. Dr. Henderson had warned him that would change, and over the last week, it had. Not agony as yet; just a quick lightning-stroke up from the gut and into the throat, like acid indigestion. It came, then faded. But it would get worse. Dr. Henderson had told him that, too.

He raised his head from the bag, opened the glove compartment, took out a wire bread-tie, and secured his dinner before the smell could permeate the car. He looked to his right and saw a providential litter basket with a cheerful lop-eared hound on the side and a stenciled message reading DERRY DAWG SEZ "PUT LITTER IN ITS PLACE!"

Streeter got out, went to the Dawg Basket, and disposed of the latest ejecta from his failing body. The summer sun was setting red over the airport's flat (and currently deserted) acreage, and the shadow tacked to his heels was long and grotesquely thin. It was as if it were four months ahead of his body, and already fully ravaged by the cancer that would soon be eating him alive.

He turned back to his car and saw the sign across the road. At first—probably because his eyes were still watering—he thought it said HAIR EXTENSION. Then he blinked and saw it actually said FAIR EXTENSION. Below that, in smaller letters: FAIR PRICE.

Fair extension, fair price. It sounded good, and almost made sense.

There was a gravel area on the far side of the Extension, outside the Cyclone fence marking the County Airport's property. Lots of people set up roadside stands there during the busy hours of the day, because it was possible for customers to pull in without getting tailgated (if you were quick and remembered to use your blinker, that was). Streeter had lived his whole life in the little Maine city of Derry, and over the years he'd seen people selling fresh fiddleheads there in the spring, fresh berries and corn on the cob in the summer, and lobsters almost year-round. In mud season, a crazy old guy known as The Snowman took over the spot, selling scavenged knickknacks that had been lost in the winter and were revealed by the melting snow. Many years ago Streeter had bought a good-looking rag dolly from this man, intending to give it to his daughter May, who had been two or three back then. He made the mistake of telling Janet that he'd gotten it from The Snowman, and she made him throw it away. "Do you think we can boil a rag doll to kill the germs?" she asked. "Sometimes I wonder how a smart man like you can be so stupid."

Well, cancer didn't discriminate when it came to brains. Smart or stupid, he was about ready to leave the game and take off his uniform.

There was a card table set up where The Snowman had once displayed his wares. The pudgy man sitting behind it was shaded from the red rays of the lowering sun by a large yellow umbrella that was cocked at a rakish angle.

Streeter stood in front of his car for a minute, almost got in (the pudgy man had taken no notice of him; he appeared to be watching a small portable TV), and then curiosity got the better of him. He checked for traffic, saw none—the Extension was predictably dead at this hour, all the commuters at home eating dinner and taking their non-cancerous states for granted—and crossed the four empty lanes. His scrawny shadow, the Ghost of Streeter Yet to Come, trailed out behind him.

The pudgy man looked up. "Hello there," he said. Before he turned the TV off, Streeter had time to see the guy was watching Inside Edition. "How are we tonight?"

"Well, I don't know about you, but I've been better," Streeter said. "Kind of late to be selling, isn't it? Very little traffic out here after rush hour. It's the backside of the airport, you know. Nothing but freight deliveries. Passengers go in on Witcham Street."

"Yes," the pudgy man said, "but unfortunately, the zoning goes against little roadside businesses like mine on the busy side of the airport." He shook his head at the unfairness of the world. "I was going to close up and go home at seven, but I had a feeling one more prospect might come by."

Streeter looked at the table, saw no items for sale (unless the TV was), and smiled. "I can't really be a prospect, Mr.—?"

"George Elvid," the pudgy man said, standing and extending an equally pudgy hand.

Streeter shook with him. "Dave Streeter. And I can't really be a prospect, because I have no idea what you're selling. At first I thought the sign said hair extension."

"Do you want a hair extension?" Elvid asked, giving him a critical once-over. "I ask because yours seems to be thinning."

"And will soon be gone," Streeter said. "I'm on chemo."

"Oh my. Sorry."

"Thanks. Although what the point of chemo can be ..." He shrugged. Part of him was marveling at how easy it was to say these things to a stranger. He hadn't even told his kids, although Janet knew, of course.

"Not much chance?" Elvid asked. There was simple sympathy in his voice—no more and no less—and Streeter felt his eyes fill with tears. Crying in front of Janet embarrassed him terribly, and he'd only done it twice. Here, with this stranger, it seemed all right. Nonetheless, he took his handkerchief from his back pocket and swiped his eyes with it. A small plane was coming in for a landing. Silhouetted against the red sun, it looked like a moving crucifix.

"No chance is what I'm hearing," Streeter said. "So I guess the chemo is just ... I don't know ..."

"Knee-jerk triage?"

Streeter laughed. "That's it exactly."

"Maybe you ought to consider trading the chemo for extra pain-killers. Or, you could do a little business with me."

"As I started to say, I can't really be a prospect until I know what you're selling."

"Oh, well, most people would call it snake-oil," Elvid said, smiling and bouncing on the balls of his feet behind his table. Streeter noted with some fascination that, although George Elvid was pudgy, his shadow was as thin and sick-looking as Streeter's own. He supposed everyone's shadow started to look sick as sunset approached, especially in August, when the end of the day was long and lingering and somehow not quite pleasant.

"I don't see the bottles," Streeter said.

Elvid tented his fingers on the table and leaned over them, looking suddenly businesslike. "I sell extensions," he said.

"Which makes the name of this particular road fortuitous."

"Never thought of it that way, but I suppose you're right. Although sometimes a cigar is just a smoke and a coincidence is just a coincidence. Everyone wants an extension, Mr. Streeter. If you were a young woman with a love of shopping, I'd offer you a credit extension. If you were a man with a small penis—genetics can be so cruel—I'd offer you a dick extension."

Streeter was amazed and amused by the baldness of it. For the first time in a month—since the diagnosis—he forgot he was suffering from an aggressive and extremely fast-moving form of cancer. "You're kidding."

"Oh, I'm a great kidder, but I never joke about business. I've sold dozens of dick extensions in my time, and was for awhile known in Arizona as Il Penisla Grande. It's true, but, fortunately for me, I neither require nor expect you to believe it. Short men frequently want a height extension. If you did want more hair, Mr. Streeter, I'd be happy to sell you a hair extension."

"Could a man with a big nose—you know, like Jimmy Durante—get a smaller one?"

Elvid shook his head, smiling. "Now you're the one who's kidding. The answer is no. If you need a reduction, you have to go somewhere else. I specialize only in extensions, a very American product. I've sold love extensions, sometimes called potions, to the lovelorn, loan extensions to the cash-strapped—plenty of those in this economy—time extensions to those under some sort of deadline, and once an eye extension to a fellow who wanted to become an Air Force pilot and knew he couldn't pass the vision test."

Streeter was grinning, having fun. He would have said having fun was now out of reach, but life was full of surprises.

Elvid was also grinning, as if they were sharing an excellent joke. "And once," he said, "I swung a reality extension for a painter—very talented man—who was slipping into paranoid schizophrenia. That was expensive."

"How much? Dare I ask?"

"One of the fellow's paintings, which now graces my home. You'd know the name; famous in the Italian Renaissance. You probably studied him if you took an art appreciation course in college."

Streeter continued to grin, but he took a step back, just to be on the safe side. He had accepted the fact that he was going to die, but that didn't mean he wanted to do so today, at the hands of a possible escapee from the Juniper Hill asylum for the criminally insane in Augusta. "So what are we saying? That you're kind of ... I don't know ... immortal?"

"Very long-lived, certainly," Elvid said. "Which brings us to what I can do for you, I believe. You'd probably like a life extension."

"Can't be done, I suppose?" Streeter asked. Mentally he was calculating the distance back to his car, and how long it would take him to get there.

"Of course it can ... for a price."

Streeter, who had played his share of Scrabble in his time, had already imagined the letters of Elvid's name on tiles and rearranged them. "Money? Or are we talking about my soul?"

Elvid flapped his hand and accompanied the gesture with a roguish roll of his eyes. "I wouldn't, as the saying goes, know a soul if it bit me on the buttocks. No, money's the answer, as it usually is. Fifteen per cent of your income over the next fifteen years should do it. An agenting fee, you could call it."

"That's the length of my extension?" Streeter contemplated the idea of fifteen years with wistful greed. It seemed like a very long time, especially when he stacked it next to what actually lay ahead: six months of vomiting, increasing pain, coma, death. Plus an obituary that would undoubtedly include the phrase "after a long and courageous battle with cancer." Yada-yada, as they said on Seinfeld.

Elvid lifted his hands to his shoulders in an expansive who-knows gesture. "Might be twenty. Can't say for sure; this is not rocket science. But if you're expecting immortality, fuggeddaboudit. All I sell is fair extension. Best I can do."

"Works for me," Streeter said. The guy had cheered him up, and if he needed a straight man, Streeter was willing to oblige. Up to a point, anyway. Still smiling, he extended his hand across the card table. "Fifteen per cent, fifteen years. Although I have to tell you, fifteen per cent of an assistant bank manager's salary won't exactly put you behind the wheel of a Rolls-Royce. A Geo, maybe, but—"

"That's not quite all," Elvid said.

"Of course it isn't," Streeter said. He sighed and withdrew his hand. "Mr. Elvid, it's been very nice talking to you, you've put a shine on my evening, which I would have thought was impossible, and I hope you get help with your mental prob—"

"Hush, you stupid man," Elvid said, and although he was still smiling, there was nothing pleasant about it now. He suddenly seemed taller—at least three inches taller—and not so pudgy.

It's the light, Streeter thought. Sunset light is tricky. And the unpleasant smell he suddenly noticed was probably nothing but burnt aviation fuel, carried to this little graveled square outside the Cyclone fence by an errant puff of wind. It all made sense ... but he hushed as instructed.

"Why does a man or woman need an extension? Have you ever asked yourself that?"

"Of course I have," Streeter said with a touch of asperity. "I work in a bank, Mr. Elvid—Derry Savings. People ask me for loan extensions all the time."

"Then you know that people need extensions to compensate for shortfalls—short credit, short dick, short sight, et cetera."

"Yeah, it's a short-ass world," Streeter said.

"Just so. But even things not there have weight. Negative weight, which is the worst kind. Weight lifted from you must go somewhere else. It's simple physics. Psychic physics, we could say."

Streeter studied Elvid with fascination. That momentary impression that the man was taller (and that there were too many teeth inside his smile) had gone. This was just a short, rotund fellow who probably had a yellow outpatient card in his wallet—if not from Juniper Hill, then from Acadia Mental Health in Bangor. If he had a wallet. He certainly had an extremely well-developed delusional geography, and that made him a fascinating study.

"Can I cut to the chase, Mr. Streeter?"

"Please."

"You have to transfer the weight. In words of one syllable, you have to do the dirty to someone else if the dirty is to be lifted from you."

"I see." And he did. Elvid was back on message, and the message was a classic.

"But it can't be just anyone. The old anonymous sacrifice has been tried, and it doesn't work. It has to be someone you hate. Is there someone you hate, Mr. Streeter?"

"I'm not too crazy about Kim Jong-il," Streeter said. "And I think jail's way too good for the bastards who blew up the USS Cole, but I don't suppose they'll ever—"

"Be serious or begone," Elvid said, and once again he seemed taller. Streeter wondered if this could be some peculiar side-effect of the medications he was taking.

"If you mean in my personal life, I don't hate anyone. There are people I don't like—Mrs. Denbrough next door puts out her garbage cans without the lids, and if a wind is blowing, crap ends up all over my law—"

"If I may misquote the late Dino Martino, Mr. Streeter, everybody hates somebody sometime."

"Will Rogers said—"

"He was a rope-twirling fabricator who wore his hat down around his eyes like a little kid playing cowboy. Besides, if you really hate nobody, we can't do business."

Streeter thought it over. He looked down at his shoes and spoke in a small voice he hardly recognized as his own. "I suppose I hate Tom Goodhugh." Although there was actually no suppose about it.

"Who is he in your life?"

Streeter sighed. "My best friend since grammar school."

There was a moment of silence before Elvid began bellowing laughter. He strode around his card table, clapped Streeter on the back (with a hand that felt cold and fingers that felt long and thin rather than short and pudgy), then strode back to his folding chair. He collapsed into it, still snorting and roaring. His face was red, and the tears streaming down his face also looked red—bloody, actually—in the sunset light.

"Your best ... since grammar ... oh, that's ..."

Elvid could manage no more. He went into gales and howls and gut-shaking spasms, his chin (strangely sharp for such a chubby face) nodding and dipping at the innocent (but darkening) summer sky. At last he got himself under control. Streeter thought about offering his handkerchief, and decided he didn't want it on the extension-salesman's skin.

"This is excellent, Mr. Streeter," he said. "We can do business."

"Gee, that's great," Streeter said, taking another step back. "I'm enjoying my extra fifteen years already. But I'm parked in the bike lane, and that's a traffic violation. I could get a ticket."

"I wouldn't worry about that," Elvid said. "As you may have noticed, not even a single civilian car has come along since we started dickering, let alone a minion of the Derry PD. Traffic never interferes when I get down to serious dealing with a serious man or woman; I see to it."

Streeter looked around uneasily. It was true. He could hear traffic over on Witcham Street, headed for Upmile Hill, but here, Derry was utterly deserted. Of course, he reminded himself, traffic's always light over here when the working day is done.

But absent? Completely absent? You might expect that at midnight, but not at seven-thirty PM.

"Tell me why you hate your best friend," Elvid invited.

Streeter reminded himself again that this man was crazy. Anything Elvid passed on wouldn't be believed. It was a liberating idea.

"Tom was better looking when we were kids, and he's far better looking now. He lettered in three sports; the only one I'm even halfway good at is miniature golf."

"I don't think they have a cheerleading squad for that one," Elvid said.

Streeter smiled grimly, warming to his subject. "Tom's plenty smart, but he lazed his way through Derry High. His college ambitions were nil. But when his grades fell enough to put his athletic eligibility at risk, he'd panic. And then who got the call?"

"You did!" Elvid cried. His voice was rich with jovial commiseration. "Old Mr. Responsible! Tutored him, did you? Maybe wrote a few papers as well? Making sure to misspell the words Tom's teachers got used to him misspelling?"

"Guilty as charged. In fact, when we were seniors—the year Tom got the State of Maine Sportsman award—I was really two students: Dave Streeter and Tom Goodhugh."

"Tough."

"Do you know what's tougher? I had a girlfriend. Beautiful girl named Norma Witten. Dark brown hair and eyes, flawless skin, beautiful cheekbones—"

"Tits that wouldn't quit—"

"Yes indeed. But, sex appeal aside—"

"Not that you ever did put it aside—"

"—I loved that girl. Do you know what Tom did?"

"Stole her from you!" Elvid said indignantly.

"Correct. The two of them came to me, you know. Made a clean breast of it."

"Noble!"

"Claimed they couldn't help it."

"Claimed they were in love, L-U-V."

"Yes. Force of nature. This thing is bigger than both of us. And so on."

"Let me guess. He knocked her up."

"Indeed he did." Streeter was looking at his shoes again, remembering a certain skirt Norma had worn when she was a sophomore or a junior. It was cut to show just a flirt of the slip beneath. That had been almost thirty years ago, but sometimes he still summoned that image to mind when he and Janet made love. He had never made love with Norma—not the Full Monty sort, anyway; she wouldn't allow it. Although she had been eager enough to drop her pants for Tom Goodhugh. Probably the first time he asked her.

"And left her with a bun in the oven."

"No." Streeter sighed. "He married her."

"Then divorced her! Possibly after beating her silly?"

"Worse still. They're still married. Three kids. When you see them walking in Bassey Park, they're usually holding hands."

"That's about the crappiest thing I've ever heard. Not much could make it worse. Unless ..." Elvid looked shrewdly at Streeter from beneath bushy brows. "Unless you're the one who finds himself frozen in the iceberg of a loveless marriage."

"Not at all," Streeter said, surprised by the idea. "I love Janet very much, and she loves me. The way she's stood by me during this cancer thing has been just extraordinary. If there's such a thing as harmony in the universe, then Tom and I ended up with the right partners. Absolutely. But ..."

"But?" Elvid looked at him with delighted eagerness.

Streeter became aware that his fingernails were sinking into his palms. Instead of easing up, he bore down harder. Bore down until he felt trickles of blood. "But he fucking stole her!" This had been eating him for years, and it felt good to shout the news.

"Indeed he did, and we never cease wanting what we want, whether it's good for us or not. Wouldn't you say so, Mr. Streeter?"

Streeter made no reply. He was breathing hard, like a man who has just dashed fifty yards or engaged in a street scuffle. Hard little balls of color had surfaced in his formerly pale cheeks.

"And is that all?" Elvid spoke in the tones of a kindly parish priest.

"No."

"Get it all out, then. Drain that blister."

"He's a millionaire. He shouldn't be, but he is. In the late eighties—not long after the flood that damn near wiped this town out—he started up a garbage company ... only he called it Derry Waste Removal and Recycling. Nicer name, you know."

"Less germy."

"He came to me for the loan, and although the proposition looked shaky to everyone at the bank, I pushed it through. Do you know why I pushed it through, Elvid?"

"Of course! Because he's your friend!"

"Guess again."

"Because you thought he'd crash and burn."

"Right. He sank all his savings into four garbage trucks, and mortgaged his house to buy a piece of land out by the Newport town line. For a landfill. The kind of thing New Jersey gangsters own to wash their dope-and-whore money and use as body-dumps. I thought it was crazy and I couldn't wait to write the loan. He still loves me like a brother for it. Never fails to tell people how I stood up to the bank and put my job on the line. 'Dave carried me, just like in high school,' he says. Do you know what the kids in town call his landfill now?"

"Tell me!"

"Mount Trashmore! It's huge! I wouldn't be surprised if it was radioactive! It's covered with sod, but there are KEEP OUT signs all around it, and there's probably a Rat Manhattan under that nice green grass! They're probably radioactive, as well!"

He stopped, aware that he sounded ridiculous, not caring. Elvid was insane, but—surprise! Streeter had turned out to be insane, too! At least on the subject of his old friend. Plus ...

In cancer veritas, Streeter thought.

"So let's recap." Elvid began ticking off the points on his fingers, which were not long at all but as short, pudgy, and inoffensive as the rest of him. "Tom Goodhugh was better looking that you, even when you were children. He was gifted with athletic skills you could only dream of. The girl who kept her smooth white thighs closed in the back seat of your car opened them for Tom. He married her. They are still in love. Children okay, I suppose?"

"Healthy and beautiful!" Streeter spat. "One getting married, one in college, one in high school! That one's captain of the football team! Chip off the old fucking block!"

"Right. And—the cherry on the chocolate sundae—he's rich and you're knocking on through life at a salary of sixty thousand or so a year."

"I got a bonus for writing his loan," Streeter muttered. "For showing vision."

"But what you actually wanted was a promotion."

"How do you know that?"

"I'm a businessman now, but at one time I was a humble salaryman. Got fired before striking out on my own. Best thing that ever happened to me. I know how these things go. Anything else? Might as well get it all off your chest."

"He drinks Spotted Hen Microbrew!" Streeter shouted. "Nobody in Derry drinks that pretentious shit! Just him! Just Tom Goodhugh, the Garbage King!"

"Does he have a sports car?" Elvid spoke quietly, the words lined with silk.

"No. If he did, I could at least joke with Janet about sports car menopause. He drives a goddam Range Rover."

"I think there might be one more thing," Elvid said. "If so, you might as well get that off your chest, too."

"He doesn't have cancer." Streeter almost whispered it. "He's fifty-one, just like me, and he's as healthy ... as a fucking ... horse."

"So are you," Elvid said.

"What?"

"It's done, Mr. Streeter. Or, since I've cured your cancer, at least temporarily, may I call you Dave?"

"You're a very crazy man," Streeter said, not without admiration.

"No, sir. I'm as sane as a straight line. But notice I said temporarily. We are now in the 'try it, you'll buy it' stage of our relationship. It will last a week at least, maybe ten days. I urge you to visit your doctor. I think he'll find remarkable improvement in your condition. But it won't last. Unless ..."

"Unless?"

Elvid leaned forward, smiling chummily. His teeth again seemed too many (and too big) for his inoffensive mouth. "I come out here from time to time," he said. "Usually at this time of day."

"Just before sunset."

"Exactly. Most people don't notice me—they look through me as if I wasn't there—but you'll be looking. Won't you?"

"If I'm better, I certainly will," Streeter said.

"And you'll bring me something."

Elvid's smile widened, and Streeter saw a wonderful, terrible thing: the man's teeth weren't just too big or too many. They were sharp.

Janet was folding clothes in the laundry room when he got back. "There you are," she said. "I was starting to worry. Did you have a nice drive?"

"Yes," he said. He surveyed his kitchen. It looked different. It looked like a kitchen in a dream. Then he turned on a light, and that was better. Elvid was the dream. Elvid and his promises. Just a loony on a day-pass from Acadia Mental.

She came to him and kissed his cheek. She was flushed from the heat of the dryer and very pretty. She was fifty herself, but looked years younger. Streeter thought she would probably have a fine life after he died. He guessed May and Justin might have a stepdaddy in their future.

"You look good," she said. "You've actually got some color."

"Do I?"

"You do." She gave him an encouraging smile that was troubled just beneath. "Come talk to me while I fold the rest of these things. It's so boring."

He followed her and stood in the door of the laundry room. He knew better than to offer help; she said he even folded dish-wipers the wrong way.

"Justin called," she said. "He and Carl are in Venice. At a youth hostel. He said their cab-driver spoke very good English. He's having a ball."

"Great."

"You were right to keep the diagnosis to yourself," she said. "You were right and I was wrong."

"A first in our marriage."

She wrinkled her nose at him. "Jus has so looked forward to this trip. But you'll have to fess up when he gets back. May's coming up from Searsport for Gracie's wedding, and that would be the right time." Gracie was Gracie Goodhugh, Tom and Norma's oldest child. Carl Goodhugh, Justin's traveling companion, was the one in the middle.

"We'll see," Streeter said. He had one of his puke-bags in his back pocket, but he had never felt less like upchucking. Something he did feel like was eating. For the first time in days.

Nothing happened out there—you know that, right? This is just a little psychosomatic elevation. It'll recede.

"Like my hairline," he said.

"What, honey?"

"Nothing."

"Oh, and speaking of Gracie, Norma called. She reminded me it was their turn to have us to dinner at their place Thursday night. I said I'd ask you, but that you were awfully busy at the bank, working late hours, all this bad-mortgage stuff. I didn't think you'd want to see them."

Her voice was as normal and as calm as ever, but all at once she began crying big storybook tears that welled in her eyes and then went rolling down her cheeks. Love grew humdrum in the later years of a marriage, but now his swelled up as fresh as it had been in the early days, the two of them living in a crappy apartment on Kansas Street and sometimes making love on the living room rug. He stepped into the laundry room, took the shirt she was folding out of her hands, and hugged her. She hugged him back, fiercely.

"This is just so hard and unfair," she said. "We'll get through it. I don't know how, but we will."

"That's right. And we'll start by having dinner on Thursday night with Tom and Norma, just like we always do."

She drew back, looking at him with her wet eyes. "Are you going to tell them?"

"And spoil dinner? Nope."

"Will you even be able to eat? Without ..." She put two fingers to her closed lips, puffed her cheeks, and crossed her eyes: a comic puke-pantomime that made Streeter grin.

"I don't know about Thursday, but I could eat something now," he said. "Would you mind if I rustled myself up a hamburger? Or I could go out to McDonalds ... maybe bring you back a coffee shake ..."

"My God," she said, and wiped her eyes. "It's a miracle."

"I wouldn't call it a miracle, exactly," Dr. Henderson told Streeter on Wednesday afternoon. "But ..."

It was two days since Streeter had discussed matters of life and death under Mr. Elvid's yellow umbrella, and a day before the Streeters' weekly dinner with the Goodhughs, this time to take place at the sprawling residence Streeter sometimes thought of as The House That Trash Built. The conversation was taking place not in Dr. Henderson's office, but in a small consultation room at Derry Home Hospital. Henderson had tried to discourage the MRI, telling Streeter that his insurance wouldn't cover it and the results were sure to be disappointing. Streeter had insisted.

"But what, Roddy?"

"The tumors appear to have shrunk, and your lungs seem clear. I've never seen such a result, and neither have the two other docs I brought in to look at the images. More important—this is just between you and me—the MRI tech has never seen anything like it, and those are the guys I really trust. He thinks it's probably a computer malfunction in the machine itself."

"I feel good, though," Streeter said, "which is why I asked for the test. Is that a malfunction?"

"Are you vomiting?"

"I have a couple of times," Streeter admitted, "but I think that's the chemo. I'm calling a halt to it, by the way."

Roddy Henderson frowned. "That's very unwise."

"The unwise thing was starting it in the first place, my friend. You say, 'Sorry, Dave, the chances of you dying before you get a chance to say Happy Valentine's Day are in the ninetieth percentile, so we're going to fuck up the time you have left by filling you full of poison. You might feel worse if I injected you with sludge from Tom Goodhugh's landfill, but probably not.' And like a fool, I said okay."

Henderson looked offended. "Chemo is the last best hope for—"

"Don't bullshit a bullshitter," Streeter said with a goodnatured grin. He drew a deep breath that went all the way down to the bottom of his lungs. It felt wonderful. "When the cancer's aggressive, chemo isn't for the patient. It's just an agony surcharge the patient pays so that when he's dead, the doctors and relatives can hug each other over the coffin and say 'We did everything we could.'"

"That's harsh," Henderson said. "You know you're apt to relapse, don't you?"

"Tell that to the tumors," Streeter said. "The ones that are no longer there."

Henderson looked at the images of Deepest Darkest Streeter that were still flicking past at twenty-second intervals on the conference room's monitor and sighed. They were good pictures, even Streeter knew that, but they seemed to make his doctor unhappy.

"Relax, Roddy." Streeter spoke gently, as he might once have spoken to May or Justin when a favorite toy got lost or broken. "Shit happens; sometimes miracles happen, too. I read it in The Reader's Digest."

"In my experience, one has never happened in an MRI tube." Henderson picked up a pen and tapped it against Streeter's file, which had fattened considerably over the last three months.

"There's a first time for everything," Streeter said.

Thursday evening in Derry; dusk of a summer night. The declining sun casting its red and dreamy rays over the three perfectly clipped, watered, and landscaped acres Tom Goodhugh had the temerity to call "the old back yard." Streeter sat in a lawn chair on the patio, listening to the rattle of plates and the laughter of Janet and Norma as they loaded the dishwasher.

Yard? It's not a yard, it's a Shopping Channel fan's idea of heaven.

There was even a fountain with a marble child standing in the middle of it. Somehow it was the bare-ass cherub (pissing, of course) that offended Streeter the most. He was sure it had been Norma's idea—she had gone back to college to get a liberal arts degree, and had half-assed classical pretensions—but still, to see such a thing here in the dying glow of a perfect Maine evening and know its presence was a result of Tom's garbage monopoly ...

And, speak of the devil (or the Elvid, if you like that better, Streeter thought), enter the Garbage King himself, with the necks of two sweating bottles of Spotted Hen Microbrew caught between the fingers of his left hand. Slim and erect in his open-throated Oxford shirt and faded jeans, his lean face perfectly lit by the sunset glow, Tom Goodhugh looked like a model in a magazine beer ad. Streeter could even see the copy: Live the good life, reach for a Spotted Hen.

"Thought you might like a fresh one, since your beautiful wife says she's driving."

"Thanks." Streeter took one of the bottles, tipped it to his lips, and drank. Prententious or not, it was good.

As Goodhugh sat down, Jacob the football player came out with a plate of cheese and crackers. He was as broad-shouldered and handsome as Tom had been back in the day. Probably has cheerleaders crawling all over him, Streeter thought. Probably has to beat them off with a damn stick.

"Mom thought you might like these," Jacob said.

"Thanks, Jake. You going out?"

"Just for a little while. Throw the Frisbee with some guys down in The Barrens until it gets dark, then study."

"Stay on this side. There's poison ivy down there since the crap grew back."

"Yeah, we know. Denny caught it when we were in junior high, and it was so bad his mother thought he had cancer."

"Ouch!" Streeter said.

"Drive home carefully, son. No hot-dogging."

"You bet." The boy put an arm around his father and kissed his cheek with a lack of self-consciousness that Streeter found depressing. Tom not only had his health, a still-gorgeous wife, and a ridiculous backyard spread that included a pissing cherub; he had a handsome eighteen year-old son who still felt all right about kissing his Dad goodbye before going out with his best buds.

"He's a good boy," Goodhugh said fondly, watching Jacob mount the stairs to the house and disappear inside. "Studies hard and makes his grades, unlike his old man. Luckily for me, I had you."

"Lucky for both of us," Streeter said, smiling and putting a goo of Brie on a Triscuit. He popped it into his mouth.

"Does me good to see you eating, chum," Goodhugh said. "Me n Norma were starting to wonder if there was something wrong with you."

"Never better," Streeter said, and drank some more of the tasty (and no doubt ridiculously expensive) beer. "I've been losing my hair in front, though. Jan says it makes me look thinner."

"That's one thing the ladies don't have to worry about," Goodhugh said, and stroked a hand back through his own locks, which were as full and rich as they had been at eighteen. Not a touch of gray in them, either. Janet Streeter could still look forty on a good day, but in the red light of the declining sun, the Garbage King looked thirty-five. He didn't smoke, he didn't drink to excess, and he worked out at a health club that did business with Streeter's bank but which Streeter could not afford himself. His middle child, Carl, was currently doing the European thing with Justin Streeter, the two of them traveling on Carl Goodhugh's dime. Which was, of course, actually the Garbage King's dime.

O man who has everything, thy name is Goodhugh, Streeter thought, and smiled at his old friend.

His old friend smiled back, and touched the neck of his beer-bottle to Streeter's. "Life is good, wouldn't you say?"

"Very good," Streeter agreed. "Long days and pleasant nights."

Goodhugh raised his eyebrows. "Where'd you get that?"

"Made it up, I guess," Streeter said. "But it's true, isn't it?"

"If it is, I owe a lot of my pleasant nights to you," Goodhugh said. "It has crossed my mind, old buddy, that I owe you my life." He toasted his ridiculous back yard. "The tenderloin part of it, anyway."

"Nah, you're a self-made man."

Goodhugh lowered his voice and spoke confidentially. "Want the truth? The woman made this man. The Bible says 'Who can find a good woman? For her price is above rubies.' Something like that, anyway. And you introduced us. Don't know if you remember that."

Streeter felt a sudden and almost irresistible urge to smash his beer bottle on the patio bricks and shove the jagged and still foaming neck into his old friend's eyes. He smiled instead, sipped a little more beer, then stood up. "Think I need to pay a little visit to the facility."

"You don't buy beer, you only rent it," Goodhugh said, then burst out laughing. As if he had invented this himself, right on the spot.

"Truer words, et cetera," Streeter said. "Excuse me."

"You really are looking better," Goodhugh called after him as Streeter mounted the steps.

"Thanks," Streeter said. "Old buddy."

He closed the bathroom door, pushed in the locking button, turned on the lights, and—for the first time in his life—swung open the medicine cabinet door in another person's house. The first thing his eye lighted on cheered him immensely: a tube of Just For Men shampoo. There were also a few prescription bottles.

Streeter thought, People who leave their drugs in a bathroom the guests use are just asking for trouble. Not that there was anything sensational: Norma had asthma medicine; Tom was taking blood pressure medicine—Atenolol—and using some sort of skin cream.

The Atenolol bottle was half full. Streeter took one of the tablets, tucked it into the watch-pocket of his jeans, and flushed the toilet. Then he left the bathroom, feeling like a man who has just snuck across the border of a strange and dangerous country.

The following evening was overcast, but George Elvid was still sitting beneath the yellow umbrella and once again watching Inside Edition on his portable TV. The lead story had to do with Whitney Houston, who had lost a suspicious amount of weight shortly after signing a huge new recording contract. Elvid disposed of this rumor with a twist of his pudgy fingers and regarded Streeter with a smile.

"How have you been feeling, Dave?"

"Better."

"Yes?"

"Yes."

"Vomiting?"

"Not today."

"Eating?"

"Like a horse."

"And I'll bet you've had some medical tests."

"How did you know?"

"I'd expect no less of a successful bank official. Did you bring me something?"

For a moment Streeter considered walking away. He really did. Then he reached into the pocket of the light jacket he was wearing (the evening was chilly for August, and he was still on the thin side) and brought out a tiny square of Kleenex. He hesitated, then handed it across the table to Elvid, who unwrapped it.

"Ah, Atenolol," Elvid said. He popped the pill into his mouth and swallowed.

Streeter's mouth opened, then closed slowly.

"Don't look so shocked," Elvid said. "If you had a high-stress job like mine, you'd have blood pressure problems, too. And the reflux I suffer from, oy. You don't want to know."

"What happens now?" Streeter asked. Even in the jacket, he felt cold.

"Now?" Elvid looked surprised. "Now you start enjoying your fifteen years of good health. Possibly twenty or even twenty-five. Who knows?"

"And happiness?"

Elvid favored him with the roguish look. It would have been amusing if not for the coldness Streeter saw just beneath. And the age. In that moment he felt certain that George Elvid had been doing business for a very long time, reflux or no reflux. "The happiness part is up to you, Dave. And your family, of course—Janet, May, and Justin."

Had he told Elvid their names? Streeter couldn't remember.

"Perhaps the children most of all. There's an old saying to the effect that children are our hostages to fortune, but in fact it's the children who take the parents hostage, that's what I think. One of them could have a fatal or disabling accident on a deserted country road ... fall prey to a debilitating disease ..."

"Are you saying—"

"No, no, no! This isn't some half-assed morality tale. I'm a businessman, not a character out of 'The Devil and Daniel Webster.' All I'm saying is that your happiness is in your hands and those of your nearest and dearest. And if you think I'm going to show up two decades or so down the line to collect your soul in my moldy old pocketbook, you'd better think again. Besides, the souls of humans have become poor and transparent things."

He spoke, Streeter thought, as the fox might have done after repeated leaps had proved to it that the grapes were really and truly out of reach. But Streeter had no intention of saying such a thing. Now that the deal was done, all he wanted to do was get out of here. But still he lingered, not wanting to ask the question that was on his mind but knowing he had to. Because there was no gift-giving going on here; Streeter had been making deals in the bank for most of his life, and he knew a horse-trade when he saw one. Or when he smelled it: a faint, unpleasant stink like burned aviation fuel.

In words of one syllable, you have to do the dirty to someone else if the dirty is to be lifted from you.

But stealing a single hypertension pill wasn't exactly doing the dirty. Was it?

Elvid, meanwhile, was yanking his big umbrella closed. And when it was furled, Streeter observed an amazing and disheartening fact: it wasn't yellow at all. It was as gray as the sky. Summer was almost over.

"Most of my clients are perfectly satisfied, perfectly happy. Is that what you want to hear?"

It was .. .and wasn't.

"I sense you have a more pertinent question," Elvid said. "If you want an answer, quit beating around the bush and ask it. It's going to rain, and I want to get undercover before it does. The last thing I need at my age is bronchitis."

"Where's your car?"

"Oh, was that your question?" Elvid sneered openly at him. His cheeks were lean, not in the least pudgy, and his eyes turned up at the corners, where the whites shaded to an unpleasant and—yes, it was true—cancerous black. He looked like the world's least pleasant clown, with half his makeup removed.

"Your teeth," Streeter said stupidly. "They have points."

"Your question, Mr. Streeter!"

"Is Tom Goodhugh going to get cancer?"

Elvid gaped for a moment, then started to giggle. The sound was wheezy, dusty, and unpleasant—like a dying calliope.

"No, Dave," he said. "Tom Goodhugh isn't going to get cancer. Not him."

"What, then? What?"

The contempt with which Elvid surveyed him made Streeter's bones feel weak—as if holes had been eaten in them by some painless but terribly corrosive acid. "Why would you care? You hate him, you said so yourself."

"But—"

"Watch. Wait. Enjoy. And take this." He handed Streeter a business card. Written on it was THE NON-SECTARIAN CHILDREN'S FUND and the address of a bank in the Cayman Islands.

"Tax haven," Elvid said. "You'll send my fifteen per cent there. If you short me, I'll know. And then woe is you, kiddo."

"What if my wife finds out and asks questions?"

"Your wife has a personal checkbook. Beyond that, she never looks at a thing. She trusts you. Am I right?"

"Well ..." Streeter observed with no surprise that the raindrops striking Elvid's hands and arms smoked and sizzled. "Yes."

"Of course I am. Our dealing is done. Get out of here and go back to your wife. I'm sure she'll welcome you with open arms. Take her to bed. Stick your mortal penis in her and pretend she's your best friend's wife. You don't deserve her, but lucky you."

"I want to take it back," Streeter whispered.

Elvid favored him with a stony smile that revealed a jutting ring of cannibal teeth. "You can't," he said.

That was in August of 2001, less than a month before the fall of the Towers.

In December (on the same day Winona Ryder was busted for shoplifting, in fact), Dr. Roderick Henderson proclaimed Dave Streeter cancer-free—and, in addition, a bona fide miracle of the modern age.

"I have no explanation for this," Henderson said.

Streeter did, but kept his silence.

Their consultation took place in Henderson's office. At Derry Home Hospital, in the conference room where Streeter had looked at the first pictures of his miraculously cured body, Norma Goodhugh sat in the same chair where Streeter had sat, looking at less pleasant MRI scans. She listened numbly as her doctor told her—as gently as possible—that the lump in her left breast was indeed cancer, and it had spread to her lymph nodes.

"The situation is bad, but not hopeless," the doctor said, reaching across the table to take Norma's cold hand. He smiled. "We'll want to start you on chemotherapy immediately."

In June of the following year, Streeter finally got his promotion. May Streeter was admitted to the Columbia School of Journalism grad school. Streeter and his wife took a long-deferred Hawaii vacation to celebrate. They made love many times. On their last day in Maui, Tom Goodhugh called. The connection was bad and he could hardly talk, but the message got through: Norma had died.

"We'll be there for you," Streeter promised.

When he told Janet the news, she collapsed on the hotel bed, weeping with her hands over her face. Streeter lay down beside her, held her close, and thought: Well, we were going home, anyway. And although he felt bad about Norma (and sort of bad for Tom), there was an upside: they had missed bug season, which could be a bitch in Derry.

In December, Streeter sent a check for just over fifteen thousand dollars to The Non-Sectarian Children's Fund. He took it as a deduction on his tax return.

In 2003, Justin Streeter made the Dean's List at Brown and—as a lark—invented a video game called Walk Fido Home. The object of the game was to get your leashed dog back from the mall while avoiding bad drivers, objects falling from tenth-story balconies, and a pack of crazed old ladies who called themselves The Canine-Killing Grannies. To Streeter it sounded like a joke (and Justin assured them it was meant as a satire), but Games, Inc. took one look and paid their handsome, good-humored son seven hundred and fifty thousand dollars for the rights. Plus royalties. Jus bought his parents matching Toyota Pathfinder SUVs, pink for the lady, blue for the gentleman. Janet wept and hugged him and called him a foolish, impecunious, generous, and altogether splendid boy. Streeter took him to Roxie's Tavern and bought him a Spotted Hen Microbrew.

In October, Carl Goodhugh's roommate at Emerson came back from class to find Carl facedown on the kitchen floor of their apartment with the grilled cheese sandwich he'd been making for himself still smoking in the frypan. Although only twenty-two years of age, Carl had suffered a heart attack. The doctors attending the case pinpointed a congenital heart defect—something about a thin atrial wall—that had gone undetected. Carl didn't die; his roommate got to him just in time and knew CPR. But he suffered oxygen deprivation, and the bright, handsome, physically agile young man who had not long before toured Europe with Justin Streeter became a shuffling shadow of his former self. He was not always continent, he got lost if he wandered more than a block or two from home (he had moved back with his still-grieving father), and his speech had become a blurred blare than only Tom could understand. Goodhugh hired a companion for him. The companion administered physical therapy and saw that Carl changed his clothes. He also took Carl on bi-weekly "outings." The most common "outing" was to Wishful Dishful Ice Cream, where Carl would always get a pistachio cone and smear it all over his face. Afterward the companion would clean him up, patiently, with Wet Naps.

Janet stopped going with Streeter to dinner at Tom's. "I can't bear it," she confessed. "It's not the way Carl shuffles, or how he sometimes wets his pants—it's the look in his eyes, as if he remembers how he was, and can't quite remember how he got to where he is now. And ... I don't know ... there's always something hopeful in his face that makes me feel like everything in life is a joke."

Streeter knew what she meant, and often considered the idea during his dinners with his old friend (without Norma to cook, it was now mostly takeout). He enjoyed watching Tom feed his damaged son, and he enjoyed the hopeful look on Carl's face. The one that said, "This is all a dream I'm having, and soon I'll wake up." Jan was right, it was a joke, but it was sort of a good joke.

If you really thought about it.

In 2004, May Streeter got a job with the Boston Globe and declared herself the happiest girl in the USA. Justin Streeter created Rock the House, which would be a perennial bestseller until the advent of Guitar Hero made it obsolete. By then Jus had moved on to a music composition computer program called You Moog Me, Baby. Streeter himself was appointed manager of his bank branch, and there were rumors of a regional post in his future. He took Janet to Cancun, and they had a fabulous time. She began calling him "my nuzzle-bunny."

Tom's accountant at Goodhugh Waste Removal embezzled two million dollars and departed for parts unknown. The subsequent accounting review revealed that the business was on very shaky ground; that bad old accountant had been nibbling away for years, it seemed.

Nibbling? Streeter thought, reading the story in The Derry News. Taking it a chomp at a time is more like it.

Tom no longer looked thirty-five; he looked sixty. And must have known it, because he stopped dying his hair. Streeter was delighted to see that it hadn't gone white underneath the artificial color; Goodhugh's hair was the dull and listless gray of Elvid's umbrella when he had furled it. The hair-color, Streeter decided, of the old men you see sitting on park benches and feeding the pigeons. Call it Just For Losers.

In 2005, Jacob the football player, who had gone to work in his father's dying company instead of to college (which he could have attended on a full-boat athletic scholarship), met a girl and got married. Bubbly little brunette named Cammy Dorrington. Streeter and his wife agreed it was a beautiful ceremony, even though Carl Streeter hooted, gurgled, and burbled all the way through it, and even though Goodhugh's oldest child—Gracie—tripped over the hem of her dress on the church steps as she was leaving, fell down, and broke her leg in two places. Until that happened, Tom Goodhugh had looked almost like his former self. Happy, in other words. Streeter did not begrudge him a little happiness. He supposed that even in hell, people got an occasional sip of water, if only so they could appreciate the full horror of unrequited thirst when it set in again.

The honeymooning couple went to Belize. I'll bet it rains the whole time, Streeter thought. It didn't, but Jacob spent most of the week in a run-down hospital, suffering from violent gastroenteritis and pooping into paper didies. He had only drunk bottled water, but then forgot and brushed his teeth from the tap. "My own darn fault," he said.

Over eight hundred US troops died in Iraq. Bad luck for those boys and girls.

Tom Goodhugh began to suffer from gout, developed a limp, started using a cane.

That year's check to The Non-Sectarian Children's Fund was of an extremely good size, but Streeter didn't begrudge it. It was more blessed to give than to receive. All the best people said so.

In 2006, Tom's daughter Gracie fell victim to pyorrhea and lost all her teeth. She also lost her sense of smell. One night shortly thereafter, at Goodhugh and Streeter's weekly dinner (it was just the two men; Carl's attendant had taken Carl on an "outing"), Tom Goodhugh broke down in tears. He had given up microbrews in favor of Bombay Gin, and he was very drunk. "I don't understand what's happened to me!" he sobbed. "I feel like ... I don't know ... fucking Job!"

Streeter took him in his arms and comforted him. He told his old friend that clouds always roll in, and sooner or later they always roll out.

"Well, these clouds have been here a fuck of a long time!" Goodhugh cried, and thumped Streeter on the back with a closed fist. Streeter didn't mind. His old friend wasn't as strong as he used to be.

Charlie Sheen, Tori Spelling, and David Hasselhoff got divorces, but in Derry, David and Janet Streeter celebrated their thirtieth wedding anniversary. There was a party. Toward the end of it, Streeter escorted his wife out back. He had arranged fireworks. Everybody applauded except for Carl Streeter. He tried, but kept missing his hands. Finally the former Emerson student gave up on the clapping thing and pointed at the sky, hooting.

In 2007, Kiefer Sutherland went to jail (not for the first time) on DUI charges, and Gracie Goodhugh Dickerson's husband was killed in a car crash. A drunk driver veered into his lane while Andy Dickerson was on his way home from work. The good news was that the drunk wasn't Kiefer Sutherland. The bad news was that Gracie Dickerson was four months pregnant and broke. Her husband had let his life insurance lapse to save on expenses. Gracie moved back in with her father and her brother Carl.

"With their luck, that baby will be born deformed," Streeter said one night as he and his wife lay in bed after making love.

"Hush!" Janet cried, shocked.

"If you say it, it won't come true," Streeter explained, and soon the two nuzzle-bunnies were asleep in each other's arms.

That year's check to the Children's Fund was for thirty thousand dollars. Streeter wrote it without a qualm.

Gracie's baby came at the height of a February snowstorm in 2008. The good news was that it wasn't deformed. The bad news was that it was born dead. That damned family heart defect. Gracie—toothless, husbandless, and unable to smell anything—dropped into a deep depression. Streeter thought that demonstrated her basic sanity. If she had gone around whistling "Don't Worry, Be Happy," he would have advised Tom to lock up all the sharp objects in the house.

A plane carrying two members of the rock band Blink 182 crashed. Bad news, four people died. Good news, the rockers actually survived for a change ... although one of them would later commit suicide.

"I have offended God," Tom said at one of the dinners the two men now called their "bachelor nights." Streeter had brought spaghetti from Cara Mama, and cleaned his plate. Tom Goodhugh barely touched his. In the other room, Gracie and Carl were watching American Idol, Gracie in silence, the former Emerson student hooting and gabbling. "I don't know how, but I have."

"Don't say that, because it isn't true."

"You don't know that."

"I do," Streeter said emphatically. "It's foolish talk."

"If you say so, buddy." Tom's eyes filled with tears. They rolled down his cheeks. One clung to the line of his unshaven jaw, dangled there for a moment, then plinked into his uneaten spaghetti. "Thank God for Jacob. He's all right. Working for a TV station in Boston, and his wife's in accounting at Brigham and Women's. They see May once in awhile."

"Great news," Streeter said heartily, hoping Jake wouldn't somehow contaminate his daughter with his company.

"And you still come and see me. I understand why Jan doesn't, and I don't hold it against her, but ... I look forward to these nights. They're like a link to the old days."

Yes, Streeter thought, the old days when you had everything and I had cancer.

"You'll always have me," he said, and clasped one of Goodhigh's slightly trembling hands in both of his own. "Friends to the end."

2008, what a year! Holy fuck! China hosted the Olympics! Chris Brown and Rihanna became nuzzle-bunnies! Banks collapsed! The stock market tanked! And in November, the EPA closed Mount Trashmore, Tom Goodhugh's last source of income. The government stated its intention to bring suit in matters having to do with ground-water pollution and illegal dumping of medical wastes. The Derry News hinted that there might even be criminal action.

Streeter often drove out along the Harris Avenue Extension in the evenings, looking for a certain yellow umbrella. He didn't want to dicker; he only wanted to shoot the shit. But he never saw the umbrella or its owner. He was disappointed but not surprised. Deal-makers were like sharks; they had to keep moving or they'd die.

He wrote a check and sent it to the bank in the Caymans.

In 2009, Chris Brown beat hell out of his Number One Nuzzle-Bunny after the Grammy Awards, and a few weeks later, Jacob Goodhugh the ex-football player beat hell out of his bubbly wife Cammy after Cammy found a certain lady's undergarment and half a gram of cocaine in Jacob's jacket pocket. Lying on the floor, crying, she called him a son of a bitch. Jacob responded by stabbing her in the abdomen with a meat-fork. He regretted it at once and called 911, but the damage was done; he'd punctured her stomach in two places. He told the police later that he remembered none of this. He was in a blackout, he said.

His lawyer court-appointed was too dumb to get a bail reduction. Jake Goodhugh appealed to his father, who was hardly able to pay his heating bills, let alone provide high-priced Boston legal talent for his spouse-abusing son. Goodhugh turned to Streeter, who didn't let his old friend get a dozen words into his painfully rehearsed speech before saying you bet. He still remembered the way Jacob had so unselfconsciously kissed his old man's cheek. Also, paying the legal fees allowed him to question the lawyer about Jake's mental state, which wasn't good; he was racked with guilt and deeply depressed. The lawyer told Streeter that the boy would probably get five years, hopefully with three of them suspended.

When he gets out, he can go home, Streeter thought. He can watch American Idol with Gracie and Carl, if it's still on. It probably will be.

"I've got my insurance," Tom Goodhugh said one night. He had lost a lot of weight, and his clothes bagged on him. His eyes were bleary. He had developed psoriasis, and scratched restlessly at his arms, leaving long red marks on the white skin. "I'd kill myself if I thought I could get away with making it look like an accident."

"I don't want to hear talk like that," Streeter said. "Things will turn around."

In June, Michael Jackson kicked the bucket. In August, Carl Goodhugh went and did him likewise, choking to death on a piece of apple. The companion might have performed the Heimlich Maneuver and saved him, but the companion had been let go due to lack of funds sixteen months before. Gracie heard Carl gurgling but said she thought "it was just his usual bullshit." The good news was Carl also had life insurance. Just a small policy, but enough to bury him.

After the funeral (Tom Goodhugh sobbed all the way through it, holding onto his old friend for support), Streeter had a generous impulse. He found Kiefer Sutherland's studio address and sent him an AA Big Book. It would probably go right in the trash, he knew (along with the countless other Big Books fans had sent him over the years), but you never knew. Sometimes miracles happened.

In early September of 2009, on a hot summer evening, Streeter and Janet rode out to the road that runs along the back end of Derry's airport. No one was doing business on the graveled square outside the Cyclone fence, so he parked his fine blue Pathfinder there and put his arm around his wife, whom he loved more deeply and completely than ever. The sun was going down in a red ball.

He turned to Janet and saw that she was crying. He tilted her chin toward him and solemnly kissed the tears away. That made her smile.

"What is it, honey?"

"I was thinking about the Goodhughs. I've never known a family to have such a run of bad luck. Bad luck?" She laughed. "Black luck is more like it."

"I haven't, either," he said, "but it happens all the time. One of the women killed in the Mumbai attacks was pregnant, did you know that? Her two-year-old lived, but the kid was beaten within an inch of his life. And—"

She put two fingers to her lips. "Hush. No more. Life's not fair. We know that."

"But it is!" Streeter spoke earnestly. In the sunset light his face was ruddy and healthy. "Just look at me. There was a time when you never thought I'd live to see 2009, isn't that true?"

"Yes, but—"

"And the marriage, still as strong as an oak door. Or am I wrong?"

She shook her head. He wasn't wrong.

"You've started selling freelance pieces to the Derry News, May's going great guns with the Globe, and our son the geek is a media mogul at twenty-five."

She began to smile again. Streeter was glad. He hated to see her blue.

"Life is fair. We all get the same nine-month shake in the box, and then the dice roll. Some people get a run of sevens. Some people, unfortunately, get snake-eyes. It's just how the world is."

She put her arms around him. "I love you, sweetie. You always look on the bright side."

Streeter shrugged modestly. "The law of averages favors optimists, any banker would tell you that. Things have a way of balancing out in the end."

Venus came into view above the airport, glimmering against the darkening blue.

"Wish!" Streeter commanded.

Janet laughed and shook her head. "What would I wish for? I have everything I want."

"Me too," Streeter said, and then, with his eyes fixed firmly on Venus, he wished for more.

ROCKY WOOD, SKELETON KILLER

Jeff Strand

When Rocky Wood was elected President of the Horror Writers Association, the membership knew that he was a typical Australian: completely insane but in a charming way. They also knew that he had superhuman endurance because he was willing to deal with so many whiny writers.

What they did not know is that to reanimated skeletons around the world, he was ... Rocky Wood, Skeleton Killer.

Admittedly, reanimated skeletons didn't pose all that much of a threat to the populace. They weren't like vampires (averaging 47 human victims a week, worldwide), werewolves (38), zombies (33), or even mummies (2). But every once in a while, there'd be some sort of enchantment gone awry, and when the skeleton sprung to life and went on a rampage, Rocky would be there to bludgeon it into bone bits with his trusty club.

Often he would show up unannounced in biology classrooms, where he'd point at the skeleton and shout, "It's coming to life!" and then, after the students were sufficiently startled, he'd laugh and eventually shout, "Just kidding!" Most people found this to be pretty annoying, but they didn't say anything because if the skeleton *did* come to life, they wanted Rocky on their side.

Once, some kids attached wires to a skeleton, and when Rocky came into the classroom, they tugged on the wires to give the impression that the skeleton had come to life. But Rocky was not fooled. He just stood there, shaking his head and clucking his tongue in a disapproving manner. The kids sheepishly let go of the wires, came out of their hiding spots, and returned to their seats. It was very awkward for everybody.

"I wish there were more skeletons to kill," Rocky said to somebody one day.

"But why?" asked the person. "Not only are you President of the HWA, but you've written glorious books about Stephen King! It's a full, rich life! Why kill skeletons?"

Rocky stared at the person, eyes flaring with passion. "Because it needs to be done! I just wish there were more of the bony bastards around."

"Maybe you should kill clowns instead?" somebody suggested.

"That would be murder. I don't *do* murder," said Rocky, finishing his sentence with some amusing Australian slang.

"Not human clowns. The demonic kind."

"Those are even rarer than skeletons."

"Then what about vampires?"

"Lots of people kill vampires."

"Maybe you could kill them in a non-standard manner."

"That's a terrible idea. Who are you, anyway? Get out of my shower!"

Rocky was about three days from falling so far out of practice with his skeleton-killing that he wasn't sure he could even knock one of their heads off anymore ... and then it happened—a skeleton rose from the ground in a major Australian city.

But it wasn't the typical four-foot-ten to six-foot-four skeletons that Rocky was used to fighting. No, this skeleton was *gigantic*. It stood fifty feet tall. It seemed unlikely that King Kong could have been buried in the area without somebody knowing, but that's exactly what the skeleton resembled.

Rocky arrived on the scene and suddenly felt a bit uncomfortable. He'd hoped for more of a middle ground between a complete lack of reanimated skeletons and the King Kong skeleton.

"Save us, Rocky Wood, Skeleton Killer!" shouted the populace.

Rocky really wasn't sure how to go about dispatching his foe. He couldn't just start whacking his club against its leg. No, this was going to require a new technique, brains against bone.

"Hey, skeleton!" he shouted. This sounded like the beginning of some sort of clever plan that might allow him to outsmart the skeleton, though he didn't have the rest of the details worked out yet.

The skeleton looked down at him and then slammed its foot against the pavement. Fortunately, Rocky was nimble enough to avoid being crushed, though he admittedly felt bad for the eight people who were crushed next to him.

Rocky let out an Australian-sounding yelp as the skeleton bent down and swiped at him with its dry white finger bones, missing by the width of an iPhone. This still wasn't as scary as leading a writers' organization, but he had no idea how to defeat the fierce beast.

The skeleton shouted something at him that would have been easier to hear if it had lungs. Then it knocked down a couple of buildings, and Rocky snarled with rage. He knew what to do.

"Oh my goodness!" somebody shouted. "Rocky Wood has just pulled out a copy of *Stephen King: The Non-Fiction!* That book is *huge!*"

With a primal roar, Rocky flung the immense hardcover book right at the skeleton's skull, hitting it right between where its eyes would have been had they not dried up and fallen out. The book exploded into 608 pages and the skull popped right off. The skeleton collapsed.

Everybody cheered.

Rocky helped clean up the rubble from the destroyed buildings, and helped scrape the eight victims off the underside of the skeleton's foot. He was just that kind of guy.

And then he walked off into the Australian sunset, a hero.

Author's note:
Portions of this story have been exaggerated for dramatic effect.

ACKNOWLEDGEMENTS

The following stories were previously published elsewhere:

» "The Gunner's Love Song" by Joe McKinney was first published in Amazon Shorts, 2007.

» "Keeping Watch" by Nate Kenyon was first published in *Monstrous*, ed. Ryan C. Thomas (Permuted Press), 2008.

» "Like Part of the Family" by Jonathan Maberry was first published in *New Blood*, ed. Patrick Thomas & Diane Raetz (Padwolf Press), 2010.

» "The Edge of Seventeen" by Alexandra Sokoloff was first published in *The Darker Mask*, ed. Gary Phillips & Christopher Chambers (Tor), 2008.

» "The View from the Top" by Bev Vincent was first published in *Shroud* #6, 2009.

» "Afterward, There Will Be a Hallway" by Gary A. Braunbeck was first published in *Five Strokes to Midnight*, ed. Gary A. Braunbeck (Haunted Pelican Books), 2007.

» "Following Marla" by John R. Little was first published in *Horror World*, 2009.

» "Magic Numbers" by Gene O'Neill was first published in *Borderlands 5*, ed. Thomas & Elizabeth Monteleone (Borderlands Press), 2004.

» "Tail the Barney" by Stephen M. Irwin was first published in N*ew Millenium Writing*s #18, 2008.

» "Roadside Memorials" by Joseph Nassise was first published in *Lost on the Darkside*, ed. John Pelan (Roc), 2005.

» "Dat Tay Vao" by F. Paul Wilson was first published in *Amazing Stories*, 1987.

» "Constitution" by Scott Nicholson was first published in *Carpe Noctem* #16, 1999.

CONTRIBUTOR

BIOGRAPHIES

Gary A. Braunbeck

Gary A. Braunbeck is a prolific author who writes mysteries, thrillers, science fiction, fantasy, horror, and mainstream literature. He is the author of 19 books; his fiction has been translated into Japanese, French, Italian, Russian and German. Nearly 200 of his short stories have appeared in various publications. Some of his most popular stories are mysteries that have appeared in the *Cat Crimes* anthology series.

He was born in Newark, Ohio; this city that serves as the model for the fictitious Cedar Hill in many of his stories. The Cedar Hill stories are collected in *Graveyard People* and *Home Before Dark*.

His fiction has received several awards, including the Bram Stoker Award for Superior Achievement in Short Fiction in 2003 for "Duty" and in 2005 for "We Now Pause for Station Identification"; his collection *Destinations Unknown* won a Stoker in 2006. His novella "Kiss of the Mudman" received the International Horror Guild Award for Long Fiction in 2005.

He also served a term as president of the Horror Writers Association. He is married to Lucy Snyder, a science fiction/fantasy writer, and they reside together in Columbus, Ohio.

Gary is an adjunct professor at Seton Hill University, Pennsylvania, where he teaches in an innovative Master's degree program in Writing Popular Fiction.

Gary's website is **www.garybraunbeck.com**

Ramsey Campbell

The *Oxford Companion to English Literature* describes Ramsey Campbell as "Britain's most respected living horror writer". He has been given more awards than any other writer in the field, including the Grand Master Award of the World Horror Convention, the Lifetime Achievement Award of the Horror Writers Association, and the Living Legend Award of the International Horror Guild. Among his novels are *The Face That Must Die, Incarnate, Midnight Sun, The Count of Eleven, Silent Children, The Darkest Part of the Woods, The Overnight, Secret Story, The Grin of the Dark, Thieving Fear, Creatures of the Pool, The Seven Days of Cain*, and *Ghosts Know*. Forthcoming is *The Black Pilgrimage*. His collections include *Waking Nightmares, Alone with the Horrors, Ghosts and Grisly Things, Told by the Dead*, and *Just Behind You*, and his non-fiction is collected as *Ramsey Campbell, Probably*. His novels *The Nameless* and *Pact of the Fathers* have been filmed in Spain. His regular columns appear in *Prism, All Hallows, Dead Reckonings*, and *Video Watchdog*. He is the President of the British Fantasy Society and of the Society of Fantastic Films.

Ramsey Campbell lives on Merseyside with his wife Jenny. His pleasures include classical music, good food and wine, and whatever's in that pipe. His web site is at **www.ramseycampbell.com**

David Conyers

David Conyers is a science fiction (and occasional horror) author and editor from Adelaide, South Australia. He has published more than 40 short stories worldwide and been nominated for various awards including the Aeon, Aurealis, Australian Shadows, and Ditmar. With John Sunseri he is the author of *The Spiraling Worm*, a collection of Lovecraftian spy science fiction tales. His other short fiction has appeared in dozens of anthologies and magazines such as *Jupiter, Ticon4, Andromeda Spaceways Inflight Magazine, Book of Dark Wisdom*, and *Innsmouth Free Press*.

As an editor, David is responsible for the anthology *Cthulhu's Dark Cults*, was the co-editor of the anthologies *Cthulhu Unbound 3* and *Undead and Unbound*, and has remained a contributing editor with *Albedo One* magazine since 2007.

With qualifications as civil engineer, David decided early on that this career was not for him, and he now works in marketing as a corporate writer. He is married with one daughter.

His latest publication is *The Eye of Infinity*, a science fiction novella from Perilous Press. David's website is **www.david-conyers.com**

Nancy Holder

New York Times bestselling author Nancy Holder (the Wicked series, co-written with Debbie Viguié) is also a multiple Bram Stoker Award winner and a former trustee of the Horror Writers Association. With her writing partner, Debbie Viguié, she has written three young adult dark fantasy series: *Wicked, Crusade,* and *Wolf Springs.* She is also the author of the young adult horror series, Possessions: *Possessions; The Evil Within*; and *The Screaming Season.* She has written dozens of tie-in projects, including official companion guides for *Buffy the Vampire Slayer, Smallville, Saving Grace, Angel, Hellboy,* and others TV shows and movies. *Saving Grace: Tough Love* has been nominated for a Scribe Award by the International Association of Media Tie-in Writers. She writes the Domino Lady comic for Moonstone, and teaches at the Stonecoast MFA in Creative Writing Program for the University of Southern Maine.

Her latest releases are *Damned,* the second Crusade novel, and the first Wolf Springs novel, *Unleashed.*

Nancy lives in San Diego, California with her daughter, Belle, with whom she has collaborated on two stories for DAW, as well as the aerodynamic corgis Panda and Tater Tot; and a trio of psychic cats: David, Kittnen [sic] Snow Vampire; and McGee.

Nancy can be found online at **www.nancyholder.com**, on Twitter **@nancyholder,** and on Facebook at **www.facebook.com/holder.nancy**

Stephen M. Irwin

Australian novelist and filmmaker Stephen M. Irwin has won acclaim around Australia and the world for his short films and short stories. In 2009, his debut novel—the supernatural thriller *The Dead Path*—was released by Hachette Australia to great acclaim. *The Dead Path* has since been released to outstanding reviews in the UK, the US, Germany, and China. *The Dead Path* was a 2011 Book of the Month Club First Fiction Award winner; it was nominated for the Aurealis, Ned Kelly, and Bram Stoker Awards, and was named Top Horror title in the American Library Association's 2011 reading list. Booklist summed up *The Dead Path* by saying it is 'one of the scariest books of this or any other year'.

Stephen toured Australia in 2009 when *The Dead Path* was named the August selection by The Big Book Club, and was a panellist at the Brisbane Writer's Festival.

Stephen's onset into long form fiction came after many years of work in Australia's film and television industry. He has written and directed several documentaries for Australian television, and is regularly engaged by film and television producers as story editor and screenwriter. He is currently co-writing an adaptation of a noteworthy autobiography into an international action feature film.

Stephen's second thriller novel, *The Broken Ones*, was released in late 2011.

Stephen lives with his wife, two young children, and a quite needy black cat in a pleasantly ghost-free house in Brisbane's inner-west. He can touch type, fix a leaky jumper valve, has memorised his credit card number for impulse purchases, and makes a very passable Mojito.

Stephen's website is **www.stephenmirwin.com**

Gary Kemble

Gary Kemble has published more than 20 short stories in Australia, the UK, and online.

In 2007, his mind-bending time travel tale "Untethered" won $6,000 and a spot in the *One Book Many Brisbanes 3* anthology. He repeated this feat two years later with "Bug Hunt", which benefited from the input of fellow Australian authors Stephen Dedman and Trent Jamieson. He is currently writing a novel with the help of an Australia Council new work grant.

Gary lives on the side of a mountain with his wife, two kids, and a couple of diligent scrub turkeys.

You can find him on Twitter @garykemble and from time to time at The Kemblog **http://garykemblenews.blogspot.com**.

"Dead Air" received an honourable mention in *Year's Best Fantasy and Horror 2008* and was reprinted in *Australian Dark Fantasy and Horror Volume Three* (Brimstone Press).

Nate Kenyon

Nate Kenyon is the award-winning author of *Bloodstone, The Reach, The Bone Factory, Sparrow Rock*, and *Prime*, as well as dozens of short stories. His novel *StarCraft Ghost: Spectres*, based upon the bestselling videogame franchise from Blizzard Entertainment, was released in 2011 from Pocket Books. Kenyon is a three-time Stoker Award Finalist, and two of his novels have been optioned for film. He is currently working on a new novel based on Blizzard's Diablo videogame franchise.

Visit him online at **www.natekenyon.com**.

Daniel G. Keohane

Daniel G. Keohane's first novel, *Solomon's Grave* (2009), was a finalist for the Bram Stoker Award. Since then he has released *Margaret's Ark* (2011) and his next book is *Destroyer of Worlds*. His short stories have been published in a number of major horror magazines and anthologies over the years, including *Cemetery Dance*, *Apex Digest*, *Shroud Magazine*, *Fantastic Stories*, and many others, and have received multiple Honorable Mentions in the annual *Year's Best Fantasy and Horror* and *Best Horror of the Year*.

Dan's website is **www.dankeohane.com**

Stephen King

Stephen King was born in Portland, Maine in 1947, the second son of Donald and Nellie Ruth Pillsbury King. He made his first professional short story sale in 1967 to *Startling Mystery Stories*. In the fall of 1973, he began teaching high school English classes at Hampden Academy, the public high school in Hampden, Maine. Writing in the evenings and on the weekends, he continued to produce short stories and to work on novels. In the spring of 1973, Doubleday & Co. accepted the novel *Carrie* for publication, providing him the means to leave teaching and write full-time. He has since published over 50 books and has become one of the world's most successful writers.

Stephen lives in Maine and Florida with his wife, novelist Tabitha King. They are regular contributors to a number of charities including many libraries and have been honored locally for their philanthropic activities.

Stephen's official website is **www.stephenking.com**

Sarah Langan

Sarah Langan is the three-time Bram Stoker Award winning author of the novels *Audrey's Door* (HarperCollins), *The Missing* (Harper Paperbacks), and *The Keeper* (HarperTorch). She has published short stories and essays in *F&SF*, *Lightspeed* and *St. John's Humanities Review*, and the anthologies *The Year's Best Dark Fantasy and Horror 2011*, *Brave New Worlds, and Creature!*. Her most recent novel was optioned by the Weinstein Company for film. She lives in Brooklyn, NY.

Sarah's website is **www.sarahlangan.com**

John R. Little

John R. Little has been writing horror and dark fantasy stories for 30 years. His first stories were published in magazines like *The Twilight Zone, Weird Tales*, and *Cavalier*. In 2007, he switched his attention to longer works. *The Memory Tree* was John's first novel and was nominated for the Bram Stoker Award. He's written a half dozen subsequent books, all of which have been very well received. *Miranda* won the Bram Stoker Award as well as the Black Quill Award. His most recent book is Ursa Major, from Bad Moon Books.

John's website is **www.johnrlittle.com**

Jonathan Maberry

Jonathan Maberry is a *New York Times* bestselling author, multiple Bram Stoker Award winner, and Marvel Comics writer. His novels include the Pine Deep Trilogy: *Ghost Road Blues, Dead Man's Song*, and *Bad Moon Rising*; the Joe Ledger thriller series: *Patient Zero, The Dragon Factory, The King of Plagues*, and *Assassin's Code*; the Benny Imura Young Adult dystopian series: *Rot & Ruin, Dust & Decay*, and *Flesh & Bone*; the film adaptation of *The Wolfman*; and the standalone horror thriller *Dead of Night*. His nonfiction books include the international bestseller *Zombie CSU, The Cryptopedia, They Bite, Vampire Universe*, and *Wanted Undead or Alive*.

He has sold over 1200 feature articles, thousands of columns, two plays, greeting cards, technical manuals, how-to books, and many short stories. His comics for Marvel include *Marvel Universe vs the Wolverine, Marvel Universe vs the Punisher, DoomWar, Black Panther*, and *Captain America: Hail Hydra*. He is the founder of the Writers Coffeehouse and co-founder of The Liars Club; and is a frequent keynote speaker and guest of honor at conferences including BackSpace, Dragon*Con, ZombCon, PennWriters, The Write Stuff, Central Coast Writers, Necon, Killer Con, Liberty States, and many others.

In 2004, Jonathan was inducted into the International Martial Arts Hall of Fame, due in part to his extensive writing on martial arts and self-defense. Visit him online at **www.jonathanmaberry.com**, Twitter @jonathanmaberry, and **www.facebook.com/jonathanmaberry**

Joe McKinney

Joe McKinney is the San Antonio-based author of numerous horror, crime, and science fiction novels. His longer works include the four part Dead World series, made up of *Dead City, Apocalypse of the Dead, Flesh Eaters*, and *The Zombie King*; the science fiction disaster tale, *Quarantined*, which was nominated for the Horror Writers Association's Bram Stoker Award for superior achievement in a novel, 2009; and the crime novel, *Dodging Bullets*. His upcoming releases include the horror novels *Lost Girl of the Lake, The Red Empire, The Charge*, and *St. Rage*.

Joe has also worked as an editor, along with Michelle McCrary, on the zombie-themed anthology *Dead Set,* and with Mark Onspaugh on the abandoned building-themed anthology *The Forsaken*. His short stories and novellas have been published in more than thirty publications and anthologies.

In his day job, Joe McKinney is a sergeant with the San Antonio Police Department, where he helps to run the city's 911 Dispatch Center. Before being promoted to sergeant, Joe worked as a homicide detective and as a disaster mitigation specialist. Many of his stories, regardless of genre, feature a strong police procedural element based on his fifteen years of law enforcement experience.

A regular guest at regional writing conventions, Joe currently lives and works in a small town north of San Antonio with his wife and children.

Joe's website is **http://joemckinney.wordpress.com**

Lisa Morton

Lisa Morton is a screenwriter and is also the author of four books of non-fiction (including *The Halloween Encyclopedia*, recently released in a 2nd edition). Her short fiction has been published in numerous books and magazines; recent appearances include *The Mammoth Book of Zombie Apocalypse!* and *The Dead That Walk*. Lisa is a three-time Bram Stoker Award winner, and in 2011, she received Stoker Award nominations for her novel *The Castle of Los Angeles* and her novella *The Samhanach*. She is also a renowned expert on Halloween who has appeared on The History Channel and in the pages of *The Wall Street Journal*.

She lives in North Hollywood, California, and can be found online at **www.lisamorton.com**

Joseph Nassise

Joseph Nassise is the author of more than a dozen novels, including the internationally bestselling Templar Chronicles series (*The Heretic, A Scream of Angels, A Tear in the Sky,* and *Infernal Games*) He has also written several installments in the Rogue Angel action adventure series from Harlequin/Gold Eagle.

He's a former president of the Horror Writers Association, the world's largest organization of professional horror writers, and a two-time Bram Stoker Award and International Horror Guild Award nominee.

Joseph's website is **www.josephnassise.com**

Scott Nicholson

Scott Nicholson is author of more than 20 books, including the bestselling thrillers *Liquid Fear* and *Disintegration*. He's also written six screenplays, three children's books, and four comics series. He works as an organic gardener and freelance editor in the Southern Appalachian Mountains of the United States.

Scott's website is **www.hauntedcomputer.com.**

Weston Ochse

Weston Ochse (pronounced 'Oaks') lives in Southern Arizona with his wife, and fellow author, Yvonne Navarro, and their three Great Danes. For entertainment, he races tarantula wasps, wrestles rattlesnakes, and bakes in the noonday sun. His work has won the Bram Stoker Award for First Novel and been nominated for a Pushcart Prize for short fiction. His work has also appeared in anthologies, magazines and professional writing guides. He thinks it's damn cool that he's had stories in comic books.

Weston's website is **www.westonochse.com**

Gene O'Neill

Gene has seen over 120 of his short stories published, several novellas, three short story collections (including the Stoker winning *Taste of Tenderloin*), and five novels—the most recent, *Not Fade Away*, debuted at WHC 2011. He is hard at work finishing up his Cal Wild Trilogy: *The Confessions of St Zach*, *The Burden of Indigo*, and *The Cal Wild Chronicles*. Upcoming from Bad Moon Books will be a collection of his most recent short fiction: *Dance of the Blue Lady*. Also expected soon will be the novellas *Rusting Chickens* and *Doublejack*.

Alexandra Sokoloff

As a screenwriter, Alexandra Sokoloff has sold original horror and thriller scripts and written novel adaptations for numerous Hollywood studios. Her debut ghost story, *The Harrowing*, was nominated for both a Bram Stoker award and an Anthony award for Best First Novel. Her second supernatural thriller, *The Price*, was called "Some of the most original and freshly unnerving work in the genre" by the *New York Times Book Review*. *The Unseen* is based on real-life experiments conducted at the Rhine parapsychology lab on the Duke University campus; and *Book of Shadows* teams a cynical Boston cop and a beautiful, mysterious witch from Salem in a race to solve a Satanic killing. Alex is also the author of two writing workbooks based on her internationally acclaimed workshop and blog: *Screenwriting Tricks for Authors*. She writes erotic paranormal on the side, and is an avid dancer and a diehard fan of Rocky Wood.

"The Edge of Seventeen" won the International Thriller Writers' Thriller award for Best Short Fiction. Alex recently adapted the story as a full-length supernatural YA: *The Space Between*, available now. She can be found online at **www.alexandrasokoloff.com** and **www.screenwritingtricks.com**

Jeff Strand

Jeff Strand is the author of a bunch of books, including *Pressure, Wolf Hunt, Benjamin's Parasite*, and *Lost Homicidal Maniac (Answers to "Shirley")*. He and Rocky Wood once had smoothies together. Hank Schwaeble paid for them. It was awesome.

You can visit Jeff Strand's Gleefully Macabre website at **www.jeffstrand.com**.

Peter Straub

Peter Straub is the author of seventeen novels, which have been translated into more than twenty languages. They include *Ghost Story, Koko, Mr. X*, two collaborations with Stephen King, *The Talisman* and *Black House*, and his most recent, *In the Night Room*.

Peter's website is **www.peterstraub.net**

Bev Vincent

Bev Vincent is the author of *The Road to the Dark Tower*, the Bram Stoker Award nominated companion to Stephen King's Dark Tower series, and *The Stephen King Illustrated Companion*, which was nominated for a 2010 Edgar® Award and a 2009 Bram Stoker Award and won the Reader's Choice Black Quill Award.

His short fiction has appeared in places like *Ellery Queen's Mystery Magazine, Evolve, Tesseracts Thirteen, From the Borderlands, The Blue Religion*, and every even number in the *Shivers* anthology series. In 2010, four of his stories were collected in *When the Night Comes Down* and his story "The Bank Job" won the Al Blanchard Award in 2010.

He is a contributing editor with *Cemetery Dance* magazine and a member of the Storytellers Unplugged blogging community. He also reviews books at Onyx Reviews. For more, visit his website **www.bevvincent.com.**

David Niall Wilson

David Niall Wilson has been writing and publishing horror, dark fantasy, and science fiction since the mid-eighties. An ordained minister, once President of the Horror Writer's Association, and multiple recipient of the Bram Stoker Award, his novels include *Maelstrom, The Mote in Andrea's Eye, Deep Blue, the Grails Covenant Trilogy, Star Trek Voyager: Chrysalis, Except You Go Through Shadow, This is My Blood, Ancient Eyes, On the Third Day, The Orffyreus Wheel*, and *Vintage Soul. Heart of a Dragon*—the chronological first book in the DeChance Chronicles is now available. The Stargate Atlantis novel *Brimstone*, written with Patricia Lee Macomber is his most recent title in print—upcoming is *The Second Veil*, Tales of the Scattered Earth Book II. His most recent novel, *Hallowed Ground*, written with Steven Savile, is now available.

He has over 150 short stories published in anthologies, magazines, and five collections, the most recent of which were *Defining Moments* published in 2007 by WFC Award winning Sarob Press, and the currently available *Ennui & Other States of Madness*, from Dark Regions Press. His work has appeared in and is due out in various anthologies and magazines. David lives and loves with Patricia Lee Macomber in Hertford, NC with their children, Billy, Zach, Zane, and Katie, and occasionally, their genius college daughter Stephanie.

David is CEO and founder of Crossroad Press, a cutting edge digital publishing company specializing in electronic novels, collections, and non-fiction, as well as unabridged audiobooks. Visit Crossroad Press at **http://store.crossroadpress.com**

F. Paul Wilson

F. Paul Wilson is the award-winning, bestselling author of forty-plus books and nearly one hundred short stories spanning science fiction, horror, adventure, medical thrillers, and virtually everything between. His novels regularly appear on the *New York Times* Bestsellers List. *The Tomb* received the Porgie Award from *The West Coast Review of Books; Wheels Within Wheels* won the first Prometheus Award. His novella "Aftershock" won a Stoker Award. He was voted Grand Master by the World Horror Convention and received the Lifetime Achievement Award from the Horror Writers of America. He also received the prestigious Inkpot Award and is listed in the 50th anniversary edition of Who's Who in America.

In 1983, Paramount rendered his novel *The Keep* into a visually striking but otherwise incomprehensible movie with screenplay and direction by Michael Mann.

The Tomb has spent 15 years in development hell at Beacon Films (*Air Force One, Thirteen Days*, etc.) as Repairman Jack. The plan is to make Repairman Jack a franchise character. Godot might arrive sooner.

Over nine million copies of his books are in print in the US and his work has been translated into twenty-four languages. He also has written for the stage, screen, and interactive media. His latest thrillers, *Ground Zero* and *Fatal Error*, star his urban mercenary, Repairman Jack. *Jack: Secret Vengeance* is the last of his YA trilogy about Repairman Jack as a teen. Paul resides at the Jersey Shore and can be found on the web at **www.repairmanjack.com**

Chelsea Quinn Yarbro

An award-winning professional writer for more than forty years, Chelsea Quinn Yarbro has sold more than eighty books and more than ninety works of short fiction, essays, and reviews, and also composes serious music. She lives in Richmond, California with three autocratic cats.

Her website is **www.chelseaquinnyarbro.net**

Shane Jiraiya Cummings

Shane Jiraiya Cummings is an Australian editor and author. He is the editor of several anthologies including *Australian Dark Fantasy & Horror Volume One*, *Shadow Box*, and *Black Box*. Shane has co-edited (with Angela Challis) the magazines *Black: Australian Dark Culture*, *Shadowed Realms*, and *Midnight Echo #2*. Shane was also the founder and Managing Editor of the award-winning zine *HorrorScope*.

As an author, Shane has been acknowledged as "one of Australia's leading voices in dark fantasy". He is the author of *Shards*, *Phoenix and the Darkness of Wolves*, the four volumes of the Apocrypha Sequence (*Deviance, Divinity, Insanity*, and *Inferno*), the Ravenous Gods cycle of stories (including *Requiem for the Burning God*) and the Adventures of Yamabushi Kaidan (*The Smoke Dragon* and *The Mist Ninja*). He has had more than seventy short stories published in Australia, USA, and Europe, and his work has been translated into Spanish, French, and Polish. Shane has won two Ditmar Awards, and he has been nominated for more than twenty other major awards, including Spain's Premios Ignotus.

Shane is an Active Member of the Horror Writers Association and former Vice President of the Australian Horror Writers Association. When he is not writing, Shane is an editor and journalist by day and a sword fighting instructor by night.

Shane's website is **www.jiraiya.com.au**

Other Brimstone Press titles

Anthologies

Macabre: A Journey through Australia's Darkest Fears

Australian Dark Fantasy & Horror Volume Three

Australian Dark Fantasy & Horror Volume Two

Australian Dark Fantasy & Horror Volume One

Book of Shadows Volume One

Collections

The Last Days of Kali Yuga, by Paul Haines

Shards, by Shane Jiraiya Cummings

CD-ROM anthologies

Shadow Box

Black Box (Shadow Box 2)

Magazines/e-zines

Black: Australian Dark Culture

HorrorScope

Shadowed Realms

Order online now at www.brimstonepress.com.au

CPSIA information can be obtained
at www.ICGtesting.com
Printed in the USA
LVOW12s1014070916

503534LV00001B/109/P